C000177989

THE BLACK SPRING CRIME SERIES CURATED
BY EDITOR LUCA VESTE

Praised and endorsed by some of the biggest names in Crime Fiction...

'Time to strap yourself in.' **- IAN RANKIN**

'I love, love, love great new crime fiction. How do I find it? Usually I ask my friend Luca Veste. I owe him hundreds of hours of great reading. Now he's doing it for real, not just for me - he's working with Black Spring Press, which means they're going to have a crime list that everyone will get excited about - and everyone will buy. Luca Veste is our genre's best talent spotter - Black Spring Press will be one to watch.' **- LEE CHILD**

'Crime fiction is going through a new Golden Age, finding readers looking for strong stories that explore the world around us and the problems we face. An independent publisher like Black Spring is the perfect fit for these fresh new voices and ways of seeing - and in Luca Veste they have a crime editor who knows the terrain like a skilled tracker. A great writer himself, he has an eye for the brightest and best. It's going to be an exciting and enriching journey for readers. Time to strap yourself in.' **- IAN RANKIN**

'I know nobody with their finger more acutely on the pulse of crime fiction. I value his recommendations; they show a great eye for what's worth my reading time.' - **VAL MCDERMID**

'Nobody knows more about the world of crime fiction than Luca Veste. He knows the business inside out and he knows all the movers and shakers. Most importantly of all, he knows a great crime novel when he sees one.' - **MARK BILLINGHAM**

'I have known Luca for over ten years and am incredibly impressed by his wide knowledge of modern crime fiction. Not only is he an excellent writer and editor who understands the many sub-genres that are currently popular and commercially sound, he has excellent people skills and is highly respected amongst his peers. He is a strong asset to the team at Black Spring.' - **SJI HOLLIDAY**

'Luca Veste is honestly the most knowledgeable person I know about both the crime fiction genre and the publishing industry. He has an acute sense of what makes a successful book, and the vision to make it happen.' - **DOUG JOHNSTONE**

'Luca Veste has a razor-sharp sense of the market at all levels, from the writers worth watching to the movers and shakers at the editorial and sales departments.' - **STUART NEVILLE**

THE SCOTSMAN

THE SCOTSMAN
ROB MCCLURE

BLACKSPRING
CRIMESERIES

This edition published in 2023
By The Black Spring Crime Series
An imprint of Eyewear Publishing Ltd.
The Black Spring Press Group
London, United Kingdom

Cover design by Juan Padrón
Typeset by Subash Raghu
Cover photograph by Getty Images

ISBN 978-1-913606-47-3

Black Spring Crime Series Curated by Luca Veste

www.blackspringpressgroup.com

CONTENTS

1 WEDNESDAY

It hits harder when they're as young as this. Not even in her teens. And she's gone.

She has red hair and milky blue eyes, opaque from corneal clouding. The slab is cold. He thinks about her parents then stops thinking about them. It's too difficult, this grief of others. Death is born to us with light, our only mutual inheritance, the dark thread sewn deeply in every breath. Thinking this, Cowan realises he probably needs to quit thinking. Completely. He quit drinking, so why not thinking as well? How hard could it be? Most people in the world seemed to live perfectly happy lives without any thoughts to speak of at all. He met them every day in his line of work. Some he helped, some he consoled, some he threw down on the concrete, kicked in the balls and handcuffed to railings.

Webster hunches over the body. Preoccupied, the doctor scarcely acknowledges Cowan's presence. His special spectacles give him an owlish appearance. When he speaks at last, it is very Kelvinside, like he just popped a hot potato in his mouth for fun.

'I'll keep it brief, Detective Inspector,' he says. 'My opinion is that death was due to suffocation.'

Webster bends and touches throat, hands and wrists in sequence. Cowan observes the careful fingers move, wonders how soft the skin would feel ungloved. He wonders why he wonders that.

'There are, as you can see, no visible wounds, no puncturing, virtually no bleeding.' Webster sighs. 'However, the girl was sexually assaulted. You'll notice the bruising here, here and here.'

The men pause for a moment to consider all that is obvious. The young girl lying there, naked, on a cold slab. Neither of them speaks. Lost in their own thoughts.

She is truly gone.

'I'm down here for the good news but,' Cowan says, breaking the silence.

Webster adjusts his gloves. The gloves seem to be of white linen, but that can't be the case. So what white material would it be, then? Cowan feels he should know. He is confused. The overhead light keeps flickering, forcing him to blink against its yellow staccato stutter. There's a big fluorescent bulb that needs changing. The latest round of budget cuts kicking in, probably. Dark shadows crawl across whitewashed walls.

'She bit him. All she could do. Trace of skin on the incisors.' Webster lifts open the girl's mouth to show. His white glove runs the length of her teeth. The gums are red. Against the red, the thumb of the glove is whiter than the teeth. 'She didn't have all her big molars in yet, even.'

'Good wee lassie, well done.' Cowan is feeling queasy now. 'What else?'

'On the clothing, I found short hair, dark pigment. Solid

fingerprints. Not the best but enough to be working with. Also, have a look at this.' Webster stretches across the slab and splays his fingers over her throat, their compass almost matching the purple bruises. 'See? Thick fingers, widely spaced. You're looking for a big man.'

'Or a wee man with huge hands.'

'That fit any known descriptions?'

'Aye, about half the male population of this city.' Webster yanks the cloth up over her face. The winding sheet descends. Cowan can still see the girl's hair though, stray red strands falling delicate over the fold, red on white. A body like any other, but younger. He has seen his share of corpses but still…

'For sheer badness this takes some beating,' Webster says. The doctor clinks his little steel instruments into the metal sink. 'The man that did this must be key-cold.'

'I've seen worse,' Cowan says, lifting the sheet for another look.

'What did I miss this time, then?' Webster asks him, laughing nervously.

Cowan examines the girl's face again and feels the sweat pool damp around his collar. What he missed is that she has blonde hair and is in her early twenties. How could he have been so mistaken? Some policeman he is. Cowan turns to chide the doctor, but Webster is gone now. The light-flicker is worse and the walls strobe into darkness. He recognises the girl on the slab now: Catriona. He watches her eyes slide open.

'What happened, Daddy?' she says, although her lips are not moving at all. A pale hand steals out from under the plain white sheet to clutch ice-cold at his wrist, causing him to flinch, freezing the blood in his veins. 'Who was it that did this to me? Why?'

***

The hot sun came streaming through the window of the aeroplane like a brass band. The back of his neck was burning something fierce. He tugged the shade down over the window, angry and embarrassed. The fingers of his left hand still circled the little plastic cup of coke and ice. Fuck's sake! Everything was up in the air. Literally.

'You were dreaming,' his seatmate announced. He was forgiven his earlier *faux pas*, then. 'You were jerking around like a snoozing cat. It was very peculiar.'

'I was?'

'And snoring, also.' The elderly woman was glaring at him in disgust now, and he supposed he was unforgiven after all. 'Quite loudly, too.'

Cowan set about reassembling the real. So, he was back at the dreaming again? No, wait, that wasn't dreaming. That was remembering. The case of the Graham girl in Dennistoun a few years back. That had been an awful business. For a moment, waves of relief swept over him, tingling his skin, soothing. Then back with anvil weight came the knowledge that his daughter was dead. Cowan felt her chill touch again on his wrist and the reality of her being gone forever seeped into his bones. That's the reason he was stuck on this damn plane, six months after her murder, flying into Washington DC for the first time. The compassionate leave he guilt-tripped out of the Chief Constable gave him one fucking week to find her killer. And here he was starting out his big investigation by nodding off. What a total loser he was, what a defective detective.

Just seven days. God's sake, what were his chances? But then Cowan recalled that God achieved quite a bit in a similar timeframe. You even managed a day off, old boy, didn't you?

The plane shuddered through a cloudbank on the descent and he flicked the shade up again. They were looping across the low skyline of the city and over the serpentine Potomac, the Doric columns of the George Washington Masonic National Memorial off to the northeast. The sky was cloudless, a clear November blue, all drunk on vapour trails. Cowan wished himself back in Glasgow dealing with an evil he understood. He should never have come here in a thousand years. This was all madness. Far below, the sun glittered on the roofs of cars in a sprawling suburban lot and stitched a thread of yellow tremor along the blue. No, he was where he had to be. It was what he owed her. It was true what the poet said then – in dreams began responsibilities. This new world he would remake in seven days, or die trying.

It had already been a dreadful trip, with a three-hour delay at Heathrow. The pilot's seat had broken and the passengers were grounded until the airline flew in a replacement from Gatwick. Why there were no pilot seats available in all of London was a mystery to those delayed. Cowan wondered if a newer generation of pilots had begun to fly standing up. He shared this sentiment at the time with his seatmate, the older woman from Essex sporting hair of an orange hue unknown to nature. She was initially startled by his accent, but then supposing it unlikely that a thuggish Glaswegian would mug her on an actual aeroplane, and having no one else available in the vicinity to berate, commenced ranting at him. Her daughter was going to be bloody livid, apparently. Kimberley was waiting at Reagan National, and now it would be a long wait, and her kids would be flipping out something awful, and by the time Grandma got there all hell would have broken loose. The children were monsters, she explained, brought up the 'American way' at the insistence of their father, a delusional Yank. A sneak attack on the airport by an Al Qaeda suicide squad with a small arsenal of portable nuclear devices strapped to their naked torsos couldn't hope to wreak the havoc those hell-spawn could. 'No discipline,' she spat at him. 'They've been over-indulged.'

Cowan suspected the flight delay was what really upset her. She even had her own theory about the seat. 'I saw him, you know, the one who broke it. He was downright massive. It's ridiculous, a human that size piloting an aircraft.' Cowan remarked that he didn't see what girth had to do with your ability to fly a plane, and she explained all about the small cockpit. The only co-pilot able to fit in there with that elephantine figure at the controls would have to be some kind of midget.

'And what if it had given way while we were taking off or landing or something? That man might have fallen over and damaged some crucial instruments. Not to mention how they would have ever got him upright again. I saw him. It would have taken a bloody great enormous crane. No wonder modern aircraft use so much petrol.'

The old orange bat kept up her harangue for two hours straight before asking him anything about himself. Cowan thought that was standard for most people, given the opportunity. Still, he did feel seriously inclined by then to start chewing his own leg off.

'I'm so glad you're staying with us.'

'Excuse me?'

'Your region. I'm so glad you're going to remain part of the United Kingdom. You Scots still have so much to contribute.'

He didn't respond to that. There was a lot he could have said, but he was making a serious effort to be on better behaviour. Ever since the unfortunate head-butting incident at his nephew's wedding reception the year before, Cowan had been on his last warning. He looked out of the little oval window and saw the flaps on the wing slotted diagonally by gusts of wind. Were they supposed to do that? Christ, he surely hoped so.

'I think we're better together,' she opined.

'The way I see it,' Cowan said, stupidly yielding to

temptation, 'is that a Yes for independence vote would have been a total economic disaster, a national catastrophe. Rivers of sewage spewing through the streets, chaos, anarchy, pollution, mass murder and rape. A whole country reduced in no time at all to the status of some third world nightmare banana republic, like Florida. A No vote just meant we stayed hooked up with you English.' He smiled broadly at her. 'Which is why I voted yes.'

The woman beetled her brows and snorted like an asthmatic seal. 'Are you visiting family in the States?'

'No,' he said. 'Not anymore.'

'Oh, so you're doing the tourist thing, then?'

'Aye, I suppose so.' Cowan crammed the in-flight magazine back in the seat pocket. He'd been temporarily entranced by a wire wine-bottle holder made to look like a frog. 'You see, I decided, in my mind, to visit all the places my wee lassie visited right before she went and got herself killed.'

That proved to be a conversation killer. Mention of sudden death tended to put a damper on things. Sometimes it could be useful though. Cowan remembered this one God-awful dinner party his ex-wife had hosted where he'd ended up half in the bag, discussing a recent murder spree in graphic detail with two dentists, on the principle that they well understood the inclination to cause random pain to strangers. That was another life ago now. The person he had been. His remark shut the tangerine gasbag up for the duration of the Atlantic crossing though, which he considered a modest success. Her revenge was the recent insinuation that he snored like a chainsaw.

From the runway, in the distance you could see the white dome of the Capitol and haloed around it another chill blue dome of sky. It was 2pm Eastern Standard Time.

Waiting to disembark, Cowan got to thinking about a Sunday afternoon long ago. Memories came thick and fast these days, unbidden. It was the grief. The two of them used to fly her kite up the hill behind the old place on windy weekends. The far side of the hill sloped down to a quarry's sheer cut sides. Cowan used to worry himself sick about his wee girl playing up there by herself. She was that wild and reckless. She took daft chances, her knees perpetually skinned. The old quarry was nearly exhausted by then, the eastern ridge long abandoned, and on Sundays the quarry-men didn't work it, which meant there was no explosive rumbling to undercut the father-daughter bonding experience. That Sunday, he was sitting beside her on a slope of the hill in a deep clover bed above the old boots chemist factory. While he unspooled the tangled kite line, Catriona ripped up a buttercup by the roots and cupped it under his chin. 'You like butter,' she said, all excited. 'But nothing too sweet.'

'I like sweet things fine.'

She commenced plucking daisies to make a chain, a little yellow-white wreath for her pretty hair. Cowan thought she looked like some Greek goddess.

'Did you know that your mother is dead scared of clowns?'

She started up giggling. 'Mummy is scared of clowns?'

'Aye, see she went to a circus, when she was a wee girl about your age, Billy Smart's it was, probably, and she saw this clown knock another clown's head right off. It wasn't his real head, obviously. But she's had terrible nightmares for years since about this clown without a head. He goes chasing her around an ice rink, screaming at her like a banshee. The ice is making it awful slippery for her too, when she tries to run away from him and that, which isn't helping her situation any.'

Catriona was thoughtful for a while. 'Daddy?'

'Uh-huh?'

'How can a clown scream at you if he's not got a head?'

'Well, it's a dream. A dream doesn't have to make sense, does it? I mean do your dreams always make sense?'

'Aye.'

'Your dreams make sense? Really? You're serious about that now?'

'Aye.'

'Well, that's weird. I've had some right humdingers of dreams that make no sense at all. There's a few times I've dreamt I'm dropping into this big pit that goes on and on forever and all my teeth have fallen out as well, which is depressing. In fact, I'm a lot more upset in the dream about me having to get dentures than I am about falling headfirst into this giant hole. Don't you ever get scary nightmares like that?'

'No.' Catriona scrunched up her pale blue eyes. 'There's

nothing I'm afraid of in this world.' She settled the daisy ring in her hair. 'How do I look, Daddy?'

Cowan could only stare at her. She was something else, this child of his. How Maggie and he had combined their DNA to create this creature was always a great mystery to them both. 'You look just like one of those Greek goddesses,' he told her.

'Which one?'

'I don't remember who they all are. Do you know the names of any?'

Catriona reclined on her back, pressing into the grass. A single green stalk clenched between her little white teeth. She furrowed her brow and shook her head sadly.

'Persephone maybe,' Cowan suggested, smoothing down a tufting of long blades with his palm. The blades sprang back at once.

'What did Percy Phone do?'

Forklifts went scooting across the factory lot of the chemical plant below. You couldn't hear a sound, though. They were little vehicles in a silent movie. The sky was a copper gray that day and the faraway hills, those blue-green Campsie Fells, jutted against the heaviness of it, like needles into cotton. Skylarks soared shrilling under a warm yellow sun, dropping to the wild heather far from their nests.

Sometimes his daughter's mind was a skylark too, leading him where she wasn't.

'I don't remember, hen. But she was awful gorgeous,

they say. All them handsome Greek boys were always dying to get off with Persephone.'

Catriona uttered a loud gagging noise. 'Ugh! Dad! Stop!' She pointed at the factory in the distance. 'Do you think those people way down there can see us?'

Far below them, the workers scurried like ants inside the black chain-link. Their dark uniforms made them seem like prisoners in a jail yard. In a sense that's what they were, paid by the hour and with no Sundays off. The chemists were the ones making the real money in that place. Cowan heard they were doing research with cosmetic testing, but exactly what it was he didn't know, blinding rabbits probably. 'No,' he said. 'They can't see anything.'

'Oh, that's good.'

'Why is that good?'

Catriona sat up and smoothed her little hands along her knees and looked off in the distance at something only she could see. 'Because I like it best of all when no-one in the world can see me or know about me, and it's all secret and safe,' she said.

'Well, that's as good a reason as any,' he told her.

The Irish who were the first to quarry those escarpments believed the burning white translucence of selenite was water congealed by the moon. They were wrong about that, of course. They were just being poetic in their Celtic way. But Cowan had always found quarries fascinating, regardless. When he was a boy, his uncle Alan had shown him how the silver-grey sheer surface oozed driblets of asphaltum on a hot summer's day, and the way a chisel against a bottom end of pure white limestone could sculpt out chalk-lamp shells of sea urchins, starfish and shark's teeth. History was quarried, too. Years later, a grown man, he had gone excavating in abandoned quarries himself, twice recovering corpses dumped there to rot by evil cretins. So you might say he'd gone off quarries a bit since. But that daisy chain summer day he'd been happy enough to be sitting near one with her. He'd been so very glad. Until they got home, at any rate, and she right away up and asked Maggie all about her crazy clown phobia. There had been hell to pay for his making that stupid story up, though it had been kind of a funny one.

The deplaning line at last began to slump towards the exit, bags being hauled down hazardously from the overhead bins into which they'd been crammed, much like the passengers were stuffed in their little claustrophobic rows. Cowan recalled suddenly that Persephone wasn't a goddess at all. She'd just been this regular girl stolen away to the underworld by a dark man. After that, she could only come back to visit in spring with the birds and the daffodils. He would have settled for that deal. Oh, that arrangement would have been just fine with him. But his daughter wasn't returning in springtime with the flowers. No, except in his dreams, she was never coming back to him.

Cowan only had the one carry-on, so after clearing immigration he walked straight from the terminal to National Airport Metro. He imagined himself then, rolling his wee roller bag up the walkway, wonky wheel and all, as a man set forth on an epic journey, like some fabled hero of myth and legend. But where was the dragon, what was the riddle, and would the lovely lady hung in chains even be worth rescuing? This was the way his mind worked sometimes. It was a damn strange thing to live in. But there was no getting away from it. So the daft philosophers said.

Caution, the moving walkway is ending. Please watch your step.

But the walkway wasn't ending at all, for the belt looped and kept right on going. It was him that was ending. The thing was a metaphor for life then: a ride on a moving walkway, a passage somewhere else, out from a terminal place towards the light. He was 30 seconds older stepping off, that much closer to death. He felt it too.

Caution, the moving walkway is ending. Please watch your step.

His daughter must have stood here like this, as he did now, on a day not unlike today. A lovely young girl, moving and yet not, with her whole life ahead of her.

The ticket machine sucked in his twenty-dollar bill. He studied the plastic card it spat out. Cowan needed to keep track of fares and distances. He glanced at the Metro map on the big board on the platform, although he didn't need to. He'd made a study of those lines for the past six months and could name every station in order from Glenmont to Shady Grove, Huntington to Mount Vernon Square. The mildness of the air surprised him a little. But this was Virginia, south of the Mason-Dixon line. He'd read that two inches of snow was enough to paralyze DC. The city was built on a swamp, some folks said, sweating through the summer humidity. Others just shrugged and cranked up the AC and, with a sly nod at all the silk suits slinking along K Street like bespoke reptiles, said the place was evidently still a swamp. The only talk of draining it these days came from creatures from a far blacker lagoon.

The first city-bound train was a yellow line. Cowan could switch to the red at L'Enfant Plaza, but decided to wait for the next blue line to Largo. He wanted to see the Foggy Bottom platform: the exact place she'd stood on her last night on this earth. There were only a few passengers on board until Arlington Cemetery, where a tourist mob spilled on, cameras slung around their necks like tribal necklaces. Behind those left waiting on the platform, scattered piles of leaves adjusted themselves to the wind and a plastic bag ghosted the embankments.

Safeway.

The train plunged into darkness and a strange silence descended and lingered till Crystal City. Cowan was the only passenger not transfixed by a phone. The Japanese girl opposite him gazed longingly at her little screen as if hypnotized. Big-eyed anime lovelies danced before her, pursued by a grinning green octopus. Fuck's sake! What was the appeal of that at all? Brought to you by the same folk who brought you Tamagotchi, maid cafes and the Bataan death march. The girl cradled a bright red purse in her lap. The thing looked like a man's bloody heart. Christ, that's probably what it was. Cowan felt like a man sealed tight in a vacuum tube with the nightmares of other people.

He was relieved to transfer to the busier red line at Metro Center. The escalator to the upper level was out of service and an elderly man with a cane was seriously distressed about it. 'What the fuck's with this shit?' he was yelling over and over. Everyone ignored him, racing up the stairs.

Cowan clutched the overhead rail to steady himself against the rattling jar of the carriage, bag clenched awkwardly between his legs. Catty-corner, a young unsmiling teenager with close cornrows and expensive looking shades slouched on the blue seat reserved for the disabled. The low-hung jeans exposed the elastic of his boxers, new iPhone clipped on the waistband. Cowan noted the livid scar under the left nostril. The same he'd seen often in East End bars. A trace of where a knife did its business. Maybe that's what this one's disability was. He doubted it.

'See sumthin' you like?'

'What?'

'What you starin' at, cuz?'

Nearby, a middle-aged man with a Godiva chocolate bag hooked around his wrist shifted uncomfortably in his seat as though suffering from a very fractious case of haemorrhoids. He wanted no part of this exchange, gazing out of the window as if entranced by the scenery.

They were in a tunnel.

'I don't know,' said Cowan. 'I think the label must have fallen off.'

The teenager peeled off his shades and hung them on the neck of his t-shirt. He had a lick at his bottom lip and grinned, displaying a grey metallic grille. The smile was just another scar across his face. 'You got yourself a problem?'

'Do you?'

'You serious?'

'Trying to be.'

The kid leaned forward and stared hard into Cowan's eyes. His cornrows shook like black worms. Neither of them flinched or looked away, both acknowledging the laws of the animal kingdom, which were the same everywhere.

Cowan tapped his nose. 'What happened? Did you pick it wrong?'

'Jesus, people,' Godiva Man muttered. He didn't for a second take his eyes off the window as he spoke, addressing their reflections. 'Y'all take it light here.'

'I'm just sittin' is all,' the kid said. 'Then this one all up in my face.'

'He not sayin' anythin' more about it now. We all chill now.'

The trio rode uneasily until Judiciary Square, where the young man stood to get off. He shoulder-pressed Cowan and as the doors slid open whispered in his ear: 'Y'all take care now.' He drew his hand across his neck. 'See you again, I'll dead you, man.'

Cowan began to laugh.

Step back, doors closing.

'Wasn't he just a sweetheart?' Cowan asked. 'It was all I could do not to knee his balls through the roof of his mouth.'

But Godiva Man wanted nothing to do with Cowan, shaking his head and blinking rapidly. 'He might be in the life, I don't know 'bout all that, but that was on you. Boy spoke the truth. He wasn't doing nuthin' till you started in on him.' He pointed at Cowan's bag. 'You just gettin' here, you best take care. This is my advice. Can't go round starin' at people that way on a train like that, friend.'

'I'm not your friend, friend.' As the train slowed on the approach to Union Station, Cowan jerked up his bag. 'But I'll take that under advisement.'

The opening doors made a little dual chime and it wasn't close to a tuning fork struck upon a star.

Step back, doors closing.

'You take care again now, sir,' Godiva Man said, studying his shoes.

The whole train confrontation left him feeling like shit. Who was he kidding? He was intimidating no one here. Worse, he was making people feel sorry for him. His anger had nothing to do with the kid with the scar: it was a more abstract fury targeted at all young black men on sub-way trains. Christ, didn't he have reason enough for that, though? It was one of them that had killed his daughter. But for whom was he nursing that much wrath really? Someone worthy of it: God probably.

He rode a working escalator to street level, keeping to the right. A boy greeted him at the top by attempting to cram a newspaper in his earhole while screaming, 'Help the homeless.' Cowan brushed him off as he did the well-dressed bum trying to flog him a rose sheathed in green plastic, for he had no-one here, or anywhere else, to give it to. He walked down E Street towards the awning of the Hyatt Regency on Capitol Hill, skirting the pamphleteering religious nutjobs. Steam belched hot from a sidewalk grate and his wheels rattled as he dragged them across the metal ridges. DC was bright and clean and smelled like popcorn. He stopped to buy a Diet Coke in Kogod's on the corner of New Jersey Avenue. Kogod's! What a name! One deity was more than enough in Cowan's opinion. As if monotheism didn't cause enough mayhem in this world. He gulped bland sweetness and considered his mood: not good. He really needed to get a fucking grip.

'We have you for five days?' the front desk clerk asked, fixing him with the brisk efficient smile cultivated by front desk clerks everywhere. There must be a manual. Her badge said Livia and she had a faint accent. 'And the first two nights are already taken care of by…'

'The First Secretary of the British Embassy.'

'That's right.'

'Actually,' Cowan suggested. 'I was hoping to make it an even seven nights. I'd like to stay the whole week, if that's possible?'

'Well, we do have a convention coming in.' Livia frowned and had a quick slap at her keyboard. 'It might be difficult. It's this big Family Research Council thing.'

'Oh, no,' Cowan exclaimed, grinning affably at her. 'Does that mean the hotel bar's going to be full of hookers every night, then?'

Livia looked confused. 'No. A Family Research Council conference.'

'Oh, never mind.'

If he was OK with switching rooms for the last two nights, it was doable. Cowan said he was fine with the switch and coincidentally was also doable himself, but she didn't laugh at the joke. Maybe it crossed a *#MeToo* line. Maybe, he thought, the joke was *Too Me*. The clerk, still unsmiling, handed him a note from the Consular Office. He was apparently supposed to contact someone called Gerald Bannon the minute he got in. Aye, that'd be the day. He'd get right to making that call after he nipped across to Nationals Park and hit a swift grand slam with a breadstick.

Cowan clicked open his suitcase: six shirts. Which one could he get away with wearing twice? Six pairs of socks, seven pairs of boxers, thank Christ! Toilet bag as usual stuffed to the gunnels with Gaviscon, Losac, and Rennie tablets, the essentials, him having the stomach of a man twice his age: an 84 year old, then. A thousand sun-hot Vindaloos had long since eviscerated his stomach lining and acid reflux had turned out to be not half so much fun as acid flashback. Where the hell was his green toothbrush, though? Still sitting on the sink in the flat in Pollokshields, missing him madly.

Cowan took out the blue flier. He'd been studying the

damn thing for months, like a Kabbalist. The block letters at the top of the flier announced: CONSENT IS SEXY.
Underneath *Do you want to stop?* and *Do you want to go further?*

Did he?

Still, so long after, memories of her were popping like
firecrackers in his brain. The latest flew at him unbidden,
leaving him astonished by the vividness of the recall: him
standing with an eleven-year-old leaning on a three-wired
fence, looking at a cow in a stubble field. It must have been
the year before the divorce and the viciousness. A pair of
blue butterflies fluttered between them and that plug-ugly
brown heifer.

'Look, they're fighting,' Catriona said, pointing at the
butterflies, interested.

'No,' he told her. 'I think they're making love.' Fearing
this was the beginning of something seriously embarrassing,
his daughter started thrashing dementedly at a big clump of
dandelions, lopping their heads off with the mottled birch
twig he'd cut and stripped for her earlier.

'I'm supposing you know all about that, now,' he'd said,
picking seedy white wisps out of his hair. 'They teach it at
the academy. It's on the curriculum and that.'

'Aye.'

'Well, make sure you listen. It's important what they tell
you.' By then, Cowan had been bearing down on the wire
in a way not to do it any good. 'Someday you'll love a boy,
when you're a bit older I mean, and you'll probably want to
marry him then.'

'I don't think so, Daddy,' she'd said, glancing around her, alarmed.

'Oh, I think you will,' he'd informed her gravely. 'These things happen. And then I'll probably have to pay for the wedding. That'll cost us a pretty penny, won't it?'

By now the cow was looking at them. Perhaps ugliness was relative. Or maybe she wanted to eat the dandelions. Anyway, there they'd stood, the pair of them, nine years ago, father and daughter alone together, stricken. It had been just another in a long series of awkward episodes between the pair of them, but this one captured for posterity as something slow happening inside the cold brain of a cow.

'I'll be a nurse by then,' Catriona explained to him, while angrily decapitating a daisy. 'I'll be able to pay for it all myself, Daddy.'

Aye, that had been a lovely day with his little girl and the cow and the butterflies. But those butterflies and that cow were long since gone, and now his girl was too. You couldn't make any fucking sense of what happened. It was a deeper darkness than any tunnel he had ever ridden through. There was no meaning to any of it. Not a fragment. Cowan made the discovery that he was crying. Aw, fuck it, not that rubbish again. He gave his nose a swift wipe with the corner of a bed sheet. What a wimp he was. *Aye, and you, what do you have to say to me about it? Sweet fuck all, right? Silence. Where were you that day? Whooping it up in one of your many mansions, were you?*

Cowan smoothed out the blue flier on the sheets. Was consent sexy? It seemed like a hell of a complicated question. The flier had been stuffed in his daughter's coat pocket the night she died. In its margins jotted in faint pencil:

202-225-0773 3/4/1030/IT

Underneath the scrawl of numbers and letters was what looked like a name:

Gilmartin.

So he had six numbers, two letters, a surname and a telephone number. It wasn't a whole lot to go on, unless you were a professional cryptographer. But it wasn't like he could put in a call to Alan Turing. Instead, he dialed the number again.

'Senator Factor's office,' a voice said, clipped and correct and cold as a witch's tit. 'How can I help you?'

Cowan explained who he was and how he'd called this number in September from the UK and had spoken to her before. He was still trying to find out whether his daughter had an appointment to see someone in the Senator's office on Tuesday April 3rd.

'I'm sorry,' the voice said, icing over. 'We are unable to give out that kind of information on the phone.'

'We are unable, eh? How's about just you give it out, then?'

'Excuse me?'

'Can I speak to someone who can authorise sharing this information?'

'No. No one can. I'm sorry. We don't divulge that kind of thing. It's not permitted. You could make an appointment to come in and talk to our office.'

'I'd rather talk to a human being.'

'I'm sorry?'

'I'm not sure I'd be getting much out of your stapler and mouse pad, hen.'

'I meant…'

'Could I maybe come in this week?'

There was a very long pause. For a moment, Cowan thought she'd hung up on him. There were a series of clicks on the line.

'No, I'm sorry. It would have to be early December. As you may know the Senator is up for re-election this year and it's a very busy time for us.'

It was like talking to a robot icebox.

'I'm only here for the week. I'm visiting from Scotland.'

'I can't help you with that either. I'm sorry.'

Cowan rifled the notebook with his finger. He looked again at the pencilled note on the half-torn page:

202-225-0773 3/4/1030/IT

'Is there someone works there has the initials IT? Can you tell me that, at least?'

'We don't divulge that kind of information, sir.'

'Seriously? You're being serious here?'

'I'm sorry I can't be of more help.'

'You haven't been of any help, sweetie. Just to clarify.

In case you were wondering: no help at all. Zero. Zilch. Nada.'

'I'd be happy to make an appointment in December for you, sir.'

'Would you be any more up for divulging then, though?'

'Excuse me? Is there anything else I can help you with today?'

'Is that 'anything else' business a euphemism for 'why don't you fuck off now?''

'Sir...'

'Actually, now you mention it, you could do me one huge favour.'

There followed another endless pause. 'What's that, sir?'

'Could you bend all the way over your desk and spread your legs extremely wide and try shoving your appointment book as far as possible up your rectum?'

The phone went dead.

It was perhaps understandable in the circumstances. Cowan supposed he'd have to work on being a wee bit more diplomatic. This was Washington DC after all, political centre of the universe. The folks who worked here would be into all that diplomacy crap. Look what a bang-up job they were doing in what was left of the Middle East. He flopped back on the duvet and contemplated the ceiling, which was uninteresting as ceilings went. There was a print of the Lincoln Memorial on the wall. Lincoln looked glum and marble-hard. The pillow was nice and soft, though. A nap was most definitely called for. But the room phone rang and his hand picked it up before he wanted to. It was a reflex. He was exhausted and not thinking straight.

The Englishman accentuated the estuary vowels while the consonants clicked around them like shelly beetles. 'Detective Inspector? Name's Bannon. So glad you could make it over to the States. Can you meet me in the lobby in, say, half an hour?'

'This is the front desk,' Cowan announced, in a laboured American accent. 'When would you like your wake-up call again, sir?'

'Half an hour in the lobby, Detective Inspector. See you then.'

Cowan stared for a long time at the purring receiver.

Well, bugger and damn it.

He discovered the Second Secretary of the British Embassy near the front desk conducting a thorough examination of a fern. The man was a bit of a potted plant himself. Bannon was about 5′ 6″, a little on the paunchy side, with a broad ruddy open face, light brown hair and small watery clueless eyes. A fine specimen of the breed of Englishman that had once built and sustained empires by any means necessary, and in the 21st century didn't have a fucking clue what to do with themselves. Cowan perused the perfectly cut speckled-gray suit accented with red silk fibres woven into the wool. The jacket had broad lapels and silver buttons. It opened on a peach shirt and silk tie patterned in tiny green and red geometrically proportioned hexagons, secured by a gold clip. Quite the swanky wee package was this Bannon.

'Mr Bunion?' Cowan suggested malevolently, extending his hand.

'It's Bannon,' snapped Bannon, grin set like concrete. 'Bannon.'

'Must have written it down wrong.'

'A drink perhaps?' The consul mimed the tipping of a glass while pointing towards the bar with his pinky. One of the gestures was redundant, but the man *did* work for the government. 'What's your poison?'

'I'd rather have a coffee. I'm not a big one for alcohol.'

'I don't think I've ever heard that line from a Scotsman before,' Bannon declaimed, elevating an eyebrow.

'How many of us have you met?' Cowan asked. 'Two?'

The Second Secretary, seemingly under strict instructions to be tolerant, slapped a toothy smile across the moonscape of his face. His eyes didn't change at all, though. He was going to be as solicitous as a mortician and as much use to him as a wooden compass.

The carpet in the lobby had a peculiar design of randomly intersecting and twisted yellow and orange ovals and triangles. 'It's like walking on a broken slinky.'

'What is?' Bannon enquired, querulously. 'Eh?'

Bloody hell. Cowan's long day was shaping up to be longer yet.

The men crossed D Street to the West Wing Café. Inside, the lighting was low-key and the map of

Chesapeake Bay on the wall behind the creamer bucket resembled an angry blue dragon. Cowan ordered a regular coffee while his companion demanded an elaborate mocha latte concoction that would have confounded the expertise of Dr Frankenstein in his laboratory. Bannon folded the receipt carefully before he put it in his wallet, like he was starting to make an origami crane. It must have been a recoverable expense. They sat at a window table. There was a fine smorgasbord of crisps in a rack. A couple of tourists wandered by outside, looking lost and muggable, fingers pecking at their map apps, which weren't helping. Once upon a time humans only needed to know the location of the sun. Mind you, that had been a hell of an issue in Glasgow.

Cowan nodded at Bannon's foaming cup. 'Six dollars for that concoction? That's daylight robbery, that is. What's in it? Ambrosia, nectar of the Gods?'

'My understanding is you're only staying for five days,' Bannon said, the type who got right down to business. Small talk wasn't his forte.

'Seven,' corrected Cowan. 'I wanted to make sure I could slot in a jaunt down the Lincoln Memorial. I'm a big fan. Sometimes I kid myself Abe is sitting in an electric chair, which is very American too, right enough. I'm only staying the week but.'

Bannon dipped his long spoon carefully so as not to disturb the chocolate swirl decorating his froth. 'And it's my understanding that while here, you'll only be…'

'Wandering around the city a bit. That's all I'll be doing. I'm going to see the sights a little. Do the tourist thing.'

'Because what we wouldn't, obviously, want is…'

'Any kind of bother.'

'Well, yes.' Bannon studied him. 'When you put it like that. I think, from the office's perspective, what we'd like is bother kept to an absolute minimum. Yes?'

'I have my appointment with the local police tomorrow. But they're just going to be giving me an update on their inquiries.' Cowan took a sip. 'Or lack thereof.'

'I see.'

'Then I'm going to have a gander at a few of the places my daughter went when she was here. This is a sentimental journey, is what it is. I suppose you could say it's my way of saying goodbye to her. I'm not sure everyone would understand.'

Bannon licked a skein of froth from his lips and rearranged his features into a suitable mask of contrition. Here was a man who wouldn't understand in a million years. 'I am so terribly sorry for your loss.'

'Everyone says that. I'm not even sure what it means.' Cowan shrugged, brushing a few croissant crumbs off the table edge. 'Sorry for your loss. It's like my wallet fell out my trousers when I was taking a dump in a Starbucks bathroom.'

'I'm sorry… I didn't…'

'Mean to offend? None taken.'

'It must have been very hard for you.'

'It was harder for my daughter.'

The fat white face turned paler. Bannon was doing the same nervous thing with his tie that Oliver Hardy did in the old four-reelers. 'The reason I bring this up about your visit here, you understand, is that you do have something of a reputation for…'

'Being disagreeable.'

The wee man was tightening the tie now. The damn thing was fast acquiring noose status. 'Well, that's not the word, necessarily, that…'

'You'd choose.' Cowan smiled coldly. 'Say, does it bother you that I finish all your sentences for you?'

'No. I think…'

'That I need to step lightly and not be a bother to your office.'

Bannon leaned in confidentially now, placing a hand on his sleeve. Cowan looked down at where the man's hand rested. 'If you're going to ask me out, Mr Bunion, I don't think you're my type.'

'I do want to re-emphasise to you that this is a dangerous metropolitan area, very dangerous for someone who…'

'Come on, it can't be that much more dangerous than what I'm used to, eh? From all I've read, my understanding is this is kind of like Glasgow, only with guns.'

'I wouldn't…'

'And with an underclass distinguished by skin color, rather than a struggle with the Queen's English. Race is the modality in which class is lived, eh? Wouldn't you say?'

Bannon looked a little peeved and a lot confused. 'I can't

say I'm all that familiar with Glasgow, Detective Inspector,' he offered.

'Oh, you don't know what you're missing, man. I tell you, if you haven't been in Easterhouse on a Saturday night, you haven't lived. It's an education, is what it is.'

'I'm sure that...'

'So, anyway, this fella from Glasgow gets run over by a lorry and the next thing he knows he's in the next world. He spends his first day there just walking around, see? Takes a tour, sees the sights. He's very impressed by everything. Then he bumps into an old acquaintance. 'Fancy meeting you here,' he says. 'Aye, how you settling in?' says this other one. 'Well, I've been here a day now,' the newcomer says, 'and it's all well and good, but to tell you the truth I'm kind of disappointed.' 'How's that?' says the other one, very surprised. 'Well,' he says. 'I might be blaspheming here, but I think heaven after all turns out to be only a wee bit better than Glasgow!' The other one just looks at him for a while with a daft expression. Finally he says, 'This isn't heaven.'"

Bannon stared at Cowan blankly. His bottom lip protruded. It was thick and damp and red, like an overripe raspberry.

'He's not in heaven,' Cowan clarified. 'He's someplace else.'

'Ah,' sighed Bannon, 'Celtic humour.'

Cowan drained the last of his coffee and contemplated suicide.

'You were last over here in early May, I presume?'

'No.'

Cowan supposed Bannon would have made it his diplomatic business to know that he hadn't come earlier. The little homunculus was making a point by bringing it up now. 'My ex-wife came. I was on a case at the time. I couldn't get away.'

The consular official didn't move a muscle, but somehow contrived to emanate waves of disapproval, maybe through his aftershave. Cowan understood. What kind of man was it who didn't come to recover the body of his only child? It was a question that had to be asked. In fact he'd often asked it of himself: if he'd only been able to come then, if he'd only been able to see the body, if he'd only been a better man.

'After the autopsy,' he explained, 'there was a cremation. Apparently the Yanks have taken to calling the ashes 'cremains' these days. Jesus Fucking Christ! Anyhow, my wife has my daughter's cremains in this big ugly jar. She brought it home on the plane. It was probably a carry on. So, it wasn't like I didn't get to say goodbye to a big jar.'

'I…'

'You know it's just a day ago that I was in Glasgow! It's hard to believe. I was walking towards a taxicab on Queen Street and I swear to God I thought there was a ferret sitting in the back of it. I remember thinking to myself, 'Ah, the cab driver has a wee ferret with him.' But then, when I got nearer, I realised it wasn't a ferret at all. It was a woman. It was a little woman looked just like a ferret.'

Bannon plucked a napkin out of the dispenser on the table. He was perspiring now and the red sheen of his complexion was deepening into rouge.

'It must be awful hard to go through life looking like a ferret.' Cowan studied the dregs in his cup. 'Unless you are a ferret, that is. Then, it would be fine.'

Bannon shifted in his chair, looking itchy as a bear in spring. 'To tell you the truth, Detective Inspector, I haven't given the question much thought.'

'No, I wouldn't imagine you have.'

Bannon checked the time on his phone. No one wore wristwatches anymore. The things were way too practical, being attached to you. The brunette at the next table was watching herself in a mirror as she texted. Then she took a series of duck-face snapshots of herself in the mirror and texted some more. What a wonderful virtual world we lived in today. Somebody once said the unexamined life wasn't worth living, and now life wasn't worth living unless everyone else examined it.

'I'm afraid I have to be getting back over to Massachusetts Avenue,' Bannon announced, sliding the phone back in his pocket.

'Do you have Ying-Yang on yours?'

'What's what?'

'It's this new smart phone application from China. It's a cross between Yik Yak and Instagram. The way it works is, every time you answer your phone it takes a snapshot of you, puts an obscene caption under it, and sends it to everyone in Beijing.' Cowan winked at Bannon. 'Even if it's just a picture of your ying yang.'

'I'm not entirely sure I like your manner, Detective Inspector.'

Cowan examined his reflection in the curve of a turning spoon. He was upside down. Now he wasn't. 'Well, to be honest, I'm entirely sure I don't like your face, but I'm persevering regardless. And if you're going to get stroppy, go ahead. Don't hold back, sunshine. I can deal with it.' Cowan clattered the spoon in the saucer. 'I imagine it'd be a lot like getting savaged by a dead sheep.'

Bannon leapt to his feet, redder in the cheeks now, a cartoon Billy Bunter.

'Thanks for all your help but,' said Cowan, quietly. The abrupt change in his tone left the consul speechless for a moment. Bannon could only stand there flaring his nostrils, looking confused as a fart in a fan factory.

'Back then, when it happened,' Cowan clarified. 'Helping Maggie out with all the arrangements and that.'

'Oh,' said Bannon. 'It's what we do.' He had a chew at his lip. 'Listen…'

'You want to reiterate that I need to watch my step; not get in trouble; keep my trap shut; not be disagreeable; don't insult nobody; and leave town in a week without any fuss and make your job easy as pie, smooth as butter, hunky-dory and nice and easy does it, old chap.'

Bannon blinked at him like a broken machine. The man couldn't get a proper handle on Cowan and it upset him. 'Well, basically, something like that, yes.'

'I promise to be on my best behaviour.' Cowan crossed his heart theatrically. 'Scout's honour.'

'You were a boy scout?'

'Hell, no,' said Cowan, screwing up his face. 'I didn't want to go get myself buggered by one of them English Scoutmasters. I was in the Boy's Brigade. Way safer.'

6.30pm. Cowan wandered along E Street and up 7th to Chinatown. The Verizon Center was ugly as sin. Whose idea had it been to introduce the neon charmlessness of Times Square to this low-key city: Attila the Architect? He ordered an egg roll, a hot and sour soup and a chicken and snow peas with spicy sauce at Big Wong on H Street. When he'd entered the restaurant, the entire staff, everyone clad in a uniform the color of blood, turned and stared at him like he was Genghis Khan reincarnated. Cowan might as well have gone the whole hog and had a post-it note with 'tourist' written on it stapled to his forehead. The other customers in the restaurant tonight were all Chinese though, a good sign.

His fortune cookie read: 'It is now, and in this world, we must live.' Cowan had seen worse. In a take-out in Drumchapel a few years back he'd cracked one open that said 'Help! I am being held prisoner in a Chinese bakery.' He took it to be a joke.

There was news on the TV of another school shooting, this one at Florida State. An angry man doing what angry men did these days. The President, another angry man, was addressing immigration reform by executive order. His action immediately affected five million immigrants and there were demonstrations in front of the White House. Buffalo was buried head-deep in snow and the Bills were to play the Jets at Fed-Ex Field. None of these stories seemed to be related. The Fox anchor appeared to be suffering from some kind of brain injury. Cowan couldn't see the screen properly because a girl in a grey scarf stood in front of it, waiting for a take-out order. Her long blue coat billowed behind her like an 18th-century corseted dress. He was going to ask her to move, but decided he preferred looking at her rather than the screen. Cowan would have liked to live in the 18th-century. People back then went to coffee shops to talk and socialise, not to take photos. There would have been no televisions in Chinese restaurants, either.

The lights on the façade near the Shakespeare Theatre flashed blue, green, orange, and Cowan had a sudden inclination to visit the Capitol. It was five minutes out of his way. He intended to walk around the dome, the giant white tit that suckled a million lobbyists, and sit on the steps the way actors always did in bad movies. But the dome didn't look itself tonight, the 52 miles of scaffolding wrapped around the structure giving it a spiky demeanour. The symbol of American democracy was under repair. Standing in front, a family from Melbourne snapped thousands of selfies. This was the new age of Narcissus. Give it another hour and this shower would be hanging over the reflecting pool. The kids were all tanned, healthy, white-toothed and raucous the way Aussies are. Cowan tried to pretend he was outside the Sydney Opera House but it was too cold.

The father approached him. He was more dissipated than

the rest of the family, cigarette twiddling between stained fingers. 'Can I take a photo of you, mate?'

'Why'd you want to do that?'

''Cause it's what I do. I'm a professional photographer.' The Australian raised his camera, aimed and fired. 'Name's Shane. You've got yourself quite an accent there.'

'So do you, Shane.' Cowan nodded to where the man's family posed. 'They're so busy taking photographs of themselves, they don't even see the building.'

Shane didn't see anything wrong with that. He was half-cut and the after-burn of his breath could have sheared the fur off a beaver. 'It's a different age, see? Me and you are antiques. The kids get it, though. This is a new visual age we live in. Back in Hong Kong, your girl in her twenties, how does she spend her day? You know? I know.' Shane leaned closer whispering now, presumably so his missus couldn't hear. 'Between us, I've slipped it to more than a few little geishas in my day. Well, anyway, she spends four to six hours a day online, staring at a screen, two or three more in a karaoke bar, the rest in front of a TV slurping her noodles. That's what she does all day every day. That's it. This girl eats, fucks, and watches a screen. If she can, she watches a screen while she's eating and fucking. Which is how come doggystyle is now standard operating procedure. Is this a bad thing?'

'Yes?' suggested Cowan.

'No, this is the attaining of a field of visual sophistication we can only dream of. People like us come out of a literary culture, which is totally gone. It's dead as the fucking dodo, right? Forget it. It's expired. I mean, what person in this day and age is reading a fucking book? A book's about as useful today as an ashtray on a motorcycle.'

'What's the use of elaborating,' said Cowan, eyes closed, 'what, in its very essence, is so short-lived as a modern book?'

'Who said that, then?'

'An American called Herman. I think it might have been Munster.'

'Don't read books, mate. They hurt my eyes.' The Australian shook his head aggressively. 'So, can I take another photo of you?'

'Sure.' The Aussie recommenced clicking away dementedly. 'Say, isn't professional photographer the same as being a trainee paedophile?' Cowan inquired.

'I'll be tagging this one 'deeply depressed Scotsman sitting on steps of US Capitol' just saying. You lot blew it big time though, didn't you?'

'What?'

'Nearly your own country for a minute back then, with that referendum. Looked like you'd be celebrating your independence from the Poms, like what we got down under.' Shane shrugged. 'Must've been a hell of a big disappointment, that.'

'I'm glad we didn't get it,' Cowan said, staring off towards the red light atop the Washington Monument at the far end of the mall. He was speaking with passion now. 'We didn't deserve it. We shat in the nest. We weren't fucking worthy of it.'

'I think it's a Stockholm syndrome situation,' Shane noted, ruefully. 'You know, when you're held captive so long you get to enjoy it?'

'Aye,' said Cowan. 'You think if you get shot of the pain and the loss you'll find a new identity, only to find the pain and the loss was your identity. You enjoyed the suffering, slobbering all over the hand that beat you like an abused cocker spaniel.'

'I know why it is you're depressed, cobber.' The Australian banged a karate chop on his shoulder. 'You're a fucking philosopher. That's a terrible bleeding thing to be.'

'Naw, I'm a fucking Scot is what I am,' muttered Cowan, shaking his head despondently. 'I'm a man doesn't have a real country, or one worth the having.'

'This thing is a big bust, though,' Shane said, pointing up at the dome. 'No pun intended. It's got hundreds of cracks, see? Sixty million dollars it'll take to fix. I come here to take a photo and the thing looks fucking ridiculous. You can't get it in frame without the scaffolding sticking out like a greyhound's balls. Come, check this out.'

He ended up following the Australian all the way around the dome to the other side. They walked for a good ten minutes. 'It's getting cold,' Cowan said.

'That's that Superb Court place over there,' Shane said, nodding at it. He wheeled and raised his arm Nazi salutestyle towards the back of the Capitol upon which had been strapped what looked like an enormous plaster.

'God almighty, it's like they've stuck a giant Elastoplast on it.'

'More like a big sanitary pad, I've been saying.'

A photograph was taken of Cowan squinting at the bandaged dome.

'Depressed Scottish Tourist Distressed at Condition of American Democracy,' Shane said, clicking away. 'Standing out tonight like a shag on a rock.'

Cowan thought of something funny to say in reply, and then didn't, recalling that it is now and in this world that we must live.

He walked back to his hotel in the chill, studying clouds adrift in a shine of stars.

2   THURSDAY

Cowan woke at 6am, showered, shaved, and took a moment to consider his receding hairline and its relation to the universe. Why was it when you hit 40 you couldn't grow hair up top any more, but the stuff gets to sprouting vigorously out of your nose and ears? Is it supposed to make you heed larger cosmic ironies: how something came once from nothing, a singularity before space-time? Cowan was addressing the God he didn't believe in again. It had become a habit this year. *Do you want us thinking about quark-gluon plasma while contorting before a hotel shaving mirror that shows every clogged pore in microscopic detail with a nail scissor shoved halfway up our left nostril? Infinitely dense, are you? A circle whose centre is everywhere and circumference nowhere. What does that even mean? Talk to us. Give us a sign. Come on. Give her back. Give her back to me.*

It was cold as fuck. The cab drivers clustered on the corner the day before were now isolated in their cabs. Cowan strolled down an expectant row, disappointing in turn Diamond, Yellow, Lincoln, Capital, Elite, Luxury, Silver, Liberty, Icon, Wonder. He had read someplace that due to the disruption in their industry, cab drivers were becoming suicidal. These days it was Uber *uber alles*.

He bought a *Post* in the Starbucks on the corner of E and New Jersey Avenue and spilled muffin crumbs between the pages as he flipped them. No crime report on the front page, bar the usual delinquencies of politicians. He scanned the roundup on page 3 of the Metro section:

> *A 19-year-old man found with multiple gunshot wounds in Southeast Washington died early yesterday at Prince George's County Hospital centre, police said. The unidentified man was found just after 2am behind the Barry Farm apartments in the 300 block of Anacostia Road and pronounced dead at 4am.*

Local entrepreneurs in competition: raw, unbridled capitalism leaving its usual trail of collateral damage. But police statistics indicated violence was well down from its 1980s peak, a consequence of gentrification: a frivolous word that, like all the best euphemisms. Gentrification slid problems out of sight, out of mind. In 1970s Glasgow, they'd levelled the Gorbals and kicked deprivation to the margins, to new grim council estates, grey concrete wastelands, deserts with windows. In DC, skyrocketing real estate values drove the underclass northeast, sliding poverty and vice into Prince George's County. Violence was portable and when push came to shove, as it always did, you could get violent about violence. You didn't use the police or army. You didn't call out the National Guard. You deployed the realtors. *The poor you will always have with you. That was another of your greatest hits. All we ever do is push the wretched of the earth around the map, like you did the moneylenders out the temple that time.*

His daughter's murder had been on the front page for so long because she was an aberration. Her death brought a nice frisson of fear back to a complacent city. A young, attractive, white exchange student shot dead in a meaningless random mugging. It was inconceivable. *'Omigod, it, like, could have been ME!'* It was the return of the repressed, a reminder of what lurks under the veneer of a gentrifying metropolis.

The frightened ones needed to linger on her death, sift its hidden meanings. They needed their ritual mourning, time to break the sprig of evergreen Acacia, so they might forget. For six weeks, Catriona was remembered, her face haunting page one; she was that cute, adorable, photogenic. She was that white. Then she was disappeared again, a disturbed dream fading into wakefulness. That nameless black man gunned down on a street in Anacostia was buried deeper still though, never having existed. Out of sight, out of mind forever. The bogeyman we shunt to the dusty corners of the imagination. The unacknowledged. It was one of the forgotten that had killed her. He was somewhere walking these streets breathing the same air Cowan was. That had to stop.

Cowan recycled the newspaper, being on a sustainability kick, and walked up C Street to the Metropolitan Police Headquarters on Indiana Avenue. He looked up at the high blue ceiling and sucked slivers of chilled air into his lungs. It was a hell of a blue day to feel this blue on. What on earth had happened to the weather? An empty sleeve of a day and sparrows so cold they huddled for warmth beneath the bushes, frozen feather balls. A dwarf on crutches outside Judiciary Square Metro nodded at him in sympathy. At least the wee man had on a proper jacket. Cowan wasn't dressed for this weather at all and was as frozen as Walt Disney.

The Second District Commander had suggested they meet downtown instead of in his office on Idaho Avenue. For convenience's sake, he claimed. But for whom was it most convenient? Cowan detected the soft pliant hand of PR, and was bothered by it. On the corner of 3rd and D, he paused by the Albert Pike statue. Pike, bearded and long-haired as Jerry Garcia, was holding forth from on high, a copy of his *Morals and Dogma of the Ancient and Accepted Scottish Rite of Freemasonry* clutched in his left hand. The bronze Athena on the pedestal below carried the banner of the Rite with that double-headed, scary-ass eagle of Lagash emblazoned on it. The thing was weird as fuck.

The Daly Building was an ugly seven-storey art deco number that would have given Charles Rennie Mackintosh a nervous breakdown. It looked down at heel. The District was trying to unload it for $175 million, a snippet in this market. The private sector would go bananas for its prime downtown location. The current occupants had issues with rats, cockroaches, burst pipes and ceiling collapses. Cowan remembered similar problems with the old Pitt Street head-quarters: that Frankenstein horror – part handsome 30s brick, part 70s concrete and glass. There had at least been one sober architect involved with the Daly Building, although he wasn't the demented individual who'd stuck the creepy eagles up on the stone pillars framing the entranceway.

Waiting in an anteroom, Cowan killed time by looking up Albert Pike online. A man who said he'd give up Freemasonry rather than recognize the Negro as a Masonic brother, yet who declared every man should be free, for a free man is an asset, a slave a liability. The author of the Confederate war song 'Dixie', Pike's poetry had been praised by Poe, probably when little Eddie was shitfaced. Still, it was just as well the only Confederate General given a statue on Federal property was represented in his civilian clothes. Cowan even found a Pike quote: *The true word of a Mason is to be found in the concealed and profound meaning of the Ineffable Name of Deity, communicated by God to Moses; and which meaning was lost by the very precautions taken to conceal it.* The moral being that some secret societies were so secret they forgot what their secrets were.

Cowan was at last ushered into a small room. A paper sheet taped to the door outside read IR2. It was obviously a temporary deal. A net curtain was slung across the window on a plastic hook-and-wire. There were four chrome-framed chairs either side of a big veneered desk, in which were etched long narrow white scratches, like a cat had been the last one in for interrogation. The desk took up much of the room. This was never a District Commander's office. This was a space designed to show that work was being done, that investigations were ongoing, that police were policing. There was a big HD Sony television hooked to a hard drive. Cowan was going to be getting a picture show.

Darius McDonald, Second District Commander, entered carrying a manila folder and a set of discs. He was tall and around fifty, African American. He carried his excess weight well, the features thickening but still attractive, and seemed to glide upon a podium of self-assurance. He was bald, but seemed to be bearing up well under the circumstances. McDonald held out his hand. His smile was open and friendly. It had damn well better be, though. 'Detective Inspector Cowan.'

Cowan lifted the proffered hand up and down and McDonald sat behind the desk. He inched his seat forward till his stomach nudged the drawer.

'I'm not sure whether I address you as Commander or Inspector,' Cowan said.

'Oh, Inspector is fine. I've never taken to being called a Commander.'

'I might try to get upgraded to Commander when I get back home,' Cowan said. 'It has a certain ring to it. It'd be like I was in Star *Trek*.'

McDonald tented his hands as if in prayer. 'I'm sorry for your loss.'

'Aye, everyone is.' Cowan looked McDonald up and down, assessing. 'You're not what I expected. I thought you'd be different.'

McDonald's eyes glazed over, indicating the offence taken. 'What were you expecting?'

'I thought you'd be taller.'

McDonald smiled, probably despite himself.

'What are you, Commander? 6′ 2″?'

'6′ 3″.'

'What's your fighting weight then?'

'I'm 270lbs.'

'See, that means nothing to me. I'd need that converted to stones and ounces.'

'I'm surprised you didn't do research on me, Detective Inspector.' McDonald commenced riffling through the folder, absent-mindedly. It was a clean file. No notes scribbled on it. No fingerprint staining the manila. 'I was informed you're very thorough.'

'Sounds to me like you're the one has been doing the research.'

'We were sent over some material by your consulate.' McDonald lifted a pair of spectacles with light-blue speckled frames out of his breast pocket. He put them on, becoming instantly more professorial. 'From a Mr Bannon?'

'Hope he said nice things about me. They say if you can't say something nice about someone, don't say anything at all.'

'You subscribe to that?'

'Absolutely.' Cowan nodded enthusiastically. 'By the by, that Bannon's a total English wanker. I wouldn't piss on him if he was on fire. He's probably hanging out with his old Eton chums from the Embassy even as we speak, betting on which of the blindfolded hobos will successfully make it across the frozen lake.'

McDonald laid the folder down on the desk and regarded Cowan seriously. 'So,' he said, 'what would you like us to cover today?'

'Your career began in Gary, Indiana,' Cowan said, closing his eyes. 'You came to the MPD in October '88. You worked a foot beat in the First District. By '99, you were promoted to lieutenant and worked Homicide. You also worked Prostitution Enforcement Unit. Good work if you can get it. By '07 you were Captain and working Internal Affairs. Now, here you are, big chief of the Second District. You've reached the top and had to stop and that's what's bothering you. You got degrees from Indiana and Johns Hopkins, are a graduate of the FBI national academy, and every day you wonder if you got to where you are because of affirmative action. I think that about covers it.'

McDonald took off his glasses. His eyes had acquired a crocodilian cast. 'You have done your research.'

'Your people have a very informative website.'

'My people?'

'Uh-huh.'

McDonald picked up a tiny yellow pencil and tapped it on the desk as he spoke. 'Correct me if I'm wrong, but do I detect a certain hostility, Detective Inspector?'

'That must be the FBI training you're putting to use.'

'No doubt.'

'You have a Scottish name, Commander: McDonald. Makes me think of the Glencoe massacre. How the Campbells did your clan in, a bad business that. What with it being a massacre and so on. That's probably where them Campbells got the idea for the tomato soup. Then again, the name also makes me think of that clown in the hamburger ads.' Cowan shrugged. 'I don't suppose you'd be related to him either?'

'Well, to be honest, Detective Inspector, I think the name came from some slave overseer, and he was probably a relative, yes.' McDonald fixed Cowan with his stare. 'My great-great-great grandmother was probably raped by one of your countrymen. That's what Ancestry DNA tells me at any rate. I'm 11% Scottish. But I try not to give it too much thought. Let bygones be bygones, as they say.'

Cowan nodded. 'Fair enough. I can still get you the clan tartan if you want but.'

The blue radiator in the corner hummed like a trapped insect. It was pleasantly warm in the little room but with a chill fast descending.

'Detective Inspector, the fact that I'm black bothers you, doesn't it?' McDonald rattled the pencil on the desk in a staccato rhythm. 'But here's what I'm going to do, I'm going to give you the benefit of the doubt.'

'That's big of you.'

'I'm going to assume the attitude I'm getting is because you lost your daughter and you're extremely upset and it's not just because you're some racist fuckhead.'

Cowan tapped a finger on his temple. 'Holy smokes. There's that FBI training kicking in again. It's truly a thing to behold.'

'I can't do anything about being black,' McDonald said. 'I can do something about your daughter. Maybe it's time you got to prioritising.'

McDonald tossed the pencil into the drawer and removed a little yellow cloth. He unfolded it and began gently cleaning the lenses of his glasses. 'We thought you'd have come to recover your daughter's body.'

Cowan sat back in his chair. 'I was indisposed.'

'You were?'

'That's right.'

'How so?'

The District Commander gazed phlegmatically at him, wiping methodically. A minute came and went. Cowan succumbed and shook his head ruefully, laughing. 'Well, actually, to tell you God's honest truth I was stuck in this rather cushy rehabilitation centre in April and May dealing with a relapse into alcohol abuse.'

McDonald sat very still. 'A lot of us have been there.'

'Have we?'

'Yes.'

'Aye, I suppose Bill has friends the world over?'

'So I hear. Especially where policemen gather.'

'Which would, in my experience, mostly be in bars, right enough.'

Cowan splayed his hands on the desk and examined the knuckles. Near where his thumb rested, was a word carved with a penknife: Boaz. He traced the letters with his finger. Sounded biblical. Maybe they'd arrested Job at the same time as the cat. Maybe it was Job's cat. Now there was a fellow who seriously needed a pet. 'I could have left early, obviously. They encouraged me to go. I was told I had some serious grieving to do. It's funny, people always have opinions about how best to grieve. That's the worst part. But I was almost finished with the programme by then, and my daughter was dead. I couldn't bring her back. I couldn't do anything. I did the memorial service.' Cowan shrugged. 'End of the day, I felt safer there. I don't know what I'd have done with myself otherwise. Actually, I take that back. I do know. I would have walked into the nearest local tavern and got pissed as a newt.'

'It was a lot to put on your wife.'

'My ex-wife. Aye, it was, and she'll likely never forgive me for it. But there's a hell of a lot of things that she'll never forgive me for anyway, from way back. I wasn't much of a husband to her. So it's all a wash.'

'You're not drinking now?'

'Not yet.'

'You've been over here before?'

'Aye, I've been to Florida on holiday. Chicago as well, for a big conference on the community policing of tomorrow, which was worse than useless. Nice lake though, full of water as I remember.'

McDonald laid the cloth on the desk and rested his glasses on top of it. He re-opened the folder and commenced leafing through the contents. 'You have some concerns about the investigation?'

'Naturally.'

'So do I, obviously.'

'Obviously.'

'So, there's something else we can agree on.'

'Aye, at this rate we're practically twins. How's about I call you Big Mac, if that's all right with you? Just to be friendly, like. A nickname if you will.'

'Fine by me,' McDonald said, grimly. 'So long as I get to call you 'small fries.' Is that OK with you, Detective Inspector? Just to be friendly.'

'Small fries! Hell, that was nearly a right good comeback, Commander.' Cowan gave a thumbs up. 'You should have been on the stage. You could have done stand up.'

'I could never have dealt with the hecklers,' McDonald muttered, not looking at Cowan. 'I'd have been wanting to jump down and smack them upside the head.'

There was a faint smile threatening to break across the District Commander's face now, but it was Cowan who smiled at him first.

McDonald walked Cowan through the investigation. Metrorail video surveillance showed Catriona arriving on the Foggy Bottom station platform at 10pm. Cowan watched the tape for the hundredth time. There she stood. His one and only, whom he'd loved so very much, wearing jeans and a long trench coat, staring at her phone, oblivious, alive, smiling at some message, warm blood fizzing through her veins. A minute later she was being bundled onto the Orange Line train to Vienna by two African American males, never to be seen alive again. It was a commuter, boarding at East Falls Church, who came upon the body thirty minutes later. His daughter was slumped, seemingly asleep in a corner compartment. The other passenger became alarmed only after seeing blood pooling on the floor. Catriona had been shot three times at close range by two different weapons. Her purse and mobile phone were gone.

The killers left the train at Ballston, seven minutes before the discovery of the body. Descriptions were vague. No eye-witnesses to the killing. The two men concealed their faces on the platform. Dark North Pole hoodies and baseball caps, scarves pulled over mouths. No witnesses at Foggy Bottom either. The passengers seated at the far end of the compartment noticed nothing unusual, idiot cyborgs so plugged into their stupid electronic devices they hadn't seen or heard a thing. Unbelievable! The main video surveillance camera at Ballston was broken, the footage grainy and unusable.

Catriona's murder horrified the city, that horror deepening when there was no initial breakthrough despite extensive publicity. But the investigation turned five weeks later, when an informant identified one of the men in the video as Carlton Sammons, a 26-year-old convicted drug dealer from Naylor Gardens. Sammons had a long criminal record and now nothing further to add to it, having himself been found dead from gunshot wounds in the Anacostia River a week before the positive ID. It was assumed to be a gang killing, part of a turf war. The police remained convinced from the evidence of the surveillance tape that Sammons had indeed been one of Catriona's killers. Despite canvassing friends and acquaintances, the other man had not been identified. The guns used in the murder were likely bought in Virginia or Maryland, most likely by some young girl with no priors, a straw purchase on a form 4473. This was true of 60% of the guns recovered in DC. The guns would be a dead end then, as guns tended to be. They'd be in a river by now, along with the mobile phone. The consensus was still a street mugging gone wrong.

'I hate consensus,' Cowan interrupted. 'Now, typically, murders here happen in specific neighbourhoods?'

'Yes, we're talking east of the river.'

'And black on black and drug-related?'

McDonald exhaled wearily. 'Nearly half the black men in DC have been incarcerated or are now. Was a time, we had more violent criminals per capita than any other city. Things are a lot better now. Chicago's gotten well ahead of us: Chiraq, they're killing it. They took the throne.'

'Murders of young white females by black males are unusual?'

'Very. And murders on the Metro even more so. I can't recall one before this. It's safer than church.'

'I wouldn't know anything about church. I quit worshipping Bronze Age idols a while back.' Cowan pattered his fingers on the desk. 'There was massive coverage of my daughter's case. I've got a stack of *Washington Posts* that reaches the ceiling of my flat. As a policeman, you couldn't have asked for more publicity.'

'That's true.'

'How does that make you feel?'

'How does *what* make me feel?'

'The amount of publicity this case got?'

'It makes me feel I don't like having unsolved murders in my district.'

'That's it?'

'That's it.'

'But if this was a black girl in southeast got killed in a mugging gone bad, it wouldn't be front and centre?'

'No.' McDonald nodded. 'It would be forgotten. Cases get cold quick.'

'How does that make you feel?'

'I already answered that question, Detective Inspector,' McDonald said, vexed. 'Can I get you a coffee or something?'

'I'm fine. So, nothing bothers you about this murder, about it not making sense?'

'There are always things about murders that don't make sense. They're murders.'

'But I'm asking, policeman to policeman, in this little confessional of yours here, no one else around, if you believe in your heart this was a mugging got out of hand?'

'In my heart?'

'Well, if you don't have one, whatever part of your anatomy you want to look inside.' Cowan shrugged. 'Maybe have a quick peek at your pancreas?'

McDonald smiled obliquely at him. 'While the investigation is still ongoing I'm not prepared to make that call. You're sure I can't get you that coffee?'

'I said I was fine'. Cowan's right hand had balled into a fist. 'So, you've been sitting around on your fat arse up on Idaho Avenue waiting for someone to squeal all this time and nobody's come forward?'

'My ass isn't fat, son,' McDonald drawled. The Commander held Cowan's glance for an uncomfortably long time. 'Maybe you haven't been looking at it closely enough.'

'I think I will have that coffee.' Cowan threw his hands up in mock surrender. 'I do seem to be a wee bit on the touchy side today.'

McDonald returned with two plastic cups. The coffee had that fresh-from-the-machine synthetic taste. The Commander looked like he'd calmed down some. Cowan wondered if he'd gone and popped a couple of valiums in the bathroom. 'Would the plural of valium be valiums or val-iaa?' he blurted.

McDonald looked at Cowan a long time in a way that intimated he might be thinking himself dealing with a lunatic, which was fair enough.

'Shaking down suspects to give up others is always the way to go?'

'Beats ballistics and forensics every time.' McDonald leaned back in his chair, which creaked meaningfully. He looked tired. He sipped and wrinkled his nose. 'OK, Detective Inspector. Here it is, straight. I did think something would turn up by now. We've chased down every informant and neighbourhood contact, canvassed and re-canvassed. We've had more publicity than Kim Kardashian's ass. And nothing. But we'll get it. Something will get pinned on our second shooter by a snitch in some half-ass plea deal. We might be waiting a while on it. But it'll happen. Maybe the cellphone, maybe the credit cards will turn up. I doubt they will. We'll never find the guns. They're deep sixed in a river. But this will get solved. I will get that other man who killed your daughter. You have my word. I will put him away.'

Cowan pointed at the cup and grimaced. 'Tastes like goat urine.'

'That's probably what it is.'

'One of the guns used was a Glock 17. Two of the bullets were from that one. That's what the MPD uses, right?'

'What can I say?' McDonald shrugged despondently. 'The knuckleheads like the same weapon the police have. It's comforting to them.'

'And do your knuckleheads usually shoot a civilian three times like that?'

'No.' The Commander looked distressed now, tonguing his bottom lip. 'They don't. And I don't get that. I can't fathom how a straight up robbery went that bad.'

Cowan leaned forward, excited. He had at last elicited a glimmer of indecision. 'I've been trying to imagine how it went down ever since. If you shoot someone in the head, why would your buddy go and shoot them two more times? That's overkill. And if you shot a girl twice during some thieving because you bolloxed it up and there was a struggle, why would you then go ahead and shoot her execution style? What kind of fuckery is that? See, I don't know anything about guns. 'I come from Europe where we're more civilized and all that, but shooting someone in the head that way seems…'

'Professional.' McDonald uttered the word molasses slow.

'How do you mean?'

'The headshot was from the twenty-two. Twenty-twos are often used by professionals who like to work close in. See, I have given this some thought.'

'And your conclusion is?'

'I don't have one. The man we know for sure was there that night was no professional. He was all kinds of twisted, but limited: a gangbanger, a street thug.'

'I'd like a list of this Sammons' friends and acquaintances.'

'You know I can't do that.' McDonald slipped his glasses back on. 'And if you went anywhere near southeast with this, you'd be dead in five.'

'Maybe I'll take my chances.'

'Don't bother them they won't bother you. They're like spiders in that regard.'

'I always make a point of never bothering spiders,' Cowan noted, shivering theatrically. 'What kind of a person is it, who does that anyway? Who gets up in the morning and thinks, 'Aw, I'm fucking bored today, I think I'll go annoy that spider.''

McDonald sighed. 'Tell me what else is bothering you, Detective Inspector.'

Cowan took the old metro card from his wallet and laid it on the desk. 'That was in the pocket of her jeans the night she died. It indicates how far you travel, right? I had it examined. So, the last two trips she made were for $1.90, which meant she took a trip to somewhere and back that day that was $1.90 away from the station beside the university.'

'It didn't have to be that day. It could have been earlier.' McDonald shrugged. 'And why assume she started out from Foggy Bottom?'

Cowan nodded, thinking. 'But it would be possible for you to get me a list of the metro stations which are that far away from Foggy Bottom? $1.90 away?'

'I can do that. I'm not sure how knowing where your daughter was earlier that day will help…'

'Just send me the list. I've got a hunch.'

McDonald crinkled his empty cup and sniffed. 'Do police investigations in Scotland mostly involve hunches?'

'Aye, they usually do. Sometimes, I also get notions when the rheumatism in my left knee gives me gyp. By the way, what happened to her computer?'

'We returned it to you with the rest of her possessions.'

'Aye, but the thing was tampered with.'

'Excuse me?'

'So, it wasn't your people did it, then? I wondered about that. See, I was trying to recover her emails. So I took it to our cybersecurity boffin. We call him Q, for obvious reasons. Q told me her drive was tampered with. I can't explain all he said. I'm not an expert on the jargon. Just that some fuck had been nosing around in there, looking at her files and mail and so on, and whoever this snooper was, he was pretty sophisticated, seeing as how he tried to remove indications of said unauthorised activity, had debugged the bugs, altered system times, whatever that means.'

'You're saying that your daughter's computer was hacked?'

'No. I'm saying this person had direct physical access to it at some point.'

McDonald looked more perturbed now.

'Which is how come I need to talk to her roommate, also. See if she has any ideas about who else had access to the computer. But that sweetheart won't return my calls.'

'She's not obligated to talk to you.'

Cowan shrugged. 'Also, the coat Catriona was wearing on the night she died? It was a Burberry Brit: a Felden Trenchcoat. I had it priced: fifteen hundred dollars.'

'Expensive.'

'Aye, and two weeks before she was begging her mother to wire money because she was down to her last two hundred.'

McDonald crushed his cup and dunked it in the trash can. 'Maybe that's because she spent all her money on a coat. Or maybe she came into some money?'

'How would she do that?'

'There are ways. Some students sell their blood and plasma for money,' McDonald suggested unconvincingly. 'My son used to do that.'

'Does your son do drugs?'

McDonald's eyes narrowed. 'What?'

'The traces of marijuana and E that showed up in the autopsy?'

'Well, where there's drugs, there's money.' McDonald picked up a random sheet of paper and studied it like it was an exam. 'That's true. But we found no evidence your daughter was involved in drugs beyond the recreational.'

There were other ways a young attractive woman could make money quickly in a metropolitan area and McDonald, ex-vice, would know it. He probably didn't bring it up now to protect the delicacy of a grieving father's feelings. What Cowan didn't feel comfortable sharing with McDonald right then, was how little he really knew about his own daughter. He hadn't even seen that much of her after Maggie booted him out on his arse eight years before. Weekends, those two summer holidays in Ibiza. He hadn't known she used drugs, although that was hardly unusual for a student. He didn't even know she smoked, until that half-empty pack of Virginia Slims showed up in her coat pocket.

What else didn't he know? The reason he was even there. That was a riddle too. Was he really trying to find her killer or was he here in search of the daughter he'd lost, not this year, but many years before? Why the need to go back to the crematorium and sift the ashes? Was it all about him, really? Was it just that Calvinist guilt, the curse of a nation? Maybe he should just let it go, get the first flight out. He was a man clutching at straws and drowning as they floated away from his flailing grasp. The pain he was now forgetting. It had even eased some in recent months, but the blank whirl-wind of emotion, the horror of great darkness, the sense of total desertion, those were the things he couldn't forget. But he was doing something now, damn it, making amends. Trying. He pulled the blue flyer out of his jacket and placed it on the desk. He smoothed it out. 'This was in the pocket of her coat along with the pack of cigarettes.'

'I saw it. Distributed on the GW campus.' McDonald shrugged slightly. 'This sexual consent thing is a big issue for undergraduates. They put up posters about it.'

'Young adults have to be told how to give sexual consent? How stupid are they?'

'It's a political issue: sexual assault on campus. The White House was involved at one point. Not the current regime, obviously. They'd offer tax breaks for sex traffickers.'

'Did you need a government to tell you what consent was at that age?'

'I could figure it out.'

'They'll soon be wanting twenty-year-olds to fill out a bunch of paperwork before they jump in the sack.'

'No doubt.' McDonald smiled. 'Who was it that came up with the idea that you need lawyers in the bedroom with you when you're hitting it?'

'Lawyers.' Cowan pointed to the flyer. 'See here? There's a phone number and what looks like an appointment time. See it? In pencil, a bit faded.'

McDonald picked up the flyer. He moved his glasses lower on his nose as he scanned it: 'March 4th. 10.30. IT. Cryptic.'

'April 3rd, you mean.'

'March 4th.'

'No. See, Catriona would have written down the day

and then the month. She was Scottish. If it's a date then it's April 3rd.'

'I see. You write things backwards in Scotland too.'

'We're backward in every possible way. This is an example of you detecting though, is it? I take it no-one followed up on any of this?'

'You take it correctly.'

Cowan sniffed derisively. 'Aye, why doesn't that surprise me? Because this was an open and shut robbery case, right? Anyhow, I called the number to save you the bother and it's the office of a US Senator. Now, what would she have to do with him at all?'

McDonald considered, eyeing the flyer. 'Your daughter was taking classes in the Elliot school, right? Political science. Maybe it was an assignment? Talk to a politician and see how stupid a person has to be to get elected?'

Cowan didn't laugh. 'Thing is, this office won't talk to me about it. Won't even tell me what IT stands for.'

McDonald squinted. 'It's IT? Isn't that a period? Instructional Technology?'

'Never thought of that. Maybe these were the same boys hacking her computer for her then, eh? Case solved already. You're brilliant, Hercules.' Cowan stuffed the flyer back in his pocket and leapt up abruptly, shoving the chair back. 'Well, I can't be sitting around here chewing the fat with you all day, though. All you do is ask question after question. I've got to get going to see a man about a dog.'

'I hope it's not a pit bull.'

'Why is that? Are you afraid I'd bite it, Commander?'

McDonald stood up and the men shook hands again, albeit considerably warier of one another now. The Commander palmed Cowan a small card. 'I've written my home number on the back. If you need to talk.'

'About the case? Or me needing a drink?'

'I never specify. One word of advice, though.'

'If you must. If it's choosing between Mastercard or Visa though I…'

'You've seen those old Westerns on the tube, Detective Inspector? You know how in those movies there's an outsider who comes to the town to straighten things out?'

'I think I did see that film. Say, did this fellow have a horse, by any chance?'

'And he ends up shooting the place up.'

'I don't carry a gun. I hate the damn things. I've had terrible experiences in my family with them, quite recently also, to be frank. Did you hear about that? You probably forgot already. I seriously think you ought to lay off them cowboy films though, Commander, they're screwing with your ability to make an effective analogy.'

'Please don't be that man. That's all I'm saying to you. I don't have any patience for that cowboy attitude.'

'You sound like the bad head cop in a worse TV show.'

'I wouldn't appreciate you conducting any kind of private investigation that interferes with our own inquiries. I'm sure as a policeman you must understand that?'

'Come off it, do I look like a troublemaker to you?'

'Yes.'

Cowan looked hurt. 'Oh no, I think I've been rumbled.' He scratched his head. 'What do you make of it all then, Commander?'

'What do I make of what all?'

'Oh, you know, life.'

'Life?' McDonald commenced doing peculiar things with his eyelashes. 'I have no idea even how to begin answering that.'

'Does it strike you as not being, when all is said and done, worth the bother?'

'Life? No. But I don't think all is said and done here, now, in this place.'

'You mean you believe there's another place then! That's so fucking cute! You're a religious person then, faith in things unseen and all the rest of the transcendental jazz. What's your considered opinion on the status of the Easter Bunny, then?'

'I do think there's another world.' McDonald looked grimly at him now. 'I'm not going to apologise for what I believe. I think we see glimpses of it here. Even in this room if you're willing to get over yourself and look.'

Cowan glanced around the little interview room nervously, feigning apprehension, then broke into a broad grin. 'Anyway, if you could text that list of DC Metro stations to me asap, I'd appreciate it. Rest assured, I'll also be in touch with you directly if I need to have another murder case mishandled.'

Cowan rode the red line to Metro Center and switched to the blue. He walked to the place on the Foggy Bottom platform where his daughter had stood the night she died and felt nothing but pain. The lights throbbed and an orange line train to Vienna wormed in. The same one that had carried his daughter to her death. He considered getting on it. Maybe he could go hear a few Strauss waltzes, take in a few of the spooky Egon Schiele drawings, or get himself into serious therapy with Sigmund Fraud. Ah, Vienna. How did the song go again? This means nothing to me. That's how the song went.

12.10pm. Cowan was twenty minutes early. He ordered a black forest ham and cheddar sandwich and another coffee and sat at a corner table of the I Street Au Bon Pain. He'd read somewhere that Oscar Levant drank 40 cups of coffee a day. He was becoming Oscar Levant. There were worse people to be. He took out the flyer and looked at it again. He was getting obsessed, it was true. Why contact a Senator's office? What was she doing? Why wouldn't they talk to him? What does any of it mean?

'Charles Cowan?'

'That's what my driver's licence says.'

The young man had told Cowan in his last email that he'd be instantly recognizable due to his red scarf. He was. An ostentatious cashmere number slung casually over his left shoulder. The scarf matched his eyes. He looked like he'd been up all night on a serious bender. Cowan knew that look, from the mirror mostly. He took in the tight Levis and black boots, the Ralph Lauren down-stuffed leather vest over a shirt like an action painting. The Louis Vuitton man-bag was a dead giveaway, so was the short-in-the-front-longer-in-the-back undercut chopped at an angle on the neck. Deyon Ferguson was clean-shaven and loose-limbed. Cowan wasn't the only customer looking at him now, but if the boy was conscious of the stares, he didn't care. He was used to the scrutiny, as beautiful people tended to be. The case file identified him as a 'former boyfriend' of Catriona, which was further evidence that the DC police were as useless as a carpet fitter's ladder. Deyon took a seat opposite him, swept croissant flakes off the tabletop, grimacing slightly. He commenced massaging the back of his neck.

'You want to get yourself something to eat, son?'

'No.' Deyon looked around warily. 'I feel like throwing up, actually,' he whispered, hand to his throat. 'I'll try to restrain myself.'

'How did you know who I was?'

'I looked for a middle-aged man who seemed out of place and awkward and foreign.'

Cowan raised his hand. 'Present.' He was grateful there was no sorry for your loss exchange. He couldn't put up with much more of that crap. 'I like your vest thing.'

The young man stroked the leather on his shoulder.

'Salvation Armani,' he said.

Cowan tapped his saucer. 'This is my fourth coffee today

and it's not even noon. I'm going to be a right basket case at this rate.'

'Can I write that down?' Deyon extracted a tiny red notebook from his bag. 'I love those phrases. What was it again? A right basketcase? Cat had a lot of those.'

'Aye, I suppose she must have.'

'You look like her, which is also how I knew who you were.'

'She was adopted.'

Deyon's mouth clicked open and shut like a trap-jaw ant. 'Umm.'

'I'm just messing with you, son. Her looks come from her mother. Obviously.'

'You're not terrible looking.' Deyon performed a swift evaluation head to toe and puckered his lips. 'Just a bit run down and pale and rough around the edges.'

'Maybe I've still got a modelling career in my future. I'll call IMG when I get back to my hotel and see if they've any openings.'

'I wrote down all Cat's sayings too. God, a lot of them were awesome.'

'Like?'

'Excuse me?'

'What sayings of hers did you like?'

Deyon riffled the pages. 'I'm totally blootered, the night.'

'She was piss-drunk when she said that?'

'She'd quaffed a few rum and cokes, yes. Here's another one: I wouldnae give that peely-wally chanty wrastler the time of day.'

'Who was that?'

'What's a chanty wrastler? What's peely-wally mean?'

'It's complicated.'

'That was Cat talking about Matt Cleverly, her writing professor.'

'She didn't care for that individual then?'

Deyon was at once perturbed. 'God, that's right.' He threw up his hands like a gun was pulled on him. 'All the questions! I forgot. Cat told me her old man was a cop.'

'Guilty as charged.'

'I'm not too big on policemen. I don't know if you noticed, but I'm black.'

'You're kidding me.' Cowan feigned surprise. 'I'd never have twigged that.'

'I've been stopped by police for walking while black, for driving while black, for shopping while black, for public urination outside a fraternity house while black.' Deyon was thoughtful. 'Well, maybe they might have had a reason for that last one.'

Cowan laughed. 'I've been done for that myself, son. Outside a hostelry in Hillhead it was. When you've got to go, you've got to go.'

'Let's just say I'm not over-fond of the police in general.'

'No one is. We're absolutely appalling individuals. But then again if you keep your hands up, I probably won't shoot. Aye, I've read all about that crap. Fucking America, right? Anyway, you were just spilling the beans to me about this Professor chappie. What did Catriona have against him?'

'Now I feel like I'm gossiping.'

Cowan already had the decided impression that Deyon might enjoy a good gossip, what with him being camp as a row of pink tents.

'The man used to hit on her some. See, Cleverly is the type who makes women feel like shit about their writing. Says he doesn't know if they're good enough for his class, to even be in there. Then when they're totally depressed about having no talent, he gives them special one-on-one time. Before they know it, they're having vodka martinis at his place in Dupont Circle with their legs pinned behind their ears. Although the rumour is,' Deyon leaned in, 'it's a bit disappointing, the endowment not being all that.'

'He gets away with it?'

'Oh, he's a big deal at school. See, he writes these violent southern gothic novels that get reviewed in the *New York Times*, places like that.' Deyon put a finger in his mouth and pretended to vomit. 'All dwarves, necrophilia and kudzu, right? He got a MacArthur genius grant. Teaches two courses a year, that's it, and they're hard as hell to get into, like a white country club. He's worshipped, with him being a genius and all.'

'But he's really an arsehole of the first water?'

Deyon smiled delightedly. 'That's what Cat said too. That wee poser is such the colossal arsehole. I wrote that one down as well.'

'You're a writer?'

'God, no. I just collect phrases to trot out at parties. I enjoy being waspish as fuck, kind of like a black Truman Capote. You don't know who that is, do you?'

'No. Wasn't he a gangster?'

'I don't think so. Not in the sense you mean.' Deyon yawned, covering his mouth quickly with his hand. 'Sorry. You're thinking of Al Capone.'

'Right.'

'Anyway, she made him back the hell off. She was quite the intimidator.'

'It runs in the family. Why the hell was she taking a writing course with this wanker in the first place though? I thought she was doing political science. Where's the creativity in politics? I haven't seen much evidence. Nor of science now I think about it.'

'It was an elective, a graduate level workshop. You need to submit a writing sample to get in. The great man only selects the crème de la crème. Cleverly liked Cat's writing a lot. He liked her too. But then he wasn't her type, obviously.'

'What was her type?'

Deyon regarded him oddly. 'Well, different.'

'What else you write down in your commonplace book there?'

Deyon licked a finger and turned a page. 'Ah'll jist have a wee drop tae be sociable; You're cruising for a bruising the night, Jim; Whit's wi your face?; Have you rice pudding for brains?; You look like you've been sucking on a bag of sour plums.' Deyon had the Glasgow accent down pretty well, a good mimic.

'She probably said it soor plooms though, right?'

'That's right! Listen, I think I am going to eat something to settle my stomach. I don't feel like puking anymore.'

'Glad to hear it,' Cowan said. 'It's my first time wearing these trousers.'

Deyon came back with a bowl of French Moroccan Tomato and lentil soup and a Black Angus steak and cheese sandwich.

'I'd have had you pegged for a vegan.'

'They do have a vegan option, but it's that you can fuck off and eat elsewhere.' Deyon laughed. 'Sometimes, though,' he added, 'I just crave something's flesh.'

'Why doesn't that surprise me any?' Cowan noted.

Deyon wagged a forefinger at him.

'The local constabulary is labouring under the delusion you were a boyfriend.'

'Well, I'm a boy and I'm friendly.' Deyon chucked a sliver of sandwich in his mouth and chewed meditatively. 'They're definitely onto something.'

'You're also gay as a daffodil.'

'You're very direct, Mr Cowan.' Deyon made a clucking sound with his tongue. 'Also, very inappropriate. Some people might take that as a very offensive remark.'

'Are you offended?' Cowan asked. 'If you are, I sincerely apologise. Permit me to rephrase. How's about you're gayer than a Judy Garland sing-along?'

Deyon sipped his soup, the colour of blood. 'For the record,' he said, 'these little sayings of yours are what's known in civilised society as micro-aggressions.'

'Was it a micro-aggression when those vicious fuckwads fired three bullets into my daughter? Or was that something else? Was that society being civilised?'

Deyon ceased slurping abruptly. 'I'm so sorry.' He looked right at Cowan, his eyes stricken. 'The police really told you that I was Cat's boyfriend?'

'Aye, it appears to have been a highly thorough investigation. And I'm starting to think the police in these parts couldn't hit an elephant whose bum was on fire with a heat-seeking missile. Did she have one, though, a boyfriend?' Two glances met now in mutual incomprehension. Cowan couldn't fathom what was being communicated to him. He was supposed to be seeing something he couldn't.

'You don't know, do you?'

'Know what? Enlighten me.'

'This is not good.'

'What's not good?'

'Cat was a lesbian.'

Deyon resumed his quiet sipping, watching his interrogator carefully. Cowan could feel his arm trembling a little. He'd never even contemplated such a thing before. It struck him at that moment also as a complete absurdity. 'No,' he managed, eventually. 'You're mistaken about that, son. She always had boyfriends, starting in high school. She was normal. She liked boy bands, for Christ's sake.'

'She was the most normal person I knew, it's true.' Deyon examined the remnants of his soup as if contemplating licking the plate. He put his spoon in the bowl instead. 'I liked boy bands too. I'm kind of an expert if you want to quiz me on that.'

'I'd rather not, son. I fail to see how your wanting to be in a threesome with Harry Styles and Justin fucking Timberlake is exactly relevant right this minute.'

One table over, a young couple held hands. The man was scrolling his laptop with his free hand, the woman her cellphone with an index finger. Modern romance.

'I'm sorry,' Cowan muttered. 'I'm a bit stressed out the day.'

'That would be one fucking amazing scene, though.' Deyon grinned at him with mock salaciousness. 'Now you're going to have me thinking about that all day. Listen, the Cat I knew was gay. Not straight. Not bisexual. She told me her mother knew.'

'For fuck's sake!' Cowan rested the weight of his jaw in an upturned palm. 'I'm the last to be told everything. Some polis I am.' It was really too much. 'So, she wasn't interested in men? She wasn't ambisextrous?'

'No. Give it up. Not remotely.' Seeing Cowan's forlorn expression, Deyon relented a little. 'Well, I'm sure she was interested in her father. She did mention you, a couple of times, at least. Didn't she say you recently assaulted someone at a wedding?'

'Aye, my nephew. It was at the reception though, not the

actual wedding. Cut us some slack.' Cowan was a little embarrassed by the turn in the conversation. 'That eejit had it coming, believe me. He has a mouth like a Malahide cod.'

Deyon smiled coyly. 'I'm sure you attacking your relative was totally normal.'

'Honest to God, that wee bastard wasn't even unconscious very long at all after I stuck the head on him that night. That yin was back up in no time doing the slosh.'

'The slosh?'

'It's kind of a dance, except it isn't.'

'I thought Scottish people did that thing where they hopped over swords.'

'Aye, that's the reason most of us have no toes.'

'I remember Cat did say that head-butting people is quite common in your primitive land.'

'It's what's known back home as a Glasgow kiss. It's all very ritualistic.' Cowan shrugged. 'Girlfriends then?'

Deyon looked like he was being led against his will into an area where he shouldn't be divulging. He divulged anyway. 'She had a couple of hookups I remember; casual, flingy, fuck buddy deals, but lately she was into something more serious. That's what she said. She said, 'I think I'm in love, D, and it's horrible.''

'Horrible?'

Deyon contorted his face. 'It's always horrible when you're in love. Haven't you ever been in love?'

Cowan considered if he ever had been. He wasn't sure.

'It's like having indigestion and cramps and food

poisoning, all at once. Love is a sucker's game. No pun intended.'

'None noticed. And who was she in love with?'

'She never told me.' Deyon shrugged. 'It was her secret thing. Someone she'd met in her workshop, she told me that much, said Cleverly didn't even notice, how the great writing genius was that oblivious to what was right in front of him. But it was Cat's thing. She wanted to keep it to herself. Not for public consumption.'

'She didn't look gay,' Cowan offered, returning to form.

'Holy fuck!' Deyon was the one who looked exasperated now. 'You're still wrapping your mind around this one, aren't you? It's giving you a real hard time, eh?'

'I think so.'

'That's your homophobia talking, Mr Cowan.'

'I wouldn't have cared,' Cowan mumbled, defensively. 'She could have told me. I'd have handled it fine.'

'Seems like you're handling it real well right now, chief.'

'You're quite a smart young man, aren't you? What's your major?'

'Fashion and marketing.'

'Oh, Christ, that's not a fucking stereotype at all.'

'Yes, I'm as gay as a Gucci bag full of rainbows. Want to add that one to your collection?' Deyon laughed, seeing Cowan's expression. 'I'm messing with you. You had it coming, though. I'm political science too.'

'You want to go into politics?'

'God, no. What are you suggesting? I might be sleazy. But I'm not that sleazy.'

'Tell me then, hypothetically, say I wanted to get into a Senator's office, at very short notice, on Capitol Hill, how would I do it? Hypothetically, mind.'

'You'd offer him money,' Deyon chafed his fingers, 'for re-election. Why?'

'Because I want to get into a Senator's office at short notice, on Capitol Hill.'

'Who?'

'Factor. Republican from Kentucky.'

Deyon twisted his face like a pretzel. 'Oh, he's a real piece of work. Thinking of running for President in the next cycle. Definitely will need oodles of cash, then. I could probably make a couple of calls and have you into his office first thing tomorrow.'

'How would you even do that?'

'That's for me to know and you to find out.'

'Well, why would you do that?'

Deyon sighed. ''Cause you're Cat's father and you look a lot like her and right now I feel like I'm going to bust out crying.'

'Thanks,' Cowan said quickly. 'I think. Please don't start bubbling, but…' He scribbled his number on a napkin. Deyon made a face and copied it into his notebook. He gave the napkin back and Cowan blew his nose on it. 'You ever hear Catriona talk about going to Capitol Hill? Meeting Factor?'

'No. Why would she do that?'

'Do the initials IT mean anything to you? She wrote that down too.'

Deyon considered for a moment. 'Giant Spider? No. Information Technology?'

'Ever hear her mention a person with the surname Gilmartin?'

'No.'

Cowan flopped back in his chair in disappointment. 'Are you sure you even met my daughter? I'm starting to have my doubts.'

'I guess we didn't talk about the stuff you're interrogating me about.'

'Ever seen this flyer?' Cowan waggled it before him.

'No.'

'Christ on a bike! You're about as observant as a mole rat, son. Could you tell me about her roommate then?'

'The new one from spring? Erin?'

'That's the one.'

'Cat and her didn't get along real well. They did hang out at first, but nothing in common. Argued about refrigerator space. There were post-its left about how Cat shouldn't use a spoon on ice cream that was frozen because it would bend, usual roommate bullshit. That's why I live alone. I can't be bothered with that.'

'She won't return my calls.'

'Cat also said she's got a big pole up her ass.'

'You know this Erin well?'

'No, not at all, actually. She had a white Coach shoulder bag though. Guiseppe Zanotti high tops.' Deyon winked. 'Prada black suede knee highs.'

'This means nothing to me. It's like you've started up talking another language.'

'She has expensive tastes.'

'Come from money?'

Deyon shrugged. 'She has money.'

'How was Catriona doing in that regard?'

'She didn't have much. She bitched about it. She was always short.'

'You see her use her computer?'

'Can't say I did. But we never studied together.'

'What kind of places did you two hang out together? Do you remember that?'

'Fuego Salvaje, off 17th, the Phase in Dupont Circle, Cobalt or Town.'

'Gay clubs?'

'Uh-huh. We liked to dance. Cat was a great dancer. I am an excellent dancer too, not to boast. Do you dance? Besides the slosh?'

'Aye, like an epileptic penguin.'

'It's weird to be telling you shit about your own daughter.'

'Listen, could you write down the name of the sleaze-bag professor and an address where I could find this Erin? Since she's gone all incommunicado on me.'

'Well, I know where she'll be in forty-five minutes.

That's when International Law gets out. She'll be coming out of Monroe.'

'That's near here?'

'Academic building. About ten minutes away.'

'Draw us a map, will you?'

'Don't you have Siri on your phone?'

'I try not to bother her. We broke up, I was two-timing her with Alexa.'

'Want it on a piece of paper? Or would you prefer it on one of your napkins?' Deyon sketched the outline on a sheet torn from his notebook. 'X marks the spot.'

'Description?'

'She's about 5' 6". Longish blonde hair pulled back in a ponytail. Oh, never mind, everyone around here looks like that. She dresses down for class, jeans and sweatshirts. Oh, that doesn't help either, does it? That's everybody again. Braces!'

'Braces?'

'On her teeth. I think she's waiting to have something done to them.'

'That's something.'

'Anything else? I've got the Doctor Watson feels.'

'Hell, you get me in to see this Factor fucker tomorrow and I'll be in your debt forever. Though I'm not holding my breath.' Cowan held up the flyer. 'Actually, could you find out when this thing was hung up around campus? That'd be good to know.'

'Sure. I got this.' Deyon took the flyer and put it in his pocket. 'Mr Cowan?'

'Yes?'

'I liked Cat so very much. She was one of the coolest people I've ever met.'

'Thank you.'

'And now that I've spent all this quality time at lunch with you today and heard you speak so knowledgeably about so much, I'd have to say, with total sincerity, you're *so* not one of the coolest people I've ever met.'

Cowan shrugged. 'Tell me something I don't fucking know, laddie.'

'You're rude and unpleasant and homophobic and in general an asshole.'

'What can I tell you? I got myself expelled from charm school. I failed curtseying 101. But I'm adjusting my attitude even as we speak. I'm even remembering where the fucking fish fork goes. Right between the eyes, isn't it?'

Deyon sighed deeply. 'But I will say you've got the same sick sense of humor as your daughter, so I'm going to help you because of her. Only because of her.' He stood up, laughing, and rewrapped his red scarf. 'I'll hit you back later.'

Cowan watched him leave. He had very much wanted to dislike the kid, but couldn't the minute he'd said he saw the daughter in the father.

One of the last times Cowan had seen his daughter alive was the infamous wedding debacle, the aftermath of which led to his long-overdue disciplining. The wedding reception had been in Easterhouse, which was bad enough. Easterhouse was the kind of place Ethiopia held rock concerts for. But the reception that day had also soon acquired its own mild hysterical edge. Deep down, both families knew this was a marriage already fucked beyond redemption. Uncle Murray was leaping up that night trying to snag the microphone after every song, always to be beaten to it by one or other of the horde of half-cut Neds who seemed to comprise the bulk of the bride's family.

'For Christ's sake, Marion,' he spluttered, very frustrated. 'Them Tims have been monopolising that thing for the past half hour!'

'The mic should git shared by both sides.' Aunt Marion sniffed for emphasis. She was big on the sniffing. Her face had in recent years collapsed into itself, Cowan had noticed, with the leathery compression of an ancient accordion. 'Murray always does Scot's Wha Hae at weddings,' Aunt Marion explained to Catriona, her glass chapping the lacquered tabletop. 'Oor side looks forward tae it.'

Paddy McNamee commenced murdering 'The Killing Moon' in a strangled falsetto. The wedding band, whose accompaniment to his yowling was a deranged Indian raga, was draped in Granny-Takes-A-Trip retro shirts, and looked ridiculous. Their name was Cerebral Paisley. Catriona informed her father the band's moniker was in appalling taste.

'What if they're from Paisley?' Cowan suggested.

Catriona hadn't said anything in response to that, just looked daggers at him.

'The thinking man's psychedelia?' he suggested,

halfheartedly. 'This lot used to be The Crewsy Fixers. Now that was bad taste.'

But there was to be no amusing his daughter on that night. She just stared right through him, those oval blue eyes of hers sad as all tomorrows. 'Can we go soon?' she wailed. 'Please. I can't take much more of this. A cat caught in a mangle would be more musical than this lot. My ears are started bleeding.'

Cowan knocked back the dregs of his latest single malt, smacked his lips with satisfaction. 'We'll give it another hour, love. It's a family duty.'

'Dad,' Catriona said, nodding at his empty glass. 'You've had enough.'

'This is just situational drinking, love,' he explained to her. 'To get me through the rest of this fiasco.'

'You've had more than enough,' she repeated. 'You're getting that way you get.'

Although Catriona never wanted to come to the wedding in the first place, she had nonetheless begun bawling during the service at the Congregational, blubbering away like all his other female relatives, and black eyeliner had run to coalesce in inky globs in the pockets of her eyes. He thought about telling her she looked like a depressed MMA fighter but decided against it. 'Two rules for drinking whisky,' he said instead. 'First, never drink whisky without water. You know what the second is?'

'No.'

'Never drink water without whisky.'

'Oh, for fuck's sake,' Catriona said, thoroughly exasperated with him. 'Mummy would hate this shite.'

'Mummy's not going to hear about this shite though, is she? Mum's the word. What you don't know can't hurt you.'

Catriona's lower lip looked like it was going to melt on her chin. 'What you don't know can hurt you a lot.'

'You know something? You sound just like your bloody mother.'

Over in a musty corner, his nephews Billy and Willie were still giggling and making stupid faces into a phone, mugging over a deep pile of empties. 'That lassie's definitely got a bun in the oven,' Willie was saying.

Paddy couldn't remember all the words and so quit on the Bunnymen number halfway through. There was a smattering of applause and a cry of Fenian wanker. Uncle Murray leapt up quick, but the Paisley was back at the dancing tunes now. 'Fuckin' hell,' he declared, flopping himself down again. 'This is jist hopeless.'

'You said it,' Catriona had mumbled angrily under her breath as she got up and slouched off in the direction of the cash bar.

Aunt Marion leaned in perfume-close to Cowan. Her skin was a peculiar mottled burnt orange, like an upturned crate of Irn-Bru. 'Yir lassie is still at that uni, eh? Ah hope she's no going tae go getting all stuck up oan us, all hoity-toity.'

'She's going to America next month and staying for the year.'

'Why'd she want tae do that? Aw they folks ower in the States shooting each ither aw the time. That's aw they do ower there. Ye couldnae pay me to go there.'

'I'd pay you to go there,' Cowan muttered, watching the bride's father swaying in slow motion across the dance floor like his calves were brimful of mercury. He was a small man with a big face and his belly, bulging askew a disturbing smoking jacket, solidified an overall impression of swollen inebriated redness. He was screaming something idiotic about the Hucklebuck.

Catriona came back to the family table with her vodka and orange and sat back down beside him. 'If you can't beat them,' she said, gazing at her father meaningfully. 'Twenty more minutes. That's it.' She shivered. 'The poor brides-maids look like they were covered with manky tablecloths.'

'Can I steal yir auld man for a minute, pet?' Billy smirked cheerily at her. His incisors were urine-colored. 'The blushing groom would like a quick word with his favorite uncle on this happy occasion.'

'He's all yours,' said Catriona, pursing her lips. 'Bring him back in one piece.'

'Why ur ye going tae the States?' Aunt Marion asked her. 'Ur ye aff yir chump?'

The groom was very far gone, practically paralytic, his eyes glassy and red-rimmed with drink, bits of pink and white confetti stuck in his lapels. 'Uncle Chic,' he yelled, seeing Cowan approach.

'How's it going, Alec?' Cowan offered. 'Big day, eh?'

'Ach, I'm knackered already. But nuthin' like later the night when I'm honeymooning up a storm, eh?' Alec attempted a leer, but couldn't pull it off and explored thrusting his hips back and forth tentatively instead. He was Shane McGowan on a bad day: rheumy, leaning too close, reeking of peanuts and Bacardi. 'Naeplace I haven't been afore, mind you,' he added. 'I'm gonnae be a daddy.' Alec was suddenly disconsolate. 'Aw, fuck. Whit happened tae my life?'

'Well, go easy son,' Cowan suggested, gesturing at the groom's gyrating groin. 'Don't dislocate yourself.'

Alec was now squinting salaciously across the dance floor at the miserable looking Catriona. 'Now there's a body looks hotter than the sun the night, though.'

Cowan wondered for a moment whether it would be bad form to deck the groom at his own wedding. He considered that such a gesture might reflect badly on him. Billy was tugging wildly at his shirtsleeve by then anyway. 'I have plants, Uncle Chic,' he hissed, conspiratorially.

'What do you mean, you have plants?'

'Them's good plants,' noted Alec.

'Outside,' Billy said, looking furtive. 'The walls have ears.'

'You have plants and the walls have ears? Terrific.'

Alec was looking all around the cavernous hall anxiously. 'Youse be careful, mind. I don't want any aggro at my first wedding.'

Sitting beside Cowan on the fire escape overhanging the tarmac parking lot behind the Ex-Servicemen's Club,

Billy proceeded to extract from the pocket of his suit jacket a plastic Ziploc bag of packed dried vegetation, like roots or fungus. 'Something from your window box, Billy?'

'Mushrooms,' Billy said, excitedly. 'Fancy a hit?'

'A hit? At your brother's wedding… For Christ's sake!'

'Naewhere better. In actual fact oor Alec already dropped some. Weddings are massive downers for everybody.'

Cowan contemplated this sentiment, frowning. Then realised he agreed. Very much agreed. 'You do remember that I'm the police, right? You do recall that, Billy?'

'Aye, but you're no going tae arrest us at a family wedding, Uncle Chic. That'd be right bad form. Drug use has an unfair reputation anyway, considering aw the wonderful things in life it's given us, like rock music and aw them world records in sports.'

Cowan sighed, examining the white tubes through the plastic. 'What do I do?'

'Whit ye do is chew.' Billy giggled. 'That rhymes. Chewing is whit yir doing.'

Cowan examined his nephew's eyeballs, which were like something you'd find behind the counter in a joke shop. 'You've taken some of this already, haven't you?'

'Chew like a coo is whit you do. Hah-hah.' Billy had some difficulty composing himself. 'Just a smidgeon. Mild high. No even the buzz of hash, very mild. Mind you, I have acquired a tolerance also, but very mellow. Mellow yellow, quite rightly. Mind that Donovan song? 'Mellow Yellow.' The one goes, 'I'm just mad about sufferin'?'

'It's saffron.'

'Whitever.' Billy examined his fingernails. 'Hello there, China,' he said.

Cowan read the graffiti scrawled on the green rubbish skip rammed under the fire escape. The usual *Fuck the Pope, Celtic, 1690* and *Bethia Loves Elephant Man* type stuff. But more creatively scribbled in purple paint, *Three Things I Hate*:

vandalism 2) irony 3) lists.

A sketch of The Little Mermaid holding a submachine gun with Fight Lookism daubed under-neath her swishy fishtail. There must have been university students hanging out here recently. Cowan was considering his current predicament. He thought of his daughter waiting for him inside, wondering where the hell he was. He'd had six or eight drinks. He'd better skip the 'shrooms, then. The two of them should best flee the scene of the wedding pronto before something really bad happened.

'Would you look at that?' Billy said, pointing. 'Unbelievable!'

A black wedding limousine had pulled around the back right beneath where they sat, parked adjacent to the skip, ready for a quick getaway, a triangular white ribbon stretched out tight across its bonnet. A cardboard sign had been looped around the bumper with a clothesline. In red capitals it proclaimed, absurdly, 'JUST MARRED.'

'There ye go,' Billy said, nodding. 'Truth in advertising.'

'Well, that might just be somebody's way of reminding the happy couple that there's no 'I' in marriage,' Cowan offered, creatively.

'Aye, but do you no think it'll more likely remind them of how the bride's family are a shower of fuckin' morons?'

Walking back into the reception lobby, Cowan happened upon the deeply inebriated bridegroom attempting to perform an oral tonsillectomy on his daughter. 'Leave me alone, you evil creep,' Catriona shrilled, shoving Alec away from her with both arms. Alec staggered, wobbling like a baby deer on roller-skates on ice.

'Ah, here's the man,' said Alec, finally noticing his irate uncle standing behind him.

'I'll thank you to unhand my daughter,' Cowan noted, right before delivering the obligatory Glasgow kiss. Alec went toppling backwards, slowly, like a cartoon character.

'Whit a terrible wedding,' Billy observed upon arrival, still high as a kite and hallucinating wildly. 'Now you've went and killed the bridegroom, Uncle Chic.'

'He's not dead,' Cowan said, looking at the drooling figure on the ground. 'Yet.'

'It'd be nae big loss,' Billy observed casually while offering to the world a cataclysmic yawn. 'I cannot stand that evil fucker myself, and he's my ain brither.'

The grass outside the Ex-Serviceman's Club was water-weighted and raindrops crashed into the daffodils in the dark that night. Cowan, standing in the doorway alcove, looking up and down the wet shining street, seeing spilled petrol spool down a drain in yellow lamplight, realised that his daughter had made her escape into the dark.

It was all coming back to him now, as he trudged to the north-east making his way across the sprawling urban campus of The George Washington University, that terrible day, all the madness that was being him, the sheer exhaustion of living with this much misfiring circuitry. Truly, Cowan was a very sick man.

Monroe was built with a million-dollar grant from the Scottish Rite of Freemasonry to 33rd Degree Mason and University President, Cloyd Heck Martin. There really was an endless litany of useless things you could learn online. From the building now poured a tsunami of young blondes. It was like Sweden emptying. For a moment, Cowan panicked, blondes breaking in all directions around him. Another time this might have been the pleasantest of daydreams. But there was only the one blonde he wanted to see today. Then he got lucky. The girl in the green sweatshirt and black leggings coming alone out of Hall of Government paused to gaze lovingly at her phone. Whatever text she read caused her to smile, which is how he knew he had the right person.

Cowan followed her across a concrete patio upon which a fountain burbled without meaning. The girl's hair was pulled back tight from her scalp and ponytailed with a green cotton scrunchie. The belt cinched around her waist was black. Cowan hoped she hadn't got it for judo. 'Erin?'

'Yes?' She turned quickly, looking scared. What was she afraid of? What was it in his voice that startled her so? The girl was desperately trying to place him. She studied his face as though he were someone she really should know. Her eyes opened and closed like a doll's. Erin was attractive, high cheekbones and deep-set marine green eyes. The wind lifted her hair across her eyes and she brushed it back.

'I'm Charles Cowan,' he said, tunnelling into her eyes with his own. 'I'm Catriona's father.' Was it his imagination or did her face resolve with relief, and then tense quickly again? 'I'm sorry to have been bothering you: all the messages and that.'

'Oh,' she said. 'I'm so sorry too. I've been having problems with my phone. My parents switched carriers. I was going to call you this week.' She made a half-hearted gesture at the buildings. 'With the start of the Fall semester…'

Sure you were, honey, he thought. Sure you were.

'I was hoping you could spare a few moments?' She just looked at him, saying nothing, offering only blankness. 'Because I'd really like to see the place where my daughter stayed last spring. If you're in the same building, still?'

'Yes.' Erin glanced at her phone, nervously. 'I don't have much time right now. I have class at 2.40.' When she spoke, she seemed aware of the metal braces across her top row of teeth. She tried to keep her lip over the metal. It caused her to pout slightly. She had a very pretty mouth, but any flirtation in the moue was unintentional.

'It'll only take 20 minutes. I just want a quick look.'

'All right,' she said, without enthusiasm.

They walked together over to 2019 F Street. Cowan tried to engage her in small talk on the way, but his effort was not reciprocated. The dormitory was a converted apartment building housing doubles for junior and senior female students. Her apartment was on the third floor. It had been a double but there was only evidence of one person living there now. He supposed this one of the perks of your roommate snuffing it in junior year. They gave you a place to yourself as a senior, so you could cope with the trauma. Erin seemed to be coping fine. It was a typical student apartment: a kitchen and private bathroom, a dining table and desks, a loveseat and a coffee table. No one was offering him coffee. It was just as well. He'd had enough.

'You live alone?'

'My new roommate is abroad this semester,' Erin said. 'She's a junior.'

'That's convenient.'

'It's all right,' she said, again without enthusiasm.

She sat on the loveseat under a neo-psychedelic poster of Lana Del Rey straddling a motorbike in a billowing white dress. Erin crossed her legs and achieved a smile. Again, he glimpsed the braces across her upper row of teeth. She noticed his noticing and her hand strayed for an instant towards her mouth then down to fiddle with the straps on her backpack. He watched her fingers move and noticed a little red koi tattoo above her right ankle.

'I'm so sorry about your loss,' she said.

'You couldn't have known Catriona for that long?'

'A few months.' There was a pause. 'I really liked her.'

'Yes, she was nice.'

An air conditioner murmured in the corner. It was practically Arctic outside and the girl had the air blasting. This was a warm-blooded creature. 'You've been going to GW all four years?'

'No, I transferred. I did my first two as an Associates': Northern Virginia Community College.' He saw pride flare in her eyes. She didn't want him to think her less than academically prepared. 'My family couldn't afford the tuition here.'

'It's expensive.'

'It's insane.' Erin glanced around the dorm suite, as though mental illness lurked in a cupboard nearby.

'What does your father do?'

She was flustered. 'He does things with cars,' she said. 'Fixes engines and such. My mother's a nurse, though.'

'You mean your father's a mechanic?'

She nodded.

'There's nothing wrong with being a mechanic!'

'I guess.'

How could a girl from a working-class family, in the first year she'd had to pay tuition at an expensive college, afford the clothes Deyon had described? Scholarships? Cowan looked around her apartment, standing awkwardly. He shifted his weight from one leg to the other. Still, she hadn't invited him to sit down. She wasn't going to.

'Well,' Erin said, her eyes shying away from his. She gave a little sigh.

'I was wondering about my daughter's computer: a Mac, right?'

'I think Cat used the computer lab in Rome Hall, as long as I knew her. I didn't see her use a computer in the apartment.' The girl's mouth quirked slightly, and Cowan knew she was lying. She stood up abruptly and walked over to the built-in desk. There were loose leaf papers scattered by her own laptop and she began sorting them. She was annoyed at losing her composure and was fumbling for the right reaction. She wasn't finding it. 'The police asked me about that, too,' she said, forcing another half-smile. 'I told them the same thing. She used her phone to communicate with people, mostly.'

'You have one of those Chrome books, I see?'

'Yeah,' she smiled and touched the thing like it was a pet. Her face was preoccupied though, as if all of her hadn't arrived back from where she'd been.

'What made you switch from Apple?'

'I didn't switch,' she said, surprised. 'I've always been a PC person.'

'Isn't that an Apple cord on your desk there though?' The pause was impenetrable. You could almost hear the interference, the misaligned gears grinding the machinery to a halt. 'On the shelf, second to your right?'

Erin picked the cord up and stared at it like Cleopatra must have at her asp. Complex things were happening in those green eyes while the rest of her face set like concrete. 'Yes, it belongs to my boyfriend.'

'He likes Apples.'

'I guess.'

'Like Adam.'

'Excuse me?'

'In the Garden of Eden. It's quite a well-known story. There's a talking snake involved, I believe?'

'Oh, yeah.' Erin had decided the best possibility was to feign boredom again, and her eyelashes accordingly seemed to weigh a ton. She glanced again at her phone, which hadn't buzzed. 'I'm so sorry,' she said. 'I have to take this.'

'I'll wait till you're done.'

Erin looked up at him quickly, this time startled by his presumption. She was struggling with the question of how to be rude to a bereaved man. It was a tricky proposition. She narrowed her eyes to fluttering quarter moons. 'I'll just step outside then,' she said, pointing at the bedroom.

'OK.'

The minute she was gone, Cowan darted to her closet. He studied the labels on the rack of dresses: Roland Mouret, Balmain, Nina Ricci. He didn't need a Deyon to interpret for him. He got the gist. Expensive designer shit. Something didn't compute, and not just about the computer. A short plaid skirt looked out of place. It was something a Catholic schoolgirl would wear. Who was this girl, then? Was she the decked-out fashion plate or was she the fetish-fantasy schoolgirl? Or was she the jeans-and-sweatshirt everyday undergraduate? Maybe she had multiple personality disorder. Cowan touched the fabric of the skirt and recalled again her sharp response to his calling out her name. He sauntered back to the centre of the room just as she re-entered. Erin looked in the direction of the closet from whence came the audible clink of a swinging hanger.

'I'm sorry,' she said. 'I have to read something quickly before class.'

'Can I ask you one more thing?'

Erin studied the blank wall opposite like it was a Monet. She was thinking with relief that this was the last time they'd talk. But that wasn't the case. No, he would be talking to this little minx again. She'd taught him exactly what he needed to know.

'Did she have a boyfriend? I mean did she always come back at night? Or did she stay out overnight at his place ever?'

'She did stay out nights. She didn't talk about a boyfriend, though.'

'You didn't ask?'

'No. We didn't talk about stuff like that. We were both quite private people.'

The girl lied more than a second-hand car salesman. 'Thanks.' Cowan walked to her and took her hand in his. He squeezed it firmly feeling the small fragile bones. She flinched and he felt her tremble in his grasp. 'I'm so glad I saw this place. I guess I'm trying to come terms with her death.'

Erin nodded as if she understood, and she smiled and showed him the thin metal line along her teeth.

That evening Cowan enjoyed an excellent Moo-Shi chicken, more than anything, he could wash it down with a Tsingtao beer, but he couldn't. The phone buzzed in his pocket.

in 9am Cannon Building wear smtg smart!

Deyon had been serious about arranging the meeting, after all. Well done, son. Cowan hadn't thought to bring a suit with him, and realised that could be a problem now. He'd wing it. Back in his room, he spent five hours browsing the DC listings for call girls advertising services in downtown hotels. Customer servicing was the more accurate designation. The search was infinitely depressing and weirdly arousing. He was about to pack it in for the night when he came upon the Exclusive Companions website.

Exclusive Companions is a private agency and one of the most prestigious escort services serving VIP Clientele. Our agency was created to provide a suitable companion and to offer an Exclusive First Class Model Escort Service to Elite Gentleman who demand the very best.

Cowan doubted he fit the category of elite gentleman, but he could always dream. He certainly demanded the best, though. He scanned the portfolios of some of the *hottest women in the world*, women who were not only *extremely beautiful and fun loving* but *carefully selected to meet the highest standards of appearance, attitude, enthusiasm and overall perfor-mance.* Enthusiasm would be a must right enough, especially at $600 an hour for in-call. Most of the high-class hookers in the airbrushed photos were blonde with plastic busts. Their faces were blurred, but they probably all looked the same, plastic faced too. There were a few who cultivated a different look though, catering to more peculiar acquired tastes, like the little debauched Catholic schoolgirl in the plaid skirt routine. Smiling, Cowan reached out to the screen to trace the red koi above an ankle and whistled through his teeth. He was long overdue a break like this. 'Well, Sammi,' he said aloud. 'Aren't you quite the fishy package?'

'Hello.' The voice sounded very sleepy.

'How's it going?'

'It's going.' There was a long pause. 'Who is this?'

'It's me, Cowan, your Glasgow detective. A sleuth sprung like a dandelion from the banks of the stintling Molendinar; a man on a mission to shoot up this hideous metropolis and expose its quivering underbelly of rank cor-ruption; a man hell bent on exposing a history of DC police incompetence, ineptitude, incontinence and...'

'Jesus Christ, man. Do you know what time it is?'

'It's ten to twelve.'

'Tell me you're not in a bar.'

'I'm not in a bar.'

'You sound like you're in a bar.'

'I'm in my hotel room. I made them remove the mini bar as well. Just in case.'

'Is this urgent? Or did you just wake me up to shoot the shit?'

'Hell, no. I need something from you. I want to book a call girl for tomorrow night. Here at my hotel. But it's a very exclusive agency and I need to be screened by them. You know, full number and contact information, and all that jazz.'

'You have been drinking. Listen, I'm going to hang up now.'

'No! Hold on, Mac. I'm dead serious. I remembered how you used to work vice back in the day. I thought you might have a name I could use to make the process easier. Maybe one of your vice boys can send me info to use when I'm making the booking: a fake name and address to clear the screening?'

'Are you fucking with me, Cowan? Because...'

'This is an absolutely crucial part of the cowboy investigation I'm not doing.'

'You need me to help you book a prosti, as part of your investigation? What did I tell you? Were you even listening to me, man? You can't be doing this. You can't.'

'I just want to have a quick wee chat with one of the girls. I won't be availing myself of her services, though.' Cowan yawned into the mouthpiece. 'I don't think I will, anyway. Not unless I get really bored. I'll tell you, the cable service here is not the best, seems to be a lot of fat Neanderthals wearing helmets, keep running into one another. They've knocked the ball out of shape too. One of them must have went and sat on it.'

'What makes you think I'd even consider for a minute such a thing?' McDonald didn't sound at all happy. 'You must be a raving lunatic, Cowan. Or think I'm one.'

'I've considered both possibilities seriously. See, here's the thing. I met today with my daughter's elusive roommate. I think her name is Marie Celeste. So I now have a new and very productive lead in the case. In a nutshell, it involves what that young lady puts behind her ears in order to attract men.'

'Her perfume?'

'No, her ankles.'

There was a long silence.

'You think your daughter's roommate is a call girl? Seriously?' McDonald sounded exasperated. 'Let me get back to you tomorrow. I need to think more on this.'

'OK. Make it early, I'm going to see a Senator first thing. It isn't to complain about you, though.'

'Jesus, God!'

'Say, did you happen to know perchance that my daughter was a lesbian?'

'Yes.'

'Well, fuck me in the arse with a big pogo stick. You were way ahead of the game on this, after all, Big Mac. Didn't you think to mention the fact?'

'I assumed you knew, being her father and so on.'

'It didn't say anything about that in the file.'

'It wasn't relevant.'

'Do you happen to know the name of her last girlfriend?'

'Not off the top of my head. The relevance of this I fail to see, also. Do I need to remind you that we actually have a surveillance tape of two men on a train…'

'Yeah, yeah, yeah.'

'I'm not investigating a crime of passion here.'

'But every crime is passionate, Mac, in a sense.' Cowan sighed. 'OK. I'm going to hang up now. I could use a warm shower. I'm right grungy from walking all over town investigating everything you overlooked. Cleanliness is next to Godliness, they say.'

'Cowan?'

'Yes?'

'Don't ever call me again at this hour. I mean, ever.'

'Oh, don't be like that, Mac. I was hoping we'd go out and have a pop together at the soda fountain before I take off. I'd bring two clean straws and everything.'

McDonald hung up on him.

That night Cowan dreamed of Flannelfeet again and woke terrified, sweating the sheets damp. It was the same recurrent nightmare he'd been having as long as he could remember. Its origins were an old rhyme from somewhere back in his childhood.

Why do I weep?
For Flannelfeet
Is up a close in Stonefield Street.

As a wee boy, he hadn't known where Stonefield Street was, if it was nearby or not, or if there was any street in Govan of that name. There was a Stonefield Street in Bearsden, but that wasn't it. Flannelfeet wouldn't want anything to do with toffs who didn't live places with dark closes to hide up. Back then Cowan wondered if Stonefield was the name of a street in hell. He'd been scared shitless of Flannelfeet as a child. That he didn't know what the thing looked like only made it worse; he imagined. What he imagined never quite came together in the dreams that shook him awake. His mother would come and take him into the big bed until his shaking and crying stopped. She'd whisper there was no bogeyman, no Flannelfeet, and she'd stroke his hair till he pretended to sleep. But he couldn't ever sleep after that dream. He'd lie, burrowing in her warmth, and pray to God his eyes wouldn't shut tight and take him back to that dark manky close up which Flannelfeet was waiting, always waiting for him.

His mother had been dead wrong. He'd been a policeman long enough to know there was a Flannelfeet. There was forever and always a Flannelfeet. He saw its minions in the High Court and he saw its victims in the mortuary. It assumed many forms, and did all the horrible things he'd imagined and more, and he saw its sinister work splayed veined and bloody on tables under the glint of the coroner's clinking instruments. In time, the shards of a little boy's dreams came back again.

Cowan rose dripping with sweat, and poured a glass of water from the tap. He hauled back the heavy curtains and looked out at the city: the Capitol white in the distance, a luminous spiked mushroom, and a poisoned one at that. The sky was like tar and thin gauzy clouds ventured nothing against the star-pocked black. He thought about his daughter and how infinite that sky was. Nothing matters to the dead, that's what was so hard for those left behind and stranded here. The way we know that there is no dark in this world as dark as the secret place in our own heart.

3   FRIDAY (MORNING)

Cowan woke feeling the need for a ritual cleansing, a puri-
fication by water. Watching his softening belly rise above
the waterline like a Trident submarine in the Holy Loch,
he recalled how a few years ago he'd caught himself pulling
his stomach in around attractive women. He'd gone so far
as to contemplate a gym membership at that time, but had
trouble finding one adjacent to a bar. He decided then and
there just to get fat. A policeman needed weight to throw
around anyway. But he couldn't even pack the pounds on
right. He was a man failed at practically everything. He ran
his tongue across his teeth and showed them to himself in the
mirror. The smile was a right killer still. It was just that he
didn't have much cause to deploy it anymore. Women would
soon look at his naked body the same fearful way retirees
looked at snow. By the time Cowan got to brushing his teeth
with his finger, since he'd forgotten to buy a toothbrush,
he'd concluded you had to go some time. The corpse was a
fine fertilizer and, at least until you were one, you just had to
work at being the best fuck up you could be.

Cowan was glad he'd have Deyon's company for the
meeting in the Senator's office. He was used to working with
a partner during interrogations. The Longworth Building
was on the corner of New Jersey and Independence; neo-
classical in structure, a white marble front with eight Ionic
columns, and a clean American flag flapping on a marble

balustrade. Inside were a warren of congressional offices and the mysterious doings of the Ways and Means Committee. If you had means there were usually ways. The Rayburn Building was more impressive, except for the goat statues outside. The beasts looked like they had giant trumpets coming out their arses. The paired Doric columns and pilasters of the Cannon Building faced the Capitol oval windows, sun-glinted this morning under the limestone edifice.

Deyon waited on the sidewalk outside, a beautifully cut suit over his powder blue shirt. His tie had subtle geometrics of red rhombi shaded in aqua to pick up the blue of the suit, and his black shoes were shiny as a pitbull's head. Deyon was the type who liked to hide his bushel under a light. 'Antithesis,' he said, running his finger along his sleeve and striking a pose.

'That's a swanky suit.'

'It's all that.'

'Dead spiffy.'

'I had an internship on the Hill last year,' Deyon explained.

'So how you doing, D?'

'I'm making out.' The young man's face contorted into an expression of abstract pain. 'God,' he said, covering his eyes. 'What in the name of fuck are you wearing?'

'It's the jacket, isn't it?'

'You calling that a jacket?'

'Aye, it's a donkey jacket.'

'Why? Because it's something a donkey would wear?

3 FRIDAY (MORNING)   113

You ask me, a respectable donkey wouldn't be seen dead in that. Where'd you get it? A dumpster?'

'Kind of. Glasgow. I'll have you know this is very fashionable there.'

'It must be a regular Milan. Remind me never to go there. Don't even let me have a stopover. I'd just die.'

Deyon wet his thumb and began rubbing it back and forth experimentally along Cowan's upper lip.

'Is this one of those gay mating rituals I've heard about?'

'Toothpaste!' Deyon said, looking thoroughly exasperated with him. 'Brushing your teeth is not splitting the atom.'

'It is when you do it with your finger.'

'Why did you use your finger?'

'Because my dick doesn't quite reach that far?'

'Don't be crude.' Deyon straightened his tie and fixed the knot. 'You could have made more of an effort, or an effort. You look like a scarecrow that escaped the cornfield.'

'We're meeting a Senator, not entering the Mr America Pageant.'

Deyon draped a conference badge around his neck.

Cowan read the nametag.

'Pastor Jerry Stuart. Asheville, North Carolina.'

'Probably short for Jeremiah.'

Cowan fingered the badge. 'Where'd you get this?'

'You don't want to know.'

'Actually, I do.'

Deyon shrugged. 'There's a convention in town this

week, see? FRC. It's this big crazy Christian thing over at the Hyatt Regency. "Jesus in the Age of Social Media." I stopped by the conference registration and picked these up.'

'You mean you stole them?'

'Semantics.'

'Theft.'

'Policemen are so judgmental. I thought you'd appreciate that I went to the trouble of finding one that had a Scottish name on it.'

'I do,' said Cowan 'I'm rapturous with admiration for your thievery. But how am I supposed to pass as a minister? Tell me that. I've got no religious spiel.'

'Oh, leave that to me,' Deyon said. 'I'm very religious.'

Cowan regarded him skeptically.

Deyon grinned back at him mischievously. 'I worship Baal.'

They climbed the two tiers of steps to the entrance. A pair of K Street lobbyists in black bespoke suits came down vituperating into their cellphones. 'I think that might have been them Koch brothers,' Cowan said. 'Did you know that politicians who don't give those rich dicks exactly what they want are known in these parts as Koch-blockers?'

'Technically,' Deyon said, ignoring him. 'We're watchmen on the wall.'

'We're what?'

'Watchmen on the Wall. You and me.' Deyon intoned: 'We stand strong on the controversial issues because God hates cowards. And the cowards that the Lord is referring to are the men who know the truth but refuse to speak it.'

'You've been reading their little pamphlets, haven't you?'

'Very informative about homosexuality too, let me tell you, which is the moral issue of our age. Now, this is a free country, friend, don't get me wrong, and you can do what you want to do, however much it turns my stomach. But it's a sin against God.'

'And who are you supposed to be when you're at home?'

Deyon arranged a badge carefully around his neck. It said: Reverend Otis Moss III, Alabama. 'You can call me OT. Don't sweat it. I can pull the minister thing off.'

'I'm more concerned about you pulling the straight thing off.'

'I can be straight. Being cis is no big thing.' Deyon dropped his voice an octave: 'It done give me no pleasure to say that the sodomites and such will be consumed in the lake that burns forever with fire and brimstone and also those little charcoal fire-starters for barbecues. Which is the second death. Revelation 21.'

Cowan sighed. 'I don't get it, D. It's hard enough in life to be gay, why'd you have to go and choose to be black as well?'

'You do any more research on Factor before you flew over here?' Deyon was glowering at his jacket still. 'Do you even have the Internet yet in Scotland?'

'Aye, but it's slow as hell due to the steam power. Factor's a compassionate conservative, right? Classic oxymoron. Like military intelligence. But he's a careerist, mainly. Reeks of ambition. Like you said, lots of speculation about him running for higher office. Forming exploratory committees and all that palaver. Seems as well to be a total bastard, which, mind you, is the primary trait of the political animal. Also sounds like he'd pick a penny out a dunghill with his teeth. Ditto.'

'Needs his campaign financed, which is how it's so easy to get in for a meet. By the way, we're seeing the Administrative Assistant or the Legislative Assistant. Can't remember which. It'll probably be a fifteen-year-old girl. So don't be rude. Just try to pretend you're normal. Dial the comedy routine back about 200%.' Deyon looked at Cowan's unfortunate garb over again and sighed. 'It's bad enough you're going in there looking like a tramp who had an accident in a wind tunnel.'

'You know how to make a man feel good about himself, D. Anybody ever tell you that?'

'Lots of men. I'll spare you the details.'

'That's much fucking appreciated.'

'It so was too.' Deyon smirked at him. 'Appreciated by them I mean.'

They passed through security and up to the third floor. In the long corridor, offices were being emptied, young men with trolleys wheeling boxes out. It was like the end-of-term emptying of a student dorm. In fact, the offices weren't much bigger than the student apartment Cowan had visited the day before. It was strange, the Free World being dependant on such pokey office spaces and this much black leather. In the cramped reception area of Factor's office they were seated in a pair of black barrel-back chairs. On the walls were a disturbing number of trippy red sunsets. One painting was of a river valley, towering firs, with a black bear centred in the frame. An intern brought coffee and said the Legislative Assistant would be out directly. Ms Thomson had to fly to Jerusalem later that day for a meeting with Bibi but would squeeze them in. This was supposed to make the visitors feel grateful. Deyon told Cowan the back office was called the leg shop and there could be as many as six people working in there. With luck, they might be able have the meeting in the Senator's office.

There was a continual frantic coming and going of staff, most scarcely out of adolescence. These kids sprang sporadically from cubicles plastered with post-it notes, like demented jack-in-the-boxes, always with phones clamped to their ears. The appointments secretary was on the phone also, and raised a finger in the air to hold them off as they approached. She was in her 40s and wore a green blouse open three buttons down and tucked into a short grey skirt, black stockings and grey pumps, brown eyes, fuchsia lipstick, and an expression that would stymie a saint. There was an open *Washingtonian* magazine on the desk before her, a cover profile of Representative Dale Schock of Arizona.

Deyon whispered, 'Hotter than the sun. Dude could be President someday.'

'You mean America's next big war is going to be over hair gel?'

They waited till she'd finished her call. 'Can I take your names?' she asked.

'Why?' Cowan asked. 'What's wrong with yours?'

'We're with Watchmen on the Wall,' Deyon said, nudging Cowan's elbow. 'We spoke to Lauren Thomson yesterday regarding the exploratory committee.'

'Not to be confused with Watchers on the Wall,' Cowan added. The secretary looked like she wanted to bite him. 'The ones keep the wildlings out.'

She picked up the phone again. 'Those gentlemen from the FRC are still waiting.'

'And giants also,' Cowan added. 'You don't want that lot clambering over the top of the wall. That would be a regular disaster. NBA draft would never be the same.' Deyon elbowed Cowan in the gut and he quit.

'Miss Thomson will be with you soon,' the secretary said. She scrutinized Cowan's jacket, and then turned towards Deyon with slanted eyes. Something didn't add up. In a few seconds her intruder alarm was going to go off and explode her cranium.

'Yours in Christ,' Deyon said, grinning inanely. He looked hopefully at Cowan, who had gone totally blank. Ten years of Sunday school had gone right out the window. He couldn't recall a solitary hymn, psalm or scripture verse.

'Jesus loves you, this I know,' he blurted idiotically. Deyon was making a small moaning sound. 'For the Bible tells me so. Isn't that right, Reverend Otis?'

'If you gentlemen would just take your seats again, she'll

be right out.' The secretary still looked as if a mongoose had gotten loose in her panties.

'I meant to ask,' Cowan said, leaning across her desk and smiling. 'Are there IT people who work with this office? Or is there someone who works here with the initials IT?'

Something interesting was happening to the secretary's nostrils. 'Why?'

Deyon tugged Cowan's sleeve, pointing at the desk nameplate. Ms Irene Torok. He hadn't noticed. Some detective he was. Well, there was one mystery solved at least.

'Never mind,' Cowan said, smiling inanely. 'I think we've found you.'

'Found me?' The secretary followed his eyes. Her own settled on the plate and commenced flickering like frightened beads. 'Well, I don't think IT would necessarily have to be me.' She was acquiring a granite smile now.

'Aye, that's true. It could stand for Interstellar Tortoise,' Cowan suggested, 'or Incorrigible Tease.' The secretary stared at his badge. 'Or Incredible Twat.'

'Jeremiah,' Deyon said. 'Perhaps if you wouldn't…'

'Look here,' Irene Torok spat. 'What's this about?'

'While I'm visiting the Senator on behalf of my parishioners,' Cowan explained, 'I wanted to check if my niece might have had an appointment on Tuesday the 4th.'

'Tuesday the 4th?'

'Of April this year.'

'You called before,' she barked, accusingly. 'You were

the one was on the phone yesterday. I remember your funny voice. I remember exactly what you said too.'

Cowan inclined further over the desk to peruse her screen, so many little icons. 'If you could just have a wee gander at your Google calendar there.'

'No,' the secretary said, decisively. 'She didn't have an appointment then.'

'You looked already?' Cowan assumed an expression of wild incredulity. 'How'd you do that Irene? Magic? It was 10.30, this appointment.'

He stood drumming his fingers atop her computer. Irene Torok kept looking frantically in the direction of the leg shop with Marty Feldman eyes. Still, no one emerged. Miss Thomson was ghosting them. Two minutes passed and the secretary wilted, tapping slowly on the keyboard. 'The Senator had a meeting at that time,' she announced triumphantly. 'About the upcoming election, with senior staff.'

'Who was he meeting with that day? Specifically. Got names?'

'I'm afraid I can't divulge that.'

Cowan thought quickly. 'What about the previous Tuesdays that month? Any record of a meeting with my niece then?'

'There are privacy laws. I've already told you way more than I should.'

'Well, could you have a quick look? It's right in front of you, isn't it? Who's to know, Irene? The fucking calendar police? What will they do? Arrange it so you're never able to go on a date?'

She presented him with a smile that showed no teeth. 'That's not possible.'

'Well, I wouldn't altogether rule out the possibility of you going on a date, Irene. You've still got most of your own hair.'

'I can't help you anymore with this nonsense.'

'You do know, Irene,' Cowan said, pouting sadly at her, 'that you only have two expressions and they're actually the same fucking one?'

Miss Thomson arrived at a jog trot: a pale young woman with a pinkish big mouth, a jot pinched. She had straight bangs and square-rimmed glasses. Everything about her intimated money. She even slightly resembled Benjamin Franklin. 'Reverend Stuart and Reverend Moss?' she said, extending her hand. 'Lauren Thomson. I'm so pleased to have the opportunity to meet you on behalf of Senator Factor today. We feel so fortunate to have your support as we move forward.'

'Delighted we are,' Cowan said, rolling the r like a wino from Airdrie.

'Oh,' she said. 'Where's your accent from?'

'Same place as me.'

Ms Thomson looked quickly towards the secretary, who was still sending panicked semaphore blinks her way. 'Is there a problem?'

'He has a question about an appointment with the Senator in April.'

'What?'

'I was explaining to this gentleman that his daughter did not have an appointment with any member of our staff on this week in April, and he's asking…'

'I didn't say my daughter actually,' Cowan informed her. 'I said my niece. IT here is getting herself in a right fankle now.'

Irene Torok was looking as if she might commence projectile vomiting any moment. 'His niece…' she began.

'See, if Irene here could look up for me if my niece or my daughter or whoever it was, had an appointment in the weeks and months beforehand, it'd be way cool.'

Lauren Thomson was now spooked too. 'I don't believe we divulge…'

'Well, could you run inside the inner sanctum yonder and find a body who could? Because the next person uses the word 'divulge' to me I'm going to be sorely tempted to insert the latest edition of Webster's Dictionary in their arsehole.'

'This,' she almost hissed, blanching visibly, 'is a Congressional office.'

'I didn't think it was the DC morgue, sweetie. Mind you, the corpses would probably be a hell of a lot more helpful than you folk have been.'

'Call security, Irene.'

'Do you really think that's a good idea, Irene?' Cowan asked. 'Seriously? With you already so mad confused about whether it was my niece or my daughter was never here?'

The two women exchanged a significant look suggestive of abject fear and then Miss Thomson left hurriedly at the same jog trot.

'She's got herself an anecdote to share with Bibi now, all right.' Cowan grinned at the secretary. 'So, Irene, if you could have a wee look at that calendar for me?'

Irene Torok folded her arms across her chest and stared like a basilisk.

Cowan and Deyon settled back into the barrel chairs. 'Now what?'

'We wait for the fucking calvary.'

'Cavalry,' Deyon corrected. 'You said Calvary.'

Cowan shrugged. 'We're ministers, right? Master the lingo, son.'

Two men emerged from the back room along with the frenzied Miss Thomson. They had the demeanour of men performing a mildly disagreeable obligation. One was young and thin and solemn, and the other was older, thickset and solemn. The younger man wore a charcoal suit with chalk stripes and a very powerful tie. The thickset man had small deep-set eyes, cold as marble.

'Now, we're for it. They've gone and summoned the gruesome twosome.'

'You might want to quit that shit now,' Deyon whispered. 'You can't go around being a jerk 24/7. You know what they say: *Softly, softly catchee monkey*.'

'Why would I want to catch a monkey? What would I ever do with a fucking captured monkey?'

'Is there a problem, Irene?' the younger man asked, ignoring the visitors.

'I think we have a quorum now,' Cowan said to Deyon, getting to his feet. 'We can probably get started.'

'This gentleman…' Irene began.

'I'm not a gentleman. Stop saying that, Irene. It's stupid.' Cowan was addressing the younger of the two men now. 'I was inquiring about the Senator's appointment calendar. But now I'm here, I suppose I'd like a chat with the man himself.'

'Craig Doyle, Legislative Director for the Senator.' Up close, Doyle was boyish, clean-shaven and straight featured, light brown hair gelled to perfection.

'I'd still rather see the organ grinder than the fucking monkey,' Cowan explained. He turned to Deyon. 'Actually, D, you might have been right about softly, softly.'

Doyle's eyes clouded, but his expression didn't change. 'This is Mr Reem, another of the Senator's aides. The Senator is on a trade mission to Indonesia. What exactly is it we can help you gentlemen with today? Has there been a problem?'

No one was shaking hands.

'I'm not here to answer questions,' Cowan said. 'I'm here to ask them.'

'This is Detective Inspector Cowan,' Deyon explained. 'He lost his daughter earlier this year. She was the exchange student from Scotland who was killed?'

Someone had changed the thermostat. The temperature

suddenly went through the floor. Doyle's posture was increasingly that of a member of the audience who had accidentally wandered onto the stage. He was still waiting on a prompt. Any prompt.

'I'm suspecting these folks knew that already, D.'

Doyle decided it best to usher them back into the Member's office. Irene Torok joined the mass exodus. Lauren Thompson trotted away, probably for a lie down.

There was a desk and a chair near the red-curtained window, two generously sized Lincoln sofas with small scroll arms and piped facings, and a coffee table with two pristine books and a white-whelk decorative ashtray. Doyle looked quite at home seated behind the desk, an ambitious boy in training, perhaps. Behind him was a trophy cabinet, black cowboy hat perched jauntily on top, and a framed copy of Factor's law degree. There were another dozen framed photos on the aqua-blue wall of the Senator meeting with constituents, revealing a proclivity for posing with fire engines; a photo of him at his alma mater receiving an Honorary Degree; and snapshots of him in uniform or posed with assorted dignitaries, including the last two Presidents. On camera, the Senator always unleashed the same wide-toothed grin. There was also a small statue of Lincoln on a pedestal, before a framed copy of The Bill of Rights, and what looked like the head of a mop in a glass case. It couldn't be a mop though. Maybe it was Factor's wife's high school pompoms. On a small side table were a collection of smaller awards, a poster of a boy in a basketball uniform, alongside a handcrafted postcard from a junior high school constituent, a miniature Israeli flag and an ugly drawing of a swooping eagle. On the desk itself, were an antique candy dispenser and a Remington typewriter, presumably for show, and two hand-wash dispensers, for cleaning up after dirty business.

'Did you know,' mused Cowan, 'that the word politics is derived from the Latin poly meaning many and the Anglo-Saxon ticks meaning small blood-sucking parasites?'

'I'm sorry for your loss, sir.'

'Uh-huh.'

'How exactly can we help you?'

'My daughter had an appointment here, in this very office, the week she died. But here I am asking what it was about and there's no record of it. How come?'

Doyle turned to Irene. 'Is there?'

'No.'

'This lady here,' Cowan noted, 'has been a suppository of information.'

'I'm afraid there wasn't a meeting, then.' Doyle shook his head. 'See, it's impossible. It would have been recorded. We'd like to help, obviously, but...'

'You're unwilling to.'

'Not at all.' Doyle employed the tone of voice one uses soothing a tantrum-throwing child. 'But if I were you, I'd...'

'You're not me. I'd require substantial cosmetic surgery.' Cowan turned to Irene. 'Was the Senator at the meeting that day?'

'Well, that's neither here nor there, is it?' It was the first time Reem had spoken. His hair was shaved short back and sides and he had the bearing of a military man, built low to the ground, broad-shouldered and thick. He was a man who looked like he could do some substantial damage and enjoy doing it.

'If something is neither here nor there,' Cowan inquired, 'where the fuck is it?'

'We can't help you. So I think you should perhaps go now, Mr Cowan,' Reem suggested. The little man was reaching into the inner pocket of his suit jacket while contemplating Cowan in a manner that might be characterized as vaguely homicidal.

'I think you should go ahead and try and make me, Napoleon.'

'We're not looking for unpleasantness here,' said Doyle, darting a concerned look in Reem's direction.

'This one here looks like he'd be up for something like that, though,' Cowan said, nodding significantly at Reem. 'Unpleasantness, I mean. I can see he's not here for his intelligence. I've seen smarter looking things hanging in a butcher's window.'

'We aren't looking for any unpleasantness.' Reem folded his arms across his chest and smiled as he spoke. The eyes were dead above the smile.

'What are you?' Cowan asked, pointing at Doyle. 'His fucking parrot?'

Reem took a step towards Cowan. Everyone else had taken to imitating furniture.

'Don't frighten me, please,' Cowan pleaded. 'I hate to burst into tears in public.'

'Look, Mr Cowan,' Doyle said. 'I don't want you to get yourself in a situation you can't handle. You're obviously very upset today. You've come here very upset.'

'I'm not afraid of him.' Cowan pointed at Deem. 'Wee man seems to be labouring under the delusion I might be. A good fart would blow that one away.'

Deyon pawed at his sleeve. 'I'm thinking maybe we should go.'

'I think that's a good idea,' Reem noted. 'A fine suggestion. Go.'

'Or what?' Cowan asked. 'What'll you do, 'roid rage? Don't give us it. You couldn't hit a cow on the arse with a banjo.'

Doyle turned to the secretary. 'Call downstairs for security, Irene.'

'Good idea. Because this yin here would lose on points shadow boxing.'

Reem advanced another step towards Cowan, his face darkening. 'Listen, you…'

Cowan leapt to his feet. 'Come on then, Tiny,' he said, lowering his hands and sneering. 'You looking to take your face home in a plastic bag?'

'Reem!' shouted Doyle. 'No. Stop!'

'He talks to you like you're a dog,' Cowan said, provoking the other man still. 'Are you housetrained even?'

A uniformed Capitol policeman entered the office.

He was not a smiling individual, and appeared physically equipped to go fifteen rounds with Behemoth if he were so inclined, or if Behemoth were, which seemed unlikely. Behemoth wasn't daft. On his shoulder, he wore a capitol badge. On his hip, he wore a capital gun.

'These two gentleman were just leaving,' Doyle explained. 'A bit of a misunderstanding is all it is.'

Cowan held his hands out, palms up and wrists together. 'I was asking yonder wee fellow with the anger management issues out for a drink and a bit of buggery, and everything got out of hand. He was leading me on something awful too.'

'They were just leaving,' Doyle repeated. 'A bit of confusion is all.'

'He heard you the first time,' Cowan said. 'He's not deaf. Big man here's not Vincent Van Fucking Beethoven, are you?'

'No,' said the policeman.

'This was all a misunderstanding,' Doyle offered again, smiling remotely.

'Aye, and so is murder to you people.'

'We're sorry we couldn't have been of more help.'

'Oh, I'm sure you aren't.'

On the back wall was a painting of a smiling blue-shirted Ronald Reagan playing poker with other Republican Presidents. A black-coated Lincoln had his back to the viewer. Bad idea. What if John Wilkes Booth came in to talk about the Second Amendment?

'Watch you don't trip over your mouth on the way out,' Reem suggested.

Doyle made an angry throat-slitting gesture towards him.

'I'll be seeing you around,' Cowan said, blowing the little man a kiss.

'You're seeing me now, asshole.'

'Reverend Stuart,' said the policeman, gripping Cowan's arm hard and steering him out the office. 'That's more than enough fun for today, don't you think?'

'Aye,' Cowan said to him. 'We should let these two get back to masturbating to *House of Cards*.'

'The Pastor gets very excited about his causes,' Deyon was explaining. 'For him salvation is a mission.'

The big Capitol policeman was nodding at him as politely as he could manage. 'This is some bullshit. Long as I don't see him near here again, it's all good.'

'I think that went well,' Deyon suggested. The policeman was disappearing back inside the Cannon Building.

'Really?'

'Of course not really. Are you actually serious? That was a disaster! No one ever tell you how you use honey to catch bees?'

'I liked your monkey thing better. Why'd I want to catch bees? There's a way to get seriously stung.' Cowan assembled his features into a facsimile of chagrin. 'Next time we do something like this I'll be the soul of discretion, though.'

'Next time?' Deyon shrilled. 'You must be joking. This is it for me, unless you plan on having a brain transplant.'

'Come on, D. Don't be that way.' Cowan patted him affectionately on the shoulder. 'Don't take that attitude. I'm just getting started.'

'Well, it was definitely a good one about the cow and the banjo, I'll give you that. I'm going to write that one down.'

'It was. Listen, can I call you later today?'

'That's what all the hot boys say.'

'Seriously, I could still use your help. I've got some other things to look into while I'm here. I'm impressed by your aptitude for deception.'

'That's also what they say. You dipping out then?'

'Got to see a man about a writing class.'

Young women scuttled around them on the sidewalk. It was still cold but Cowan had the impression they'd be moving quickly even in midsummer. There was a lot of black, much grey, and a dearth of heels. The girls here dressed mannishly in their pursuit of success and bore expressions of glassy-eyed hopelessness.

Deyon was reading his mind. 'This has never been a fashionable town.'

'No kidding?'

'I got a very bad feeling about you going to see Cleverly, though. You're not someone who should be spending much time around people. You're prickly as a cactus.'

'Ach, I'm fine.'

'More like a ticking time bomb that's going to go off.'

'Don't talk shite, son. I go out of my way to avoid conflict whenever possible, which is the reason I hardly ever vacation in Aleppo anymore. I might need to visit southeast Washington soon though. Which I hear is not dissimilar.'

'Why'd you want to do that?'

'I'd like to have a wee chat with the family of the goon who killed my daughter, if possible. I'll make it more than worth their while to talk to me, too.' Cowan solemnly handed Deyon a thick white envelope. 'The name and the address of the relevant party is in there, also satellite photos.'

'Good God, you might actually be a detective after all.' Deyon narrowed his eyes suspiciously. 'What do you want from me, though? Why are you giving me this?'

'You've got a car, right? Also, I figure you might know the lay of the land.'

'Because I'm black? You think that means I know everyone else who's black?'

'You mean you don't? Damn it, there goes my champagne brunch with Beyoncé.' Cowan wheeled away from him. 'Cheerio then, D. I'll call later with more details.'

'Please try not to hurt anyone today,' Deyon called after him. 'I'm serious.'

'It's all good,' Cowan yelled back. 'It's all just verbal with me. I'm a massive fucking pussycat at heart. And I know what it is you're thinking now! 'Me, how?''

'Unbelievable,' Deyon said, turning away from him. 'Unbelievable.'

Cowan had turned in the wrong direction and found himself by the Library of Congress. The city was subdued by an icy wind. Four policemen, bundled in black mufflers and ski masks against the cold, made a parallelogram on The Supreme Court steps. By the Capitol, a reporter in a bright red coat addressed a semicircle of cameras. Either that or Little Red Riding Hood was giving a press conference. Right enough, there were wolves in these parts. He skipped the metro, thinking a walk on such a brisk day would clear his head. The National Mall was the Grand Avenue envisaged by Charles L'Enfant as the centerpiece of his planned city. DC's layout was a right-angled grid overlaid by a pattern of plazas, from each of which avenues radiated as spokes from a wheel's hub. The odd diagonal angles created were purposeful. For if the District was a perfect square ten miles on a side, rotate it 45 degrees and the square and compass appeared. Then again, if you tried hard enough you could always find sinister shapes in clouds and inkblots. It was like the old joke: *What's so special about that painter Rorschach? All he ever did was paint pictures of me fucking my mother.* Your conspiracy theorist could make anything of nothing. But it was also true that L'Enfant had been a freemason. And his employer, General Washington, he was a funny hand-shaker too.

The tourist horde ebbed west, as Americans tended to do, moving en masse towards the Washington Monument as if intent on prostrating themselves before that giant phallus. That was one way to remember your first President:

memorialize him as a big white dick. L'Enfant died penniless. All he left were three watches, three compasses and a few surveying tools. The lesson being that it's always better to be the employer than the employee. George just chopped down things he was bored with, like trees and England.

Cowan was at the Constitution Gardens within sight of the Lincoln Memorial before he turned north. People walked quickly, like ants running home. He passed a pale woman in a bear hat sawing ferociously at a cello. He lobbed a few quarters into an upturned cap. A homeless man in a trench coat with an earmuff secured by scotch tape nodded deranged approval. On 21st Street, a girl strolled by him wearing a harness from which four fishing lines rose to a cluster of red balloons above her head, a wireless camera suspended from the balloons. Cowan hoped to God it was performance art. He turned along H Street and noticed two students having difficulty unchaining a bicycle from a rack. Sometimes he had cause to question evolution. There was construction all around George Washington University, cranes tilting across the skyline above pyramids of yet to be laid drainpipes and coils of cable. Cement mixers churned. Drills drilled. Hammers hammered. The university was adding to its special collection of glass and concrete horrors. Rome Hall was evidently the work of another dud architect, or perhaps his dog. Cowan arrived at the front entrance accidentally, further proof that all roads led to Rome…

He consulted the faculty directory in the lobby and took the elevator to the third floor. Cleverly's office door was closed and the only posted hours were on a Thursday. There was a secretary in the department office. She was in her late 40s, and preoccupied with a coffeepot. She had a complex weave designed to hide the damage done by too many years of the hot comb. Her face was lined, but it looked like she'd got that way having fun, at least.

'Hi,' he said. The secretary looked surprised. You could tell she was used to dealing with a younger clientele. 'I'm looking for Professor Cleverly.'

'He only comes in on Thursdays,' she said, appraising him.

'Man's only in one day a week? There's the kind of work I want.'

'You said it,' she said, smiling. 'He only has one class a semester: his seminar.'

The secretary pronounced seminar the same way she would shitpile. Her nameplate said Connie Williams. Connie wasn't a fan of the MacArthur Fellow.

'Nice work if you can get it.'

'Where you from?' she asked.

'Glasgow, Scotland.'

She looked at him with interest now. 'I know Scotland. My nephew is married to a girl from Kirkintilloch. She sounds like you.'

'Been there?'

'No,' she said, sadly. 'I'd like to, though. In all those books when a woman goes to visit, she meets some guy in a kilt and he always fine and he always sweeps her off her feet. You know how they do?'

'Aye, lassies like you cannot resist your kilted highlander. You know what those boys wear under their kilt, don't you?'

She smiled flirtatiously. 'I heard nothing.'

'Naw, that's a myth. You Americans believe anything you're told. They actually wear a smaller kilt. And under that another one, smaller still.'

She was laughing now.

'There's dozens of them. It's a whole big Russian doll situation, only with kilts.'

'Where's your kilt then?'

'Dry cleaners. Had to get the dried blood out of it. It's so hard to get English bloodstains out of tartan. It's enough to make you think about not using a sword.'

A bearded graduate student in sandals came in with an inquiry about a jammed photocopier. He looked at them oddly, having overheard part of the conversation.

Cowan leaned his elbow on top of a filing cabinet. 'But you should visit. The lads will be freaking out when they see you. Scottish lassies have way too much body hair.' She began laughing. 'I'm telling you, they look like Yetis. It's a thing. Back in high school, I went out with one who looked like Sasquatch.'

'We had a lovely Scottish girl here last year,' the secretary said. 'I don't know if you heard about that?'

'Say, do you have a phone number for this Cleverly chap? Or does he spend the rest of his week on a beach in the Seychelles?'

Connie leaned towards him, confidentially. 'I shouldn't

tell you, but he's in there now, conferencing. With the door closed. Which is a big no-no these days. We're not supposed to let anyone know he's here. Unofficial office hours.'

'Maybe I'll knock on his door, unofficially.'

'If you want I can call ahead.'

'No. It'll be a nice surprise. I'm sure a writer likes surprises.'

'Not that one,' she offered, with a slight sneer.

Cowan pressed his ear to the office door. Then he rapped on it. There was a scuffling inside. He knocked again, harder. 'Yes,' called a nervous voice. 'What is it?'

'Professor Cleverly,' Cowan shouted. 'Can you come out to play?'

The door opened and a slightly dishevelled Professor stood in the frame, wound tighter than a three-day clock. He was smallish, pale and reed-thin with a fledgling beard, un-tucked long-sleeved, red-striped Brooksgate button-down shirt, and unlaced Timberland boots. He also wore a scarlet bandanna. Maybe he aspired to be a comical bandit. Cowan noted that his jeans buckle belt missed a front loop.

'If you held that expression for long enough in a hospital bed,' Cowan told him, smiling. 'They'd probably turn off the machine.'

'Can I help you?' Cleverly attempted a smile, failed. 'This is not an office hour.'

'I'm Catriona Cowan's father.' He waited a beat to let that register. 'I wonder if you have a minute.'

Cleverly's expression mutated from mild annoyance to serious regret. He looked Cowan over like he was a marked down flannel shirt. 'Oh, just wait a second,' he said. 'I have to get finished up with a student.'

He closed the door. Taped to it was the jacket of his last novel, a solitary barn against a hellish skyline. *Southern noir... despair-filled, hickory-smoked, swamp-damp literature echoing the matter-of-fact cynicism of Cormac McCarthy and the conspicuous immorality of Jim Thomson. Cleverly has looked in the abyss and writes like the devil was after him.*

Well, the devil was after him now.

The door reopened on a typical faculty office, narrow bookshelves high on the wall either side, packed tight and over-spilling, implying the weight of narrative could become an avalanche. More books were scattered across the desk and chairs like a fungoid growth. A couple of chairs were upholstered in yellow. Arranged on the desk were a brown-stained coffee cup, a metal water bottle, a black phone with a twisted and knotted wire, a Munch's scream doll, a stapler, and a shoe polish tin full of paper clips. The smallish cake with centred candle on the desk was out of place. So was Cleverly, who looked like a ferret had just got up his trouser leg.

The girl who'd opened the door this time was tanned with a thick mane of honey-blonde hair. She looked flushed and mussed, but not embarrassed. Maybe she thought this creep a notch on her own belt. You never knew what a nine-teen-year-old was thinking. Sometimes they just weren't engaged in that fatiguing process at all. She saw Cowan looking at the cake. 'It's Duke's birthday,' she explained.

'Were you giving him a present? In my day we used to bring teachers apples, but that was kindergarten.'

'We were conferencing,' Cleverly said, hoarsely. 'Jill's a talented writer.'

'What you writing about, Jill?'

The question seemed to unsettle the student. She tried to make eye contact with her Professor, but he'd begun an intricate study of the Poe bobblehead on his radiator. 'It's complicated,' she ventured.

'You had problems getting started, but now it's going like a house on fire?'

'I have to go do that thing,' Jill announced. In one fluid motion she offered the office a mouthful of blinding white teeth, and went bounding out the door like a rabbit. It took all her self-control not to break into a sprint in the corridor.

'They have a lot of energy at that age. Places to be. People to do.'

'I'm so sorry about your daughter,' Cleverly said, with a faint southern twang. Cowan had read online that he was born in Cleveland and was an Oberlin graduate. 'It was a terrible thing. We were very cut up about it. How can I help you?'

'I wanted to ask you a few questions about her, if that's OK?'

'Of course. It was a tragedy. I can't imagine how hard it must have been.'

'I'd imagine you could imagine it,' Cowan said. 'You being a writer. Isn't that what they call empathy?'

Cleverly made a miniscule adjustment in his bandanna.

'You two didn't get along that well.'

Cleverly had a quick scratch at his little soul patch. 'Where did you hear that?'

'I keep my ear to the ground.' Cowan grinned at him. 'You must keep your ear to the ground too.'

'Being a writer?'

'Being so short.'

Cleverly put his elbows on the desk. He clasped his hands together, fretful.

'This is a great setup,' Cowan said, looking around. 'Teach one class, no office hours. You have a place in the Hamptons as well?'

'I can see you're upset, Mr Cowan.'

'You're right. That's dead observant. That's what must make you a writer: being observant. Must come in handy when you're writing about swamplands and dwarves and southern crackers buggering sheep or whatever the hell it is you do.'

Cleverly's eyes glazed over. 'What was your question?'

'This class she was in with you. I need to talk to someone else who was in that class with her. But I don't know her name. Could you give me a look at the roster?'

Connie knocked on the door and poked her head in. 'Oh, Duke. I didn't know you were in. Everything all right?'

'It's fine,' Cleverly hissed through gritted teeth. 'We'll

talk about it later.' He called her back in. 'Could you bring my lunch? Back of the refrigerator in the office?'

'Duke?' Cowan sneered. 'Seriously? You go by that?'

Cleverly ignored him. 'It's a very exclusive seminar. You apply to get in. You need a strong writing sample. Your daughter was in political science and not a writing major, obviously, but her sample was just amazing. She has serious talent. Had.'

Connie returned with a plastic container. Cleverly took the lid off. It was a tofu concoction. She hadn't closed the door.

'What's that?' Cowan asked. 'Looks like fungus.'

'It's actually very good.'

'Could you give me a copy of that roster, then?'

'I'm sorry,' Cleverly said, forking the white rubber in his mouth. It was like he was eating tiny pieces of elastic band. 'That's contrary to what I can do. That's covered by FERPA. College privacy regulations and so on.'

'No-one would know if you slipped us a copy.'

Cleverly dabbed his mouth with a napkin. 'More than my job's worth.'

'How much is that?' Cowan asked. 'You do all right. No teaching. Screwing dumb wee co-eds. That a fringe benefit?'

'I'm going to have to ask you to leave,' Cleverly said, getting up. 'I understand grief can cause one to do things one normally wouldn't and...'

Cowan stood up too. He walked to the door, closed it and came back.

'Wait a minute,' Cleverly yelped. 'Who do you think you are?'

'I'm the man's going to put you in the infirmary, fuck-face.'

Announcing this, Cowan grabbed the Professor by the scruff of the neck and slammed him face down into the tofu container. He held him there as he choked, suffocating on the stuff. It would be a cholesterol free death, anyway. 'Still good?'

Cleverly made a panicked snuffling noise and his fingers scrabbled desperately. Cowan put his entire weight across the man's back. When he at last pulled him out, gasping and flailing, he jammed his nose up hard against the computer screen: wet stringy snot on the pixels now. 'What I need you to do is to call up that old roster.'

'I can't do that... I...'

Cowan swept the tofu container off the desk. He ripped the candle out of the cake. 'Dessert?' This time, the face of the genius was plunged into his own birthday cake, his nostrils and mouth deep-sixed in cream cheese, submerged in marzipan. Cleverly sputtered, drowning in sweetness, blacking out on sugar, falling down a deep dark chocolate well. 'See,' Cowan whispered. 'Who was it that said you can't have your cake and eat it?'

After a while of the suffocation routine, Cowan extracted the Professor from the cake and thrust his head back against the screen. Sticky icing gummed his eyelashes shut. Cowan tore off the stupid bandanna and wiped the splurge away with it. 'Why no picture of this one?' Cowan said, pointing.

'She was odding,' Cleverly mumbled.

Cowan's elbow smacked the Professor on the side of the head. 'Ice cream giving you a brain-freeze, dipshit?'

'She was auditing,' Cleverly sputtered. 'She's not a regular student, part-time. I let her in because she's so good.'

'At what? Fellatio?'

'Creative nonfiction. She was a journalist.'

Cowan commenced cramming the bandanna into the Professor's open mouth. 'Honestly, I think I've heard quite enough from you.'

The Professor made muddled crying noises. A strand of saliva dripped on the desk.

'Print it.' Cowan commanded. 'Where does it come out?'

Cleverly nodded at the door. 'Wa Wawa.'

'The office? Fair enough. Well, thanks for your time, Duchess. It's been an education.' Cowan dragged the man's contorted face up to his own, the bandanna protruding like a huge tongue from his mouth. 'If you leave in the next ten minutes, I'm going to come back and chop your testicles off and feed them to a budgerigar. Got it?'

Cleverly's teeth ground together squeakily.

'Also, I'm going to talk to that Jill girl. These days a 21-year-old is practically a baby. Come near her again, even breathe in her vicinity, I will fuck you up so bad. I'll drive you into the ground like a fucking tent peg. Comprehendez, shithead?'

'Ah Wawawa.'

Connie retrieved the roster from the office photocopier for him. 'Oh,' she said, surprised. 'Duke actually helped you.'

'That's one menacing person,' Cowan said, giving a little shiver. 'I can see why he writes all that dark stuff.'

'Really?'

They began laughing.

'Seriously, Connie, I think you could knock him down with your eyelashes.'

'He's quite a hit with our young ladies,' she said. 'Believe it or not.'

'Aye, you'd suppose that one couldn't pay a drunk monkey to go interfering with him. Listen, I'll be sending you a postcard soon as I get back to civilization with a list of eligible kilted bachelors want to marry a naïve young US lass.'

Connie blushed. 'Only if they got big estates. That's my deal clincher.'

'Every one will be a laird or a marquis, I promise.' Cowan was whispering now. 'By the by, Professor Grant Genius is going to come belting in here in about ten minutes flat screaming bloody murder and asking for the police.'

'Why would he be doing that?'

'I'll be frank with you, Connie. There was an altercation. No one got hurt, much. It involved tofu.'

Connie looked at him and shrugged.

'And cake.'

'Have you been a bad boy, then?'

'Slightly. But it's been so difficult for me here in the future ever since I teleported from Culloden. They said to me don't ever touch that ancient creepy standing stone at night in a lightning hailstorm, but then that night during that big lightning hailstorm…'

'Oh, for God's sake.' Connie was laughing again.

'But I was definitely a bad boy. So, should I shove a book down the back of my trousers now? Am I due a spanking?' He winked. 'I wish.'

'I don't switch little kids don't know any better,' Connie said, staring at him.

'I didn't hurt the man at all, Connie.' Cowan crossed his fingers, nodding contritely. 'I promise you that. He's somewhat intact. Plus it's worth considering that the Great American Novelist is this massive shithead.'

Connie frowned, looking mildly disappointed at Cowan's misbehavior. 'I'll check on Duke when you're gone and if it's all good and there's no serious damage done, I'll make sure campus security knows where not to find you.' She leaned forward and looked along the corridor towards the office. 'Didn't you even hurt that white boy a little bit?'

Cowan pointed both forefingers at her, remorseful no more. 'I'm upgrading you to Viscount or Earl.'

4   FRIDAY (NIGHT)

1.30pm. In the UpTowner Café, Cowan ordered a Carlyle
sandwich and a Pepsi and studied the roster. There she was
again: smiling, happy, lovely, living. There were only three
other women in the class. One was a mature student, late
40s. Another girl just wasn't Catriona's type. Cowan considered this assessment. Only twenty-four hours ago he'd
found out his daughter was gay, and here he was deciding her
taste in lovers. The likeliest suspect, Mary Barnham, was the
one who had no ID photo. He used his PeopleFinder program to find an address in Alexandria, Virginia. There were
no photographs on her Facebook page. Her public profile
hadn't been updated in three years. No employment status.
The profile picture was a Disney princess. No Linkedin
page. An abandoned Twitter account with a few cryptic
tweets: *I wish I were a wittier Twitterer too, Toto*. Her profile:
*My Mission is simple: make order out of chaos and wear cute shoes
while doing it*. So, he'd be looking for a goddess-come-prin-
cess in Louboutins then. Didn't she know a digital native in a
new millennium of social-mediated post-reality was obliged
to share her deepest darkest secrets with the world, or at least
with him?

Google images were a boon, giving him two photographs five years apart. The first, from the GW Alumni magazine of 2011, identified her as a college senior in political science, which made her about 28 now. The article was about

student internships on the Hill and the smiling young Mary posed by a photocopier, stapler in one hand, ribbon cartridge in the other, one leg in the air, looking daffy. In the second, from four years later, that goofy girl had mutated into a grey-suited professional, senior legislative assistant to Congressman Bill Griffith of Louisiana. There you go. That had been one rapid political ascent from intern. Mary stood alongside the staffers in a Congressional office, arms draped on each other's shoulders, leaning forward into the lens, all smiles, the cats that got the cream. Yellow balloons bobbed behind them, streamers streamed. Birthday party? Christmas? Election celebration? Mary was a tall, attractive, dimpled blonde and looked like good fun. Cowan could easily see himself going for that if he were a younger man, or a younger woman. Did that mean he had the same taste in women as his daughter? It might be true, he'd married her mother right enough. God help him.

McDonald had texted him a list of metro stations $1.90 distant from Foggy Bottom. He checked it again. King Street was a possibility, the Metro for Alexandria.

Cowan walked 20 blocks from the station, first looping by a huge yellow crane blocking the entrance to Joe Thiesmann's. King Street began as a boutique district (shops called Belecara, Decorium, Olio, Coco Blanca, seemingly named after inhabitants of Dante's Inferno), and ended in Old Town, a tourist trap of overpriced restaurants and cafes. At the intersection of Washington and Prince was Buberi's Appomattox bronze statue. The lone defeated

Confederate soldier stood, back turned solemnly against the north. His arms were crossed, a wide-brimmed hat clutched tight in his hand. The Reb looked dour, or maybe constipated. Beneath the statue were carved the names of 100 dead Confederates, a memorial to their sacrifice. Robert E. Lee's boyhood home was close by too, a big attraction to some. Cowan supposed everyone needed their Flodden, Culloden, Mons Graupius, some terrible loss or other to keep the juices flowing. There was pleasure to be had in wallowing in defeat, so long as you didn't have to do anything about it. Polish the bronze and keep the bird shit off. That was enough.

He recalled sauntering across George Square years ago with DC Milroy, scattering a feathering of dirty pigeons from its manicured parterres. They were headed to an autopsy. Good times. Milroy had pitched the dog-end of his fag against the figures at the base of the Equestrian Monument to Queen Victoria that day. 'I've often wondered which one's the fucking horse,' Milroy had said. Cowan laughed, remembering now. He was currently strolling past another horse, a fake grey one stood up in the back of an antique truck. By the Torpedo Factory art gallery, an elderly man in blue overalls pushed a rusted bicycle with only one wheel along the sidewalk. It could have been another YouTube performance piece. It wasn't.

The address was an apartment above an antique store opposite City Hall. Number 3 would be one of four apartments on the upper level where a rust-red metal fire escape hung. He got to the back door down cobbled

Ramsey Alley, under a brick arch and up a small flight of stairs to a rock garden. The door had been painted cream with purple trim. The letterbox was purple too. There was a realtor's rent sign on a crate beside an aspidistra and a lockbox on the handrail, and a pile of firewood with a carved owl perched on top. Cowan rang the doorbell. An immaculate silver fox appeared unsmiling in the frame of the door. His hair was a perfect helmet of grey, moustache impeccably trimmed. A slight plastic veneer also, that telltale tightness around the corner of the eyes. Soon everyone of a certain age in this country was going to resemble an Inca death mask.

'Hello,' Cowan said. 'I'm looking for Mary Barnham.'

'She no longer lives here.' No suggestion of a smile, only the subtle intimation of an inconvenience. 'Miss Barnham left town three months ago.'

'Did she leave a forwarding address?'

'No.'

'Are you the landlord?'

'I rent apartments in this building. We are currently renting. I live here, also.'

Cowan took out his wallet. He held a photograph of his daughter out to the man. 'Can I ask if you ever saw this woman?'

'This is none of my business,' was the immediate response.

This Botoxed contrarian wasn't even going to look at it. Cowan decided not to push, though. He'd already got himself in enough jams for one day. 'Look, I'm sorry that I'm interrupting you, but…'

'I have nothing more to tell you. I don't know anything else about Miss Barnham. I can't help you.'

The misanthrope was on the cusp of shutting the door in Cowan's face when a woman entered the vestibule behind him. She must have come down the back staircase. A sheeny redhead in pale pink lipstick who looked so sour you could have hung a jug on her lip. She was in her early 30s. With her was a child of about four. 'Mr Gorham,' she said.

Gorham gave her a curt nod. The woman manoeuvred her little one past him and under the arch. 'Excuse me.'

Cowan watched her fingers move as she fastened the mittens on the child's little hands. The pair set off pigeon-toed down the cobbles, in the direction of the river. He liked the way her skirt swayed over her black boots. He felt as if he'd seen the woman somewhere before and yet knew he hadn't. He also felt strange and unhinged.

Gorham was regarding Cowan oddly. He must have been presenting an even more peculiar expression to the world than usual.

'You can't help me any further?'

'No. Miss Barnham no longer lives here. I have nothing more. I cannot help you. I have to be somewhere.'

I. I. I. There was the mantra of 21st Century Man. 'Thanks for all your help,' Cowan told him. 'I hope the pills kick in soon.'

Cowan strolled past the Old Town Gallery and Candi's Candles, a sign advertising new luxury condominiums from the upper $1 millions. He turned, his mind changed, setting off down the alley in pursuit. Turning right on South Union, he saw the pair up ahead. The woman went into a health food store. He followed them. It was called Cornucopia, naturally, and had an extensive display of organic pre-packaged food. The day's blackboard special was eggless egg salad. Cowan wondered if that was just salad then, and commenced studying a packet of Ezekiel Sprouted Grain Tortillas, while an earnest young woman with short blue hair quizzed the server about mother's milk tea and fenugreek. The redhead was next in the queue, and a second server was summoned from the bakery to ring her up. From the other counter came a discussion regarding lactation support capsules.

'Can I help you?' a multiple-pierced young woman asked him. The gauge in her nose gave her a mild resemblance to something you'd see with its snout in a trough.

'God, I hope not,' Cowan told her.

The redhead left, child in one hand and a packet of breadsticks held against her chest like bagpipes in the other. He kept a discreet distance until they entered an ice cream parlour called The Creamery, swirling cones etched on its window. Through that window, he watched the woman order. The little girl pointed at the row of tubs, excited, and her mother gave a fragile smile. The shroud concealing her beauty was lifted and, momentarily unaware, she offered the world a fleeting glimpse of someone else, a person Cowan, unaccountably, wanted very badly to know. She slid into a booth under a Girardelli's Chocolates poster and took off her child's mittens, putting them in her pocket. He wondered, watching, about the sadness he saw in her eyes.

Cowan made as if to sit in an adjacent booth with his dish of strawberry. The little girl was consuming an elaborate cream truffle smothered in chocolate. 'That looks good,' he said. 'What do you call it?'

'Ice cream,' she said.

'Well, I know that. I mean, does it have any other name?'

The girl examined her dish and pressed her lips together and shook her head. 'No, just ice cream.'

The woman said, 'It's a triple chocolate fudge cone.'

'It looks good,' he offered.

'It is good,' said the girl. 'It's ice cream.' She looked at him. 'You talk funny.'

'Emma,' her mother said. 'That's rude.'

'It's true. I do talk funny.' Cowan shrugged. 'Didn't I just see you? Don't you live in one of the apartments above the antique store on Fairfax?'

The woman's eyes flickered slightly, but then she seemed to recall him from before. 'Yes,' she said. 'That's right. You were outside talking to Tal Gorham.'

'He's the landlord?'

'Yes.'

'Quite a character.'

'Old money,' she said. Her eyes were a subtle colour.

Cowan decided he'd have to look at them more. 'The type still talks about the War of Northern Aggression. He used to work for the government.'

'As a doorman, was it? I was actually looking for someone who used to live in the building, a woman called Barnham.'

'She was in the upstairs apartment. She moved out.'

'What happened?'

'I think she moved jobs. She was a journalist.'

'You didn't know her well, then?'

The woman was staring up at him now, concerned. He realised he was pushing too hard with a stranger. It was inappropriate. He was a much better policeman than that.

'No, I didn't really know her.' She turned away, a signal to end the conversation.

The girl sat watching the exchange, spooning her ice cream at the same time, causing a spectacular mess. 'Are you almost done?' the woman asked.

For a moment, Cowan thought she was talking to him.

He hoped he wasn't.

'Almost.' The girl rubbed a smear of chocolate across her mouth. Her mother moistened a napkin and gently rubbed it off. When she put the napkin to her lips to wet it, Cowan felt something slide away inside him. He was standing still by their booth, as immovable as those statues he liked to contemplate. The redhead reached down to scoop up her shoulder bag. Her face was a vision to him then.

'I believe Mary knew my daughter,' he said, quickly.

'My daughter was the girl from Scotland. The one was killed here on the Metro last spring?'

'I'm so sorry.' The woman looked at once a little stricken.

'I was her father,' he mumbled at her, hopelessly. 'I am her father.' All Cowan wanted was for her to stay sitting where she was, to linger there. 'I don't know why I'm telling you this. I'm just trying to talk to everyone who knows her. Who knew her. I'm trying to make my own peace with her death.'

'I understand.'

Her eyes were looking deeply into his now and he felt her sympathy swell and crush him like a wave. It was a palpable throbbing fearful thing coming at him. Her eyes were the kind that seemed to see something just beyond your face. It was too much. They were so blue he nearly burst into tears right in the middle of the stupid ice cream shop.

'You're all right,' she said very quietly, and laid her hand on the sleeve of his jacket, his hideous repulsive jacket. 'You're all right now.'

Was he? He got out his wallet, this with difficulty, his fingers trembling, and gave her his card, his cell number scribbled on it. 'If you think of anything more about Mary,' he told her. 'I'd love to talk to you. I mean, her. You about her.' He was become a gibbering idiot. Words didn't work.

'Sure.' She stood up and eased her way out of the booth, her smile uncertain. It was a lovely smile though, slow and unselfconsciously strange. He was still all lost in the spatter of freckles on the bridge of her nose. For the life of him, he didn't know what he'd meant by 'love to'. He'd intended to say something quite different.

'I'm sorry I was so strange there,' he ventured, sounding stupider still. 'My life collapsed around my ears and I'm trying to rebuild it.'

'You weren't strange.' The woman bent towards her child and a strand of red hair fell across her cheek like a scar. She took his card. 'You were bereaved.' She caught her daughter by the hand. The girl wouldn't let go of the long spoon. The ice cream had been that good. 'Goodbye,' the woman said to him. 'Everything will be all right.'

'You should have that,' Emma said, pointing at the long-tapered glass. 'It was Lucy scrumptious.'

'Goodbye,' Cowan said, and let desolation sweep through him. He sat in a booth unmoving till the ice cream was a pink puddle in his cup. He threw it in the trash and walked into sunlight. The afternoon warming, yellow light was speckling bare trees. Cowan considered the depths of his loneliness, how in this place he seemed to drift into a new state of being, too sentimental and ramshackle for his tastes. Was he still sifting the ashes, making believe he was some-place else, with a compulsion to find out what all others reasonably knew was not there? Did he only want to make order out of the chaos that he was? *That was your bailiwick wasn't it, order from chaos? A person pledges to uphold law and order and then finds the law of chaos is all there ever was. That was on you.*

Cowan addressed these thoughts not to God but to an antique cigar store Indian outside a tobacconist's called *The*

Scottish Merchant. It was the kind of place that would advertise itself as quaint. Cowan went inside to be hideously swaddled in tartan. Hundreds of patterns and colours of tartan scarves and ties, tartan clan crests, tartan lighters, rows of shelves of tartan shot and beer glasses with clan names and tartan, always tartan. *Nemo me impune lacessit.* A cardboard sign on a back door said *No Bags In The Humidor*. Cowan had never seen those words arranged in that order before, and never would again.

'This place wouldn't look out of place on The Royal Mile,' he told the cashier.

'Huh?'

'They do say woollen plaid is not woollen plaid unless it reeks of smoke.'

'Eh? Can I help you find something?'

'Aye,' he said, leaving. 'A smidgeon of Celtic dignity.' On South Fairfax were pretty blue, white and red colonial townhouses. Some hung American flags outside; others had rows of miniature pumpkins ranged on their lintels. On a black door was a bright orange wreath wheeled like a galaxy. On a red door was a wreath of green apples. Under a grey-shuttered window was a spray of purple celosia. There were For Sale signs in the windows of a few, a consequence of the recent election, a Republican wave. From an open window a saxophone came keening: Bill Clinton in mourning. In his wandering he stumbled upon an old Presbyterian Meeting House, founded in 1772, the plaque said. Round the back was a cemetery through which he strolled, impressed by the antiquity of the grave-markers, the gravity of the marble inscriptions. With his finger, he traced the faded lettering of canted stones. Lindsay. Henryson. Dunbar. Old Scottish names, all, an ocean from home, like him. He hunkered on the sparse grass by embedded black slabs all erased now, silent, unreadable colonial histories. Years ago now, he'd wandered up to the Necropolis to look at the Knox memorial statue. The old Thunderer high and gloomy on his Doric column—cylindrical pedestal, wide-pedimented abacus, dog-ear acroteri—draped dark in Geneva cap and gown. The King of the city of the dead glared stone-faced at the city of the living. Beneath Knox's statue was written these words: *there lieth he who never feared the face of man; who was often threatened with dag and dagger, yet hath ended his days in peace and honour.* Cowan could read that inscription because Knox had preached that the Scottish child should be a literate one.

It was while sitting on a peculiar and ancient red sandstone, a curiosity there, that he called the office of Congressman Griffith. This call affirmed what Cowan suspected. Mary Barnham hadn't worked for the Congressman in some years and the office had no current address. Didn't Mary work for *Capitol Inquirer*, the political magazine? Had he contacted them? They did have a website. In fact, they were a website, mainly. This was shaping up to be just another dead end in a cemetery. By his left knee, letters carved into the stone by a vandal's penknife: JACHIN. Sounded biblical. What was the story of Ruth again? It was long gone. He remembered nothing. The graffiti was probably gang-related.

Two colonial soldiers approached him where he sat. It was quite disturbing, like he'd come staggering into some curious historical dream space. The pair had the uniforms: tricolour hats, black jackets with red waistcoats, white pants. One carried a replica musket, the other an American flag and a crate of orange juice, no pulp.

'Hello.' Cowan couldn't think of anything else to say. Nothing surprised him anymore. He surrendered to the surreal.

'There's a wreath laying later,' one of them explained. 'On the tomb of the unknown soldier of the Revolutionary War.'

'Who was that?'

'We don't know,' the other soldier told him. 'He's unknown.'

The soldiers explained to Cowan that they were representatives of the Children of the American Revolution as they set up plastic tables and chairs and lined up the juice cups. 'You're welcome to stay,' one of them said.

Cowan didn't stay. Near the fountain in the square, Columbian street musicians shrilled on panpipes and by Capital Bikeshare, a young man in mirror sunglasses tried to get him to pay to look through a massive telescope. 'The sun, moon, three planets and the dwarf planet Ceres are aligned, man.'

'Uh-huh.'

'It's Mercury, Saturn and Venus. It's a conjunction: New Moon and everything, man, sunspots too.'

Cowan walked on beyond the din and the hawking to the Carlyle House, a monument to the Scottish mercantile spirit built in 1753 for John Carlyle's new bride, Sarah Fairfax of Belvoir. The Palladian-style house was the headquarters for General Braddock in the French and Indian War. Now it could be rented for private functions. Remembrances of home, no matter where he went. He'd crossed the Atlantic to escape himself and connect with something different, a new world, and everywhere he wandered he found reminders of the old, dropped randomly like sweet wrappers in the street.

His mobile buzzed at his groin as if a metal insect was trying to pollinate him. A staffer for Senator Factor said that the Senator would very much like to meet him. The distinguished gentleman had been most distressed to hear of Cowan's bereavement, having a particular and longstanding interest in crime and victims' rights. He was also incredibly upset about what he heard had transpired, a most unfortunate misunderstanding, in his office on Capitol Hill yesterday. The Senator was on his way back to Washington tonight. Could they meet for a light brunch tomorrow? Did Cowan by chance know Alexandria, Virginia? The Senator had a residence there. Cowan said he would be delighted to stop by. Maybe he could discuss politics with the Senator. It was, after all, something in which he was fast acquiring an interest.

It was 4.10pm. In the shadow of a townhouse on Duke, a man sat fiddling with a shoe and a screwdriver. What could a man possibly be doing with a shoe and a screwdriver? Cowan cut back towards King when he saw the Masonic Monument loom like Pompeii's Pillar. Back on the train, a young woman punched digits on her phone. It wouldn't work in the tunnels, so she kept re-dialling, which wasn't easy. Her red fingernails were so long they curled like the talons of a bird. By the time the train escaped the dark into late afternoon Arlington, the swollen sun was beating a tattoo on the windowpane.

Cowan was in his hotel room contemplating where to eat an early dinner when the knock came. He opened the door to McDonald in a brown suit, carrying a long manila envelope. He wondered if it might be an extradition document. 'I can't come out,' he said, sadly. 'My mammy says it's my nap time.'

'I wanted a word.'

'I hope it doesn't start with C and end in a T.'

The Commander brushed by him and sat on the edge of the bed. He wasn't smiling any. 'Crumpet?' he sniffed.

'Make yourself at home,' Cowan suggested.

The Commander motioned for Cowan to sit also, so he did. 'How's your day been, Detective Inspector? Doing the tourist thing, were you?'

'Aye. I wandered all over. Went to Alexandria. It's a fascinating historical place. I wanted to see the library, but they tell me it burned down. Have a good day yourself?'

'I've had better days at the dentist. Do you know a Professor Cleverly?'

'I didn't recognise you at first without your clothes on; your uniform, I mean.'

'Cleverly.'

'That's a suit and a half that is. It suits you, that suit.'

'Cleverly?'

'Oh, in every possible way.'

'Well, this Professor person says he knows you. As a matter of fact, he was thinking about filing assault charges.'

'I think it's coming back to me now. This has to do with a cake?'

'I told you to be careful.'

'I'll try to be more so.'

'You will be more so.' McDonald held his gaze. 'I talked him out of it. It wasn't easy. I explained all about grief; yours, not mine. I apologized on your behalf. I also noticed a pill bottle on his office desk in the course of my inquiries: Vicodin. No prescription, apparently. The Professor was quite agreeable after I brought that up. How you and he just had a misunderstanding. Quid pro quo as they say.'

'Thanks, Mac. I owe you big time. One week. Then I'll be gone, lickety-split.'

'That a promise?'

'Absolutely! Soon as I'm done here, I'm heading off to Switzerland. Always wanted to go there.'

McDonald looked skeptical. 'What's so special about Switzerland?'

'I want to see how their army manages to fight with those little red knives.'

'Are you ever serious, sir?'

'Did you follow up on that call girl info for me? I want to get that wrapped up.'

'I assumed you weren't serious on that, too.'

'I. Thought. I. Was.'

McDonald shook his head sadly.

'Wouldn't it be worth it for you though, Big Mac? Just to get me the hell out of what's left of your hair?'

McDonald observed Cowan grimly.

'Baldness is a sign of virility, Mac. First time I saw you, I thought to myself, now here's a big man practically leaking his manhood all over the place.'

'It must be wonderful to be you, Detective Inspector.'

'I still have to go the bathroom every day, like the next man.'

'You do?' McDonald slapped the envelope against his leg. 'I'm surprised.'

'Though I hear they do have those special cotton panties now. No one even knows when you're wearing them, they're that discreet. I could be going to the bathroom right now, and you'd never even know.' Cowan smiled. 'In fact, I am.'

McDonald tossed the envelope in Cowan's lap and stood up. 'I know nothing about what's in there,' he said, pointing. 'Nothing!' He picked up the electric razor attachment on the dresser table. 'What's this gizmo?'

'It's for trimming the hair in your ear.'

McDonald frowned. 'I don't understand that, from an evolutionary perspective. Why would we start growing hair in our ears? Warmth?'

'I think it's so as we get older, we don't have to listen to other people.'

'You must get a lot in your ears then? That explains a lot.'

'My sense of hearing is practically hirsute.' Cowan pointed to his ear and then to McDonald. 'Hey, check this out. Hirsute and his suit. Get it? It involves wordplay.'

'God, give me strength,' McDonald muttered at him.

'Well, He's what gives your life meaning, or so you were saying the other day.'

'Detective Inspector, to me life is like a box of chocolates.' McDonald observed Cowan's expression, and smiled. 'It doesn't last that long if you're fat.'

'That was a good one. I might have to use that if I'm stuck and I can't think of anything funny.' Cowan accompanied the Commander to the door of the hotel room. 'But I'm seriously almost out of here. You'll be free at last, Mac. Free. At. Last. Thank God almighty, free at last.' McDonald was glaring at him angrily. 'Just saying.'

'With your attitude, someone is going to knock the checks off your Nikes sooner or later,' McDonald observed. 'I'm just hoping it isn't me.'

Cowan rummaged through the papers McDonald had left him. He was a Mr Leung visiting from Hong Kong, identity verified and approved, looking for a hell of a good time tonight. Well, here was hoping Mr Leung would find it. He decided to skip his Chinese meal, him being Manchurian enough already. He called room service. His alter ego had called in the order for his servicing at 9pm. The vice boys had set up a fake email too. The password was moron-scotsman1! In this at least Cowan detected the hand of the Commander.

She contacted him at 8.30 by email to say she was on her way. That was a relief. Cowan was worried about having to put on an accent and sounding like Fu Man Chu. He sent her his room number and the location of the elevators in relation to the entrance. Then he dropped the envelope's contents in the trash bin, put a pile of twenties inside and laid it on the table beside the TV. It would be the first thing she'd see coming in. He reread the sheet titled Companion Protocol downloaded from the agency: *Your companion is a human being, with emotions, feelings, desires, and a life outside providing professional services to clients. Respect her, treat her as you'd expect to be treated. True, you are paying for her services, but that doesn't give you licence to treat her like dirt or non-human. Respect her boundaries.*

Cowan had never paid for sex. He wasn't sure how he'd expect to be treated as a call girl. His daughter had been doing something like this too. He was sure of it now. He imagined Catriona entering a hotel room to find her father waiting and felt sick to his stomach. He turned off every lamp but the one by the bed. The room was dim now.

She called at 8.50pm. Cowan kept his end of the conversation monosyllabic. He then observed her arrival through the peephole. She flicked her hair back and widened her eyes before knocking, no doubt suspecting she was being watched, performing for his hidden male gaze. He unlatched the door and retreated, turning his back and walking towards the window, as if shy, overcome by nervousness.

'Hi,' she said, closing the door behind her. It clicked. She felt safe. He was pre-approved, like a credit card, which is all he was, really. 'I'm Sammi.' She was going to be nice and gentle with him then. That was considerate of her.

Cowan turned around to examine her more closely. She squinted at him through the murk, pursing her lips, a bee-sting scarlet, deep red lipstick so labial as to be obscene. There was to-be-expected tension in the air. She looked classy in that knee length coat, but underneath would be the requested plaid skirt, the white shirt and check tie of a Catholic schoolgirl. She'd been bad in class today and needed a right spanking. Spare the rod and spoil the child was Mr Leung's special kink. She smiled coyly at him and her braces glinted.

'I hope you got your homework all done, Erin.'

Her most recent expression was that of a camel eating sherbet. Erin spun, groping for the door handle, but Cowan was too quick for her. He snatched her arm.

'I'll scream,' she hissed at him.

Cowan clamped his hand over her mouth. 'No, you won't. That would be stupid.' Her breath was warm on his fingers and she whimpered slightly. 'I got a few more questions for you, little girl.'

'Please,' she said, trying to pull her arm free. 'I just need the money.'

He threw her down on the bed. She lay there, snuffling, her mascara spiked with tears. 'How long you been doing this, then? You must be pretty good at it by now.'

She threw him a look like a spear. 'Two years,' she mumbled.

'You started back in community college?'

She nodded. Her eye-makeup had run and she looked a bit like a startled raccoon.

'This was what Catriona was doing too? Did you get her started on it?'

Erin looked surprised by the accusation. Shook her head. 'God, no.'

'She wasn't into this?'

'No.'

Cowan handed her a tissue, speaking evenly. 'OK. Here's what's going to happen now: I'm going to ask questions and you're going to answer them without lying this time. Got it?'

The girl's coat had fallen open and he caught a glimpse of schoolgirl plaid and her long, bare white legs. 'I didn't lie,' she whispered.

'See, that's a fucking terrible start. There you go again. Here's the deal. You lie to me again and everyone finds out about your extracurriculars. I mean everybody: your school, your friends.'

'My friends know,' Erin said, still hard as nails through the tears.

'Your parents?'

Her face turned grey. 'Please, no. It would kill my dad. You can't do that.'

'What about the damn computer then?'

'I don't know.'

'Who else had it?'

'I don't know anything.'

'Too bad. I'll let your folks know that when I talk to them. I'll reassure them that their wee hooker-lassie knows nothing about nothing.'

Erin's face seemed to come apart, the eyes the prelude to a scream, but no sound could force its way between her lips. 'Please!' The word was little more than a hoarse whisper

Cowan sat on the bed beside her and ran a finger carefully through her blonde hair. She ventured a hopeful smile, her upper lip exposing the silver braces. 'I've got nothing to lose.' Cowan left a pause between the words. 'Who. Had. The. Computer?'

Her smile vanished. 'I don't remember his name.'

The blanket of rippling lamplight cast shadows across the wall, etching tide pools of darkness.

'I don't want to do this to you,' he whispered. 'I really don't.'

'I just don't recall that name. Honest to God.'

'I don't believe in Him, Erin sweetheart, or you.'

Then came the tears,

Cowan sat impassive, watching the girl sob quietly into his pillow. Was she buying time to think? She practiced breathing for a while.

'One answer and you're out of here. I don't want to hurt you. Not much anyway.'

She was staring at the picture of the Lincoln Memorial on the wall. The Great Emancipator wasn't going to help her. No freedom there. Her eyes had a faraway look. 'Two days before everything happened, I got a call.'

'Everything? You mean the murder? That was everything?'

'Yeah.'

'This call was from someone you knew?'

'Yeah.'

'A client?'

She smiled with her eyes, without moving her lips.

'Do you need those things on your teeth or is it part of the act?'

'They like it: the clientele. It's a kink. I had to have it done.'

'They like it. Jesus, this is a fucked-up world, right enough. This customer of yours wanted a good look at that computer, didn't he?'

Erin nodded.

'Keep going. You're doing good.'

'He asked me if I could get her computer for an hour or two. I didn't understand why, how he even knew Cat, but that's what he wanted. I told him she'd be gone all weekend. If he came by on Friday, he'd be able to do what he wanted with it.'

'But he took it.'

'This other guy did. I don't know who he was, techie type with a beard. They always got beards, you know? He came Saturday morning and looked at it and said he needed to take it, but he'd bring it back Sunday afternoon.'

'How did you feel about that?'

'I was scared Cat would come back early and it wouldn't be there, obviously. How was I going to explain that?'

'Did they ever say why they wanted to look at it?'

Erin shook her head. 'I didn't ask. I didn't want to know. I was afraid.'

'They paid you, though?'

'Yeah.'

'How much?'

'It wasn't much.'

'I'd like a name.'

'Please,' she said.

'Give me one name and we're done forever.'

Erin looked like a desperate thing now. 'The techie guy brought it back on Sunday, but then the thing that happened, happened.'

'You mean the murder.'

She nodded. 'I was worried sick, but no one even asked about it till you came creeping this week.'

'What does he do? What makes this person you know so scary?'

Erin sighed, composing herself, shriven. 'He works for the government.'

'You mean he works for a US Senator?'

She looked surprised. 'He said if I told anyone about it, he'd destroy my life.'

'That's a coincidence. Here I am now telling you the exact same thing. It's not your day, Erin.' Cowan touched her cheek gently. 'Sounds like you're between a rock and a hard place, eh? I'll give you time to think about it. I paid for the whole hour.'

Erin began crying again. She stretched out on the bed, exposing her legs. She was narrow and white as a knife's pearl handle. At the top of her thigh there was a bruise the same shade as her plum toenails. Cowan turned on the television and watched the news. There were protests in DC about the immigration bill. Talking heads were talking now. They were expecting Missouri to explode after the latest grand jury verdict. The panel was practically creaming their pants at the thought. Race war meant ratings through the roof. Cowan had no patience for racism. He wasn't done hating all the white people yet. The Vice President was filmed at a prayer breakfast being prissy as a eunuch vicar.

'He can't know it was me,' she whispered up at him.

'It's not like you're in a position to discuss terms, Erin. When the firing squad gets all lined up, the prisoner doesn't get to negotiate a price on the blindfold.'

'Craig. Craig Doyle.'

'He and I are acquainted. Anything else?'

She gave him a blank look. Cowan could try applying thumbscrews, but he wasn't going to get anything else out of her.

'Was he an in-call?'

She nodded.

'Here,' he said, pushing a hotel notepad towards her. 'Write down his address.'

'I don't remember it.'

'Yes, you do.'

She scribbled something and pushed the pad back and he glanced at the address. 'It didn't give me any pleasure to do this,' he told her.

'Yes it did.' Erin was regaining her composure and a fixed meaningless smile had settled on her face. 'We good now?'

There was something in the girl's expression made Cowan angry at himself. 'I wouldn't call you or me good.' He pulled her face close to his, smelled her scent. Inhaled it deeply. 'No,' he said. 'I'm for sure not. So go in there, get yourself cleaned up and get the hell out of my hotel room.'

After five minutes Erin came out of the bathroom composed and sleek and walked to the door, changed her mind and came back. She picked up the envelope and stuffed it in her purse, glaring at him. The look she gave wished him dead.

Cowan knew he badly needed to get the hell out of the hotel room: time to think, time to breathe. He went to the bar off the lobby and after deliberating for a long time ordered a Sprite. He was struggling. The girl was right. He had enjoyed intimidating her. Some days he felt so frail he longed for utter oblivion, to close his eyes on the past and the future alike. But he didn't know til a few minutes before, what he was capable of doing to another.

The lounge was a wasp nest of buzz-chatter. The FRC members were unloading from the escalators after the big 9pm keynote speech. The male conferees wore suits and conference badges and engaged in the acts of networking expected of those so wilfully self-identified. They cackled at each other's jokes, impressed and impressing, and sneaked peeks at the badges of passers-by, ever on the lookout for a more valuable person. It was a conference just like any other, then. Except no one was drinking at this one, or having any fun, and everyone had a personal relationship with their Lord and Savior, everyone except him. Cowan had read someplace that a subordinate monkey derives great pleasure from the act of looking at a superior monkey's ass, and will actually forgo food for the opportunity so to do. There you go.

'Excuse me,' a woman said, looking concerned, 'but are you aware that your nose is bleeding? It's getting on your shirt.'

Cowan saw that it was. 'I think I was listening too intently to that amazing sermon,' he told her. 'It was so inspirational I didn't feel a thing.'

'Did you enjoy it?' she asked, suddenly enthused. The woman was plain and uptight in what looked like a blue housecoat. Her eyes were much too close together. She looked like the type who would keep herself and everyone in the immediate vicinity cleaner than the White House lawn.

'Can't say I did,' Cowan said, sadly. 'See, my philosophy is, if thy morals make thee dreary, depend upon it they are wrong. That, and also never trust anybody who only reads the one book. I'm having a crisis of faith, you might say.'

The woman's eyes were open wider now, telegraphing mild alarm. She looked around the adjacent sofas, in case an intervention or conversion was necessary.

'Hold up,' Cowan said, pretending to be startled. 'You aren't a call girl, are you?' He shook his head apologetically. 'Sorry. My mistake. It's just that, between you and me, this hotel is full of them. Did you know that pussy,' he whispered, sotto voce, 'is the second most abundant commodity on earth? After water?'

It was at this juncture that the poor woman jumped up and ran away very quickly towards the lobby, looking all around the bar with the startled eyes of a chicken. Cowan knocked back his Sprite, the ice clacking his teeth, and reviewed everything that had happened since that morning. He thought it best to leave out all the people he had insulted or assaulted. There was something wrong with all this. He'd always thought it. He knew it for sure now. What the hell had his daughter been doing in this place? Why were these people so interested in her? Why was her body now buried so deep in lies? He sucked on an ice cube and thought about ordering something else.

He got himself out of the bar before it was too late.

5   SATURDAY (MORNING)

The curtains held the scent of stale heat and, when he punched the pillow, a puff of perfume rose. He inhaled it: *Opium*. Sickened and sad, he began trying to stuff himself back into himself, turning in his mouth the aftertaste of ashes, his eyelashes sticky. Cowan stared into the bevelled bathroom mirror, considering the state of his life: concluding that this morning, it was an empty carousel at sunset filled with snow.

7.50am. His phone was chirruping. Hateful thing. It was Bannon, yet another hateful thing. Downstairs. Brief chat in order: concerns, anxieties, mistakes had been made, make him part of the conversation. The usual bumf.

In the lobby, the staff was, with some difficulty, attempting to erect a big Christmas tree. The original Druids wouldn't have had that problem back in the days of Alban Arthuan. Those were the boys who built Stonehenge. Bannon was observing the struggle diffidently, perhaps contemplating his own difficulties controlling an unruly nature. 'Ah, there you are,' he announced, looking plump and prosperous and panicked.

'Here I am,' shrilled Cowan. He nodded at the tree, now at a 45-degree angle. 'Are they going to put you on top when they're done?'

The corners of the consul's mouth drew down and his

face got sulky. 'I thought we could have a quick word, old man.'

'No-one wants a slow word these days.'

'I was talking to McDonald.'

'Old McDonald? The one can't spell?'

'Spell?'

'Aye, he thought you spelt farm E I E I O.'

Bannon frowned. 'No. The other McDonald.'

'Ramsey MacDonald? Ronald McDonald? There's so many. They must breed like fruit flies them McDonalds.'

The consul's tiny pig eyes receded into their flesh sockets. 'No, the police chief of the 4th District.'

Cowan gave up. 'Oh, that one.'

'Look, do be a good chap and try to keep out of trouble a smidgeon. It's a terrible annoyance. There have been calls, a lot of calls. Couldn't you maybe see your way to leaving the professional inquiries to the, well, professionals?'

'I've been a bit wound up,' Cowan explained. 'It's a natural part of the grieving process. If I had a way to relax, you know? Any suggestions for local massage parlours?'

'No.' Bannon wasn't getting the sarcasm, but did look more engaged now. 'I'll tell you, know what I'm into these days?'

The consul commenced beating on his chest like an ape.

'Martial arts? Gay martial arts like cricket and that?'

'Dahn yoga. It's changed my life. It's all about breathing. I never knew about breathing. You wander through life every day, oblivious, and you're not even breathing. See, you work on getting the body positioned right and then work your way into the postures.' Bannon began demonstrating a basic posture, right there in the lobby, craning his neck and pushing down on his knees. It looked like he was defecating. The concierge was staring at him concerned that he was. 'There are five key postures you learn. What all the stretching does, is help release the stagnant energy in the lower abdomen.'

'Back in Glasgow we call that farting.'

'Down here,' continued Bannon, pawing meaningfully at his lower stomach, 'is the Dan Jeon. It's like the energy centre. Get more in touch with it every day, I do.'

The consul exploded abruptly out of his awkward squat. He extracted from his pocket a black and gold card and handed it to Cowan. 'There's even a centre in Georgetown now. Say no more. They're getting to be all over these days. This offshoot of Dahn is spreading like a good cancer. That's the best I'm giving you there. It's more exclusive, invite only, but you should call ahead.'

Cowan twiddled the paper rectangle between his fingers. 'I'm going to check this out for sure. Gets me looking trim as you.'

'Awaken the healer within,' Bannon intoned. 'Develop it. Master it. Heal yourself, your family, society, and the earth.'

'That's a mouthful of good life philosophy, right there.'

'A colleague said she'd read in a magazine that Dahn

started out as a Korean cult. But you just take from it what you need, you know? It's yoga, right?'

'Yoga,' said Cowan. 'No need to get all bent out of shape about it.'

'Now, about you staying out of bother and so forth…'

'I'm on it,' Cowan told him. 'Like a fly on shit.'

'Well, good. It can't be all that terribly difficult not to irritate everyone.'

'I'm just adjusting to being in this country. I think the time difference must be contributing too. I'm six hours behind and living in the past. I'm like a Pilgrim Father.'

'What's your plan for today? Something non-confrontational, we'd hope?'

'I've got an appointment with a journalist at a large circulation online political magazine. Wait a minute, can you circulate online even? Now there's a question worth pondering. Then, after that, I'm having brunch with a US senator.'

'Good,' said Bannon, looking goggle-eyed and hysterical. 'Good, good.'

'I've got another question for you though.'

'Yes?' Bannon acquired a look of panicked expectancy, his smile plastic.

'If the meal between breakfast and lunch is brunch, would a meal taken between dinner and supper be sinner? Or would be it dupper? It's really bothering me, that.'

'Dahn yoga,' said Bannon, patting his stomach. 'It'll change your life.'

★ ★ ★

The Capitol Inquirer office building was a three-tiered glass case within walking distance of the Crystal City Metro in Arlington. The lower entrance level was an open contiguous space that even at 9am was a hive of activity, the editorial staff punching keypads dementedly in a brutal symphony of muted clacking. The keyboard bangers were flanked on each side by enclosed recording studios with glass walls and large video screens tuned to the crucial channels (Fox, CNN, MSNBC). C-Span wasn't an option here. Real politics moved in time, not at the virtual speed of gossip. Real politics was way too boring for the ADD crowd. Cowan had been reading how this magazine had accelerated news inside the Beltway from days to minutes. It had become the daily must-read for political professionals, and every day paper copies were delivered to the White House and Capitol Hill and eagerly devoured in the office of any K-street lobbyist with a pulse. Then again, most of that lot were vampires, so they probably didn't have a pulse. New online media enterprises like *The Inquirer* had rendered thinking obsolete and replaced that tiresome and redundant process with a blitzkrieg of dopamine. These folks were journalists who didn't actually write anymore, they just typed.

Cowan was led by a young staffer up the winding, open interconnecting stairway that led from the main entry and creative collaborative zone, to the terrace on the upper level. Little yellow post-it notes were stuck on the glass walls to prevent people walking into them. The staffer walked ahead of him and he glimpsed a reckless tattoo at the base of her spine drifting up the ass of her jeans. The light inside the building was blinding. Upstairs, there was an open-plan cafeteria with pillow-fluffed blue futons located at each corner. There were also two ping-pong tables, currently not in use. It was too bad; Cowan could have used a quick set of table tennis to get the interrogative juices flowing.

Paul Belardo was seated on one of the futons chewing meditatively on the remnants of what appeared to have been a cheese bagel. He was looking at two mobile phones simultaneously, glancing quickly from one to the other on the table in front of him. The man dressed like a journalist, at least. That fact was reassuring amid all this babble of new media. Cowan was at once nostalgic for the old Press Bar down on Albion Street. He used to drop in there on his way to Central Station and down a few lagers to sedate himself. The Press Bar clientele was journalists who drank like journalists: quietly, methodically and rigorously. He had once seen the rugby correspondent of the *Evening Times* drink till he toppled over backwards like a great Douglass fir, down with an almighty crash in a big puff of sawdust. The regulars all turned to look at the giant stiff where he lay, and then resumed drinking, the quicker to join him. It was that kind of place. Cowan missed the Press Bar. You could spit on the floor, and no one cared.

You couldn't spit on the floor of the *Capitol Inquirer*. It had beige carpeting. But here at last, after all this time in the city, Cowan met a man who could actually make him feel good about his own fashion choices. The journalist greeted him cheerily enough, shaking hands and spilling crumbs down the front of a cardigan that was a bright chemical green like that of a dyed Easter egg. Besides being grotesquely ugly, it was buttoned obliquely. Belardo had three-day stubble although he had no more chin than a bird. His big eyes drooped like Deputy Dawg and he clutched his Red Bull like it was a hand grenade. He also had a plaster strapped at an angle across his nose. Cowan liked him immediately.

'Sorry about the mess,' Belardo said, swishing yellow flecks around the futon. 'I've been up since 4.30am putting together our newsfeed.'

'I've often wondered why these things are called futons when you don't put your feet on them.' Cowan was quizzical. 'It's mostly the arse in my experience.'

'Yes.' It was Belardo's turn to look quizzical now. 'I guess so.'

'Do you really think people are reading what you write at 4.30 in the morning?'

Belardo nodded enthusiastically. 'Political junkies don't sleep. They're an Adderall generation. They're lit 24/7. Arlington and Rosslyn are totally OCD.'

'Oh, DC is OCD?'

'What?' Belardo was puzzled anew. 'I'm really sorry, but I've only got fifteen minutes, Mr Cowan. Everything is crazy today, what with the incipient trade war and the rumors of FLOTUS' new nip and tuck. Total madhouse. I'm so sorry about your daughter. That was just terrible. I actually met her once, you know.'

'You did?'

'Yes, it was in Filomena in Georgetown. She and Mary looked so lovely together. Those two were so out of place in this place. I mean, Washington is just Hollywood for the ugly. But together, those two looked like these amazing, gorgeous twins. I think I made a joke about it when I saw them at dinner that night. Perhaps a reference to the Olsens, something like that.' Belardo took a deep slug of his Red Bull and looked mildly abashed. He perused the side of the can, frowning. 'They had the same hair: shoulder length, blonde. Neither was remotely butch. I guess they're what people used to call lipstick lesbians before the term became unacceptable.'

'You just used it.'

Belardo crumpled the can in his hand and looked for the nearest recycling bin. The bins were everywhere. Cowan wondered if the bins were recyclable too. 'But it's acceptable to talk about how it's unacceptable maybe, I think. Isn't it? I should check. You said when you called that you wanted to talk to me about Mary though?'

'I did. I do.'

'We shared a few bylines back in the day.' Belardo shrugged a little. 'I have no idea where she is now. Mary quit last year. We kept in touch, but you know how that goes. It's DC and life moves fast. It's all very caffeinated. She must have changed her cell number. I wish I knew where she was. I like Mary a lot. I'd like to catch up.'

'You worked with her for how long? Two years was it?'

'That's right. Two.'

'Do you know why she left?'

'Yes. She quit because she wanted to write a book, of all things.' Belardo guffawed, seemingly very amused by the weird notion. 'She was even taking a creative writing class last I heard. Imagine that! That's where she met your daughter too, right? Mary told me she had to take steps to polish her prose style.' He shook his head, still incredulous. 'A book!'

'What was it about?'

'Her book? It was political, mostly an investigative piece. Mary was working some on it when she was here but...' Belardo gestured towards the cafeteria space and the surrounding swirl of perpetual motion. A ferocious rally had erupted on a ping-pong table and one of the players had no backhand to speak of. 'Who has time to write a book in a place like this? No one even has time to read a memo.'

'Before she came to work here, Mary was a Congressional staffer, right? She quit that job too? For this.'

'She was never cut out for Capitol Hill. Mary got disillusioned real quick with that kind of politics. A bit of an idealist, was Mary.'

'What was the problem?'

'Besides her being an idealist? Isn't that enough of a problem for anyone in DC?' Belardo glanced down to process an incoming text on one of his phones, holding his hand up in apology till he was done. 'They get so lonely in DC,' he added.

'Lesbians?'

'Idealists.' Belardo sniffed. 'Lesbians make out fine. You follow the lesbians you can make a fortune in real estate. Mary was working for a Louisiana Congressman, which is a tough gig anytime, but she had to be half-closeted. She was from the Midwest originally, Indiana or Iowa or Illinois. An 'I' state, definitely. It was all a bit alien to her.'

'This would have been a fellow called Griffith, she worked for then?'

'The Ragin' Cajun. One of Mary's responsibilities was environmental outreach, which was a farce, since her boss was this fossil fuel Republican.' Belardo was laughing again. 'Mary said he would frack the earth to death if he could and that he thought it was flat anyway. She told me that the old boy was a bit of a fossil fool himself.'

Cowan smiled. 'So what did she do as a staffer for him, exactly?'

Belardo carefully folded, unfolded and refolded a napkin. He was taking steps to ration his Red Bull apparently. 'Besides get disillusioned? She got to see up close and personal, every day, how much influence PACS have on the legislative process. She said Griffith spent four hours a day on call time, calls to donors, and another hour on strategic outreach. It was going to take 20 million to get him re-elected. This is today's politics.'

'It's a secret ballot still, I'm told.'

'Don't be naive, Mr Cowan.' Belardo looked disdainfully

at him, knowing what he knew. 'There's no secret ballot. I can find out which primaries you voted in. I link that to your subscription data, kind of car you drive, sub-division you live in, social media use, the rest of your consumer information. The Internet of Self means I know how you vote before you even do it. In a world without privacy, there can be no secret ballot.'

'So a politician might get corrupted by money? Since when is this news?'

'That's true. I think Julius Caesar knew that back in his day.'

'That's probably why Brutus and the Capitol boys dyed his toga red.'

Belardo took another measured sip of his drink. The stuff didn't seem to give him much energy though, for he still drooped like an aspidistra. 'There's a billion dollars of outside spending sloshing around Capitol Hill. Most of it is dark money. No one knows where it comes from or wants to know where it comes from. Now, Mary was the kind of journalist who just had to know things like that. Couldn't leave well enough alone.'

'So, she had a Road to Damascus moment? I had one of those too.' Cowan frowned. 'It was about the substantial influence of the brewing industry on my liver.'

'See, when she came to work here, that's what she wanted to write about, the corruption of the political system. But she didn't get to do it too often.' Belardo nodded significantly at the staircase. 'Downstairs wouldn't let her.

Might be treading on too many toes we might have to suck later. We've become corporate too, you know.'

'Well, this is all very depressing.'

'Still,' Belardo itched his little beard. 'It's a living, almost.'

'What happened to your nose, by the way?'

'I walked into the glass,' Belardo said, forlornly. 'It happens all the time here.'

'To you?'

'To everyone who works here.' The shabby journalist was despondent. 'It's the stupidest design for a building imaginable. But people do want transparency.' Belardo pointed at the bridge of his nose. 'It has its costs. People have been hospitalised.'

'So Mary was writing about the corporations bankrolling her Congressman? That was her version of wanting transparency?'

'That's where she started out, at any rate, following the money. You always follow the money in political journalism, ever since Watergate, right? But Mary followed the flow of that green river into some real dark woods. Honestly, she should have left well enough alone. No one would touch a book on that subject.'

'On what subject?'

Belardo quaffed a more substantial gulp of the Red Bull and shimmied his shoulders nervously. He was nervous as a porcupine in a balloon factory.

'I'd really like to know,' Cowan said, leaning in closer to him. 'It's important.'

Belardo began twiddling a wooden button on his fraying cardigan and so noticed the misalignment. He spent a minute re-buttoning while glancing at his phone.

'Did you hear me?' Cowan inquired.

Belardo edged closer to him on the futon. 'Tubalcain Services,' he whispered. 'That's what the actual book was going to be about. You didn't hear it from me.'

Cowan jotted the name down. 'And who are they when they're at home?'

Belardo at once threw his hands up in mock surrender. 'Dude, I'm so not going there. That's like the third rail. You can look them up online.'

'Will that take me to CapitolInquirer.com?'

'I hope not.' Belardo resumed the study of his ever-buzzing phone. 'I have to get back down to the hub. The President just re-tweeted a Goebbels quote. I hope I was some help to you.'

'You were. I really do appreciate your time. I might call on you again?'

'Well, you have my digits. If you do track Mary down, let her know I miss her.' Belardo looked all around the glass case imprisoning him. 'Tell her she's well out of this.'

'Well,' Cowan said, shaking the journalist's hand with vigour. 'You know what they say about people in glass houses.'

★ ★ ★

It was a pleasant late autumn morning, some relief after the cold of the day before. A warming wind swept along King

Street, rustling the little flags strung above. Cowan was near the Buberi statue when she called. He was in total disbelief, having been fantasising idly only moments before about bumping into her on the street again. It was like he'd somehow willed her call into being.

'I remembered a few things about Mary might be useful to you.'

'I'm actually walking into Alexandria right this minute. Can we meet?'

'Oh, I don't live there. I can tell you what I know on the phone though?'

Cowan had to think fast, 'I'd rather meet in person. People remember more details in conversation, you see. Little details pop better.' He said this with his fingers crossed tight. 'It's something you pick up as a policeman.'

'Ah, you feel the need to subject me further to your interrogation techniques.'

He laughed. 'Well, something along those lines. I'm staying at the Hyatt Regency on Capitol Hill.'

'There's a place across the street from there. Art and Soul? We could meet there.'

'Tonight perhaps?'

'Tonight?' There was a very long pause. 'Fine. Let's say 7.30.'

Cowan was excited by the conversation and also perturbed by his excitement. What was going on with him? Sweating, he convinced himself it was just the effect of a warm breeze on his cheek. He also realised he hadn't caught her name. Even her voice threw him for a loop.

On Duke Street, a pair of sneakers was lassoed around a wire, pulleyed by the laces, new Jordans naturally. Cowan gazed down at his own feet, watched them move that way feet do. The feet took him by an old biddy with a blue rinse trailing a terrier in a tartan coat and then, a block later, an intense young woman with a nose like a knife blade who was barking into a phone: 'Well, sometimes I'm really, like, just not where I want to be at in my, like, life, you know what I mean?' Cowan knew exactly what she meant.

The Wringhim House was an L-shaped building that, on a street of compressed narrow townhouses, sprawled to a half-acre. Around it was a high brick wall, another rarity in Alexandria. The enclosed grand brick Colonial would have been a clapboard house in the 18th century, but had evolved in the centuries since into this stately home carriage house connected to the main building by a colonnade. On the other side of the wrought iron side gate, a man in his 30s in a slim-cut grey suit and green tie was waiting for him. He wore wraparound sunglasses and was expressionless as a mannequin. 'Mr Cowan? You are expected.'

The speaker did not offer his own name, ushering the visitor along the walkway of a meticulously landscaped formal courtyard. Dead centre of the lawn was a folly, five spindly aluminum pillars and metal mesh dome. It was a bizarre looking monument to oddness. Cowan was observing the powerful build of his escort and how the man moved with the effortless grace of an athlete. The rigid carriage was suggestive of other things too, that, and how the left side of his jacket hung lower than the right. They walked past two other men of a similar build in dark suits wearing white ear-pieces. 'The Senator has quite the security detail,' Cowan observed. 'It's not even the Ides of March yet.'

The young man said nothing.

'I was just chatting to someone about Julius Caesar this morning, you see.'

Still nothing.

'You ex-military?'

The escort turned to regard Cowan warily. 'Could be.'

'I was thinking to myself it must either be that or Trappist monk.'

Near the back door, was a bronze sculpture of Thomas Jefferson seated on a bench, quill in hand, serenely crafting a document on his knee. Jefferson was looking off, thought-fully. Perhaps he was writing the Constitution. Perhaps he was thinking about bedtime with Sally Hemings. The bench had a motto: *Visita interiora terrae, rectifando invenies occultam lapidem.* Cowan's Latin wasn't up to snuff, though.

They entered a cream-walled double parlour that, despite the intricately wrought carved moldings and custom-made iron grates on the radiators, was likely part of the original farmhouse. 'The Senator hosts in the Gathering Room,' the young man told him.

A dozen prosperous-looking individuals were indeed gathered there, besuited, glasses in hand, chatting beneath the gold-leaf ceiling and Baccarat crystal chandelier. There was a black grand piano in the corner and a wall-long suite dappled with cherub throw pillows, and soft chairs no one sat in. On a table sat an elongated glass with a sprig of purple heather thrust in it. Above the fireplace hung a gallery of visual art including a Gilbert Stuart painting of George Washington and a small oval picture of the Senator with Bill and Hillary at a White House reception. He was a bipartisan soul. The image in the photograph arose from a chair. Senator Haley Factor sported a perpetually amused expression, accentuated by wide-set grey eyes and a thin nose. The hair was bouffant, if splotched with grey. The teeth were white and beautiful, and hadn't always been in his mouth. He was wearing a frayed green jumper and carpet slippers. The Senator resembled a politically connected Val Doonican. 'Please excuse the sweater,' was his greeting. 'Truth is, I think best when I'm most comfortable.'

'I have some of my best ideas in the shower myself,' Cowan told him.

Factor shook his hand. 'Come on upstairs,' he said. 'I love an excuse to get away from the congregation. They start off talking serious politics and in no time have gotten started in on Chuck Todd's haircut or such like. It's not productive.'

'Neither is the haircut.'

'Mr Hall.' The Senator addressed the man who'd led Cowan into the house. 'Have Lily bring some victuals to the library. Those fancy biscuits too.'

Cowan accompanied the Senator up the curving staircase. Factor was not as tall as legend had it, but physically imposing, poundage tightly packed, hands and head impressively large, short thick arms swinging freely as he climbed. Overweight though, no question. The wooden stairs creaked at every step and Factor exhaled creakily too.

'It's a fabulous house this.'

'It is. Eleven fireplaces. Eleven! I'm not sure who needs that many, except maybe the devil. It's not my house though.'

'No?'

'An old friend lets me use it when Congress is in session.'

'Is that legal?'

'Well, it's not illegal.'

'An important distinction.'

'I should say so, Mr Cowan. I should say so.'

They walked through the upper level, past bedrooms and a spa-like Master Bath into which a stream of water poured dreamily from the ceiling. The space opened onto a mahogany-panelled library with two Persian rugs, soft armchairs and sofas, and custom-built bookcases floor to ceiling. In the far corner was a black pedestal and on it lay an open bible, columns of chapter and verse intersected with red lines, a textual gloss or commentary. Cowan glimpsed a grey church steeple against the pale blue, outside the window.

'I think of this as my chamber of reflection.' Factor pointed at a recliner. 'Make yourself at home.'

'Oh, you wouldn't want me doing that. You should see how I behave at home.' Cowan sat down. 'I've never met a Senator before. It's quite intimidating.'

'Well, I'll let you into a little secret, Mr Cowan. We put on our pants the same way as everyone else: one leg at a time.'

Time emerged as 'tan' in a fatal collision of sibilants, like the speaker had recently come from having a root canal and the Novocain hadn't worn off. The Senator had a broad, open face, the skin around the eyes drawn tighter by cosmetic surgery. Everywhere in this city Cowan found all the same familiar facelifts.

'I must apologise for the jacket,' Cowan said. 'I didn't bring anything formal.'

'Thoreau says in Walden that it is an interesting question how far men would retain their relative rank if they were divested of their clothes.' Factor laughed.

'Thoreau also said we should beware all enterprises that involve new clothes.'

Factor widened his eyes, like he'd just caught the family cat smoking a cigar.

'Good schools in Scotland,' Cowan explained. 'It's John Knox's fault.'

'I was so sorry to hear about your loss.' Factor had become more serious all of a sudden, and was making the required facial adjustments. 'It was a bad business. I have taken a particular interest in crime in our capital city. It is a scourge.'

'It's the drugs cause it.'

'It's the culture too,' drawled Factor. 'Are drugs an issue? Yes. If it were up to me, I'd legalise, let the market take care of it. But there's a cultural degeneracy also. Harsh words, I know, but the family is in decay. I grew up in a town that was like a family. Colwan, Kentucky, population 17,000. Colwan Demons, state champions three times. Family is everything. The main thing is to keep the main thing, the main thing.'

'It's the same thing all over.'

'When I first came here, twenty years ago now, I couldn't believe I was meeting people who didn't know where their grandparents were buried.' Factor shook his head sadly. 'In the South, that's unheard of.'

'I'm not a very political person,' Cowan observed.

Factor laughed at that. Cowan didn't care for the man's laugh, which sounded like the grinding of a waste disposal under a metal sink. 'I assume you must have had some interest in the Independence question?'

'The English are south of the border whether Scotland is independent or not. If it had been a referendum on whether to drop an atomic bomb on London, I'd have been more engaged. I'd have had to weigh the pros and cons.'

'Ah, that dark Scottish humour! My ancestors were Scotch: Clan Douglass. I take a particular interest in the history of it, the Black Douglass and so on. The Scots and the American South have a great deal in common.'

'You mean we both lost civil wars and never got over it?'

Factor's frown was almost imperceptible and his fingers drummed the armrest, a shelly noise like beetle husks on a windowpane. His nails had a purplish tint. 'I'd say it's a sight more complicated than that.'

A maid knocked and came into the library with a tray

of cheese and crackers, and chocolate dainties on a dish. She arrayed the food before them.

'It's a hard thing to lose a child,' Factor noted.

'I lost my father when I was four,' Cowan told him. 'And I never found him again. My daughter, I will find again, though. There's loss and there's loss.'

Factor listened contemplatively. 'Ah, you are a widow's son.'

Hall entered the library accompanied by a young woman in standard DC uniform: silk bow blouse, long skirt, understated pumps: bringing unsexy back. Both sat. This was to be a committee meeting, then. Hall tossed a briefcase on the settee. He was the kind of person who immediately took possession of a living space. Cowan never warmed to people with that much confidence. He knew the type. The type who could sell you things you didn't want or need and then before you knew it had departed, leaving you naked in the desert with a newly purchased sandbox and a 100-year warranty stuffed in your ass-crack. In this case the type who also carried a gun.

'Can I offer you a morning cocktail?' Factor asked.

'I don't indulge.'

'A strange sentiment coming from a Scotsman.'

Cowan shrugged. 'So I'm told.'

'Perhaps I can interest you in tea, then? Or is that an English affectation?'

'I can drink tea.'

'Sugar?'

'Aye.'

'Lily, bring our guest a nice cup of Earl Grey and put lots of sugar in it.' Factor turned back to him, solicitous. 'I hope you don't mind Mr Hall joining us. He is one of my most dependable aides and quite indispensable to me.'

Hall was studying Cowan with grave seriousness. His head was shaved clean and he had a smile like a well-healed surgical wound.

'That Presbyterian graveyard round the corner is full of indispensable men, Senator,' Cowan said, smiling at Hall.

Factor guffawed. 'Ah, that dark humor again! In propinquity to Mr Hall over yonder, you will find Ms Dubino, another member of my staff. I tell you Mr Cowan, a Senator is like the groundskeeper in a cemetery. A lot of people are under you, but none of them are ever actually listening to a word you say.'

'I met a few more of your walking dead in the office yesterday.'

'I cannot apologise enough.' Factor frowned deeply. 'Mr Reem is not one of my official staff. He's on assignment, as it were. Honestly, he's a bit of a loose cannon.'

'He also looks like he might have been Special Forces at one time, right? What did Mr Reem do for fun in the Middle East?'

No one spoke. Ms Dubino licked at her lips to moisten them. A clock ticked.

'Laid Hajiis out on sheets,' Hall said finally.

Factor smiled through his teeth. 'Mr Hall also served

our country in Iraq and Afghanistan. With great distinction, I might add.'

'Glad to hear it,' Cowan said. 'You employ a lot of ex-military then, Senator?'

'You can't be too careful in the current climate. The incivility is rampant.'

'I read in *Capitol Inquirer* that you're thinking about running for higher office?'

'You read that rag! It's extraordinary how fake news gets out and about.'

'It was either reading the *Inquirer* or Pokemon and if I got started up playing that again then I'd never have made it here the day.'

'It's not practical.' Factor was depressed at Cowan's earlier suggestion. 'I have a lot of handicaps: I'm from a small state; I'm from the South; I have an accent.'

The maid returned bearing the tea in a white china cup. Cowan sipped it. An antique grandfather clock chimed the quarter hour.

'How's your tea?'

'It's a bit sugary.'

'It's the sugar that does that,' said Factor.

'How long do you plan to stay in the Senate, then?'

'Politicians always find it difficult to leave the stage.' Factor rubbed his hand on the armrest. It made a bat-like squeaking sound. 'Of course, I'd make a fortune lobbying. Or I could do the ads. They'll want to get me for Weight Watchers, no?'

The two staff members laughed.

'I'm all for term limits, myself,' Cowan announced and everyone at once stopped laughing. He put his cup down. 'I'm curious as to why you wanted to see me, Senator.'

The fingers of Factor's right hand ceased drumming and he pursed his thick lips. 'I wanted to extend my sympathies for your recent loss, of course, and also to apologise for yesterday's contretemps. Mr Reem's conduct was, I hear, deplorable, if I can still use the term. I now feel behoved to offer my assistance to you in any way I can.'

'I appreciate that.'

'I had my people thoroughly review the inquiry you made. Your daughter did not meet with anyone in my office that day. There is no record of her being there at all, actually. I never met her in person, which is something I regret. I really would like to have met your daughter. All indications are she was a fine young woman. However, I will also inform you that my staff did take a meeting with a woman who may have been acquainted with your daughter. This may be where the original confusion arose.'

'Mary Barnham.'

'Yes. That is the name. She's a young Jewish woman.'

'I fail to see the relevance of her religion, Senator.'

'Oh it's not relevant at all, Detective Inspector, merely an observation.' Factor smiled grimly at Cowan. 'Jews are like everybody else, only more so.'

'I have indeed been looking for that young woman.' Cowan laughed mirthlessly. 'And I'm sure you already know that I've been asking questions about her around town, which is how come I'm now having this powwow with the Big Chief, right?'

The Senator had begun squirming like one of the things that crawl from under trees in the rain. 'DC is a small town,' he drawled, sinking deeper into his fine upholstery and glancing anxiously towards Hall. 'You can't imagine how quickly news travels on the jungle telegraph.'

'So this Mary Barnham came to see you, did she?'

Factor nodded. 'She did, Mr Cowan. Like you, she had many questions about my supposed political ambitions. Many questions.'

'She was doing a story for *Capitol Inquirer*?'

'An article about the next Presidential election, yes, my intentions regarding and so forth, which are of course limited, as I've indicated. Laying all my cards on the table, I was also interested in what I could learn from her, particularly any insights she had about Bill Griffith, for whom she used to work. Quid pro quo: I'd provide her with a few juicy quotes about my political ambitions, all publicity being good publicity in that regard, and she'd fill me in about the dubious fundraising methods of her former employer.'

'Because he'll be a Presidential candidate too. So, you were digging for dirt.'

'I admire straight talking,' said Factor, picking up a little biscuit and crunching it with a satisfying snap. 'Just a very minor excavation in the way of opposition research.'

'I like to be on the level,' Cowan said. 'I think that's important.'

'Prince,' Factor twiddled his fingers in Hall's direction. 'How would you describe my distinguished colleague from Louisiana?'

'Someone who'd solicit Satan if he had money for a campaign contribution.'

Factor shifted his weight from one buttock to the other. 'Yes, quite. Griffith could sell Fords to Chevrolet dealers and charm the skin off a snake. He's a mean-spirited, tea-party-funded, negative ad-spewing, cracker-barrel aphorist and so, sadly, in this nation, also electable to the highest office in the land. There is precedent.'

Cowan dipped his spoon, rotated it thoughtfully. 'And the sudden disappearance of this Barnham woman, almost immediately after my daughter's murder? You think this Griffith knew she had been talking to you? Are you intimating foul play, Senator?'

'Good Lord, no.' Factor appeared deeply offended at the suggestion. 'This is the United States of America, not Russia.'

'I'm in charge of the Senator's security,' Hall announced. 'You and I have a common goal here.' He pointed at himself and then Cowan, clarifying the identification. 'We hope there's room for collaboration. We're both looking for the same person.'

'I work alone,' Cowan told him. 'But feel free to tell me what I don't know and I'll feel free not to tell you what

I do know. One thing I do know for sure is that I didn't come all the way here today to be given the third degree. No offence.'

'If I was a man in your shoes…' Hall began.

'You wouldn't be seen dead in my shoes. I got them on sale at Marks and Sparks. You've got way more expensive taste, son.'

'It might be in your best interests to help us find her,' Hall suggested. The aide's phrasing carried with it the slightest intimation of menace.

'Well, I said no already.' Cowan held Hall's stare for a long and uncomfortable moment, grinning obliquely. 'Was I talking too soft for you?'

The female staffer spoke up for the first time. She'd been taking copious notes. 'Detective Inspector, we can offer you financial support, the resources of our office, to help you locate Miss Barnham.' Ms Dubino had very outgoing teeth and her eyes were shadowed. There had been sleepless nights in these parts. This lot had the wind up.

'Sorry, sweetheart, I'm a DIY guy.' Cowan shook his head at her. 'No person in their right mind would want to work with me, anyway. I'm awful company. If you had a recent photograph, I'd take it. Of her, I mean, not you. Anything else, no.'

The room was deathly still now. The old clock chimed the half hour.

'I don't suppose you're going to tell me why it's so important you find her?'

'I don't suppose so,' Hall said.

The chamber of reflection was no longer reflective but silent as the grave. Only a sharp knock broke the silence. A small unassuming woman stuck her head around the jamb. She looked meek and apologetic and Japanese. 'I'm sorry to interrupt,' she said, timidly. 'Haley, Lily said you were eating those chocolate biscuits again?'

The Senator's face at once flushed beetroot red. 'The wafers are for my guest, dear. Mr Cowan, this is my better half.'

The Senator's wife half nodded, half curtsied and retreated into the hallway. She was younger than her husband. She carried an aura of demure weakness. Would a politician like Factor need a submissive younger partner as continual daily affirmation of his power? Perhaps the ideal political wife was diffident and unassuming and shy. Then again, Factor was the one who looked chagrined now, afraid even.

'Yet another arena of pleasure that has been closed off, I'm afraid, Detective Inspector,' Factor mumbled, with a tight grin.

Who knew what went on in a marriage?

'We are somewhat hamstrung,' Factor continued, 'by the need to be discreet. It is a delicate time for me. A person even remotely contemplating running for higher office in the current environment can be seen to step on his dick occasionally, but he can't be seen jumping up and down on it.'

'I'm still trying to work through that metaphor, Senator,' Cowan told him. 'It was a right beezer.'

'Griffith is well financed by PACs on the fringes of the Party. I am reassured by the axiom that putting wings on a pig does not an eagle make, but not comfortably so.'

'I'm sure you'll do just fine in your election, Senator,' Cowan offered, with an insincere smile. 'You can still talk the hind legs off a donkey.'

Factor stood up. 'I think we have some understanding of our mutual interest.'

'What was the nature of your daughter's relationship with Mary?' Hall inquired.

'They were on the same synchronised swimming team,' Cowan said.

Ms Dubino wrote that down.

'Did Mary just come by that day to ask about you running for President, Senator? See, I heard a rumor she was investigating other things. Just on the jungle telegraph, like.'

'I must re-join my guests now,' Factor announced, with another meaningful glance at his staff. 'They will have moved on from immigration to the Missouri grand jury business by now. It's very exciting obviously, the possibility of riot. Riot is in our nature, is it not? And the report on enhanced interrogation techniques still to come later!' Factor shook Cowan's hand again, clasping it firmly and pressing below the thumb. 'If you change your mind and decide you need more tangible backing, Mr Hall will give you his number as you go. Godspeed, my friend.'

Hall led him back across the courtyard to the wrought iron gate. He closed it behind him and stood staring at Cowan through the ornate grating.

Cowan shrugged. 'Was I supposed to tip you or something?'

Hall smiled with his eyes without moving his lips at all. 'There are things you should take seriously, Detective Inspector. DC can be a mean and dirty town.'

There was a sharp edge to the remark, turned toward Cowan like a flashing blade.

'Oh, believe me, I take politicians and their sidekicks very seriously. You lot would disembowel your own grandmother with a fishhook given the opportunity.' Cowan laughed. 'I'll be sure to give you a buzz if I ever need the help of anyone indispensable though.''

Walking back to the Metro, Cowan contemplated what he had got himself into. How much had been said, really, and how much implied and insinuated? All he knew for certain, was that the woman closest to the secret of his daughter's death was still out there. She had to be found and he had the impression it would be best if he found her first.

There was a for-sale sign by Tartan Properties outside a light-blue townhouse on Duke Street. There was no escape from home here, everywhere he turned. He felt very frail and had a longing to close his eyes on the past and future alike. He'd thought for some time that he was in fact two persons and that the self upon whom the world acted, violently and randomly, walked beside another who quietly wished for nothing more than to dissolve itself in utter oblivion. There were days he assured himself that this other being had made itself known to him for the first time, on that cold morning in rehab when he was informed of his daughter's death. But that was not so. That other self had walked with him from the day he was born. Cowan looked up. A cloud-dappled ceiling offered nothing, the ways of heaven as ever, inscrutable. A few black specks of birds strung like notes on the stave of sky, nothing else. A sprinkler doused the postage-stamp lawn in front of a lime-green townhouse. Sprinkling lawns in November! Just then, the sun broke through a cloudbank and its rays struck the dense spray and were refracted. Cowan was at once struck by the loveliest of illusions: a blue haze of spray like a dense smoke had risen in a semi-circle above his head. Tiny droplet spheres shone in their lovely millions, offering the appearance of a bright halo as a pale rainbow above him, like the casting of some fairy web. Had he not come here a seeker after such signs and portents? Had he not prayed for a revelation like this?

'Catriona,' he said aloud.

But the rapture of his vision was at once erased and replaced. Within that limpid cloud lurked the face of another. For a moment, Cowan supposed it himself, that he was witness to an uncanny reflection, a curious trick of light. But it was not him. This thing had its eyes fixed fast upon him and was in its aspect both terrifying to behold and terrified of being seen. It cowered in the spray, concealing itself, hiding red burning eyes, and he knew it to be not human, not of this world. The features in the wet mist crumpled and faded and vanished before him, leaving only sparse beads of water lit by sunlight. Some people had beautiful epiphanies, Cowan just had scary frights. He slumped on, morbidly depressed, head down, disturbed by all he thought he'd seen, by all he didn't know. At Roundhouse Square, by the Society of American Florists, he stopped and leaned his elbow against the façade. He felt dizzy and defeated. A small insect whizzed by his ear and collided with the brickwork, displacing a tiny piece of plaster that fell crumbling on the sidewalk at his feet.

His body knew before his mind. He dropped to the ground. A sharp crack and a second bullet flattening itself against the wall clarified everything, the echo reverberating between the buildings. Cowan was moving like a bat out of hell when the third bullet snapped in the air and shattered the window behind him. The gunman was in a car on the other side of the street. The weapon in his would-be-killer's hand was glinting in the sun. Cowan sprinted down Daingerfield in the direction of King. There seemed to be no one else around. That was most unfortunate. His breathing was nervous and shallow, each inhalation painful. Cowan was concerned that he'd been shot and didn't yet know it, that he was still in shock. The car had been green, an old one, rusted. This same car had now looped round Dechantal and sat by the curb at the intersection.

Cowan swivelled and bolted back. He was soon

scrabbling around on his hands and knees behind a dumpster in Reinekers Lane. He thought about hiding in the dumpster, then remembered he had a date that night. He couldn't show up smelling of garbage. It would make a terrible first impression. It occurred to Cowan that he wasn't thinking straight. Being shot dead in a dumpster would have its drawbacks too. The busiest street in Alexandria was a block away. Cowan just had to find a way to get to it alive. What he needed was a diversion. From Diagonal Road, as if in answer to his prayer, came a phalanx of tourists, heading to the Metro.

'You hear firecracker?' one man said to him. 'We hear firecracker! Someone is having fun!'

'Aye,' said Cowan, wildly enthusiastic. 'Tons of fun.' The green car came to a slow stop at the meeting of Diagonal and Daingerfield. Cowan ambled towards it with his tourist group, locating himself deep in the middle. He was explaining to them how Mount Vernon was an absolute must-see. He didn't know anything about Mount Vernon. He told them Ben Franklin had arranged to have the body of George Washington stuffed and put on display there in a big glass case. They loved it. They were going to go see it tomorrow. If the fuckers in the green car were going to take him out, they would have to mow down a few tourists too. Cowan considered the morality of his actions, endangering this many innocent bystanders, and then decided to stop considering it. His life was complicated enough.

The tourists approached the death car. Its windshield was tinted black. Cowan waved. You had to maintain your sense of humour. The tourists waved too. It was all very surreal. Then a black-gloved hand emerged from the passenger side window and waved back. It was just business, then. Nothing personal. Murderers punched clocks too.

Cowan remained enmeshed in the protective custody of the phalanx of Japanese tourists until the Metro entrance. The woman whom he walked beside bore some resemblance to Factor's wife. Everything confused in his mind.

Three men stood by the ticket machines, watching passengers approach. All now seemed menacing and sinister. The first was a surly young man in Timberlands and a napkin bandanna. The second was a middle-aged guy in bespoke suit and dark sunglasses. The third was a skinny kid in tight jeans and a leather jacket, sleeves rolled. Cowan was realising now that he didn't know who to be afraid of anymore. He wheeled around at once and sauntered back over to the taxi rank. He ignored the first two taxis in line and spoke to the driver of the third. 'How you doing?'

'Doin' OK.'

'Can you take me to the Hyatt Regency in DC?'

'For real?' The cabbie was incredulous. 'From here? Why you be wantin' to do that, man? It's cheaper you get on that train there.' The cabbie pointed in the direction of the station.

'You want my business or not? You want me to try your buddy over there instead?'

'That's fine. Y'all do what you have to.' The cabbie punched at the meter. 'I'm down with taking your money. Don't mean shit to me, no way. Just saying is all.'

Safely on the GW National Parkway, the waterfowl sanctuary blue and rippling to their left, Cowan dialed McDonald's number. No answer. He left a garbled message. The Commander called back five minutes later, sounding both exhausted and exasperated. It was true, Cowan would try the patience of a saint. 'So someone's trying to assassinate you, now? That the story for today?'

'Aye, and it's a compelling narrative. Some fuck just took a potshot at me outside the offices of the Society of American Florists in Alexandria. I don't think the location is significant. I don't believe he was trying to send me flowers either, before you ask.'

'Were you speaking to this individual by any chance, Detective Inspector? Being your usual charming self? Because there is such a thing as justifiable homicide.'

'I'm fucking serious! There were three bullets. One near took my ear off. Another went through a window. So the odds are, your people should be able to bring their usual efficiency to bear and maybe find it. Follow the big trail of broken glass.'

'What kind of a car? Can you describe it?'

'Green. It had four wheels and windscreen wipers. Made of metal.'

'What make was it?'

'Haven't a clue. I'm not a car person.'

'You're not a car person?'

'It wasn't a Honda Accord. It was one of those American cars from the 90s looks a bit like a boat. You could have roasted a duck in the trunk.'

'That narrows it down.'

'Are you taking me seriously, Mac? You'd think the information that someone is trying to knock off yet another UK citizen might elicit some concern.'

'I'm concerned.' Cowan heard another exaggerated sigh on the other end of the line. 'There are reports of shots fired. Property damage. I checked already. But I warned you. I told you. You get started poking around the business of some of these bamas without knowing what you're about and they'll murder the fuck out of you.'

'I know, I know. Listen, just send somebody out there to get the bullets, alright?'

'I'm on it.'

'Also, give us some advice.'

'Seriously? You want my advice? This is a red letter day.'

'Do you think it's safe to go back to my hotel?'

There ensued a long static pause. Eventually, McDonald said: 'The odds of someone shooting you outside the Hyatt Regency on Capitol Hill I'd put at less than 2%, unless you try to have a conversation with them, in which case more like 40%.'

Cowan hung up. 'The comedic stylings of the DC police, ladies and gentleman,' he said aloud.

'Someone shootin' at y'all's ass?' the cabbie said, looking more interested in his fare now. 'You don't be needin' that.'

'No,' Cowan observed. 'I don't. Got any advice? The police are all out of it.'

'Walk away fast.' The cabbie laughed, but not in the good way. 'Is all I got. That way y'all don't get yourself seriously dead.'

Cowan jogged quickly across the hotel lobby and sprinted past the elevator bank. He took the stairs to his room, locked and set the chain on the door, and breathed lung deep. Sitting on the bed, he texted Deyon to meet him tomorrow morning somewhere near Massachusetts Avenue. Deyon texted back suggesting the Smithsonian American Art Museum and added that the blue flyer was hung around the GW campus in early March. That was not altogether unexpected. His next text was a revelation, though. Deyon had taken it upon himself to make a few calls on his behalf and pull a few strings and also arranged the meeting they'd discussed for afternoon on the following day. An interview with the girlfriend of the late and unlamented Carlton Sammons was going to cost him big time, though. Cowan always expected that to be the case. Truth came at a cost. Deyon really was remarkable. He was the more efficient detective. Cowan didn't know what he'd have done without the kid's help. He'd lucked into his acquaintance. The next day was going to be a day and a half.

It was 2.17pm. He still had to get through today.

Cowan reviewed all he knew. He knew bugger all. But someone thought he knew something. That someone was wrong. So, he knew that someone was wrong about what he knew. Therefore, he did know something. He knew that he knew less than someone thought he knew and he knew that was to his advantage. In a chess game, he'd be way ahead in terms of board position. He'd be up on pawn exchanges or something. Cowan hated chess. He'd go with cards instead. He was ahead strategically in whist because he hadn't played the Tubalcain card. But was that the ace? On Wikipedia he read more about them. Tubalcain Services was an American private military company specialising in security contracting. The company had acquired its current moniker in a rebranding operation in 2014 after its acquisition by a group of private investors. The company was founded in 2000 as Wringhim Security under the leadership of one Gil Martin. So it was two names then. There you go. And Cowan was just this minute back from visiting Wringhim House, owned by an old friend of the Senator's, with ex-military types crawling everywhere. There was a definite tissue of connection. Cowan was getting somewhere now, although he had the awful suspicion that the somewhere was shaping up to be his own grave, which was unfortunate. Cowan's death had the potential to seriously interfere with his inquiries.

But he couldn't do anything now except nap for a bit and then get ready for a date that was not a date. The redhead from Alexandria might be able to help him out too. Whatever she'd remembered recently about Mary Barnham could bring that mystery more into focus. Or not. Truth be told, Cowan didn't altogether care what the woman knew. He just wanted to see her face again. He wasn't being rational about that either. Someone had just tried to off him, and all he could think about was seeing a smatter of freckles and a shy smile. Maybe it was the adrenaline pouring through his veins still confusing him. Maybe he was a fucking idiot, like everyone kept telling him. But there was something about that woman's face. Something. That was a mystery to him as well. As if there weren't mysteries enough for him already. He had so far still to go and was so tired already of this mad pursuit, all this talking in circles, all these confessions of a justified sinner.

6   SATURDAY (NIGHT)

Art and Soul was attached to The Liaison on Capitol Hill. Usually, Cowan would avoid an overpriced hotel restaurant. This one was owned by Oprah's old chef, which was supposed to be a recommendation. He hoped to God it wasn't the same guy who made the recommendations for her book club. Art and Soul was trendy and upscale; contemporary décor with dark finishes, neatly textured walls, herringbone wood floors, and artsy twisted light fixtures. The Yelp reviews said it combined a contemporary urban market feel with true Southern warmth and hospitality. What this seemed to involve was taking an artful mélange of glass, metal and wood and sticking some hand-painted farm signs on the walls. Postmodern rustic. Facade Farm. The Liaison was at the heart of the so-called corridor of influence that included Georgetown Law School, the AFT, and National Association of Realtors. The restaurant was next door to the International Brotherhood of Teamsters. Its usual clientele didn't need a drink then: that crew was well intoxicated with power long before they sashayed in off a New Jersey Avenue sidewalk.

Cowan sat in the lounge on a plush black leather sofa, waiting, nervous as a watch, his left leg jittering under his fingers. He'd put on a nice button-down shirt, a pair of black jeans and black boots. This would be him making an effort. Sitting there, dry-mouthed and anxious, he realised he could barely remember what she looked like. Cowan supposed he'd already made her over into some storybook creature of his imagination. The noir detectives rescued damsels in distress. For him, it was all about being rescued by them.

Aye, he would be the errant gumshoe who did everything arse backwards.

Then she came in from the cold night air. She didn't look remotely distressed. He liked how she carried herself, the way she moved, the effortless fluidity of her limbs. She floated at him, even prettier than he remembered. Stray strands of red hair fell across her eyes, the slight crook of her nose tilting gently away, lips full and moist in a natural pout. A lovely wee thing, a burning beauty. Her eyes were pale blue and as she came closer seemed flecked with green in the artificial light. The lipstick was so dark it seemed almost black against the oval paleness of her face. She made you want to take off your shoes and wade around a little in her. Maybe drown a bit, too. Cowan had noticed before she wore no wedding ring. Divorcee?

He stood up to greet her. She smiled at him. He would have given anything to fix that smile in place. It was the velvet depression left by a jewel.

'Hi,' he said. 'Charles Cowan.'

'Kris. Kris Guthrie.'

They shook hands politely. It was all very formal. She was casually dressed in an orange jumper and tight blue jeans. Her shoes were curious. He realised she was not treating this as anything like a date. Cowan wondered at his own sad need to. This woman wanted to be at ease and wasn't making too much of an effort. She held his glance for a moment longer than was comfortable for him, though. She had a sunken, waterlogged beauty and the faint waft of her perfume caught in his throat: Chanel.

'I thought we could maybe have something to eat while we talked?'

Cowan nodded agreeably and followed her into the bar, watching the sway of her hips. She sat at a table assembled from three pieces like a giant Jenga. It kept coming apart as they sat there, needing constant reassembly, like the fragments of his thoughts.

'I was a little worried about us meeting at a place called The Liaison,' he said.

'Why?' Her smile hinted playfulness. 'Were you worried that's what people would think you were having?'

'No, I was more concerned about being next to the Teamsters building. I mean Jimmy Hoffa could be buried right underneath where we're sitting now.'

'I wouldn't be surprised.' She took her mobile phone from her clutch purse and laid it on the table before her. 'Are you enjoying the city?'

'Aye. I've been all over, like a cheap coat. I went to the American Art Museum.'

'I've never been there.'

'You should go,' he said. 'I had a fabulous time.'

'What did you see?'

'Mostly paintings,' he lied.

'Maybe I will go some time,' Kris said, with polite insincerity. She looked in the reflecting glass of the bevelled mirror and gently scooped a loose strand away.

'I wonder what people did before there were mirrors?' he asked her. 'There couldn't always have been mirrors available.'

She examined him more curiously now, squinting slightly, a more thorough evaluation being performed. 'They probably looked in pools and ponds,' she suggested.

'Aye, and fell in like that Greek eegit.'

Kris gave him another half-smile. 'You live in this city long enough, you get used to narcissism.'

'I've met a few politicians recently. So, the narcissism angle had occurred to me.'

'Everyone in DC is a politician,' she said, dryly. 'Of some kind.'

'Are you?'

She shrugged. Their waiter slunk over obsequiously and Kris requested a glass of the house burgundy. Cowan was sticking with water.

'You don't drink?'

'No.' Cowan considered the strategic importance of reticence and concealment then blurted: 'I'm an alcoholic, which is how come. I'm also a complete and total fuck up as a human being.' He laughed ruefully. 'That's all my cards on the jiggly table now.'

She was regarding him with interest now. 'You're very honest.'

'Not always. Like I told you on the phone the other day, I'm a policeman. So I deal with liars all the time. I have a facility.'

'Should I be careful around you, then?'

'Always. But as long as you stay honest with me, you'll be fine.'

'Are you going to read me my rights next?' The waiter brought their drinks. Cowan dipped a finger in the water and wet down each corner of the napkin to anchor it. He didn't want the napkin to come up with the glass and make him look ridiculous. 'Is it just me or is this a really weird conversation?'

'This is a really weird conversation.'

'Just checking.' She glanced down at her phone. 'So, should we talk about what we came to talk about? I have to be somewhere a little later.'

'Eventually. I'm kind of having fun.'

'Kind of?'

'Kind of.'

'What would you like me to be honest about, Mr Cowan?'

'My friends call me Chic. That's with a C and not a K. I wouldn't want you thinking it was short for chicken.'

She regarded him with amusement. 'Or Chickpea?'

'Aye,' he laughed, embarrassed. 'That neither.'

'So if I call you Chic for now, I'm your friend, then?'

'For the duration.'

'Well, here's some honesty for your collection, Chic.' Kris pressed her lips together lightly. 'I got dressed up for this tonight like it was a date. I spoke to my sister earlier. I told her I was meeting a strange man for a drink.'

'I'm not that strange. I'm just a wee bit askew.'

'A stranger, I meant. I haven't decided if you're strange yet. My sister said, just go and enjoy yourself. Be entertained and let him pay for everything. And if he seems like a serial killer go to the bathroom and don't come back. Climb out of a window if you have to.'

'What do you mean I'm paying for everything?'

'I didn't tell her I was actually going out to be quizzed by a British policeman. That might excite her actually. She loves those rumpled PBS detectives from the UK.'

'As a matter of interest, how big is the window in the Ladies loo, exactly?'

'It's gender neutral, actually.'

'Jesus,' Cowan said, grinning inanely at her. 'I didn't even know you could get gender neutral windows. Society is evolving way too fast for me.'

'Oh, windows aren't gender neutral.' Kris smiled coyly. 'They're always male.'

'How do you figure that? Is it because they have a little handle on them?'

'No. It's because I can see right through them.'

'I feel like I'm losing this conversation.'

'I didn't know it was a competition.'

'I'm already down five- zero, and it's not even half-time yet.'

'I'll ease up after the first timeout.'

Cowan laughed. 'I'm relieved you were able to find a sitter for your daughter. Otherwise, I'd be missing out on this cerebral drubbing tonight.'

'You mean my niece?' Cowan's face must have conveyed his sudden confusion, his addled expression amusing her. 'Emma is my sister's daughter. You're looking at the sitter. I drive over to Alexandria when she needs me.'

Cowan settled back on his stool, with a lot to reassess now. 'See, I thought you were the one lived in the apartment below Mary Barnham.'

'No, I live in Eckington. It's a turning neighborhood north of the Capitol.'

'A what?'

'That's what they say. The neighbourhood is turning.'

'Is it turning quick enough for you?'

'Well, let me see, there's still a murder every six months, which is a drawback. I paid $350,000 three years ago for a brick row house. I refinanced it last month and the value was $600,000.'

'What do you do when you're not a house flipping demon?'

'I was Communications Director for a teachers' union for a while. But now I'm with a public relations firm. We specialise in crisis consultation.' She smiled ruefully. 'Ethically, it's not all it could be.'

'You mean you explain how oil slicks are actually good for penguins.'

'But they are,' Kris said eagerly, fluttering her eyelashes at him. 'Petroleum products spruce up their feathers.'

'You're good, lady.'

'You have no idea how good I can be. Chrysler brings me in when airbags start decapitating people.'

'You'd probably come up with a public relations explanation for the benefits of commuting headless too.'

'Yes, probably. It's a variation on the new driverless car, the headless driver.'

Kris laughed at that, albeit she looked shocked. 'I can't see you in a burka though.'

'I think that'd be the idea,' Kris said. 'People not seeing me in a burka.'

'Aye, but them randy Wahabbis would still be able to see those eyes of yours. That'd be quite the problem for them.'

'This is me flirting,' Cowan explained.

'I figured that.'

'Should I stop?'

'Yes. I kind of like it though.'

'Kind of?'

'Kind of.' Kris shrugged. 'I'm easily amused sometimes.'

Saying that, she took a deeper swig of wine and looked infinitely sadder. Cowan contemplated the extent of her last putdown. Was the situation irretrievable? The waiter came back to take their order. Kris suggested they get appetizers and recommended the snack board and the andouille stuffed smoked quail. Who was he to disagree? When he was visiting Chicago, he'd stayed at a hotel whose restaurant was an uberkitchen specialising in gourmet German cuisine. He ordered a wiener schnitzel and said he feared the 'wurst' was still to come. The waiter hadn't even attempted a smile.

'Chris with a C?' he asked.

'K. It's the opposite way from you.'

'I thought it'd be a C for some reason.'

They sat in silence. Cowan had many other questions, but didn't feel like asking them. He wanted to hear her talk, about anything really. He liked the very sound of her, feeling pillowed by her voice, the shaken timbre, the cracking of soft. What he wouldn't give to hear her voice stretching out to him in the dark. She looked up at him and he asked a question of her. A question he had no business asking. 'Are you happy?'

'Excuse me?'

'Are you happy? In your life, I mean. With where you are right now?'

Kris looked annoyed at him, and he knew he'd gone way too far. She made as if to lift her glass and then didn't bother. It was still very full, and her hand didn't seem steady. 'Why do you ask?'

'Because I'm curious. I know it's rude of me. But sometimes you can say things to a stranger you know you won't ever see again that you couldn't say to anyone else.'

Kris was looking hard into his eyes. It was a look tinctured with a deeper hurt. 'If I want a therapist, I'll get my own,' she said.

Cowan could see soft glistening, a wet misting. She'd cried a lot. He could tell. He was paid to notice things like that, other people's pain and denial of. 'I'm sorry,' he said. 'That was way too forward.'

'Well, if you must know, I haven't been happy in a long time.' She looked aghast at what she'd said, thought it over, and accepted the fact that she'd said it. She looked down at where her hands rested on the table.

Cowan couldn't think of what else to say to that. How did you follow that one up? He watched how she examined her wrists, turned them over, blue veining across white. Now she was looking at her fingers and he was looking at her fingers too.

'Are you happy?' she said, bitterly.

'Hell, no.'

'What does your wife do?'

'Throws darts at our wedding photo. We're divorced. I was a complete arse to her and she didn't notice till the honeymoon. My ex actually was a therapist. I'm not kidding. I don't think she managed the transference very well. How about your husband?'

'My ex-husband now enjoys the family he said he couldn't have with me.' She moved her finger around the clouded rim of her glass. 'So, we're a pair of fuckups, Chic.' It's good to know. And here we've come together like two straws floating in a puddle.' She looked around the bar. 'I think I need another glass,' she said.

'Does that mean he has to come back and mispronounce all the specials?'

'Well, it's not like I can sit here telling you all about

myself all night…' Kris waved the waiter over to her with a brisk hand motion.

Cowan couldn't always tell when she was kidding. A lot of people had the exact same issue with him. 'Someone once told me,' he said, 'that marriage is just a funeral where you can smell your own flowers.'

Kris stared at him.

'In retrospect, I think it might have been my wife.'

'So, anyway,' she began. 'What I wanted to tell you tonight. I didn't know Mary well. Neither did my sister. Mary kept to herself. She was friendly, but no intimacy. But here's the thing. My brother-in-law is a political consultant. He travels a lot with his work, and sometimes on early flights. There are times he'd leave at five in the morning.'

Cowan was resisting the urge to start taking notes.

'So, this one night he calls my sister from San Francisco. He tells her that when he'd left that morning, he'd seen a man coming down the stairs from the upstairs apartment. This was at 5am. A man who looked like he didn't want to be seen.'

'Would that be unusual? Barnham is a young, unmarried woman.'

'I suppose not. But the thing was, Alan recognized this man. He'd seen him on television. The man was a US senator.'

'Haley Factor.'

Kris looked more than surprised. 'How did you…?'

'The honourable gentleman from the blue grass state.

I had tea with the sleazy old bastard just today. Like Alice with the Mad Hatter.'

Kris lowered her lashes, contemplating the fact that her information had not been nearly as valuable as she supposed. 'Yes, but him being seen leaving Mary's apartment at that hour just seemed…'

'Downright strange.'

'Right.'

'Mary was a lesbian. So I think you're barking up the wrong tree here.'

Kris looked disappointed. 'She could have been bisexual though, right?'

'It's a possibility. I'll keep it in mind. Everything else about this business is fluid, so why not that too? Haley F and Mary B doing the bone dance upstairs, who knows?'

The waiter brought their food, ranging it before them: deviled eggs, pimento cheese, cured salmon and pork rinds. Cowan took an unconscionably long time repositioning a miniature bottle of tartar sauce. 'Your sister it was, told you this?'

'My brother-in-law. Last year. He works for the Republican Party.'

'Jesus,' Cowan muttered, processing the hints. 'You're a Republican too, aren't you? I just realised. I'm so fucking out of here.'

'You said you wanted me to be honest,' Kris said, spearing a boudin ball and looking amused by him again.

For a few minutes, they ate quietly and awkwardly. But

Cowan was not unhappy. A man could be perfectly content sitting here in silence with a woman like this. It was that nice quiet, not the kind that isn't. There was something about her eyes, how they held you still and calm in the blue. He didn't feel like moving, secretly wished he never would again. She was a challenge and a half this one. 'Factor is supposed to be this great family man too, right? I met the wife.'

'His second wife that'd be: Yumi Ishiku. She's a big deal in DC as well. Assistant Attorney General in a previous administration. Very well connected.'

Cowan was surprised. 'That's all you have on Mary, though?' he asked.

'Yes.'

Cowan didn't know what else to say to her. Kris had said what she came to say and was embarrassed because it turned out to be gossip. She hadn't felt comfortable gossiping on the phone. So he'd heard what he came to hear. She crunched carefully on a salted butter cracker. He liked her crunching. He'd have let her crunch like that forever.

'You want me to show you the dress I nearly wore tonight?' she said, abruptly.

'What?'

She typed on her phone, showed him the photo on a website.

'That is an amazing dress,' Cowan said. 'Now, I'm disappointed I missed out.'

'It's kind of fit and flare.'

'That's apt.'

She looked at him, blinking rapidly. 'How so?'

'You look fit and you have flair.'

'Ugh,' she said, cringing. 'Don't you know puns are the lowest form of wit?'

'This coming from the girl wants to meet up at Art and Soul.'

Kris laughed. 'By the way, in case you want to order one for your girlfriend, it's called Plays Well with Others in Poppy.'

'I haven't seen much style in these parts. It isn't Paris exactly.'

'This is the shittiest city for shopping.' She stuck out her tongue slightly, and he nearly lost it. 'The idea of buying something at Anne Taylor or Banana Republic is so depressing. DC style is all beige and black, plain Jane. There are no prints.'

'Why is that?'

'There's a fear of expressing who you really are. All you see is black and grey. Short jackets and button down skirts. I don't even own a suit.'

'Where do you shop?'

Kris touched her hair gently with her open palm. 'You're the first man ever asked me that.'

Cowan shrugged. 'I'm a policeman,' he said. 'I ask point-less questions.'

'Online mostly. That's where I got these.'

Kris held her shoe out for him to look at. It was all he

could do not to touch her instep. The shoe was purple and strapless with a little orange flower, a thin heel.

'I noticed those when you came in.'

Kris scrolled her phone. He wondered if she were getting bored with him. 'Look.' She handed the phone to him again.

'What am I looking at now?'

'The current favourite. I have to keep myself from getting this.' She turned the screen back towards him. 'Frames and Fortune Dress. Pleated black fabric.'

'You really need a life. Are those glasses frames on the print?'

'Yes! It's like you've imprinted the male gaze on yourself.'

'Not to mention the bad pun.'

'Well, that's me all over. I'm attracted to bad puns and heels.'

He had to laugh at that. It was the way she said it. Then came one of those moments of intimacy when a man and a woman realise they make each other laugh. It's not put-on, when you don't have to force yourself and it just happens somehow, spills out and rings like silver, an accidental thing. They were both embarrassed at this.

'Why heels?'

'I want to be tall.'

'I used to be that way myself. $250 for those shoes?'

'I have money to burn.'

'Do I even want to know your salary?'

'No. It would make you even more depressed than you already are.'

That one hurt.

She turned her phone off. 'Any more questions?'

'So, how do you assemble an outfit for meeting a fascinating person like me?'

'Like you?'

'Yes.'

'Well, I don't know you. I have no idea what you're like or what you like. But I want to look as good as possible anyway. I would for anyone.' Saying this, she licked her lips. 'No offence. Something tight-fitting. At my age, the stomach is the big issue.'

'Tell us about it. I've got friends that look like Jabba the Hut.'

'I wanted some pop, something a little off. Orange is a good colour for me.'

'Goes with your hair. I love your hair.'

'Thanks. I don't accessorize much. So, the one bracelet.' She held it out to him. 'I got it in Peru.'

'I've only been to the Peruvian palindrome.'

'Huh?'

'U Rep.' He touched her bracelet. 'What were you doing in Peru?'

'Looking at ruins.'

They held each other's eyes again for a while, an odd entanglement of isolates. Was it the sad need of the lonely, that expanse of want? She turned away, rested one hand atop the other, an interlacing of fingers. Her bracelet spun around her wrist like a hoop and Cowan felt more aroused than he ever remembered feeling before in his life.

The waiter began clearing their plates. Kris explained that she didn't have the time or inclination for dessert.

'Are you seeing someone?' he asked.

'Yes.'

'Is it serious?'

'Kind of.'

'Kind of?'

'Why do you ask? He's a Capitol policeman.' She grinned. 'He's armed.'

'I met one of those boys the other day,' Cowan told her, shaking his head. 'Big fellow looked a bit like Frankenstein's monster. The reason I ask is because I wanted to take you to that museum I mentioned tomorrow. And I didn't want you to think it was…'

Kris shook her head. 'Sorry. I can't do that.' She glanced at the time on his phone. 'I have to go. I'm sorry I wasn't more help.'

She said he didn't have to, that it was beyond unnecessary, but he walked with her to where she'd parked her car two blocks away. They didn't talk, just strolled together in the paling moonlight. He watched the tendons of her feet tighten as she walked. He wasn't himself at all.

Finally, she spoke. 'It's a chilly night.'

'Winter's coming.' Saying this, he looked at her quickly, caught the retreating dimples of an amused smile. 'You probably knew that.'

Kris looked up at the sky then, and inhaled deeply, as if she might inhale all of it. Her eyes were wide and the starlight was in them. 'Will you look at all those stars up there tonight,' she said.

'That's where you usually find them.'

She pointed at the lady's ellwand in Orion, the sparklit sifting there. 'You think people live on the planets there?'

'People like us?'

'Yes.'

'I hope not.'

'I think there are.' She hugged herself. 'People like us, only happier.'

Cowan felt the deep bruise of the sentence, a vast pin-prick of darkness. Kris had her fingers on the car door handle now. He was looking at her and she was looking at herself being looked at. Neither knew how to say good-bye. Cowan noticed a solitary tear on her cheek. Why the sadness beneath it all? He wanted so much to catch that tear, salty wet on his tongue, would have given a lot for five more minutes with her, his very soul. He knew it was wrong, the timing fatally flawed, but at that moment, didn't seem to care. He would never see her again. He swooped quickly to put his lips on hers, to see if that salt trace still lingered there. He wanted to taste that remnant of tear. But she turned away from him and his lips brushed only her cheek. 'Now, what good does that do?' she asked, pushing him away.

Cowan staggered into the roadway, looking hopeless. Feeling hopeless. An ambulance went wailing by, lights spinning blue and red. Kris got in her car and turned the ignition. He still stood there stupefied, still as masonry. Kris stared dead ahead, working her mouth a little. She turned and wound her window down. She couldn't leave it at that either, a last word then, a consolation.

'I'm awful sorry,' he said at her, shaking his head. 'I don't know what I was…'

'Come home with me,' she said, and that was all, and as her window slid up, she disappeared in the glare and he could see only his own reflection clarifying in it.

The narrow townhouses loomed silver in the moonlight and the square shadows of them were black to the south and west. Lights burned in a few windows and a scurry of leaves gave the faintest rustle in the night breeze. Then the moon got lost behind a skein of cloud and the night leaked its velvet dark into the street. They walked together along the street not touching, with nothing more to say, their silence perfected under a beclouded moon and star-sheen. Kris climbed the steps ahead of him, her hand on a black railing, to the red door of a brown brick rowhouse.

'I think people live up there,' he said to her, with sudden vehemence. His fingers scraped her jacket. 'I do. I lied. They must. Otherwise it would all make no sense.'

'Maybe it does make sense though,' she said very quietly, 'if you only look for it. Can you even believe in Him?' Kris was looking at him intently, and he could not hold her gaze.

'The man would turn in his grave like a rotisserie chicken if he knew what they do in his name today,' he said, bitterly.

Kris disarmed her alarm system and a lock clicked with meaning. 'But He doesn't have a grave,' she reminded him.

Cowan gazed up into the night sky, the everywhere deep darkness of galaxies, cold and distant, the light of stars dead and gone, coming still to his eyes, and it was his turn to tear up. It was pathetic. He was this ridiculous wet thing.

'Hush now,' Kris said, gripping his hand and leading him inside.

In a hallway alcove against the stairwell, Kris held Cowan close till he quit his wild trembling, but she wouldn't let him kiss her. 'No,' she told him, adamant. 'I have to change.' She turned on the overheard light and a fan began its synchronous slow turning. Kris pointed to the grey sofa under the window. 'Wait,' she told him. She went on up the stairs to the upper level.

She's going to her bedroom, Cowan thought. Her bedroom.

The downstairs level was open space, living room leading into a small dining room and kitchen. Checkered throw rugs lay on the floor and a yellow cupboard with books lined on top offered a strong contrast to the bare brickwork. On one wall hung a few African masks, a black metal grate, a few western hats on pegs, and a blue bicycle. Against the other wall stood a bench, a stool, and a glass cupboard on which rested a coke bottle with two roses in it. The old steam radiators bled and hissed like snakes. Houseplants were scattered along with black and white prints and a bowl of blue plums. The ceiling fan whirred on, causing a jangly mobile to chime. A few framed family photographs ranged on the bench. Cowan got up for a closer look at them. He wanted to investigate this woman to death. So, this was her sister, and this the brother-in-law. He was still examining the photographs when she came back down the stairs. She wore long leather boots and a blue shirt. It wasn't clear if she was wearing much else. She looked different too. He thought she'd dabbed mascara on the top lashes to make her eyes look bigger, and the lips were fire engine red. Cleopatra crushed carmine beetles and ants to get her pigmented hue. How did he even know that? Holy fuck, he needed a life.

'You were slipping into something more uncomfortable, I see.' His voice sounded strange to him, like it came from a dybbuk.

Kris turned off the light and the room went blacker than he thought it could. He picked up a brass ornament from the dresser, a Hawaiian dancer in a hoop skirt. It was a bell. He shook it. It rattled, the clapper inside the skirt was rusted.

'It's dark now,' he said, redundant as ever.

Kris sat down on the sofa and crossed her legs, leaving the question of whether he was to sit to him. The boots creaked.

Cowan stood very still and his stillness disturbed the silence. 'What now?' he asked, and was startled again by the sound of his own voice. 'I'm not sure what it is you want here, lady. Honest to God, you're weirding me out more than a little.'

'I think… what I want is to go to bed with you,' she said. 'I'm still deciding.'

He put the ornament carefully back in its place. His fingers felt like worms.

'Is this too quick for you?' she asked.

He covered his mouth with his hand and even in the dark could see the blue veining on the back of his wrists, knuckles paling above. He should really go, wanting no further part of this strange ritual. But there was fat chance of that. 'No,' he said.

'But you have to do everything exactly as I tell you. Understand?'

'OK. As long as I'm still amusing you.'

'Take off your clothes then.'

It was a request that felt like a command and he was overcome with a sick longing for her as she switched the lights back on. He began unbuttoning his shirt and saw her smile. His arousal was intense and it weakened him. She hadn't moved at all. 'Here?'

'Here.'

She still hadn't touched him, nodding her head, perverse as a fairy tale princess, indicating precisely where she would take her pleasure. Cowan took off all his clothes, as requested. He felt the cold rug pushing soft into the soles of his bare feet. He felt like a fish working its jaw deeper into the reddening hook.

'Very nice.'

'I'm glad I meet with your approval.'

Kris stood up now and came around behind him. He waited. He felt her lips cool against his back and a finger touching him, the slightest impression of sharp nail. He wanted her to scratch him. He shivered.

'You have a rash.'

'Yes. It's a nervous thing.' Cowan could feel her breath warm on his skin. 'Do you mind?'

'No.'

'I'm nervous.'

'Good,' she said. 'It's good that you're nervous because I'm going to fuck you hard enough to rattle your teeth.'

'What?' he mumbled, hoarsely. He was wondering if he would awake from this dream anytime soon. Not that he wanted to.

As the tip of her tongue touched his spine he flinched. She said, 'Don't move.'

He kept his hands by his sides. His erection was so fierce it hurt. It was like he was eighteen again. He had never wanted to be eighteen again. But there would be no trouble with that, though. It was good there'd be no trouble with that. You never knew.

Kris walked slowly around him and unbuttoned her shirt carefully, enjoying his eyes upon her. She was naked but for her boots. The boots were lovely brown Italian leather thin and soft as peeling skin. There were thirteen boot-holes top to bottom, sheathed with silver catches. He'd counted them. She unlaced them, one foot on a stool, instep pendant and arching, the laces snakelike against her wrists. She unlaced them one loop at a time, running the laces through her fingers. She peeled the boots off slowly, her eyes on him. The suck of the leather felt like a shedding of skin. She was enjoying this, her power over him, her control of the situation. She was showing him something he needed to see.

Kris handed the boots to him, smiling. 'There you go.' Cowan threw them hard against the wall. 'My,' she said.

'Can I move now?'

'You can do whatever you like.' She parted her lips. 'It's your funeral.'

They lay entangled, slippery with sweat on the bunched carpet, not speaking, pulses clarifying. He ran his fingers through her hair. It was softer than he imagined. The tenderness of aftermaths, the return from a place beyond words.

'Do you always make that much noise? The realtor should have warned your neighbours about that. It'd be like living next door to an air raid siren.'

'Sometimes I do,' she laughed. 'Not always. I might have been a little pent up.'

They were giggling, huddled together on the floor, verging on a strange hysteria.

'What about you? Do you usually make that much noise?' she asked.

'No.' She was touching a thumb to his bloody shoulder with an expression of bewilderment as he spoke. 'I should mention that actually I'm not edible either, by the way,' he pointed out. 'For future reference.'

'Are you sure?' she asked, smiling. 'If you were a chocolate bar, I think you'd eat yourself.'

'You didn't come?'

'No. It's hard for me, the first time, with someone new, to feel that safe.'

'Maybe I could…'

'No, thanks.'

'Do you want me to leave? We started off tonight being honest with each other and, honestly, I'd like to spend the night with you. Not for this. We're done with this. I just want to hold you is all it is. The smell of you does something weird to me.'

'My smell?'

'I mean that in the nicest possible way.' Cowan could see her eyes in the dark: thinking eyes. 'I just want to lay beside you tonight. I want to watch you sleep and to see your face beside me when I wake up. Is that too much to ask? That's all I want now.'

'That's all? So my pheromones aren't going to be a problem for you anymore?'

'That's it.' He pushed her hair back over her ear, studied the softness of the lobe. 'I think we got everything else well out of our systems now, anyway.'

She patted his shoulder. 'I think so too.'

Her hair was damp against her cheek and her eyes matted with black. A bead of sweat dropped from her cheek onto his arm. She was in glorious dishevelment. He had done that to her. What had she done to him? He should get up and check. Would there be anything left in the mirror to see? It must have been 4am. There was no clock in her bedroom. Cowan didn't want a clock in any bedroom of his again. A bedroom was a place he might step outside clock time and into the real thing.

'I'm such a hot mess,' she said, a laugh becoming a yawn.

'That you are.' Cowan slid lower, down the length of the bed, his hands covering her knees. 'You can say that again.'

'I'm such a hot mess,' she repeated. 'Hey, what do you think you're doing?'

His tongue tip ran the length of her leg.

'Oh, for Christ's sake,' she moaned. 'Quit it already.'

'Shhh. But you're still one behind me. We're playing catch up now.'

'No one is keeping score. It's not a football game. I don't think I can…'

'Oh, you're as indefatigable as the Queen of Sheba, ma'am. We've already established that tonight. Now, mouth shut please.' He pressed his lips against the soft skin of her inner thigh. 'See, I think you have a major crisis consultation coming on.'

Whether it was feeling his hair brush her thighs, or the wetness of his sweeping tongue, or the spasm of her legs against the damp sheets, keeping her mouth shut just then seemed to be the last thing on earth Kris was able to do.

Afterwards, lying propped on a pillow watching her sleep again, the prettiest sight he'd ever seen in his life,

Cowan made the discovery that he was, for a moment, happy.

7   SUNDAY (MORNING)

He was dreaming he was a little boy again, at a summer-time wedding, scrambling on his knees for pennies in the cobbled street behind the old Congregational Church. The best man's prank had been to heat the copper coins red-hot in the oven. So when Cowan jerked awake it was to a dull aching in his palms. He didn't have a clue where the hell he was. It was like being a hungover student back in the day, when he'd wake up in a strange bed-sit in the West End facedown in a pool of his own vomit, or somebody else's if he was unlucky. This looked nothing like a West End flat. And the sun warming his cheek told him this was never the West of Scotland. Her indentation in the bed beside him, sheets juiced and damp. A shirt hung strange from a chair. On the floor, panties lay crumpled and surprisingly dainty. His trousers and underpants at the foot of the bed were one truncated garment, like lined shorts. The t-shirt she slept in chucked to a windowsill in the flailing maelstrom of their ridiculous lust, an eyelash on the pillow. On the side table stood an antique wooden jewellery box, and an ornamental pelican pecking its breast.

He texted Deyon to remind him of their meeting at the Smithsonian American Museum at 10.30am. Come look for him on the ground floor. Was it the first floor here, though? Cowan could never recall. What he did recall, was that when he was through with that slippery Craig Doyle, the fuck would be wearing his own arsehole as a collar.

In a tiny bathroom no bigger than a closet, with a green-tiled floor and orange walls, a mirror with six bare bulbs above it like an unsuccessful actor's dressing room, Cowan looked into the glass at a man who seemed to have gone through some profound and delirious experience. He reassembled his clothes, dressed, and came downstairs, through the dining room – a glass table and four chairs – into the kitchen. The floor was mosaic tile. The built-in cupboards around the white appliances were painted dark red and the set of knives high on the wall were long enough for a circus thrower.

Kris was typing on a laptop at the butcher-block kitchen table, sipping coffee from a green mug, in a blue bathrobe. Barefoot. She looked up at him. 'I wanted to let you sleep,' she said. 'There's coffee in the pot.'

He poured a mug, sat down, waited a few seconds, leaned in and kissed her on the cheek. His chair creaked longingly. He felt a great and unreasonable affection for her.

'I just have to finish this,' she said, seeming distracted. Above the dishwasher was a graffiti blackboard, with words in coloured chalk: *Year of listening! Do no harm? Hair! Benevolence! Trash Friday t/wk. Dont fgt eggs.* She had her ciphers too. Rickety wooden steps led down from the back door to a small, enclosed backyard, scrappy lawn and a plethora of potted plants. Cowan watched her type, brow creased in concentration. She was comfortable with him seeing her like this. He wanted to touch her, but didn't. Things done in darkness seemed like daylight impossibilities.

She hit a key forcefully. 'Done,' she announced.

'Work?'

Kris read earnestly from the screen: 'St Clair and Abif deploy uniquely qualified teams – armed with the instincts, influence, and experience needed to win your battles in an increasingly complex and challenging world.'

'Like the Knight Templars back during the Crusades,' Cowan suggested. 'Doing what? Explaining how it's not that big a deal your gas pedal got stuck on the floor and you ended up doing 95 in the Walmart parking lot that time?'

Kris held up a finger. 'In today's hyper-connected world, crises spin out of control in seconds. An activist reporter, a savvy blogger, or a smartphone-enabled citizen, can change your brand's trajectory with a single tweet…'

'Is this you talking or the copy?'

'That would be our PR speak. This is how I earn the big bucks.'

'I was terrified for a minute that was how you sounded in daylight hours.' He drew her head towards him, his hand upon her neck, and kissed her on the lips.

'I can't make this a thing,' she said, pulling back. 'I have a boyfriend.'

'Would your boyfriend be OK with what we did last night?'

'No,' she said quietly. Her hair was a dusky red, the colour of a controlled prairie fire. 'No, he wouldn't.'

'You said he was a policeman?'

'Yes.'

'What's your therapist say about this thing you have for law enforcement?'

Her eyes fixed on the metal base of the table like it reminded her of something she should be remembering. Cowan cupped his mug in both hands. If he pressed hard enough, it would shatter and the broken shards slash his hands bloody. The pair of them avoiding eye contact now. The sad awkwardness of the morning after, mistakes made and regretted. But the truth was, he regretted nothing.

'Do I remind you of your daughter?' she asked him.

'No,' he said, annoyed. 'Don't be like that.'

'I was just wondering.'

A long and difficult silence, for the first time she'd irritated him. Kris had wanted to, of course. She was coming to terms with what she'd done and hurting him now would be part of it. She was picking at the scab of regret. He could wait it out. 'Is your family from DC originally?' he asked.

'No one I know calls this town home. Most everyone comes from someplace else. They pass through to get a quick buzz off the Pennsylvania Avenue grid. Everyone is term-limited, except the politicians.' She took a sip. 'There's a lot of hate in DC.'

Kris said this with some passion.

'Why are you angry?' She didn't reply. 'Are you mad at me or yourself? I need you to make up your mind on that score soon. Because I want you to spend this morning with me.' He touched his hand to hers. 'No matter how fucking cranky you get.'

'That's not going to happen,' she said, inching her fingers away.

'I want you to come with me for an hour just. I'm meeting a friend downtown, well he's a pal of my daughter's really. He's been helpful to me since I came here. I could use a ride to tell you the truth. But then you could come to that museum with me. That's where he's picking me up, see? I want you to do it to humour me. Hey, look at me.'

Kris did look at him, sorrowfully. Her eyes really were extraordinary. He felt himself falling deep into those irises, and not caring.

'Because right this minute,' he continued, 'I can't imagine being apart from you and need time to get used to the idea. I think I'm a bit deranged about you already and it's all I can do not to get down on my knees and beg like a spaniel.'

'You do that,' she told him.

Cowan right away dropped to his knees before her and plopped his head in her lap, looking up at her with puppy eyes. 'I'm not leaving till you fucking say yes.'

Kris shoved his head away from her, and he put it back.

The bathrobe was soft against his cheek. She tried again.

'You seem to be labouring under the delusion that I'm not serious.'

'You're not serious.'

Cowan opened his eyes as wide as he could and began panting.

'Oh, for Christ's sake,' she said.

'If that's what it takes.'

'You're going to wear those same clothes? You're not going to change?'

'These clothes reek of you. I'm never taking them off again. That way, if you ever get lost, I can track you by scent. I'll come and rescue you like a St Bernard, only I'll have a barrel of red wine round my neck instead of brandy.'

'You're not right in the head.'

'No,' he said, looking up at her. 'I'm not. But then again neither are you, ma'am. Isn't that obvious? We're both odd, so I suppose that makes us even.'

The morning rain had left a wet jewellery of cars and gelatinous leaves in scummy puddles. Underfoot, was a blue mud with sky in it. In daylight, the street looked different. It was a neighbourhood of two-level houses with porches and tiny front yards, a mix of Victorian buildings with steeply pitched roofs and flatter Federal structures. The houses were a palette of pink, yellow, gray, vermillion, red, slate and blue. In summer, elms draped their canopy of shade.

'That house over there,' he said, pointing, 'is the colour of your eyes. I'd like to live there. I'd like to live in that colour, to live in your eyes.' Kris didn't respond. Was it a compliment even? 'This all looks weirdly familiar to me,' Cowan added.

'They use this street in the credit sequence of a TV show.'

'That's it!' He felt a crushing disappointment. 'I knew I'd seen it before.'

'You're standing,' Kris said, unlocking her car door, 'in a fictional space.'

'I have a confession to make.' Cowan was sitting in the passenger seat looking very ashamed. 'Don't hate me please.'

Kris turned over the engine. 'Don't tell me,' she said. 'You just this second remembered that you're engaged to that Hooter's waitress?'

'No, it's that I've never actually been to this museum. I walked by it the other night, but I never for a second was inside looking at paintings and so on.'

'Why would you lie about that?' she said, exasperated. 'Put your seatbelt on.'

'I was trying to impress you.'

'You don't need to try so hard.' Kris hooked a left onto Rhode Island Avenue, heading downtown. 'Believe me, you make enough of an impression.'

'You know a lot about the politics of DC, right? The PR and lobbying stuff?'

'That's part of my job. I need to know where the bodies are buried.' Kris looked at him quickly, realising. 'Oh, God, I'm sorry.'

'It's OK. I'm not scared of metaphors. You ever hear of Tubalcain Services?'

'God, yeah. They were all over the news a few years ago when they were still Wringhim, very controversial. There were congressional inquiries and everything.'

'What is it they service exactly?'

'They provide security services to the federal government on a contractual basis.'

'What does all that mean in English though?'

Kris laughed. 'Basically, that's bureaucrat-speak for the way the government hires out mercenaries to do the real dirty work. Whenever you hear of a 'contractor' being killed in the Middle East, it'll be one of their people. And whenever you hear of an unfortunate massacre of civilians in Afghanistan, that'll be them too.'

'There's a lot of money in that mercenary game?'

'You kidding me? Wringhim must have had more than a billion in government contracts, including one for $250 million with the CIA for God knows what.'

'That would be for the massacre, most likely. That's the going rate for random slaughter.' Cowan stared straight ahead, thinking. 'So there is money in that game, then.'

'Their whole shtick a few years ago was how they were going to do for national security what FedEx did for the postal service.'

'Which was?'

'Disrupt it. Do it cheaper and better.'

'Kind of a coalition of the billing?'

'Tubalcain claim their main business is providing training support to military and law enforcement organizations, that kind of thing. But during the Congressional hearings it seemed mainly to involve hiring ex-Chilean commandos to shoot Arabs in the back.'

'Interesting.'

'Actually, I know someone who could tell you a lot more about them than me.'

'Who's that?'

'My sister's landlord.'

'Oh, him! Mister I know nothing about nothing. Now there was a damn cold fish. I'd rather you arrange an in-depth interview with an ice sculpture.'

'Oh, Tal was just being protective of Mary. I'll have a word with him about speaking to you. Maybe he will and maybe he won't. He's a strange old bird is Tal.'

Cowan stood before the apse, lost in the numinous whitish glow of the shimmering metallic foils in the recessed niche. What a strange glowing thing it was, enchanting as a child's Lego castle: *The Throne of the Third Heaven of the Nations' Millennium General Assembly*. It was constructed out of aluminium and gold foil, shreds of cardboard, old light bulbs and shards of mirror, coffee cans, jelly jars, electrical cable, desk blotters, all pinned together with tacks, glue and tape. The monarch's seat was a maroon-cushioned easy chair on a wooden platform. The detail was exquisite: mercy seats, pedestals, plaques and offertory tables; foil-wrapped bulbs representing Christ as the light of the world. It comprised 180 pieces in total, a few inscribed with texts from Revelation. Smaller objects sprouted wings, suggesting sky-bound angels. The Throne's architect was a lunatic visionary, his junkyard revelations recorded on the tablets around it. By day, he'd been a janitor cleaning Federal office buildings. At night, he shuttered himself in a garage with the detritus he scavenged, and laboured on the holy masterwork still unfinished at his death. Above his masterwork, James Hampton daubed these words: '*Fear Not.*'

Fair enough.

Kris seemed more intrigued by the other artworks in the gallery. She lingered by the bottlecap giraffe and the skeleton riding in a wagon near the African statues and death's heads. Cowan joined her in front of Malcah Zeldis' *Miss Liberty Celebration*, oil on corrugated cardboard. Zeldis painted herself in a red dress standing alongside Elvis and Miss America. 'It's all about the company you keep,' Cowan said. 'You like it?'

'I'm still thinking about it.'

'Fi! Contentious woman.'

'I saw that too,' Kris said, laughing. 'Wasn't that *Every Foul and Every Unclean Spirit*? Why do outsider artists always get so obsessed with Revelation?'

'Why is anyone?' Cowan shrugged. 'You can make of it what you will'.'

They moved on to Finster's THE LORD WILL DELIVER HIS PEOPLE ACROSS JORDAN. The bottom of the frame was a compressed space of text and figures representing the nature of life in a fallen world. A place of FALSE PROPHETS and FORNICATORS and LONG TONGUE LIARS; of LOVE OF THE DARKNESS RATHER THAN THE LIGHT; of WINE BIBBERS and DRUNKERDS.

'There's where I am,' Cowan said, pointing. 'I'd be a total wine bibber.'

A white-robed Jesus walked on the dark blue. The text on the river said: *I WANT HAFTO CROSS JORDAN ALONE* and *THINGS MUST BE BETTER JUST OVER JORDAN*. On the other side was a green expanse and light blue sky and angels soaring above the spacious mansions of the celestial city, skyscraping masonries. On the shoreline of Paradise was NO SUFFERING, NO PAIN, NO FUNERALS.

Kris traced the paths of *LOVE* and *PEACE* and *KINDNESS* and *FREEDOM*. 'I'm going this way.' She measured with her span the long road of *ETURNAL LIFE*. 'You're not coming?'

'Why can't these weirdos ever spell right?' Cowan asked, scowling at her.

Kris pressed her lips together and turned back to the artwork. She was irritated. Cowan wanted to touch her shoulder. He wanted to kiss her neck. He did neither.

Deyon was sitting on the bench before the Throne where Cowan had been sitting minutes before. Leather jacket collar popped like antennae. 'I didn't recognise you,' Cowan said in greeting. 'What are you being today? The hip-hop James Dean?'

'I didn't recognise you either,' Deyon said, sneering. 'Dressed all in black like that. I thought you must be an imitator escaped from a Johnny Cash convention.' Deyon pointed at the installation. 'Now, that there is one serious weird-ass piece of work.'

'I'm not going to disagree.'

'Even the wings have wings. The artist must have been batshit insane.'

'It's a distinct possibility.'

'When there is no vision, people perish,' Deyon read. 'That's deep.'

'When there is no vision, you should get yourself a pair of specs. That's deeper.'

'I see you got yourself a lady friend.' Deyon nodded at Kris. 'You move fast, Mr C. She's fine. And of an appropriate age for you, mid 30s is ballpark. I didn't have you figured for a *playa* though. My man!'

'Careful, son.'

'Just saying, is all. It's a compliment. Well, sort of.'

'She's just a very nice woman who happens to appreciate a distinguished older man, someone with a few splashes of grey, nice wrinkles.'

'She must really adore elephants,' Deyon said, smirking at him.

'Fuck you.'

Kris joined them at the bench. The men stood to greet her. 'Hi,' she said shyly.

'Kris, this is D. He's the friend of my daughter I was telling you about in the car. We're on a mission. He's helping me out with my inquiries today. Not in the bad sense.'

'They,' said Deyon. 'That's the pronoun I go by.'

'You're putting me on.'

'No. It's a thing. Respect the pronoun.'

'He's like my black sidekick.' Cowan sighed. 'I'm

sorry. That comment was way disrespectful. Permit me to re-phrase. They's like my black sidekick.'

'I'm not your fucking black sidekick,' Deyon snapped.

'Sure you are. You're the Tubbs to my Crockett, the Robin to my Batman.' Cowan scratched his earlobe. 'The Muttley to my Dick Dastardly.'

'This racist white man,' Deyon explained to Kris, 'manages to embody the quintessence of toxic masculinity. He's so talented at insult. It's quite extraordinary.'

'Then again, Robin isn't black,' Cowan said, musingly. 'Batman kind of is. And Muttley is a dog.'

'Yes,' Kris said to Deyon, shrugging her shoulders. 'He redirects the anger he feels at himself out into the world as humour. That way he never has to look in his heart.'

Cowan could only stare at her. That was some seriously sobering insight.

'I love your shoes,' Deyon said to Kris. 'Girl, you got some serious style.'

'Thanks,' said Kris, blushing.

'I drove over here in the Corolla rust bucket,' Deyon informed Cowan. 'I'm parked illegally by the Verizon, but I'm supposing you'll pay if I get a ticket.'

'I'll be right with you,' Cowan told him. 'I just need five minutes with Kris.'

'You guys can go,' Kris said. 'We're done. I have to be some place at 11.30.'

'Where do you have to be?' Cowan asked.

'It's Sunday. I'm going to church. That's where I have to be.'

Cowan grasped her by the arm and frog-marched her to the corner of the room. Behind her left shoulder was Almon's *Hell*, with its border of red flames and Jesus in a yellow bubble enclosed by scarlet devils and the cartoon faces of the damned, like a row of sad gingerbread men, mouths down-turned in sorrow. 'Can I see you tonight?' He detected the faint crack of desperation in his voice.

'No.'

Cowan touched her cheek, staring into a blue deeper than Jordan. 'Please.'

'I can't.'

'You can.' He kissed her, her lips so soft it pained him.

'I told you I'd come here with you,' she said. 'I did. I can't fall into this. Not where I am now. I'm all messed up. Last night was last night. I was in another place.'

Cowan didn't know what to do and now he had Deyon tugging at his sleeve also. 'I hate to interrupt, but we got to get.' Deyon addressed Kris now. 'I know this strange and terrible man acts semi-deranged and seems semi-deranged, but don't let that fool you, he really is semi-deranged. But if you can scrape away all the layers of that macho jont under-neath, he's kind of almost OK. Well, almost.'

Kris fought off a smile.

'So,' Deyon continued, 'if you could say you'll see him for, like, five minutes later, we could get out of here and do our thing. Seeing him could mean a lot of different things, too. It could be through a pair of binoculars. Best way to see him, if you ask me.'

Kris nodded, that gesture seeming to cost her a lot, her shoulders slumping a little.

'Also, if you could put aside a little time soon to speak to him also about the way he dresses? The clothes! I mean can you even believe this down-and-out hobo shit?'

'Fuck you, again,' Cowan suggested.

'Plus he swears like a veritable trooper, makes a spectacle of himself in and out of Congressional offices, assaults Professors with tofu, tenured professors at that. It's all quite shocking. You should say a prayer for him today too if you can. He so needs it.'

Kris looked at Cowan and smiled. 'I think you're right. So I will.'

'You owe me,' Deyon said to Cowan. They were halfway across F Street. 'That woman was looking to run away, like most everybody who meets you.'

'I suppose.'

'Wait up.' Deyon stopped by a hot dog wagon. 'I want to get a half-smoke.'

'Couldn't you have eaten before?' Cowan asked, exasperated.

'Couldn't you have got it on with your lady before?'

★ ★ ★

'You must be seriously messing with me again.' Deyon wasn't being a regular smart-ass anymore. He looked frightened now.

'No. I wish I was.'

The two men walked along Massachusetts Avenue, north of Chinatown. A crane wheeled across the skyline above a chorus of blasting jackhammers. No Sunday rest here. Monday must be trash day, for, on the far side of an apartment building, a dumpster over-flowed with week-end detritus, cardboard boxes of Bud and Corona Light, red cups, bags from Trader Joe's.

'You're seriously telling me that the same people who killed Cat might also have killed her girlfriend too?'

'Uh-huh, and it's getting to be my turn now, which bothers me. For one thing, it's fucking inconvenient.'

'That's what you say when someone tries to kill you? That it's inconvenient?'

'Well, it's perturbing as well? Causing major perturbation, most definitely. I tell you, D, it for sure makes me downright shifty-eyed walking down a street like this.'

'I thought that look just came natural to you.' Deyon chucked the remnant of his hot dog in a trash barrel and discreetly sucked a smear of ketchup from his thumb. 'This sounds like some deep conspiracy movie stuff here. Could it be you're just imagining it? Crazy people make up all kinds of stuff. Look at the Throne Man back in the museum.'

'I'm only telling you this,' Cowan said, reasonably, 'so you can get out. Whether it's real or I'm imagining it, doesn't matter a damn. You don't have to be involved.'

'But I'm up to my neck in it, Mr Cowan. These people

saw me with you in the Cannon the other day. I'm your accomplice. They probably think I'm your rent-a-boy.'

Cowan contemplated this prospect for a while and then made a choking sound.

'You could do a lot worse.' Deyon was offended. 'I'm Frank Ocean classy.'

Cowan scanned the sixth floor of the Acacia apartment complex. 'There's a wee shithead up there has some answers about all of this, though.'

'This is the same white boy was in the office the other day? I don't know anything about killers, but he doesn't seem the killer type to me. More like a barista.'

'Appearances are deceptive, D. I caught this man one time, cooked his wife in a big pot. Never did say why. I assume they'd had a disagreement. It was a steel pot too. He looked like a librarian, bald little punter with big side-burns, totally innocuous. Only one leg though. Just goes to show you never can tell. Then there was this other fella...'

Deyon was looking at him now, disturbed. 'You can stop whenever you want.'

'So.' Cowan held his arms akimbo like an avenging angel. 'Tell us what we're looking at. Give us the skinny. You're the expert on local colour.'

'Boomtown is all.' Deyon sighed. 'Sometimes my father just shakes his head and goes, 'Where all these white people coming from?"

'This is a turning neighbourhood?'

Deyon laughed. 'Yes, it's turning for sure. Millennials,

right? The whole of DC is a turning neighbourhood. They come in to Columbia Heights, to NoMa, to Capitol Hill. They're like Caucasian cockroaches. Don't want to live in the suburbs anymore. Want a central location and condos and ugly apartment buildings with rooftop pools and gyms and coin laundries in the basement. They want cool nightlife a Lyft ride away.'

A deeply toned young woman in a pink headband emerged from the Acacia; sunglasses and earbuds, yoga mat, a big bottle of orange Gatorade tucked beside her hip.

'There you go,' Deyon said, frowning at her. 'The world of the echo boomer: Zipcars and tablets, pinot noir and P Street Whole Foods, bike lanes and skinny ties, deep talk about slow food and global warming and sustainability drives over double espressos in Baked and Wired. Overpriced restaurants shooting up like dandelions. 24-hour fitness centers for 24-hour health fanatics, survival of the fucking fittest of the fit. Varsity vegans. I think therefore I Instagram.'

'Shite, D, cool your jets. You should have been a preacher, son. You have a vocation for creative ranting.'

'I have flow. My father was a Baptist preacher. Now he sits around retired, watching Judge Joe Brown and saying 'Where all the white people coming from?"

'You said that. You're repeating yourself. I'd never have figured you for a minister's son, though.' Cowan punched Deyon's shoulder, smirking. 'By the by, did I ever tell you that the only one who could NEVER reach me was the son of a...

'You know what gets me?' Deyon said, ignoring him, gazing up at a blank ugly expanse of windows. 'These are white liberals. Get all bent out of shape about police brutality and black profiling. Say the right things, talk a good game, beat themselves up about their privilege. Talk and talk about their privilege and how much they hate having it, the way privileged people do. The type is all over a 'hands up, don't shoot' meme on Tumblr, retweet stuff about the evils of racism, know all Kendrick lyrics by heart. White folks who seriously love them some poor oppressed black people. But when the woke drop $300,000 on a condo downtown, some of those same black people got to move and make room for them. See, liberal hipsters love their black person in the abstract. We're a concept. We're people of colour. What does that even mean? Like we're in a cartoon, like we're different in HD? These white people are so into diversity, love it everywhere but where they live. I hear the word ally used seriously one more time online, I'm going to puke.'

'For me it's two words: Ally McLeod.'

'I have no idea what that means.'

'It's complicated and Scottish and traumatic. That the end of the sermon?'

'Amen.'

'Thank God for that. I thought I was going to have to commit hari-kari by swallowing my own tongue. So, this place?'

'Dorm rooms for the postgrad set, college without the

college. You'll notice these apartments got no balconies.
They have sunrooms instead. So you get a one-bedroom,
one-sunroom unit for $3000 a month, cheaper than a two
bedroom. The sunrooms have cable, outlets, the lot, 12 by 9
and glass enclosed. You never need to leave your little glass
box except to go to work, get stoned and hook up. We're
talking about some serious pod people here. A lobotomized
gerbil leads a more interesting life.'

The men proceeded to the front of the complex. It was
massive, hideous, another architectural abomination. A thir-
ty-something with a receding hairline in slacks and a green
dress shirt drove up on a blue Stella scooter. He was wearing
a pretty little backpack. Three flags outside, including the
United Nations. The UN was always hip. No one knew what
the fuck the UN did, really. Blessed are the peacemakers.
Rows of little scrub bushes were placed symmetrically.
A fountain. There was always a fucking fountain. These
people adored running water. They were like trout in that
regard.

'Doorman?'

'Don't sweat it. I know him. He's a friend, sort of.'

'Seems like you're friends with everyone.'

'For you I'll make an exception, Mr Cowan.'

The WIFI enabled lobby had sleek dark furniture, a vom-
it-colored carpet, and a chandelier like an inverted mushroom. Large white ornaments rested on the tables like bul-
bous growths. While Deyon chatted up the concierge,
Cowan picked up flyers from the desk. Apt. 502 had won

the Ugly Sweater Contest and Apt 701 the Jellybean Count. The Pet selfie winner was Perri. Honorable mention went to Henry. Perri was a shiatsu dressed up as a pumpkin. Henry wasn't pictured.

The concierge rode in the elevator with them. He and Deyon giggled, sharing some private joke. It was about Cowan probably.

'What was the jellybean count?' Cowan asked, flapping the flyer.

'284,' said the concierge, without turning around. Outside Apartment 663, Cowan smudged his finger over the spy-hole.

'Too bad they don't have an ugly jacket contest,' Deyon said. 'I think I see a definite winner.'

Cowan beat on the door with his fist.

'I wonder who's in 666?' Deyon inquired, open-eyed. 'Care to speculate?'

Craig Doyle looked a lot more relaxed on his day off: red shorts and a black bro tank with *Here Come the Irish* in green on the front. There were discreet tattoos on his ankle and shoulder blade and hipster black-frame glasses balanced on his nose. 'Yes?' he said, looking at once shifty and worried and petrified.

Well, so much for relaxation then. Cowan had seen a salmon look more relaxed in the mouth of a bear. 'Remember us?'

Doyle squinted slightly at Cowan and then at Deyon. He had acquired a face like a burst tomato. 'Yes,' he managed.

'We were hoping for a chat,' Cowan said. 'Won't take up much of your time.'

'About what?' Doyle was working on edging the door closed. Cowan was working on inching his foot further in.

'Senator Factor. We think he's been having this passionate affair with Mitch McConnell. We have incriminating photos, involving margarine and other sex toys. We're thinking of tipping TMZ off. Also a missing girl called Mary?'

Doyle's eyes clouded over. He took off his specs as though those were the problem. 'Well, I was about to go up to the pool for a dip.'

'Well, we'd be happy to join you, right, D? You wouldn't have an extra pair of Speedos lying around for him, would you? I'm fine diving in fully clothed. I swim like an eagle in the eye of noon.'

Doyle kept his eyes on Cowan, his face hard as a chisel. 'I have ten minutes,' he said eventually. 'I'll listen. Then I'm going.'

Cowan waved Deyon forward through the open door. 'After you, Macduffer.'

The apartment was scantily furnished. In the narrow living room was a white sofa with two red pillows facing a white chair, two black leather cubes with books piled on top in lieu of tables, a checkered rug like a chessboard beneath them. There were sporadic ugly yellow lamps and the black shelves screwed into the wall had framed pictures balanced on them with figurines and a plastic clock. There was a chrome lava lamp for retro-chic irony. The lamp was two feet tall and inside it a red liquid twisted and spun around a floating luminous yellow wax pillar. The adjacent sunroom was used for dining. Its large picture window overlooked Mount Vernon Square where another crane swung lazily in the empty air. The big green plant stuck inside the sliding doors of the sunroom was about the size of a Triffid. The outlets were inexplicably high on the walls.

'I'd offer you something to drink. But I haven't been able to get the shopping in yet.'

They sat on the sofa opposite him and said nothing. This wasn't helping relax him.

'If you've come here to ask about your daughter again,' Doyle blurted, 'I still know nothing about her. After you left the office the other day, I checked. I looked into it myself. I called and told the Senator all about it. There is no record of a meeting.'

So Doyle hadn't been kept in the loop about yesterday's big confab with his boss in Alexandria. This was either a good or a bad thing, depending. 'What do you know about one Mary Barnham, then?' Cowan asked.

Doyle fidgeted his fingers against the lining of his shorts. His legs were smooth and hairless. 'Very little. I believe she's a journalist, works the Hill.'

'You believe?'

Doyle grimaced. 'I know.' Saying this, he had a quick nibble at his lower lip.

'You ever meet this young lady in the course of what-ever the fuck it is you people do every day, Mr Doyle?'

'No.' Doyle moistened his lips again. 'I do believe she may have come into the office to take a meeting with us at some point, but I wasn't present for that meeting.'

'Who would have been present on that occasion then?'

Doyle sighed. 'I just remember her name coming up in some context or other. This would have involved the staff working the campaign detail. Devlin Reem is the person you should really be speaking with about that.'

'Well, I'd rather watch the 1978 Scotland- Peru game on a loop than talk to that dipshit again. I'd also be con-cerned he'd get angry and rip himself in two like fucking Rumpelstiltskin. So, what do you suppose that little arse would have wanted with her then, Mr Doyle? That's my starter for 100.'

Doyle considered this for a moment. 'Wait, wasn't she the Wringhim person?'

'Wringhim?'

'They're not called that anymore. They've got a new name now. I forget what it is. Been rebranded. I believe it had something to do with Wringhim, though.' Doyle was nodding at them now like a mechanical drinking bird. 'Yes, I think so. Gil Martin is a major donor to the campaign. The Senator has enjoyed their corporate support.'

'Keep going.'

'It's really not my area of expertise.' Doyle was back to picking nervously at his shorts. 'Look, Barnham was employed for a time by a major political rival. There's a Presidential election in two years. I guess we were trying to get information from her? I'm not sure what it was. She must have been bringing something to the table.'

'You know she's missing?'

Doyle's jaw tightened imperceptibly. 'No, I didn't know that.'

Cowan picked up a glass ashtray off one of the black cubes. 'You smoke?

'Of course not.' Doyle looked mortally offended.

'Now, this question's a bit more awkward, Craig. Could you fill me in about what you were doing screwing around with my dead girl's computer? What was that about?'

There was a faint glitter of sweat showing on Doyle's forehead now. 'I'm sorry. This time you've completely lost me.'

'That so?'

Doyle stood up. 'Look, what's this all about?'

'It's about Erin.' Cowan pointed at Doyle's tee. 'And I don't mean the Emerald Isle. You have any thoughts on that sweetheart, the GW student? Cool wee blonde lassie with braces on her teeth? St Ninian's schoolgirl outfit ringing a bell?'

Doyle's face was a mask. 'I don't know any GW students. We may currently have an intern in the Congressional office who goes there. But I've barely spoken to her. I think she's Georgetown anyway. I don't know anyone called Erin.'

'Also goes by Sammi. Her name when she's doing her afterhours call girl gig?'

Deyon was acquiring a deeply perplexed expression too. He was hearing about all this for the first time. 'Erin's a hooker? Little Erin with all the clothes?'

'Where's this going?' Doyle looked to be having an especially difficult bowel movement where he sat. 'I have seriously no idea what you're talking about here.'

'You're a client of hers, Craig,' Cowan said, accusingly. 'You've been serviced by her, which is kind of sad seeing as how it's not like you look like the back end of a bus, exactly. Is dating too much bother for you politicos? Tender is the night become Tinder is the night, has it? Anyhow, you've been a bad boy, Craig, and you're busted.'

'You're totally off your head!' Doyle was looking at Deyon, wild-eyed. 'You know this is all bullshit, don't you? Why don't you tell him?'

Deyon was looking even more confused now, glancing from one to the other.

'Look,' Doyle said, gesticulating at Cowan abstractly. 'This is what I'm going to do for you. I want all this nonsense cleared up right now. I'm going to get my phone and give you the numbers of the people who can maybe help you with this. Maybe is the operative word. You've got everything ass backwards so far.'

When Doyle stalked off into the sunroom, Cowan turned to Deyon. 'What did he mean with the 'you know it's bullshit'? Tell me what?'

'Yeah, I was going to say. It's just that he's…' Deyon's eyes were the size of dinner plates now, like a bunny with myxomatosis. 'Uh-oh. This is so not good.'

Doyle had come back not with his phone but with a semi-automatic pistol, which he aimed directly at Cowan's forehead. The hand holding the gun trembled slightly.

'Did you find that thing in your man purse, Craig?'

'I need you to leave,' Doyle snarled unconvincingly. 'Now.'

'Or what? You're going to shoot us with that popgun? Here in your apartment? Going to stain this gorgeous monochrome carpet, are you? Then what, you going to drop our bodies out the window and tell the police that we fell while buildering up the wall outside? Give me a break. Put that stupid thing away before you get yourself hurt.'

'I need you to know,' said Doyle, his voice quavering. 'That I know how to use this. I have a permit. I've been to the range in Manassas. I have the badges. I don't want to hurt anyone. I just want you to leave. Right this minute.'

'Is that that new Bersa Thunder?' Deyon inquired.

Cowan was looking at Deyon incredulously. 'Yes,' said Doyle. 'And I sure know how to use it.'

'It's like the Walther PPK,' Deyon explained. 'Cheaper. What's the retail?'

'You Yanks and your fucking guns,' Cowan moaned. 'I seriously give up.'

'You need to go,' Doyle repeated, agitated, waggling the

pistol side to side. 'I have a right to protect myself in my own home. I have a right to stand my ground.'

'Ugh,' Deyon observed. 'Why'd you have to go there, sweetie?'

'I think we'd best do like Cunt Eastwood here says, D.' Cowan was shaking his head sadly. 'The poor boy looks more liable to shoot himself with that thing than us, but why take the chance?'

Cowan got up and strolled to the front door of the apartment, eyes fixed on Doyle the whole way. Deyon was still sitting on the sofa as if paralyzed, left hand resting on the table with the lava lamp. 'For the record,' Cowan noted, 'I consider this dick-waving episode to be an admission of guilt on your part, Craig.'

'Leave. Now!'

There was a loud shattering of glass and red spattered across the coffee table and carpet and dripped down the wall sticky and wet. Doyle tipped backwards onto his carpet in a blur. Time crawled treacle slow, everything moving in slow motion. Then with a sudden jump cut, Doyle was staggering back to his feet, looking dazed and in shock, no longer holding the gun, the idiot somehow contriving to shoot himself after all. Cowan wasn't going to linger on figuring out the details. Instead, he hurled himself headlong at Doyle's torso causing both men to crash backwards onto the kitchen floor. It was hard, as kitchen floors went. They wrestled each other back to their feet, something unpleasant smacking Cowan repeatedly hard behind the ear. He fell to one knee, shaking his head to clear it. The tiling on the floor was rippling in waves, which probably wasn't good. Crouching, balled with pain, he presumed it might be productive to drive his fist hard into Doyle's groin, and now they were back writhing on the floor. It was all like a terrible dream. The dishwasher door fell open and smacked Cowan's shin. It really hurt. That was so unfair.

Doyle for a while seemed mainly interested in trying to bite his nose off or in gouging out his eyes, but he had settled for merely choking him so vigorously that the inside of his eyelids began pulsing green and red. Doyle's attempted strangulation only ceased when Deyon cracked him in the skull with a glass cutting board. The hollow thud caused Doyle to sag, his sweeping hand lifting a tumbler off the counter. Cowan elbowed him hard on the temple to help him on his way down. There was something very silly about the way Doyle fell. The glass shattered, Deyon muttered, 'God!' Doyle stretched out full length on the tiles, his open mouth making the same sucking sound a fish makes flopping on rocks.

Cowan took the opportunity to kick him viciously in the liver. Deyon was in his face immediately though, waltzing him out of the kitchen like they were doing a rumba on *Dancing with the Stars*. Deyon still had the cutting board clutched in his left hand. 'Enough,' he shouted. 'Quit it. Calm the fuck down.'

Cowan could taste blood in his mouth, salty, thick and tangy. 'That little shit,' he said, struggling to extricate himself. Eventually Deyon had to tumble him over onto the carpet where he sat for a while, like an infant on a play mat, pawing at his mouth. His tongue felt thick and hard when he tried to move it. His face really hurt.

'Get your act together.' Deyon looked down to notice the cutting board was still in his hand. The board had a vintage carousel design embossed, rearing ponies in blue ribbons, sticker still attached. He began reading the sticker aloud: '*With custom design and heat-resistant, tempered glass, this cutting board beautifully reflects your good taste.*' He shrugged. 'May also be used as a weapon in an emergency, apparently. These hipster kitchens got them some well-made dangerous shit.'

Cowan was looking up at him, chagrined. He ventured a faint smile.

'Better now?'

'Yeah.'

'Feeling less homicidal?'

'A smidge.' Cowan stood up, squeezing at his throat. 'Let's assess the damage.'

'For the record, if you're going to start up kicking that defenseless man again…' Deyon gripped Cowan's arm. 'I will rip your tongue out and make you eat it. I mean it.'

'Aw, that's sweet. I didn't know you cared.' Cowan was hunkered over the prostrate Doyle now, trying to gauge where the man had shot himself. His fingers drabbled in the red sticky liquid where it coagulated on the t-shirt, warm and waxy to the touch. 'This isn't blood,' he announced, ridiculously.

'No,' Deyon said, looking chagrined. 'It's the goop was inside that lamp thing.' Cowan stared at him. 'I threw it at him while you two were making eyes at each other.'

'Don't ever do that again!' Cowan spat, angrily. 'That was stupid. Did you happen to notice that this fucker had a gun pointed right at my head?'

'Well, I wouldn't have attempted it if the gun had been pointed at me.' Deyon watched Cowan poking around the back of the unconscious man's skull. 'I hit him first with a lava lamp and then with a cutting board,' he said dreamily. 'You don't get to do stuff like this every day. In another life I could be some kind of urban assassin.'

'It's a concussion I think,' Cowan noted. 'He might need the hospital.'

'Is that a good idea?'

'Probably not for us. For now, let's get him into his bed. Your pal downstairs can look in and check on him. We'd best never have been here. I'm just saying.'

The men dragged Doyle into the bedroom and hoisted him onto the bed. The duvet was tasteful and comforting. Doyle's face was a mask of fragile white tissue paper. Deyon folded the top sheet neatly and winked. 'Hospital corners,' he said.

'You'll make a man a fine missus some day, D.'

Deyon wandered into the sunroom and came back in waving the gun around.

'Don't point that fucking thing in my direction,' Cowan hissed at him. 'I've had enough of that being shot at crap to last me the week.'

'Yeah, a cheap Bersa for sure,' Deyon declared. 'Also not loaded.'

'Fuck me!' Cowan glared down at the unconscious Doyle, shaking his head. 'You are a regular halfwit, Craig, aren't you? Or a quarterwit.'

'Look, no offence, because you're a professional. I mean respect.' Deyon tapped a finger on his temple. 'But could be you're doing a shit-poor job of detecting here.'

'Do enlighten me, Agatha.'

Deyon nodded at Doyle who was breathing more evenly now, a peculiar aimless smile playing on his lips. 'You think that man there was using a call girl?'

'Aye.'

'No.'

'No?'

'Absolutely not. See, I knew I'd seen him before somewhere. Before the other day in the Congressional office, I mean. He looked awfully familiar to me. But I only remembered when he opened the door to us today: the Green Lantern.'

'A movie?'

'A bar!' Deyon tilted his head to one side, assessing Doyle. 'Obviously, he's not my type. I mean, for me, speaking personally, his sex appeal wouldn't buy the phlegm off a dead frog. But having said that, he's got a nice…'

'You mean he's…'

'Absolutely. 110%.'

'He doesn't look…'

Deyon rolled his eyes. 'You're seriously going to start that shit up again?'

Cowan slumped on the bed, looking defeated. 'Somebody is a serious long-tongued liar. I think I'll just assume from now on everybody I meet in America is gay. It'd be a safer hypothesis.'

'That's the first smart thing you've said today, Mr Cowan.'

'This is a fucking situation though.'

'Maybe he wakes up in a few hours and thinks it was a bad dream?'

'I hope to Christ I do.'

'There's something up with all this, though.'

'You don't say.'

'You know how little Erin lies a lot?'

'Yes.'

'Did it ever occur to you…'

'That she might be lying to me still.'

'Yeah.'

'The thought has crossed my mind, particularly in the last five minutes. She wasn't in the best frame of mind when she took to confessing. She was a bit peeved actually.' Cowan sighed. 'I happened to be threatening her at the time.'

'She sure got you good. Doyle wasn't using a call girl. It looks like the call girl was using Doyle. Not to mention playing you like a fiddle at the same time.' Deyon examined Cowan's face. 'You've also got a black eye, incidentally. I think he must have popped you with a right hook.

It's swelling up most righteously. You think Craig might have a steak in his refrigerator?'

'I'm not that hungry.' Cowan pawed under his eye. 'We ruined the poor bastard's carpet into the bargain. He's going to notice that. He'd be the house-proud type.'

'There will be cleaning supplies. We could take care of it with a little scrubbing?'

'You're shitting me?'

'I'm shitting you.' Deyon laughed seeing his expression. 'Let's get out of here before one of the other bathing beauties comes looking for him.'

8 SUNDAY (AFTERNOON)

The inside of Deyon's rusted blue Corolla had a skunky smell.

'Somebody I know been on the wacky baccy?'

Deyon started wiping his phone.

'This is hardly the time and place for you to be checking your Grindr profiles.'

'Tubalcain Services, formerly Wringhim Enterprises,' Deyon read from the screen, 'is headquartered in Manassas, Virginia.'

'The same place Craig Headache took his shooting lessons.'

'Company has been through an intricate rebranding process, changing its name and logo several times. More than a dozen affiliate companies registered offshore. Operations are shrouded in secrecy: a one-stop shopping source for world-class services in the fields of security, stability, aviation, training and logistics.'

'Fascinating. How's about you wind the windows down in the interim?' Cowan suggested. 'I'm getting baked, just sitting here. And I don't mean from the heat.'

'They have a private training facility: 9,000 acres. The Impact Training Center, with an artificial lake and a driving track, firing ranges and two airfields.'

'Anything on the leadership? I do believe Gil Martin was the name.'

'Chief Executive Martin is notoriously secretive about himself. Self-made success story, emerging from an unhappy youth, devoid of educational advantages. No college, biographical details sketchy. Age a mystery, variously given as 60 and 73. Wife unknown. Said to have one child, now deceased. Company has no phone number, email address or press contact for him. Has in the past concealed his identity as buyer with shell corporations, of which he is the sole member. Did not testify before Congress in person.'

'Retiring soul.'

'One of our most enigmatic and reclusive billionaires says *Forbes*. Few outside corporate elite know what he looks like. Never talks to reporters and fires subordinates who do. Quoted as once saying: 'No interviews, no speeches, stay out of the spotlight, it fades your white suit'.'

'I'm just glad to know that Gil Martin is two names. Now all I need to figure out is why Catriona went and wrote the fucker's name down on that damn flyer.'

Deyon read on from the screen. 'Is said to interact with business contacts using virtual online world Second Life, via an avatar named Solomon Temple, a tall, tattooed black man with no hair.'

'You're making that bit up?'

Deyon shrugged. 'The point of an avatar is to let you do the weird and wonderful things you can't do in real life. You can be anyone you want in Second Life. It's like being born again. No point being yourself, right? You can do that in real life.'

'Can you?'

Deyon considered this. 'You have a point.' He held out the phone to Cowan. 'Care to peruse a collection of images of Sol Temple using a variety of bondage apparatus in a mature-rated virtual dungeon called The Blue Lodge?'

'I'll skip it.'

'Looks like Gil boy here wants to be black online but nowhere else. Blackfishing.'

'Maybe he's trans-racial,' Cowan suggested. 'It's probably the new thing. It'll probably involve new Black and White Minstrel shows and a whole new set of pronouns for your generation to master.'

Deyon turned the ignition. 'The great mystery making any more sense now?'

'No, not one tiny bit.' Cowan offered a mirthless laugh. 'We all set for our wee foray into the ghetto then?'

'Let's not call it that.'

'Aye. Let's not call the ghetto the ghetto. Let's be sensitive. If you can change the language you can change the… well, fuck all, actually.'

'You got the money?'

'I got the money. So, you think Carlton's girlfriend will actually talk to me?'

'She'll meet with you. Whether she'll talk I don't know. I used an intermediary.'

'He was one of the fuckers that killed my little girl.'

'I know. But this is just the girlfriend we're seeing now, remember? She didn't do anything to anyone except hook up with the wrong guy. Chill. She's harmless.'

They drove east on I-695 onto Pennsylvania Avenue SE, down past Navy Yard and across the river on the 11th Street Bridge onto the Anacostia Freeway.

'You giving me the silent treatment?' Cowan asked, after a while of driving. 'Was I fucking too hard with your precious snowflake PC sensibilities again?'

'No. I was thinking about if I had an online avatar, what I'd want it to be?'

'Bette Davis?'

Deyon tapped his screen with one hand as he drove.

'I'mma be at the ET home in 5,' he drawled into the phone.

He had dropped his voice to a lower register.

'Aight bet,' said the voice on the other end. 'Where you at now?'

'Fuck me,' Cowan said after Deyon hung up. 'You're multilingual. Is there no end to your talents?'

Deyon said nothing.

'How'd you set this up again, master code-shifter?'

'I know a man knows a man knows a man...' Deyon hooked a right, back onto Pennsylvania Avenue and pulled into the parking lot of a nondescript office building. The sign outside said DMV *ALIEN ABDUCTION RESEARCH GROUP*. '...who happened to know another man. I know a lot of men. Not just from Grindr either, before you go asking.'

Cowan pointed at the absurd sign and shook his head. 'Just when I think things can't get any weirder.'

'This is just a convenient lot to pick our contact up. His real name is Norman but he goes by Ea$y Money, dollar sign instead of the S. He does this hybrid emo-metal mumble-rap mix on Soundcloud, gets a shitload of downloads.'

Cowan grimaced. 'Aye, does he have a stupid nickname but?'

They sat in silence for a while.

'How come your Department of Motor Vehicles is interested in alien abductions? Are they trying to keep their queues down? Like, arranging for half the folk waiting in line to disappear when they're renewing their plates? Speed up service?'

'Mr Cowan, will you please, please, please, try to shut the fuck up? DMV is short for District of Maryland, Virginia.'

'There's probably a bunch of right mentalists sitting in there right now, wearing tinfoil hats thinking they're communicating with Jupiter. We could go in there and fuck with them. Say we just arrived from Alpha Centauri and assumed human form.'

Deyon gave Cowan a look.

'Or not.'

A hunched figure with a flipped Nets cap slouched towards their car. He was in his mid-20s with small watery eyes and protruding front teeth, like a jackrabbit with allergies. He wore a green velour zippered tracktop, True Religion jeans and Nikes, and looked like he'd got his most recent haircut breaking up a knife fight. It was a look. It wasn't a good look, but it was definitely a look.

'You the Deyontais?'

'Uh-huh.'

'What's good, mo?'

'I just be on chill mode, dawg,' Deyon slurred.

Cowan emitted a soft groaning noise.

'Shhh,' said Deyon.

Ea$y settled in the backseat and poked Cowan with a finger, like he was checking whether he was real. 'This the money, then?'

'Uh-huh.'

'He so offbrand.'

'Right,' Deyon said, laughing.

'I'm going to need a translator,' Cowan said. 'This is starting to remind me of that time I went to Portugal by accident. Was that a crack about my sartorial elegance?'

Deyon ignored him, glancing in the rear-view. 'She down with it, then?'

'Will be,' said Ea$y. 'Roychelle. She cool. It's up to y'all make it right.'

They turned down 28th Street. A group of black youths on a street corner stared down at the pavement with half-mast eyes, looking like cowled monks at evensong.

'It's hot as a mug,' Ea$y announced.

'True,' Deyon agreed.

'Why the windows not up? You need to get that AC crankin', cuz'

'We're revelling in the katabatic winds,' Cowan informed him.

'Huh?' Ea$y tugged at Deyon's shoulder. 'What the fuck he say?'

30th Street was tree-lined and the Naylor Gardens apartment complex was not at all what Cowan was expecting. There was a park on the perimeter of the property, what must have been a summer expanse of green. Clean brick buildings set back from the road, a long flight of steps leading up. The projects it was not. It was like one of the better council schemes in Garrowhill or Coatbridge. Places habitable, if without beauty.

'Bit nice for a ghetto?'

'We're on the border here,' Deyon said. 'Hillcrest Heights that way is middle class, neat. But we're not far from the complexes over on Congress Heights, either. That's where this girl started out from.'

'She's moved up in the world.'

'Residents are not permitted to hang out on stoops or in the yards here,' Deyon explained. 'There's a security car circles around. The rent for a one bedroom is $900.'

The room they entered was small, but with hardwood floors and a high ceiling. The windows were large and there were ledges and molding around the baseboards. An apartment built at a time when people paid attention to detail, but didn't consider amenities like central air. Cowan was sweating like a rat in a sock. The room was sparsely furnished but clean and the only thing that looked out of place was the young woman. She sat in a grey armchair holding her knees like they were made of glass. She was about twenty-one, although she looked older, with an air of resignation, or surrender. She was slightly built with big brown eyes that flitted nervously and couldn't seem to focus properly. Her hair was short and dyed platinum blonde, and her mouth had a dissatisfied droop that didn't complement the cut.

Deyon and Ea$y sat down on the yellow sofa. Cowan pulled a wooden chair out from under a desk in the corner, so he could sit closer to Roychelle Watkins.

'Girl, these the ones lookin' to get up with you.' Ea$y pointed at Cowan. 'This the wack-ass going to show us the money.'

'Nobody is getting jack shit until I hear something I haven't heard,' Cowan said.

'You talk funny.' It was the first thing Roychelle had said. She unclenched her legs and regarded him with sullen disapproval.

'I have an accent.'

'You got a bruise.' She pointed under her eye.

'Yeah. I'm told I have an attitude, also.'

She was looking at him skeptically. 'You say a thousand?'

'I say a thousand.'

'Aigght.'

'How's about you start by telling me all about your man. Carlton would be your husband, right?'

'He just my baby daddy. Know him since high school.'

'How long was that?'

'Six years. Sumthin' like that.' Roychelle was downcast now. 'Not always but mostly. Man played round some.'

'He wasn't a good man?'

'He done bad things.' She thought for a second. 'He was all right.'

'The police say his death was gang-related. That he got killed over drugs, a deal gone bad, maybe? That how you see it?'

'Naw. There was a crew down there and he in with them and there was drugs. I'm not talkin' 'bout that. That wasn't it. It wasn't 'bout any of that.'

'What then?'

Roychelle sniffed. 'Other stuff. I'd like to know my own self.'

'You want to talk about that?'

'You show me cash money?'

Cowan laid the envelope on a table, watching her closely. 'There's $500 in cash to start. The rest if we get somewhere interesting.' Roychelle stared at the envelope like it was boo-by-trapped. 'So, we already established that your ex was a murdering sack of shit. What else can you tell me about him?'

'Dawg, don't talk about her man like that.' Ea$y was languidly getting to his feet.

'Sit yo ass down,' Deyon said.

'He getting me bent.'

'Sit!'

Ea$y flopped back down, looking put out. 'He keep

fuckin' around like this and I'mma have to slump his wack ass.'

'You'd make a fucking cat laugh.' Cowan was trying to hold Roychelle's focus, but she was looking away. 'Who do you think killed him, then?'

'Dunno.'

'Talk to me.' Cowan leaned forward, intent.

'If you don't get out her face, I'mma steal you slam in your jaw.'

'Seriously, Snoop?' Cowan swivelled and stared narrow-eyed at Ea$y, until the latter started up clawing at his cap. 'I mean, seriously?'

'Chill out, Joe,' Deyon said, touching Ea$y's arm. 'It's questions.'

A little girl came wandering in from outside and stood in the centre of the room looking around wide-eyed at the strangers in her home. She was about six years old.

'This your daughter?'

'Uh-huh.'

'What's your name, pet?'

'Keneesha.'

'That's a cool name. The best. You like chewing gum, Keneesha?'

The girl looked at her mother for approval. Roychelle nodded slightly and she took the stick of gum from Cowan. She had white ribbons in her hair. Keneesha watched Cowan closely as she slid the stick between her teeth.

'It's cinnamon flavored so it'll burn your mouth a bit. But that's good. It means you can breathe like a dragon after. Would you like to breathe like a big dragon?'

Keneesha nodded.

'Aye, you'd like to go out and breathe on the people around here and burn them all up? You'd like to burn it all down, wouldn't you?'

'This white boy lunchin'' Ea$y announced. Everyone ignored him.

'What you want to be when you grow up, Keneesha?'

She again looked at her mother and then turned back to him. 'A nurse,' she said.

'You be a nurse then. I think you'd be very good at it. I bet you could bandage anything up in no time. Do you think you could fix up my eye, eh?'

Keneesha smiled uncertainly at him and went back to methodically chewing.

'You go,' Roychelle told her. 'Get those hands washed up good.' Keneesha had stopped in the doorframe to look back at Cowan. He interested her. 'You go on now,' said Roychelle, sharply.

They all sat listening to the sound of splashing water poured from taps. The girl was singing a song from *The Little Mermaid* in a clear silvery tone.

Cowan smiled at Roychelle. 'I remember my daughter when she was that age. It's a good age.'

'She the white girl he shot?'

'Yes. He tell you that?'

'He tell me he shot a white girl. Was on the news. Said she need to be got.'

'Did he say it was an accident?'

'He didn't say.' Roychelle was studying her black pumps and leggings as attentively as she might a movie screen. 'But it weren't no accident.'

'He was proud of it, wasn't he?'

Roychelle looked at him and then at the others. She nodded imperceptibly.

'She liked dressing up. Even as a little girl.'

'Who?'

'My daughter.'

'Who as?'

'A mermaid.'

Roychelle looked away, her face contorting.

'Aye, she used to wear only blue clothes and pretend to limp everywhere. Her fingernails would be all glittery with silver-sparkle nail polish. When she was nine, she refused to eat anything at all but frozen fish sticks for three months. Wanted swimming lessons and all the rest of it. You couldn't get her out the damn bathtub.'

'They like that. Keneesha, she like that.'

'She'd tell the hairdresser to please cut her hair long. Her mother thought she needed to see a trick cyclist for a while. A psychiatrist, you know.'

'They like that.'

'Someone pay him to do it?' Cowan changed tack again.

'I says to the police I don't know.'

'I know what you said to the police. I read the report. Now, it's me asking. And I'm doling out cash money. Someone pay him?'

'He got money. Happened before. Went to Florida this one time; California twice; Chicago; sometimes he don't say where he been. Trip to Westbumbafuck, bitch. Why you care? Always come back with money when he goes places. Why we live here?' She looked around the apartment, smiled. 'This some expensive shit. Carlton get the money.'

'They say crime doesn't pay,' Cowan said, shrugging. 'But it's a myth. Like margarine being better than butter and that thing about the poor inheriting the earth.'

'That why he gone. He was so pressed to show everyone around how he got his money. Carlton just syced the situation. He droppin' bills like...' She hesitated, didn't finish the thought.

'He talked too much?'

'Could be someone thought that. You know how they do.' Rochelle shrugged. 'Carlton run his mouth off. Always did. He ji stupid.'

'Who killed him?'

'People.'

'Who?'

'Wasn't taking no names.'

'See, what you're telling me is worth something, Roychelle, but not a thousand.'

She shrugged. 'All I got.'

Keneesha came back in again, still chewing meditatively

on her gum. Her face was shining and bright, beads of water un-toweled on her neck.

'Hey, nurse.'

'Hey.'

'I bet you like mermaids too.'

'Sometimes.'

'But I think you really like ponies, right?'

'Uh-huh.'

'Your mama says she going to get you some pony stuff to play with, that right?'

'That right, honey.'

'Soon as she gets done talking to me here.'

Roychelle looked at Ea$y. He licked his teeth and rolled his shoulders slightly.

'You go on now.'

Keneesha went back outside to play and the quartet was left in silence. It was the quiet happens when a child leaves, the retreat of innocence and the irrevocable reminder of pasts gone, never to return.

'It don't matter none,' Roychelle said, eventually. 'He dead.'

'What was it?' said Cowan, eager. 'What didn't you tell the police last spring?'

Roychelle began working her palms into her eyes. She looked at the packet on the table for a long time. Her eyes were red where she had rubbed. 'I need to think on it.'

'I don't have time for that,' Cowan said. 'It's now or never, like the King said.'

'Thousand?'

'Uh-huh.'

Ea$y turned to Deyon. 'He shittin' us?'

'Is good.''

'This one time Carlton was supposed to go with me to the movies or whatever, but he loafed. Supposed to meet me at 2.00 and left me ass'd out. This was maybe a day after that girl got herself shot? I woulda kirked on him, I seen him that day. So I go looking for him. Thinkin' 'bout this other girl, Tia. She work at Deedee Kutz. She's a sack chaser. Got extensions make her look like a horse 'cept she look like a horse before the extensions, know what I'm saying? I mean that girl shit ugly.'

'That girl so ugly,' said Ea$y, giggling, 'she look like her face caught on fire and they put it out with a track cleat.'

'She's so ugly people go as her for Halloween,' said Roychelle, wryly.

Ea$y was giggling now. Cowan stared at him till he got through with it.

'So you went looking?'

'So I come back and see him over Alabama in a car. I think he's with Deedee the Geegee so I start slamming on the window, see? I was bugging see? But he's with this lightskin bruh. Talking. This other one faking like he's a gangsta. But he's not.'

'What makes you say that?'

'Hit the window and soon as I start in on him, screaming at his ass, he out the car and yelling and that

Mack Daddy was ghost. I mean he dive out of there like he don't want nobody seeing, but his shirt is fine, his watch is real fine. He so fine. When I see that face, I was, guh. I know it then. I know he's the one pays Carlton for those trips and shit.'

'You got a name?'

'I ain't know him.'

'What he look like?'

She shrugged. 'He just lightskin. Look like anybody. Anybody lightskin.'

'And you think he was mixed up with Carlton in this other stuff he did?'

'Hell, yeah! Carlton afraid after that day. He all nervous and shit. See his own shadow and jump like a frog on a spring. Something not right. I see he scared of that bougie. And Carlton ain't afraid of no one. The world shit scared of Carlton.'

'Anything else?' Cowan held his forefinger and thumb very close together. 'You're this close to a thousand bucks, Roychelle.'

'Had a phone. Not his regular, but a ji special one. Kept it in a drawer. Only took calls on it for 'business'. He'd get a call, he'd leave, come back, then be gone three days. So, he'd get a call on that phone, he'd leave, he's dead. But the police never give it back to me. See, that phone be long gone, or whatever. He left with it but it didn't come back, know what I'm sayin'? I get his wallet. Five hundred in it. You telling me that gang-related?

No-one taking that? When they say no phone, I was blown. Cheap ass track phone it was. Somebody take it. But I don't say nuthin'.'

'No name?'

'Naw. He answer that phone, Carlton say he got a call from royalty and laugh his ass off. I tell him royalty needed to come up with 500 by next Tuesday for the rent. This cost me nine hundred a month.'

'Royalty? That's all he says?'

'Yeah. When Carlton get that call, he in the money. So he call that the Royalty call. I know nothin' else.'

'You done good, Roychelle.' Cowan pointed at the envelope. 'That's a sizeable chunk of my pathetic polis retirement you're looking at there. I'm a man is going to end his days in rags waving a tin can on Sauchiehall Street. Anyone besides Carlton ever go on these paid trips?'

'Maybe somebody in that crew do some stuff. Yeah. I'mma give no names.'

'We cut it now?' asked Ea$y.

'What does Sleazy Dogg here get?' Cowan asked

'For bringing us together?' Deyon shrugged. 'Half.'

'Fuck that. He's just a matchmaker. He's like the old guy with the dentures on Eharmony.com. Give him 100 commission.'

Ea$y looked outraged. 'This man's time is valuable, motherfucker.'

'Five hundred dollars an hour? Who do you think you are? A fucking lawyer?'

Ea$y sneered at him. 'Why you do me that way?'

'Maybe I just don't like your face?'

Keneesha stood on the brick walkway outside, holding a jump rope. She stopped skipping to wave at the departing men.

'I suppose she can pay a month's rent with what I gave her. But what after that?' Cowan looked at the little girl in white ribbons 'What happens to her down the road?'

'They go back where they came from,' Deyon said. 'Slip down the chute. They can't live here long term. Can't sustain it. They're project bound.'

'Fuck. It's all so sad, D. That lovely wee girl doesn't have a snowball's chance in hell.' Ea$y was pawing at the back door handle. 'Where you think you're going?'

'I'm getting a ride someplace.'

Cowan looked at Deyon and shook his head. He got in the car.

'I can't give you a ride, young,' Deyon said, shrugging. 'Try Uber or you short.'

'Try Uber? Huh? What the fuck, mo?'

Cowan wound down his window. 'Listen up. I hear you ask that woman for more money, I'll come find you where you at and fuck you up. Hear me Norman? I'll staple your scrotum to a ceiling fan. With you still attached. That there's a promise.'

'Y'all ain't shit.'

'No, but you are.'

Ea$y watched them drive away, working his mouth furiously.

'Home, Jeeves.' Cowan said. 'To the Regency.'

'We done with all this for now?'

'You have class tomorrow?'

'Only in the morning.' Having foolishly admitted this, Deyon at once looked very regretful and nervous. He'd messed up. More would be asked of him.

'Fancy a road trip in the afternoon? We can pack a picnic?'

'What you mean is, you want the use of my sorry-ass car.'

'And the pleasure of your charming companionship.'

'Will no one rid me of this turbulent policeman?' Deyon muttered at the air bag.

'They're trying hard enough on your behalf, son,' Cowan said. 'They've been giving it their best shot, except it wasn't. Their best shot, I mean.'

'What did you learn from this today?' Deyon asked, looking at him. 'Anything?'

'I've got solid confirmation that Catriona was never killed during any damn robbery gone wrong. That's fucking obvious. This Carlton was just a convenient tool, or smoke-screen. Someone else wanted my daughter dead and I got to find that Barnham girl pronto because she's the one knows why.'

7.30pm. Cowan shaved carefully. His left eye was partially closed and there was the faint indentation of a tooth on his jaw. That would take some explaining. He put on jeans and a green jumper. The jumper was supposed to complement his eyes but only seemed to accentuate the bruising. He tried a red one, which did complement his eyes. He rested his forehead on the cold streaked glass.

There was a row of wet cabs on New Jersey Avenue, a street running with umbrellas. The Capitol was not yet lit, the clouds above the dome a warped purple. How much time he was wasting in his life! Had it been a life even? He dialed her number. 'How'd church go?'

'It went good.'

'It's such a long running show, I'm surprised there's still an audience.' Saying this, Cowan wondered again at his malevolent heart. As if talking to her about faith wasn't already like walking through a minefield. 'Can I have my five minutes?' He thought he heard her soft breathing, but it could have been his own. 'You promised.' The hotel room remained stark and empty and hushed till an ambulance blared by. By the time it dopplered to silence he was pleading. 'Please.'

'I'll stop by,' she said, decades later. 'In an hour. Five minutes is all, though.'

'I'm in 323.' Silence. 'It's on the third floor,' he clarified, redundantly. He stared at his phone, stupid plastic on the screen creased and pockmarked. He hated it, always with him, demanding, needy; the thing would not permit his solitude.

The green jumper was back on. Go trumped stop. Lit by only the light from the bathroom he might pass for normal, a low-key guy. A film noir detective would be waiting for the femme fatale to return and betray him again. But a noir detective always knew things. Secrets. Cowan knew sweet fuck all. Doyle was well out of the loop, a mere nobody. Erin was a liar. But why had the little whore given him Doyle's address? Cowan had underestimated that one. She'd played him like a grand piano, a tough, smart little cookie. The key to everything was still the missing Mary Barnham. Cowan should have been looking more seriously for her all this time. He'd been distracted, wasting precious hours pining for a lost and broken angel who fucked him into daft dreams of some impossible tomorrows. Now he was getting another five minutes from her, time enough for an awkward goodbye. Last night was her mistake.

Waiting, he found a Gideon Bible in the drawer. Cowan opened it to the page marked by the last reader, presumably a depressed salesman:

Oh, that I were as in months past, as in the days when God preserved me; When his candle shined upon my head, and when by his light I walked through darkness; As I was in the days of my youth, when the secret of God was upon my tabernacle; When the Almighty was yet with me, when my children were about me; When I washed my steps with butter, and the rock poured me out rivers of oil. When my children were about me.

Why would a man ever want to wash his steps with butter, though? The personal injury lawyers would be all over that. Cowan read on, one eye on the clock. It was always nice to consider someone had it worse than you.

'What have you done to yourself?'

He had her pinned against the wall like a butterfly, his hands lifting up her dress. She wanted to be that accessible. He bunched the fabric up high on her thighs. Plays Well With Others In Poppy. Small lines flowered in the corner of her eyes and she looked as desperate as he and so gorgeous in her wanting. He'd so wanted that wanting. They didn't even make it into the room proper. He groped for the chain on the door. Hooked it.

'I did it shaving. My hand slipped.'

Her fingers fumbled at his crotch and he heard the zip purr down.

'But you've a black eye.'

'What makes you think it's mine?'

'Did someone hit you?'

'No.' His hands cupped her ass and he felt the cool of her skin on his wrists. 'I'm just totally inept with a razor. You should see the state of my legs.'

She contrived somehow to cause his pants to drop around his ankles. He clawed at her, tearing the panties to shreds. He heard her sigh, hearing the rip of silk. That sigh wasn't doing him any good either.

'You can reimburse me for those later,' she said, 'from your expenses.'

'Shouldn't we be engaged in extended and creative foreplay,' Cowan gasped at her. 'Like how *Cosmo* used to recommend?'

'Definitely,' she whimpered.

'I hear the female orgasm is very complicated,' he told her.

'True,' she said. 'True.'

'Like trying to solve Fermat's Last Theorem while riding a unicycle.'

'With a wombat balanced on your head. I'll give you a guided tour of my G spot later.' This, in that throaty whisper did weird things to his spine. 'If you're real good.'

'Oh, I'm never good.'

'Oh, it's good you're never good.'

He watched red slip over white in her mouth. The way her lipstick stuck to her teeth made Cowan feel as if he was losing his mind. 'Help me,' he said, sounding sad and desperate and broken. It wasn't what he had meant to say at all.

Afterwards, Kris cried. By then, the pair of them had somehow stumbled to the bed from the floor. He'd held her close and, after an hour, the sobbing ceased racking her. She asked him to make love to her, this time tender and gentle. He had, and it had been just that, a lovemaking, not the wild demented craving of before, and different, and this had complicated things for him too. Now he lay tangled with her, his limbs confused in hers again, his body drenched in her sweat and tears, for she was weeping again.

'You're not happy right now,' Cowan explained, his hand lifting her hair away from her cheek. 'And we have this weird connection. I can't explain it either. It's not normal. I understand why you want to run away. I would, from me.'

'I must be evil.'

'No. Don't say that.'

'I went to church. I sat there.'

'You're not evil,' he told her.

'I get so excited,' she sobbed, 'by how much you want me. No one has wanted me like that. Your need is awful. What I want is your wanting me. And it's too much.'

Cowan traced the curve of her lip with his thumb, trying to imagine how any living creature could ever want her any less than he did.

'Was that us?' she asked. 'Against the wall? Or in the bed? Which is us?'

'There's two sides to us, and they're both good.' He cradled her head between his hands. 'There's the animal thing, and there's this right now, here, which is good too.' Cowan contemplated the fact that he had no idea what he was talking about.

'I don't know what to do,' Kris said, pummelling his chest.

He caught her wrists. 'Quit it.' She flailed, trying to break free. He drew her closer. 'You need to break up with this guy. Look at me.' Her eyes were just glistening pools in the dark. 'You'd be doing him a favour.'

'I already did it,' she said, drawing her arm across her face.

'Did what?'

'Texted him last night. Said I needed space.'

'You texted him.' Cowan's heart was in his throat. 'That was cold.'

'Was it?' Kris covered her mouth with her hand. 'I'll see him at church.'

Then they were kissing desperately again, her tongue a wild questing thing. She had a grip on his arm like it was the oar of a sinking boat. She pushed him away. 'We can't keep doing this. It's wrong. This is not me. This person you see is not me.'

'It is,' he pleaded.

'I'm an obsession for you. I think you're grieving still and looking for something, and I don't know what it is, and I'm caught up in your thing. And I'm messed up myself. You went searching for someone as screwed up as yourself and you found me...'

'None of that is true.' Cowan wondered at his callous lie. 'I want to understand how you came to be who you are. When we make love it's like I can't get deep enough inside you. I keep trying and can't. I've never felt that.'

'You make me another mystery to solve,' she said. 'It's not fair.'

'No,' he said, stunned once again by her insight.

'I'm such a hot mess. I told you. You need to get the hell away from me.'

They lay still. Her heart thrashed against his chest. After a while the beat settled. She propped herself on an elbow. 'You're tousled as a lamb's tail,' she said, touching his hair. 'I get you all tousled.'

'Yes,' he said.

She lifted his face towards her. 'Someone hit you. Don't ever lie to me again.'

'I won't.' After a few minutes of quiet, Cowan got up, retrieved his wallet from the side-table and took out the photograph of his daughter from three years before, her first year at the Uni. He showed it to Kris. 'That's her,' he said. 'There's the reason I'm here, the reason for all this.'

Kris examined the image. 'She looked different when she was younger.'

Cowan was confused by the remark. 'Who did?'

'Mary.'

'That's not a photo of Mary,' Cowan explained. 'That's my daughter.'

'Oh, my god,' Kris said, looking stricken. 'I'm so sorry.'

Cowan was plunged deep in thought now, though. 'No, this journalist I met with yesterday told me how the two of them looked like twins when they were out on the town. I guess he was right.'

'There is some resemblance, but I was just assuming when you…'

Cowan dropped his wallet on the carpet and stared fixedly at Lincoln on the wall. Honest Abe would have figured it out days ago. So might his beard. 'I've been wearing a fucking blindfold all this time,' Cowan muttered, mechanically. 'I've been so stupid.'

Seeing his expression, Kris was concerned. 'Are you alright? What's the matter?'

'Sometimes you get so focused on details that you can't see what's right in front of you, you know? Or you don't want to see it. They were about the same height, same build.

Both were blonde. Mary must have smoked sometimes too, right?'

'Yes. Mary did smoke.' Kris nodded at him. 'I saw her out on the fire escape. She wouldn't do it in the apartment. Tal wouldn't like her doing that inside.'

'Virginia Slims?'

'I think so.'

'You ever see Mary wearing a tan trench coat?'

'Yes. I remember that. It was a Burberry type thing. A lovely coat that. Why?'

Cowan enfolded her back into his arms and kissed her tenderly. 'You might indeed be a terrible mystery, lady, but you've helped me out with my own.'

In the yellow glow of the lights from the awning they kissed madly, rain falling in blue ropes around them. The cab driver and doorman turned away, embarrassed.

'You going or not?' asked the driver, eventually. 'Y'all got specific plans? Cause I was planning to get home by the Skins game next week.'

'One minute.'

'I'm tryin'.'

Kris cracked her head getting in the cab, and rubbed at her scalp. His heart jumped in his throat for already he could not bear to see her hurt. The cab door clicked shut before he could say all he wanted. She smiled weakly at him through the window, her eyes looking like they were trying to see beyond an imaginary horizon. The bruise-blue street was shining with rain. The taxi disappeared on E Street in a slish of tires. Torrents gushed from gutters. She vanished. A petrol spill rainbowed down a drain. She was gone. Did she even exist now? Cowan opened his wallet and took out a dollar.

'She's fine,' the doorman declared, watching him closely. 'You know her a long time or just getting acquainted?'

Cowan opened his wallet and took out two dollars. 'Yes.'

'She hit herself on the head?'

'Yes.'

'Got to be careful getting in the cabs.' The doorman had a whistle round his neck and a big nose, like Jimmy Durante. 'She's aiiight?'

'I don't know. Probably not.'

'Take it light, hear? You done won the lottery.'

10pm. On the mezzanine, the tree shone with snakes of silver tinsel and green and blue ornaments, red striped candy canes slung precariously from branches. Two men in grey suits stood next to the tree. 'Rain's sure coming down tonight,' Devlin Reem announced, presenting him with a big mouthful of capped teeth.

'I've never seen it going up,' Cowan told him. 'Did the other wise man have to go to the lavvy then?'

'What I say?' Reem asked his companion, shrugging. 'All the fucking time.'

'Or are you folks the shepherds, maybe?' Cowan winked at Haley Factor. 'I know I've seen you hanging around the sheep looking mighty interested, mister.'

On this occasion the Senator looked professionally laundered, steel grey hair swept into a pompadour. His complexion was ruddy, a faint wickerwork of broken veins across his nose. Under his suit pants, he wore black cowboy boots with pointed toes curled up like elf shoes. When he spoke, his voice was hoarse, like he was getting over laryngitis. 'Mr Cowan, as you see I am tonight not in my most comfortable attire…'

'I've seen you in suits in photo ops often enough. You're a man who never met a camera he didn't like. Especially if there's a firefighter in the vicinity.'

A red butterfly shape was forming over Factor's nose and cheeks. It could have been rosacea. It could have been massive annoyance.

'Can the Senator have a minute of your precious time?' Reem inquired.

'Over there,' Cowan said, nodding to the leather sofas near the bar. 'But I'm going nowhere else with you. I'm staying alive. Like the Bee Gees.'

'Fine,' Reem said. 'Senator?'

'We could do that.' Factor was studying Cowan, and not in a friendly way.

The American Medical Association was the latest visiting conference and over by the hotel bar were many small, ruthless looking men making very precise movements with their hands as they picked up their glass stems.

'So many folks in here, you could stir 'em with a stick,' Factor offered, his accent molasses smooth. He coughed into his hand. 'I apologise, since I got back, the allergies are kicking in. I do believe I'm fixing to get sick.'

'Nothing trivial, I hope.'

'It's the corruption of this place I'm allergic to,' Factor said, choosing to ignore Cowan's dig. 'This Gotham of the South.'

'I suppose that must make you the Joker then, Senator, right?'

'I was visiting with a friend of mine earlier today,' Reem interrupted, smiling at Cowan. 'He's in hospital, you see. Had an accident.'

'I'm sorry to hear that,' Cowan said. 'I hope he has good insurance.'

'Previous administrations were invested very much in the issue of heath care,' Factor declaimed, deeply gloomy. 'Great believers in universal coverage and damn the expense and the waste. Untenable of course, with the deficits.'

Reem was still regarding Cowan with wry amuse-ment. Eyes clear as ice. The eyelids drooped a little, so he looked sleepy and icy at the same time, a mixing somehow redolent of death. There was a wire-thin scar beneath his left eye. Prominent cheekbones over hollows, nose bladelike, strong chin, powerful torso. His ears were long and meaty and his face expressive as a clock with no hands. He was the embodiment of cool. Here was a man who wouldn't think of peeing even if his pants were on fire.

'Between you and me,' Factor said, more jocularly. 'Our young hospitalised friend couldn't pour piss out a boot if the instructions were on the heel. Blow on the head is the best thing could have happened to him. Might wake him up a little.'

'Craig is not pursuing charges,' Reem added. 'He's decided against it. I put in a word for you, Cowan, said you might have been dropped on your head as a baby. That would explain a lot. Craig did however indicate that you and he had a conversation.'

'Mr Cowan,' Factor interrupted. 'Can I call you Charles?'

'No,' said Cowan. 'You can call me Ishmael but.'

Factor smiled wanly, a blowtorch lit but not yet shooting flame. 'I'll tell you what's what. I've come tonight to offer you my assistance. We'd like to get this all straightened out and put to bed right quick. In this regard I am flexible as a warm tub of water.'

'That's nice, in that regard.'

Factor turned towards Reem. 'Devlin? You want to…'

'We feel,' said Reem, choosing his words with care now, 'that this whole informal investigation of yours is getting way out of hand.'

'I agree,' said Cowan. 'That it? Anything else you have to say or are we done here? There's this thrilling ice hockey game on the box later: Penguins versus Walruses.'

'Your inquiries about Miss Barnham and her whereabouts…' Reem began.

'Now, that name rings a bell,' said Cowan, leaning back

and feigning a deep bemusement. 'Like Quasimodo, you know.'

Reem's jaw clenched slightly, his patience being sorely tried.

'Mr Cowan,' Factor said, clasping his fingers solemnly. 'It concerns me very much that you may have been hoodwinked by what I can only label as darker forces. Let me tell you a minute about our friend the Congressman, for I have known that distinguished gentleman since back when snakes used to walk.'

'Those same days when Moby Dick was a minnow?'

'A long time, Mr Cowan. I was on the Ellis campaign thirty years ago. I was just a young pup, wet behind the ears. We lost that election. You hear about that? How badly that campaign got sabotaged? That's not going to happen to me. No way. No siree.'

Cowan was squinting obliquely at the bridge of Factor's nose. 'You called Griffith a cracker barrel aphorist, mind? But tell me, what exactly does that make you?'

Factor's eyes were hard and bright without any depth to them. He stared at the carpet as if trying to recall something of which it vaguely reminded him. 'You think you're slicker than owl shit, don't you?' he offered, eventually. The Senator had all along been seething like Krakatoa. It was the Cowan effect.

'Haley,' said Reem, resting a hand on the Senator's arm, patting gently, as if placating a tantrum-prone toddler.

Factor shook the hand away. 'I've enjoyed just about all of this I can stand.'

'You two are losing your routine. It was going so well, too.' Cowan was laughing now. 'Foghorn Leghorn here is supposed to be the silk and you're the steel, wee man. I've seen good cop, bad cop before. Practically invented it one day in Pollokshields, on my lunch break it was. I'm a past master. Now you're getting to acting like fucking Florence Nightingale and he's becoming the Tasmanian Devil. It won't do.'

Factor made as if to stand up and Reem eased him back down on the sofa. 'What can we do to help you here?' Reem asked Cowan. 'Serious offer we're making. You can act cooler than the other side of the pillow all you like but…'

'What are you going to be when you grow up, Devlin?' Cowan asked. 'You're not interested in helping at all. You're interested in knowing.'

'You're being a tad melodramatic here, Cowan.'

'How's this for melodrama?' Cowan said. 'I thought my daughter met with you lot on April 3rd. I was wrong. It was Mary met with you March 4th. All my daughter ever did wrong was wear Mary's coat the night she died. And what was in the pocket of that coat was Mary's too. She'd jotted your number down in a hurry, scrawled it, and I didn't even think to compare the handwriting. The folks knocked her off were genuine fuck ups. See, they followed her to the Metro all the way from the apartment in Alexandria that night thinking she was Mary. You know that apartment, don't you, Haley? You visited once I hear. Afternoon showers that day in May. I looked it up. Mary must have let my daughter borrow her coat. Rank amateurs those boys were. Small wonder Mary did a bunk after. She realised they were gunning for her. It wasn't a robbery. They were trying to kill her. They were just inept. Those incompetent bastards killed the wrong woman.'

Blood had darkened the Senator's face to the colour of beef liver.

'Did Mary bring up Tubalcain that day in the office? Gil Martin? Is that it? Did she cross a line? Did she dig too deep? You two fuckwads are accessories to murder. I do believe a current employee of yours took a shot at me the other day too, Haley. Credit where credit's due, at least he was shooting at the right person this time. He still missed. Maybe Craig can take him out to the range when he gets out the infirmary? Work on his aim?' Cowan extended a finger at the tip of Factor's nose. 'I'm coming after you, dickweed. I'll bring the walls crashing down around you like Samson at Gaza that time.'

Factor's tongue fell out as if to receive a coin. 'You really don't know shit from shinola, mister,' he muttered.

Cowan stood up. 'Are we done now? I scheduled an enema for later tonight and I'm really looking forward to it. I'm sure it'll be more fun than this, at any rate.'

'Might I suggest,' said Reem, speaking very quietly, 'that it is not your own safety you should be concerned about?'

'Excuse me?'

Reem sat motionless. 'When a person digs around blindly in things they don't understand, it's those around them who suffer, in my experience: the bystanders.'

Cowan sat back down. 'What the fuck is that supposed to mean?'

'I'd be concerned about, let's say, that woman you were with outside the hotel.'

The blood ran cold and lumpy in Cowan's veins. 'If you even think…'

'Attractive woman that,' Factor said to Reem, nudging him.

'Most definitely. Don't know what she sees in this one, though.'

'Well, I'm not a hostile midget, for one thing.'

Reem laughed loudly. 'You should have been a comedian, Cowan. That was your true vocation, no? You missed your calling.'

'You're the one keeps asking the funny questions, Devlin. What was your calling then? Being thrown at a dartboard by Snow White?'

'All I'm saying is, don't let your mouth write a cheque your ass can't cash.'

Factor stood up abruptly, brushing his hands down his pants. 'That woman of his got eyes bluer than a cross-eyed carpenter's thumb,' he said, bending to Cowan's ear. 'How's that for a cracker barrel aphorism, Charles?'

'You take care now, Cowan,' said Reem, standing too. 'Every story can still have a happy ending – if you play your cards right.'

Cowan sat for a while where they left him, his arms dangling down like useless pendula. He very much wanted a drink. By a series of very deliberate acts of will, he reassembled himself.

Cowan called Kris from his room and tried to explain everything, from the very beginning. Why he was so afraid for her. How someone had tried to kill him. It was difficult to get through to her, though. Kris refused to be afraid of anything in this world. She was like his daughter that way. Catriona had liked it when no one in the world could see her, or know about her, and all was secret and safe. 'You mean it's all a big conspiracy?' Kris sounded more amused than frightened. 'Trilateral Commission? Rockefellers?'

'Please. Take me seriously for a minute. Sometimes, I think I'm going mad here, making connections where there are none.'

'You're quite sure these men weren't, in fact, alien lizards?'

'Well, I wouldn't be surprised if they were. I did accuse them of being accessories to murder. They didn't like that one bit. They were positively peeved. But they're the type who willingly dispense with the luxury of morality. It's an inconvenience to a political career.'

'Accessories to murder? You can't be serious?'

'Maybe I am. Aren't we all accessories to murder, one way or the other? Sufficient unto the day is the evil thereof. You must know that one? It's a classic.'

Kris didn't say anything for some time. 'Why does darkness fascinate you so much?' she ventured, eventually.

'Because I see it everywhere around me,' he told her.

'And most other people wander through their lives trying to ignore it. And if they can, good luck to them.'

'Is it there?'

'It's there.'

'But what if you brought it here with you? What if it's all you?'

Kris had just articulated his worst fear to him: the suggestion that all he ever did was plumb his own depths and explore the darkness of a deeper fathomless well.

'Well, then I'd still have to deal with it, wouldn't I?'

'Yes,' she said, but this very quietly.

Cowan wanted very much to say Lux e tenebris to her, but decided not to. Instead, he lifted his hand to his nose and inhaled her lingering scent. In bed, he could never tell where the odours of her body began and his ended, all essences mixed, sweat and essential oils merged pooling, dripping on sheets. He felt again the thrill of her legs tight around him, and was at once aroused. He found himself telling her he loved her.

Kris didn't say anything in response to his blurt. She changed the subject. She said she'd talked to Tal Gorham on the phone earlier and he'd agreed, albeit reluctantly, to meet with Cowan in Alexandria. She'd introduce them. It had to be tomorrow, though.

'I'm heartily sick of Alexandria.'

'It's only for a half hour. That's all the time he's got. I'll have to drive you there before I go to work in the morning. It'll be an early start.'

'No one in this moronic city has time for anything. You don't have to come with me. I want you to be careful. I want you to stay out of this as much as possible.'

Kris told him there was nothing for her to be careful about and that in her life she always had someone to look after her. Cowan had no smart answer to that. He wanted to say that for him, the message of Christianity was that if you don't love you're dead, and if you do, they'll kill you. But he didn't say anything. He'd stopped talking to God in recent days, was well done with it.

There was now just the silence of a void.

9   MONDAY (MORNING)

Kris dropped him off on the corner of North Fairfax, having arranged everything. Cowan's meeting with H Tal Gorham was at 9.30am. With an hour to kill, he sauntered down to the Torpedo Factory. The sun was trying and failing to gouge out a break in the grey and a pearl-white fog had settled on the Potomac. A tourist-bloated water taxi cast off from the city marina to make its way across the river and the word shibboleth popped in his head like a grenade. It was his belief that the word meant the crossing of a river. Why Cowan believed this, he didn't know. Probably the same reason he believed anything, probably justification by faith alone.

There was a boxwood wreath with a looped red ribbon hung on the door of the Gorham building and under it was pinned an envelope addressed to him. Nothing was bloody easy. He ripped the envelope open and found a sheet of paper with the address of a local coffee house and an instruction to remove the battery of his cellphone. He was to put the battery in his left trouser pocket and the phone in his right. Cowan did what he was told, having decided in advance to play along with whatever floated the old weirdo's boat. There was also a small printed Google map with the precise walking route he was to follow traced by a blue line. Cowan's impulse was to ignore this and make his own way to the bizarre rendezvous. He then reconsidered. Better to be safe than sorry perhaps, given his recent near-death experience in this nightmare of a town. He duly followed Gorham's map, walking down South Royal, taking the requested route along Prince, and then another right on North Patrick. In this way he completed the square.

Large, open-squared arches connected the three rooms of the coffee house and wide-paned westerly-facing windows overlooked the street. The long serving counter in the central room was staffed by the usual array of tattooed, pierced and ponytailed hipsters. There was a community table in the second room. Cowan assumed that Gorham wasn't the community table type. He wasn't a socialist drinker. The third room featured a number of small tables. Gorham was seated at the furthest from the door, which gave him a sight line that ran the full length of the cafe. He sat there very still, ramrod straight. It was like he'd just got back from the taxidermist. Gorham was in his 60s, silver-haired, with a tall, immovable forehead, expressionless eyes and a trimmed and waxed moustache. His suit looked spanking new, charcoal gray wool, the black shoes exotic, like postmodern winkle-pickers. Gorham was lean and cold with a practiced attentiveness and, God, was his hair perfect. Before Cowan could say a word, Gorham held out his open palm. Cowan handed over the phone battery. Gorham motioned now for the phone and proceeded to balance his own phone on top of it. He examined his screen as though taking a reading. In this way, the weirdo boat floating was to continue.

'I don't want to ask why all this is necessary, do I?' Cowan asked.

Gorham said nothing then handed Cowan's phone back to him, seemingly satisfied. The roaster fired up, churning a batch of beans, a whining background grind.

'You should go get something from the counter,' Gorham said, eventually.

'I'm fine,' Cowan said.

'No,' Gorham told him, earnestly. 'You must.'

So, now he'd arranged to liaise with an actual legitimate madman. Cowan definitely knew how to pick them. Five minutes later, he was back at the table with a decaf cappuccino and biscotti. He was self-conscious about dipping the biscotti in front of Gorham, so he snapped it in half and tried to bite the end of the thing. It was hard as a brick and his molars started screaming.

'I was told you had some questions for me.'

'Yes.'

Gorham sipped at his skinny latte in genteel fashion, with pinky elevated. 'I will stay 20 minutes,' he announced. 'After that, I will leave. You will leave too, five minutes after my own departure, inverting the route you came by. You will take a taxi from outside City Hall when you return to DC. You will avoid the Metro and speak to no one. This will be the only time you and I ever meet.' Gorham had another discreet sip and sat back rigid as a Madame Tussaud's waxwork.

'And after this conversation is over, it will never have occurred. Do you understand me?'

'Were you a schoolmaster once upon a time?'

'Do you understand my instructions?'

'Yes.'

The ceiling of the coffee house was high with criss-crossing beams and the acoustics were clattery, so it would have helped to raise their voices as they talked. But Gorham wasn't into raising his voice. Cowan was forced to lean in. The slatted table between them was oval and green and made him think of cartoon planets.

'You knew Mary well?'

'Quite well.'

'You knew Mary from before she rented the apartment from you?'

'Yes.'

Cowan wanted to inquire about the nature of that earlier relationship, how the two of them had first met, become acquainted. Had it to do with the newspaper or the politics? Did they perhaps share an interest in antiquing or pederasty? But he was rationing his queries today. He only had the twenty minutes. 'Did you know my daughter?'

'No.'

'Ever meet her?'

'No.'

A barista hoisted a fibrous cargo bag of beans nearby and Gorham studied him closely. The barista had a man bun and a do-rag, which seemed like serious overkill.

'Are you ever going to move beyond the monosyllabic here, Mr Gorham?' Cowan asked, annoyed. 'This is like talking to one of them phone banks when you're trying to make sense of the gigantic electric bill.'

Gorham didn't respond at all, sipping decorously, so demonstrating that he could move beyond the one-word answer after all, that in fact his default position was silence.

'You knew what Mary was writing about?'

'She touched on it.'

'You strike me as a man who's been around a bit. If you don't mind me saying.'

'Was that a question, Mr Cowan?'

Cowan plunged his half-biscotti deep into the froth, submarining the thing angrily, to hell with manners. 'So, it's my understanding that Mary was writing a book about Tubalcain Industries, formerly Wringhim.'

'Is that so?'

Cowan decided to try another tack. This was like interrogating his voicemail. 'What would your personal understanding of Tubalcain be?' Gorham elevated a solitary eyebrow, with difficulty. 'I'm curious as to what you might have read about them, say, or heard on the political grapevine. You know? General knowledge.'

'General knowledge.'

'That's right. He's a military man, General Knowledge, went to West Point and everything. May have served in Afghanistan and Iraq, if you get my drift.'

'I believe I heard that the company provides security services.'

'What does that mean? In layman's terms?'

'You think I'm a layman, Mr Cowan?' Gorham daintily dropped a sliver of croissant in his mouth and chewed meditatively. He swallowed. 'I think not.'

'How's about you imagine for the next minute that you're talking to a total simpleton then,' Cowan suggested. 'It can't be that hard.'

'No.' Gorham didn't come close to cracking a smile, but small teeth bared in his tight slit of a mouth. 'I do believe Tubalcain hire out what are known in the trade as proactive engagement teams. A layman, I suppose, might call such people mercenaries.'

'That's what I heard, too. We must have been listening to the same NPR podcast. And the US government would have got involved in the mercenary business how?'

Gorham sighed profoundly, realising that a longer explanation was required of him. It might even necessitate formulation of complete sentences. 'Some years ago,' he began, 'the CIA decided to get out of the assassination business. So they privatized it: outsourced the jobs as black budget contracts. Consequently, CIA officers no longer had to participate in the most violent of our operations, or even witness them. Don't get me wrong, our security services can still have our enemies abducted or killed, I'm sure. It's a sad necessity in an era of asymmetric warfare. But now no one employed in those agencies would be responsible for such actions, necessarily, or provide oversight. See no evil, as it were.'

'That sounds cold.'

'Contractors are not subject to the same checks and balances as the military chain of command. That has its advantages, and, perhaps, drawbacks.'

'So the US government hires out murder and mayhem and so on to private enterprise? Aye, what the hell could possibly go wrong with that?'

Gorham shrugged. 'It saves a fortune in pensions. We outsource everything else now. Even the phone banks where you query your huge electricity bill, Mr Cowan.'

'Aye, you end up in Bombay on the horn talking to Vikram about your kilowatt hours. It's a fucking nightmare.'

'Mumbai,' Gorham corrected, cheerlessly. The man smiled as much as Lou Reed. 'But in truth it doesn't matter who holds the contract, for it's the same people, after all.'

'How do you mean?'

'Tubalcain, to take your example, would have a revolving door policy with the CIA. The agency will 'sheep dip' their active operators or, alternatively, activate 'green badgers', or cleared agency contractors, for the CIA Special Activities Division.'

'You just totally lost me with your riff on the sheep and badgers there.'

'Same people in, same people out. It's a revolving door of sorts, a rose by any other name.' Gorham tore off a segment of croissant and regarded the oozing jelly with suspicion.

'The Tubalcain board will have any number of former members of the CIA's Counterterrorist Centre.'

'So, the government wouldn't care to know too much about what they get up to?'

'I'd say our government has a love-hate relationship with such entities.' Gorham almost discovered a smile. 'On the one hand, they're reliant on them to outsource political risk and, on the other, eager to slap them in public whenever scandal happens.'

'And when scandal happens?'

'You throw someone under the bus and rename the company. Rebrand and move on. It is the millennial way.'

'And good for everybody except for the body gets flattened by the bus, eh?'

'Eight more minutes, Mr Cowan,' Gorham declared, glancing down at his phone.

'Mary was especially interested in corruption wasn't she? That was her thing?'

Gorham arranged stray crumbs around his plate with the tip of his finger. 'How I'd put it, is that Miss Barnham was a strong and impressive young woman, with passion and a good heart, who happened to want more than anything, to know how to distinguish between, say, the facilitation of large scale stability operations and,' Gorham hesitated a moment, decided to let the diplomacy drop for once, 'stone-cold murder.'

Cowan inhaled his cappuccino. It wasn't half bad even minus the caffeine rush. 'Before Mary vanished like the Cheshire Cat, what was it she was looking into?'

Gorham was, if anything, even more waxwork impassive now, choosing his words as delicately as he ate. 'I don't think it would be in your best interests to know that, Mr Cowan. It might even be deleterious to your long-term health.'

'Oh, I'm with the National Health Service, remember? My long-term health is already well screwed. Plus, they're trying to kill me.'

'The National Health Service?'

'Aye, them and Tubalcain.'

'Tubalcain?' Gorham elevated both eyebrows, a new look for him, like that on a plastic inflatable clown. It was like he'd underlined his head. His forehead didn't crease at all. It had been possible for Cowan to surprise the old codger though. That was progress.

'I think that crew makes Blackwater look like Poland Spring.'

Gorham teetered on the brink of a smirk. 'They're trying to kill you? Oh, that's rich! You're the Man Who Knew Too Much. How very Hitchcockian of you, Mr Cowan.'

'Let's just say that given the massive number of psychos living in these parts I won't be getting myself anywhere near a crop-duster plane anytime soon.' Cowan considered this for a second. 'Or hopping in the shower in my hotel.'

'You've been stumbling blindly into things you'll never understand. It's too bad.' Gorham shook his head. 'You have froth on the tip of your nose, incidentally.'

Cowan wiped his nose on his sleeve causing Gorham to

look distressed. 'I suppose that explains all the envelopes and maps and phone battery rigmarole?'

'Silly, I know, but it's too easy to eavesdrop these days. We live today in a surveillance society.'

'It's too easy to get paranoid as well.' Cowan thought hard about how best to phrase the next question. 'How's about, hypothetically, you speculate about what Mary might have been looking into, specifically, in the weeks before my daughter's murder.'

Gorham sighed cavernously. 'I want to take this opportunity, just so we're quite clear, to remind you that this conversation is not currently taking place.'

'I know,' Cowan said, grinning at him. 'I'm not even here right now. I'm currently hanging out at the Trump International downtown participating in a water sports orgy with the Vice President, two Saudi princes, and my good friends Svetlana and Natasha in a Jacuzzi of Smirnoff vodka.'

'Fair enough, it is important that you have a plausible alibi.' Gorham dabbed his lips with a napkin. 'I would speculate, off the record, that Mary may have been looking into allegations contained in sworn affidavits, given under penalty of perjury, in the Eastern District of Virginia, as part of a seventy-page motion by lawyers for Afghan civilians suing Wringhim for alleged war crimes and other misconduct.' Gorham brushed crumbs neatly off his sleeve into a saucer. 'How's that for specificity, Mr Cowan?'

'Would that be unusual though? I mean, atrocities happen, right? Aren't these Tubalcain people in the atrocity business fulltime? Isn't the war crime thing collateral damage for them?'

'What was unusual in this case, I believe, is that there may have been two sworn affidavits by former members of Wringhim's management team. Said affidavits, maybe, alleging that the corporation may have arranged the disposal of another someone who may have provided information, or who was planning to provide information, maybe, to the federal authorities about ongoing criminal conduct. Perhaps there may have been suspicious circumstances in this individual's demise.'

'That's a fuckload of mays and maybes, H. How long ago was this court case?'

'Three years.'

'And the outcome?'

'The case was dropped.'

'What about the former members of the management team?'

Gorham's mouth formed a straight line. 'John Doe 1 and John Doe 2? They had broken the big boy rules.'

'Which are?'

'Among covert operatives the big boy rules are that there are no rules, until you break one.' Gorham looked amused by the paradox. 'By, say, giving an affidavit.'

'Mary must have very much wanted to track these Doe twins down, right?'

'Sadly, they are no longer with us.'

'Doe, oh dear.'

'Both individuals shuffled off this mortal coil in most unfortunate circumstances. Lethal wrong-way crash on a Minnesota highway and zipline catastrophe in Costa Rica, would you believe? Don't get me started on the upper midwest freeways. And I'm told that those jungle ziplines can be quite lethal.'

'About as lethal as close proximity to some corporations. So what did Mary suppose was the ongoing criminal conduct? Care to speculate some more in my direction?'

'Oh, Miss Barnham knew what it was. You see, it was alleged that incidents of excessive force were videotaped and voice recorded and that, immediately after the event's conclusion, these were viewed in a session called a 'hot wash' for assessment purposes. Everyone is bedevilled by assessment these days, no exceptions.'

'Tell us about it. They assessed my division this time last year and then brought in more pencil pushers to assess the assessment, which we referred to as the art of disappearing up your own assessment.'

'Quite. Anyway, after the hot-washing, the video would, of course, be erased to prevent anyone other than Wringhim personnel seeing what had transpired.'

'One of these John Does was in possession of a tape that wasn't erased.'

'That's speculation on your part, Mr Cowan. I couldn't begin to comment.'

'Mary located a tape.'

'Again, your surmise.'

Gorham glanced at his cellphone and began consolidating his dishes. Spoon carefully aligned on the saucer nudging the cup. The interview was almost over.

'Can I have a quick-fire round to finish? Like on a bad quiz show?'

'You'll have to make it very quick, Mr Cowan. I have my bi-weekly choir practice over at the United Methodist this morning. We do a charity concert at Christmas.' Gorham corrected himself. 'The holidays, I mean.'

'The people trying to do me in are mercenaries, then?'

'The dirty work in the field is carried out mostly by Bosnians, Filipinos, South Africans, Chileans. Former commandos from the Pinochet era and the like.'

'It's nice that they cultivate diversity though. They definitely ticked that box.'

'That's the Middle East theatre of operations. But I would speculate that your species of imbecility, Mr Cowan, has led you directly into contact with Tier One contractors. These would be former members of the elite Special Forces or retired Agency, men with tattoos and SF or SEAL rings, men who put in their time in Pakistan and Afghanistan. Men also best avoided in dark alleys and, actually, pretty much everywhere else too.'

'Mary's not dead, is she?' Cowan blurted this at him. 'She came running to you in a fucking fright and you hid her away somewhere? Where'd you stash her?'

Gorham flinched, a solitary blink and then a rapid adjustment. It was enough though. Cowan knew he was right. 'Mr Cowan… Why would I even indulge…'

'I've tried to put myself in that girl's shoes. It's damn hard. I'm terrible at walking in heels.' Cowan spread his hands wide. 'Catriona is killed. Mary's really upset, but she's a smart kid. She figures out it's a fake mugging and the killers were gunning for her. What are her options? The police? I can't see her running her story by Darius McDonald. Can she go to her newspaper people with it? No, they're sitting around on the Internet in their pajamas and are as much use as a handbrake on a canoe. So, where does she go?'

Gorham shrugged, appearing indifferent, but looking discomfited still.

'The only place she can go. She comes desperate to the old friend with the right connections. To someone she thinks can help her get off the hook. She's out of options, so she runs downstairs and she chaps on the door of her land-lord mentor. The poor girl must have been scared shitless that day. How terrified was she when she came knocking?'

'Fascinating narrative, Mr Cowan.'

'How could you help her, though? What's your interest in this game?'

'I don't play games, Mr Cowan. Not anymore.'

'What's Tal short for? Talented?'

'Talmadge.'

'And the H would be?'

'Horace.'

'I see why you went with the middle name.'

A vein throbbed under Gorham's eye.

'I'm sorry,' Cowan said. 'I don't mean to be rude.'

He contemplated whether he was sincere in his apology. 'I just am fucking rude.'

'I've lived an interesting and full life, Mr Cowan, as you seem to assume. Not always salubrious. Not always edifying. And perhaps there are events in my past I'm not at peace with.' Gorham's top lip slid on the diagonal. 'You see, I don't plan to meet my maker tanned, fit and rested. I intend to be tired, battered, and bruised. It's safer that way.'

'Is Mary safe? You know where she is. I know you do.' Gorham put his phone in his pocket and stood up. 'Can I meet her? I'd like a word.'

Gorham shook his head. 'This is over, Mr Cowan. Please don't ask me anymore about this matter. Learn your limitations, man. You've learned enough. You'd best go home, I mean to the UK. Leave here. I'm sorry about your daughter. I'm sorrier than you will ever know about that sad business. But I think you'd best quit this while you're ahead.'

'I can't stop, because I'm not remotely ahead.' Cowan squeezed the table edge with his fingers. 'What about you, though? I don't get it. Won't these thugs come after you if they know what you know?'

'No.' Gorham tried to smile but it withered instantly to a snarl of teeth. 'They won't touch me. They can't, you see.'

'How come? Did you get one of them Get Out of Jail Free cards? You shouldn't have a Monopoly on that. Can I get one too?'

Gorham stared at Cowan, his moustache twitching imperceptibly.

'Oh, of course.' Cowan struck his forehead with his palm. 'I'm kind of slow on the uptake. You're ex-CIA. A high-head one.' Cowan looked down into his empty cup. 'You did get a card, from Langley. I really shouldn't trust you as far as I can throw you.'

'No. Probably not, I'd say.' Gorham did not offer Cowan his hand. 'Goodbye, Mr Cowan. Please take care of yourself.'

He watched Gorham leave. The door rattled on its hinge. The narrative he'd just constructed on the fly was creative, but made a kind of sense. Mary would have come running to Gorham in a right panic, angry, over her head, despairing, terrified. Gorham respected and liked the girl. Cowan had picked that much up from the conversation. The old fuck cared. Plus, he was atoning for past misdeeds, singing in the bloody choir, saving women's lives, and getting ship-shape to meet his maker. Cowan wondered what Saint Peter would make of his funky shoes. What kind of deal could an ex-spy have cut on the girl's behalf? Mary was to be hidden away safely for how long? Would a year or two do them? Long enough for all this to blow over. Tubalcain might be rebranded again by then as Murder Inc. And in return, she'd have had to turn over her manuscript, and whatever else she'd found. A tape. There must have been a tape. These days it would be a video file. He wasn't even angry about what she'd done. Hell, he'd have probably done the exact same thing. So there had been a negotiation and a funny handshake and a deal cut. It had all been cleaned up very nicely and swept decorously under the nearest rug along with his daughter's body. Then he'd come stumbling into town, a teetotal police officer who might as well have been dead drunk, leaving chaos in his wake, like Buster Fucking Keaton at a police parade. Cowan should have listened to McDonald that time.

Had Mary shared the file with Catriona? Did they believe his daughter had shared it with him too? If so, Cowan was damn lucky to be alive. His head felt like a turnip. Thinking did that to you. I think therefore I yam. Factor's people weren't looking for Mary at all. They'd settled that matter to their satisfaction. Mary was dealt with and incapacitated. They were looking to see how much he knew about her. And him being a right dumb fuck he'd insinuated it was a barrel load.

Cowan wasn't leaving this city anytime soon, though. Fuck that suggestion. He was taking this to the limit. He was going to make these people pay for what they did. Of course, he might end up floating in the river like Carlton with a bullet in his brain. Such as it was. That's what happened to people who knew too much about Tubalcain. So be it. Factor had it coming. This Gil Martin person, he was a piece of work. He had it coming too.

Cowan was about to make the call to Deyon saying where to pick him up when he realised that Gorham hadn't returned his phone battery. Interesting.

★ ★ ★

'Who was that woman who called me? It didn't sound like your friend Kris.' Deyon was applauding Cowan ironically as he clambered into the passenger seat of the Corolla. The clock on the dash said 12.30pm. 'I'll say it again, I'd never have taken you for such a radical playa when I first made your acquaintance at Au Bon Pain.'

'Shut it. She was just this very nice older lady,' said Cowan, flushing red. 'She happened to be in the coffee shop and made the call for me. My phone wasn't working. What took you so long anyway? She made me drink something that had a big mushroom floating in it while I was waiting. It was very disturbing.'

'Kombucha.'

'Aye, well that Kumbaya stuff tasted like fermented shoes.'

'Ah,' said Deyon, grinning. 'The old 'my phone's not working' pickup routine. Working the Scottish accent angle were you? Rolling some Rs her way? Round and round the rugged rock the ragged rascal randomly ran, and so on. You'd be the ragged rascal too, most definitely in that jacket. She a booty call for later now?'

'Fuck off.'

'That's nice language. And here's me just went out and got you a gift too.'

'I hate presents,' Cowan declared. 'My ex-wife was always buying me presents: socks, pullovers, button-down shirts of shining blue with wee horses on them, books whose spine I'd never crack and music I'd never listen to. This one time, she actually gave me a lacquered wooden box for my birthday. 'What's this?' I say. 'It's a box,' she tells me, all enthusiastic. She opens it and closes it. It clunks. 'For what?' I ask. 'For keeping things in! You know, things.' I'm like, 'What things would I keep in a little wooden box at all? A dead pygmy?' So she goes and turns all vicious on me then…'

'I really can't say I blame the poor woman.' Deyon reached across Cowan, interrupting his rant, and let the glove compartment drop open. 'This is something for your own protection.'

'I told you I don't like guns. Listen, I will never in my life fire a gun.'

'It's not a gun.' Deyon handed him a little black canister. 'It's something else.'

'Oh, my god,' Cowan said. 'It's a miniature dildo. You shouldn't have.'

'Screw you.'

'With this? Is it an actual replica of yours? You really shouldn't have! Can I get the same done for mine?' Cowan stretched his arms extremely wide. 'Mind you, that'd be more like the Washington monument in scope and colouring and…'

'Dream on. It's pepper spray. There's a tear gas component too. And also a uv dye, so you can mark your assailant.'

'Why would I want to mark my assailant? Wouldn't he be identifiable as the individual writhing on the ground choking and spewing tears?'

'I suppose.' Deyon pulled out of the parking space and turned onto King Street.

'This is kind of girly,' said Cowan, fingering the pepper spray and crinkling his nose. He gave the canister a good shake and smelled it.

'Well, if you don't want it cause you're a sexist pig, I'll keep it. I'm always having to fight guys off, especially horny bears in the clubs after midnight.'

'Sounds grizzly.' Cowan slipped the canister in his jacket pocket. 'Might come in handy. Help me disable the seductive cougars with their fungus cups in coffee shops.'

'Where we going?'

'Manassas.'

Deyon flicked on his blinker and headed towards the beltway exit. 'You're wanting a look-see at Tubalcain headquarters, I take it. We're going to their training centre place? Is that it?'

'It is. It's only an hour away and we can get our kicks on Route 66. Spend some quality time listening to Dusty Springfield.' Cowan snuck a look at Deyon. 'Just a quick gander from the outside, D. It'll be no bother. I want to get a feel on what we're up against here.'

'In that case, I'm so glad I stuffed the AK in the trunk.'

'You brought a fucking machine gun?'

Deyon laughed, 'You so wish.'

2pm. Sparse woods ran down a slope from the road where the washboard gravel slanted right, up an incline. A metal gate had to be opened and closed. The curved driveway went up past a decrepit garage, a burnt-up wheel-less trailer, an upright piano filled with rainwater, and a couple of boats sunk in a mud field moored against dead trees. At the edge of a faded field, three black horses sniffed one another's butts by an old barn, half caved in. Outside was an ancient Duesenberg with a plank stuck through its windscreen. Desolation. The cold rain had stopped, a thin blue leaking through the clouds. The two men crawled along the perimeter of the wire fence demarcating the eastern boundary of the compound and lay flat in the grass.

'I'm getting my pants all dirty,' Deyon noted, fractious. 'And you're getting the dry-cleaning bill, Mr Cowan.'

'What d'you think we're looking at, Miss Moneypenny?'

Deyon sniffed in response.

'Come on, aren't you getting a serious Dr No vibe from all this?'

'No.'

In the distance they could see the 9,000 square-foot Lodge. The brochure Cowan had downloaded described how it contained conference rooms, classrooms, a lounge, a pro shop and a large chow hall offering a variety of interesting ethnic food selections. The smaller buildings to the east would be the armory and tactical house. There were photos of the inside too, a big black bear looming over the fireplace mouth agape, with other mounted animals observing activities through plastic eyes in the gun cleaning room. Many tanned and ripped men in those photos stood

posed pointing chest-high compressed air nozzles at their
weapons, while concentrating and looking cool. It couldn't
really be that hard to focus on blowing air up a metal tube.
No one had been into mugging for the camera that day.
They'd all been working hard chiselling their rock-hard
cores earlier in the gym too. You could just tell. This lot had
abs of steel.

'I just don't see you as James Bond is all I'm saying. Bond
is cool, you feel me?'

'I am shinsherely shocked and sho depresshed at your ass-
ershun, shon.'

Gunfire and muffled explosions echoed up from the
ranges below, a persistent crackle of automatic weapons.
Cowan remembered the quarry behind his old house, the
rumbling excavations. On one range, small black figures
ran through an urban street facade in pairs, spinning and
firing. An artificial pond used for water-to-land training
was currently occupied by two small rubber raiding craft.
The helmeted figures leapt out of their boats into the water
and shimmied up an embankment in teams of four. The
attackers were weighed down by heavy equipment and
fired what sounded like real ammunition. Not that Cowan
would know the difference. A shrill whistle sounded
occasionally and the action stopped, while there was a
confab with instructors and much pointing and gesticu-
lation. Then the boats were re-launched and the exercise
resumed. Mallards lifted off in a flurry, in response to the
snarl of gunfire and resettled on the pond during breaks in

the action. The ducks were used to it by now, apparently. Ducks could adapt to anything. Cowan had been told their brains were bird-sized.

'Let's not stay too long here,' Deyon observed. 'It's like an NRA convention where someone put meth in the Kool-Aid.'

'What you're looking at here, D, is a private army for the 21st century. A private for-profit militia in action.'

'OK.' Deyon sounded unimpressed.

'What you're looking at here is the end of democracy as we know it.'

Deyon was more thoughtful now. 'And that would be a bad thing, why? I mean have you even seen what you white men have been voting for recently?'

Two helicopters lifted off like giant black bugs from the adjacent airstrip and ascended vertically, a copse of white ashes staggering in the draught of the departing rotors. In the circumstances, the men decided it might be advantageous to crawl under the sharp red stems of a protruding dogwood. 'What I've learned from recent informative conversations, D,' Cowan whispered. 'Is that militaries are capable organizations, but they're not designed to be cost effective.'

'Why are you whispering?'

'I'm fucking paranoid is why.'

'You think this bush is bugged?'

Cowan shrugged. 'I seriously don't know what I know anymore, son.'

They watched the two helicopters shrink to specks in the sky and didn't talk for a while. A rattle of gunfire persisted.

The soil under the bush was caked and frost-hardened. Cowan brushed a film of dry dirt from his jeans.

'America has always been like that,' Deyon announced, apropos of nothing.

'What are you havering about now?'

'America's always used civilian contractors. George Washington had his own contractors too – you can see them in Lafayette Park. Their statues flank the four corners in a square.'

'Not quite the same thing, D.'

'It is too. Those men, foreign officers, came over and built the capability of the continental army. They contracted. No question, those motherfuckers were major contractors.'

'It's not the same thing at all.'

'Lafayette Park should be called Contractor Park. Those men were mercenaries.'

'You're missing the...' Cowan interrupted himself, pointing up. 'Holy fuck!'

High above them, small figures commenced jumping from the helicopters, their chutes opening on the descent. They floated like dandelion seeds down towards the burnt-brown rectangular parachute landing zones. 'Now, there's something you don't see every day,' Deyon suggested.

'Thank Christ.'

'You think those paratrooper people might see us laying here behaving mega-suspiciously under a bush on their way down?' Deyon asked. 'Might wonder what we're doing? See us spying and so on?'

'I don't know.' Cowan looked around the trees and reviewed their current situation and position. 'We're not invisible. I know that much.'

'What's the first thing you'd do if you were invisible, Mr Cowan?' Deyon asked, looking at him provocatively. 'I'm just curious. I know what I'd do for sure.'

'Besides kicking a mime to death?' Cowan looked up at the sky. 'But for now I think it might be advisable for us to maybe run the fuck away, just in case.'

As if in response to this concern, one chopper descended and hovered above the black oaks fifty yards behind where the men were sprawled. Shots rang out. They lay still for a while, barely breathing, limbs trembling, listening to the thudding of branches and twigs displaced and falling, then the susurration of leaves in the wake of the departing whirr and rattle. Somewhere in the treetops an annoyed crow screamed.

'That's exactly how I feel,' Cowan muttered, his voice hoarse with fear.

10   MONDAY (NIGHT)

On Route 28, they passed a sign for Loch Lomond. 'There you go,' Cowan said, shrugging. 'We have officially entered a parallel dimension. It's a total *Twilight Zone* situation now.'

Deyon was looking at his phone while driving, which wasn't good. 'Besides Lafayette are Baron Friedrich Wilhelm Von Steuben, Rochambreau and Kosciuszko.'

'Excuse me?'

'In Contractor Park.'

They drove on as clouds to the east began bleeding in the sun's drop and a crepe ribbon settled on the broken stalks of fields. The first star occurred to the sky just north of Centreville, which was also when Deyon began shifting nervously behind the steering wheel. 'Can I say something melodramatic at this juncture?'

'You say that like it's something new for you,' Cowan sighed.

'You know how this car doesn't go real fast?'

'I had in fact noticed that. I believe it might have been when we got overtaken by the Amish gentleman in a buggy a while back.'

'Right. Everybody but trucks has been going by us except this one car, just this one. It's right behind us now again, a Cadillac Escalade, silver.'

'You must be putting me on. What a fucking cliché.'

Cowan turned the rear-view towards him and squinted. 'Two or three men, right?'

'Can't see who all might be in the back. But I let them get real close ten minutes ago when it was still light enough to see. There's one with an Orioles baseball cap driving, the front passenger is wearing a dark suit.'

'Great, now we're being pursued across country by the Odd Couple. Well, why don't you make like Steve McQueen and get us out of here?'

'The fashion designer?'

'What? No, he was a big film star. You don't know who Steve McQueen was?' Cowan shook his head. 'You seriously mean to tell me you've never seen *Bullitt*?'

Deyon clutched the steering wheel tighter now, his knuckles whitening. 'I'm starting to think I'll be seeing quite a few of them the minute we get out of this car.'

To their right, was an exit sign for the NRA National Firearms Museum. 'What did I tell you?' Deyon said, pointing at it. He shivered and became deeply contemplative. Cowan wondered if he was plotting a way out of their current predicament. 'Oh, I know!' Deyon suddenly declaimed, enthusiastically.

'What?'

'I was thinking of Alexander McQueen! That's a totally different person.'

'Jesus!' Cowan headbutted the glove compartment a few times for effect. 'You seriously can't make this horseless carriage of yours go any faster?'

Deyon shrugged his shoulders. 'The mechanic said if I go over 65, the transmission explodes or something like that. It wasn't good, whatever it was. I might be able to lose them on the Beltway, though. Everybody drives like a bat out of hell there.'

'They're after me, son. Let's cut out before then.' Cowan pointed at the latest highway exit sign. 'Is there a Metro stop in this Oakton place coming up?'

'That's Vienna.'

'You're kidding me on.'

'No.'

'That's unbelievable. I've come all the way back to where this thing started. There's maybe a hidden symmetry to things, after all.' Cowan scratched at his head. 'Here's what we're going to do, then. Take the next exit ramp, stop in town by the Metro, and I'll take my chances by myself. I think they'll follow me. You can bugger off home.'

'You sure?'

'Sure I'm sure.'

'What if I drop you and they decide to follow me instead?'

'Well, then I'm off the hook and you're totally fucked.' Cowan grinned at him malevolently. 'In which case, you roll into the nearest police station and tell them the whole crazy story. They won't believe you for a minute and think you're mad, but at least you'll be safe inside. Then just get yourself committed to a loony bin for the duration.'

'I was going to party tonight too,' said Deyon, looking disconsolate.

'On a Monday night? What are you, Jay Gatsby?'

'What difference does a Monday make?'

'Well, you still might make it. Let's think positive thoughts. Let's be mindful. You'll be at that party whooping it up like Freddie Mercury on a bender in a few hours from now and I'll, well, maybe I'll not be that deceased.'

As Cowan predicted, the Escalade followed their car all the way up the ramp to the Metro complex. Deyon pulled into the kiss and ride section of the north parking lot of the Vienna-Fairfax station. 'No smooch for me?' said Cowan, slamming the door, but Deyon had already taken off roaring back in the direction of the highway. In the circumstances, Cowan assumed it advisable to break into a jog. From the elevated walkway, he watched three distant figures exit the Escalade and walk quickly towards the station entrance. He was sprinting now and discovered that he'd mislaid his fare card. He bolted back to the ticket machine and bought a new one for $10. He was anxious and fumbled his wallet, a few stray coins spilling and rolling along the concrete. A young girl in a pink ponytail was bent over retrieving his change for him. 'It's OK,' Cowan yelped at her. 'Don't bother. It's OK.'

'But it's quarters,' the girl said, adamantly helpful. Her overweight father was nodding at her approvingly. He was wearing a t-shirt said 'Sewer Rat' and Cowan felt like he might have accidentally stumbled into someone else's bad dream. From the kiosk alcove, he saw two of his pursuers running across the mezzanine.

'Thanks,' he squeaked, pocketing the change. 'Thanks.'

'That man was funny,' Cowan heard the girl say to her father as he ran away like a scalded cat. 'His face was funny. He had a funny scared face!'

Cowan slipped the new card in the slot and half-ran, half-stumbled down the escalator onto an island platform of red tile. The train on the right side was ready to leave, the oval yellow lights on the platform edge blinking rhythmically. He leaped aboard, feeling immense relief. He'd made it. He was safe. There were a dozen other passengers scattered around the carriage. None of them looked remotely suspicious. He could sit anywhere, but chose to stand by the door, gripping the rail. The door that still hadn't closed. Cowan willed it shut and remembered that the Vienna station was a terminus. Orange line trains went one way towards New Carrolton and, in all likelihood, they did not have to depart the station right away. He was a right bright spark. Far from escaping, he'd only succeeded in cornering himself.

First, Sewer Rat and his daughter climbed on board hand in hand to be followed by the tall man in the Orioles cap arriving at jeopardy trot. He sauntered on, exhaling breathily, and sat down on a seat facing Cowan, pretending hard not to notice him. The second latecomer strolled all the way along the platform to the front of the carriage, looking thoroughly unconcerned. He loped on there, nonchalant. This one was heftily built and wearing a grey American University sweatshirt and matching sweatpants. He hadn't seen a college classroom in years. The faux student stood facing the other door, parallel to Cowan, watching him. Cowan watched him back.

After a while of mutual eye fucking, he stepped off the train and back onto the platform. The yellow lights were blinking rhythmically still. His minder at the other door did the same. Now they stood facing each other on the platform. Monkey see, monkey do. When Cowan stepped back on the train, so did his eerie doppelganger. Now he was standing alongside the open door again, looking directly along the long nose of the other pursuer. Orioles Cap chose not to acknowledge Cowan's gaze at all. Other passengers were now examining him though, intrigued or perturbed by his weird indecisiveness regarding his trip. The little girl was nudging her father, looking at him curiously. Funny face man was acting funny now too. Cowan was never going to make it off this train alive. It didn't matter how many other passengers were in the carriage. It was immaterial how much they were looking at him making a spectacle of himself. His time was up if he stayed on board. It would be like the night with his daughter all over again.

Cowan edged closer to the train door. Getting off this thing was his only shot at survival. But his timing had to be perfect. Still nothing. Sweat tingled his scalp. Then after an eternity came the invocation 'Stand back, doors closing.' Cowan waited till the final echoing chime and then leapt back onto the platform as the doors slid closed, the edges brushing and catching at his jacket. He landed awkwardly on his knees. Orioles Cap was on his feet and staring down into his eyes this time, but from the other side of a window. He looked gravely disappointed in Cowan, not to mention mildly murderous. At the far end of the carriage, his accomplice was engaged in frantically trying to pry the door open. Cowan laughed aloud, waving ironically at his would-be killers as the train began rolling away.

'See ya later, alligators,' he mouthed at the window.

'In a while, crocodile.'

The voice was right behind him. Cowan had assumed he would be the only person left on the platform following the train's departure. He'd assumed wrong. Turning slowly, he discovered Devlin Reem, looking smug and amused, dapper in that little black suit. Cowan shrugged at him, resigned. 'Well, it worked in the French Connection that time,' he explained. 'I only steal from the best.'

Reem's right hand was buried in his jacket pocket. He lifted that pocket towards Cowan and gestured towards the far end of the platform.

'Is that a gun or are you just happy to see me, Devlin?'

'Never heard that one before. You're walking now,' Reem told him. 'This here hostile midget needs a quick word with you.'

Cowan did as he was told. What choice did he have?

A light breeze from the northeast dappled his face as he tramped on into the darkness. They were the only two people on the Metro platform. They might as well have been the only two people in the Universe. 'What's the going rate for a mercenary these days anyway?' Cowan asked, over his shoulder.

'I'm not a mercenary, Cowan,' Reem said. 'I'm a loyal American working for America to protect Americans.'

'Whatever helps you sleep at night, Devlin.'

The men walked on into the gloom. What Cowan wouldn't have given to have a nice lava lamp close at hand.

'Did you know,' Reem said, conversationally, 'that the Order of Malta was formed in the 11th century before the first Crusade with the mission of defending territories the Crusaders had conquered from the Muslims?'

'I did not know that,' Cowan said, sounding impressed. 'Is that what you think you are? Fancy yourself a Malteser? I think you've sniffed too many gas tanks, Devlin.'

The two of them had arrived at the far end of the platform. Ahead, the walkway dipped at an angle. The tracks extended into the night, away from the overhead illumination and the reflected glow of the streetlights in the lots above.

'You can't get away with this, you know. Didn't I read someplace that the DC Metro has 10,000 surveillance cameras? It's a panpoticon.'

'A panopticon you mean,' Reem corrected.

'Nope. I think everything has gone to pot and I'm

definitely in the frying pan here. Anyhow, I hope you gave a big smile when you were on Candid Camera.'

'I'm sure there are indeed that many recording devices. It's very possible. And the relevant ones will, I'm also quite sure, all prove to be out of commission when reviewed later by the police.'

'Oh, that's how it's done, eh?'

'You're going to give me your phone now.' Reem held out his hand. 'Please.'

'Everyone keeps asking me for my phone these days,' Cowan said, frustrated. 'I suppose it's trackable on a network, right? Indicates my current location. That explains a whole lot about the stupid ads I get on it. The thing doesn't have a battery actually.'

'What do you mean?'

'I lost it.'

'How do you lose a phone battery?'

'Same way you lose anything else: your little girl, your sanity, your life.'

'Very good,' Reem said, sighing. His hand was still extended towards Cowan. 'Now shut the fuck up for once and give it here.'

Cowan reached into his pocket and his fingers closed around the black canister. In the dark of the platform, it might pass for a cellphone. He flicked the cap and took it out slowly, resignedly, holding it out before him at arm's length. The fluid stream blasted Reem full in the face and the .22 went rattling across the tiles as he staggered backwards, yelping and clawing at his face. One second he was there, snarling in blind anger and frustration, feeling at his face with his little stubby fingers, the next, his foot was reaching into empty air as he disappeared off the platform.

Cowan crouched over the dimpled edge, aghast at the scene unraveling below. Reem was struggling to get to his feet, moaning, still feeling at his face with his fingers, balanced awkwardly like a man trying to stand up in a pitching row-boat. He coughed and spun and took a knee, gasping for breath, emitting desperate hacking sounds.

'Over here,' Cowan shouted, wanting to get him off the tracks, at least. He didn't feel like being the one responsible for getting the man flattened by an incoming train. That would be too much. 'Come towards my voice.'

But Reem was stumbling on all fours in the other direc-tion. Then down he went in a heap. It was too late for any-thing now. The man's legs were jerking spasmodically and the torso undulated in sudden quick lunges. His face, lit by yellow sparks, appeared a thick congested purple. Cowan saw a skein of white drifting ghostlike above Reem's smoking skull.

'My God.' An old Hispanic man, newly descended from the escalator seemed to be in shock. 'Is he drunk?'

'He's out of his head on something,' Cowan informed him. 'He tripped and fell right off onto the tracks. We'll go down there and get him, OK?'

'No, tercer riel.' The old man's voice cracked. He was

searching desperately, for his words communicated danger. 'It's third rail, you know. He kicked the cover off it.'

The burnt black thing that had been Devlin Reem, was somehow making its way back across the tracks, dragging its legs, moving by instinct or muscle memory towards the sound of the voices above. Deep scarlet and white welts had formed on what was left of his face and marvellously bright gouts of blood dripped more black than red. From the upper teeth to the throat was a red mottled gap, with a few hanging strips of flesh and splintered bone. It wasn't a good look.

The lights on the platform commenced flashing, the arrival of a train from Dunn Loring was imminent. That would put the tin hat on proceedings. Cowan's tongue felt swollen against his cheek. It hurt to look at the crawling worm thing. He tried to spit, but nothing came. He was responsible for this, too.

'Oh, my God,' the Hispanic man said, grasping at his arm. 'What we do, man?'

'I'll go get help,' Cowan lied, breaking free of his hold. 'Maybe they can stop it somehow. Make it brake.' He was garbling nonsense now, knowing what was to come.

Cowan was at the top of the escalator when he heard the train roar in, the blunt thud of the impact, the echoing scream. He didn't know who it was screamed. It couldn't have been Reem, not with his face like that.

Cowan strolled briskly out of the station and hailed a taxi. He moved with deliberate casual ease but felt less than inconspicuous. He thought about 10,000 cameras recording him killing a veteran, maybe a war hero, from every conceivable angle. So he was a murderer now, too. Wasn't that just fantastic? What taboo was there left for him to break now? Cannibalism?

He couldn't in all honesty say it hadn't been coming.

8.15pm. Cowan killed two hours in a Starbucks till he had serious caffeine jitters. He'd bought a phone battery in the Walmart on H Street and left a message for Kris. She didn't pick up when he called. He left another message on McDonald's mobile then texted Deyon saying he could most definitely use a place to stay the night. Going back to his hotel room was hardly a viable option now. Who knew what monsters lurked under his bed? The police might be napping in it.

Deyon was already at his party and said he could meet him there: tell the doorman he said it was fine to let him in. Deyon also, maybe, did have a place he could stay the night. It wasn't ideal, but beggars couldn't be choosers and Cowan had been plodding all over town this week looking like a manic panhandler.

He took a taxi to the Dupont Circle address, which had the appearance of a converted industrial warehouse. Deyon hadn't mentioned the cover was $10. He hadn't mentioned it was a gay club either. Cowan palmed the bill to a muscle-bound bouncer in blue eyeliner and kohl who gave him the once over, assessing and dismissing. 'D said it was fine,' Cowan informed him, coldly.

The bouncer elevated an eyebrow. 'You?'

'What's up, sugarplum? Don't see anything you fancy?'

'Not even.' The bouncer stamped a tiny anchor under his thumb. 'I like mine a little less long in the tooth, hon.'

'Where would I find him, then?'

'God,' the bouncer said, wincing. 'Who isn't looking for that one?' He evaluated again head to foot, inventorying and objectifying. 'You're so not Licious' type.'

'Licious?'

'D-licious.'

'You'd be surprised,' Cowan smirked. 'I have hidden talents.'

The bouncer drilled a grin through him. 'Just go through the green door there, old-timer,' he said, indicating behind him. 'Look for the biggest orgy happening in there. That's where Licious will be, right in the middle of it. You might want to crank your hearing aid down a tad though and also try not to get over-excited and dislocate anything not covered by your Medicare.'

'Fuck you,' Cowan observed.

'Oh, you so, so, wish.' The bouncer gave Cowan a final dismissive eyeroll and sent him on his way.

Inside, it was difficult to see through the static flicker. Once Cowan's eyes adjusted to the wobbling globs of color, he saw the walls were painted a deep blue, which gave the space an underwater feel. A glow-silver webbing

was strung across the rafters. The old concrete underfoot had been converted into a dance floor, with a mixing
table and speakers high on a jerry-rigged platform. The
sound system was clear and crisp, set with the right bass
and soulful treble levels for the DJ to lay down his bomb
beats. The acoustics were excellent, considering. A stage
had been custom-built for the weekend drag shows, but
tonight, only two half-naked, sweat-stained go-go boys
gyrated there. Over at the bar, the staff was bow-tied
and shirtless and rouge-nippled and hustling up a storm.
Cowan commenced swimming his way through the ocean
of male bodies. It was like he'd sashayed into an alternate
Banana Republic, whose clothes were modeled by young
men snaffling martinis. The scent of sweat-tinged cologne
caught in his throat. Most of the partygoers were twen-
ty-somethings, but there were a few hefty bears and other
tight-bodied older types lurking, miniature gold-plated
gym membership cards dangling from their lanyards. A
few women were dancing too, which was comforting.
He supposed he might have trouble passing here. Cowan
decided to feel as homosexual as possible. But he didn't
even make it all the way across the dance floor. Midstream,
a heavy industrial beat dropped and the room exploded
into crazed mayhem, everyone moving as one, 300 people
partying Ibiza techno style. The lights flooded purple,
pink and green, pulsing in time to the fat thud. The warehouse sizzled, crunched, stomped, echoed, the young men
engulfing him now seemingly machines programmed

for nothing but their own rapture. He felt his feet being swept from under him. He was treading water. The beat throbbed, clogging his ears. God, he thought, spun around like a whirling dervish, even the white guys can dance here.

Cowan ebbed and flowed in the swell, floating where shafts of blue light strobed strawberry shimmer, smudges of tortoiseshell and blinding vermillion. The DJ tore it down with deep house then, keeping the bpm at a lower, teasing rate, built up again with fritzing noises that stretched the rhythms out like a long coral shelf. The man was putting the dancers in a coma, the bass so loud it rattled Cowan's ribcage. He just gave up, surrendered to the rhythm, accepting there was nothing between his body and the bodies around him, between him and light and sound. He supposed he'd wash up eventually on the edge of the dance floor as sweat-soaked flotsam. He felt at that moment as if the staccato beats and lights flowing through him flowed through everything. Connected to all of it, he suddenly imagined himself curled like a comma in his mother's womb, floating, suspended in a fluid sac. Shirtless men ground on him enthusiastically, wished him well, and drifted away. He did nothing to dissuade them. He was that lost. The hand squeezing his ass went too far though, fucking enough already with the sexual harassment. He definitely hadn't consented to any gropery. Cowan wheeled around angrily to discover a smiling Deyon, who at once caught his hand and pulled him through the milling

throng, like a pillaging Viking warrior claiming his pil-
fered bride.

'You seem to be settling in,' Deyon bawled at Cowan's
nose, gesturing towards the winding metal staircase. 'Up,'
he yelled.

A narrow soundproof room ran the length of the club
on the second floor, an elevated area with couches, where
it was actually possible to have a semblance of conversation
once your ears ceased haemorrhaging. Deyon wore a mauve
shirt unbuttoned to the waist and very tight yellow trousers.
'You looked like you were having a time,' he said, grinning.
'What did you like best? The Chromeo? Did I really witness
with my own two eyes, a rampant homophobe getting down
to Gigamesh?'

'I just got caught up in the crowd,' Cowan explained,
deeply chagrined still.

'You certainly did that.' Deyon nudged his elbow. 'You
looked right at home boogying your little ass away to Janelle
Monáe. A Scottish policeman appreciative of pansexual
afrofuturism, who knew?'

'Whose fucking birthday is it anyway?'

'I have no idea. Some girl.'

'Some girl?'

'A party's a party. Any chance to get carried away, you
know?'

'That's the attraction for you, is it? Getting carried away?'

'What's not to like about that? You felt it too. I saw
you getting the feels. It's like this big unifying experience.

A happy moment when you're all rallying together and think, 'I'm not alone. I'm with hundreds of people, feeling the same thing they are.''

'I used to get that vibe at Old Firm games.'

Deyon shrugged. 'I have no idea what that even means.'

'It's a traditional male-bonding ritual in the West of Scotland, ancient and deeply religious and with many homosexual overtones.'

'I've got you a place you can stay. I'll take you over there in a bit. You might not like it. But at least it's safe. Or did you want to hang out here and dance some more? You might get lucky.' Deyon winked lasciviously. 'I did see a few Twinks on the sidelines checking you out. I think it's the non-binary way you shimmy those hips.'

'Aye, that's what I'm afraid of,' Cowan muttered, crossing his legs. 'You'd better go grab your pink coat or whatever, before I get carried away and forget myself.'

'You know, you've always struck me as being deep down in your soul maybe a bit more pansexual than you care to believe, Mr Cowan.'

Cowan winced. 'Aye, but my deal is I'll only boink the non-stick kind.'

Deyon's father lived in a rundown row house in Columbia Heights. The wooden frame was once painted a plain chocolate brown with a leaven of jaundice-yellow trim, but the ancient oil-base had buckled and swollen, and a few peeling strips had fallen to the deck of the narrow porch. The floorboards sagged as the men walked across the porch, aggravated by the weight of the ancient sofa padlocked to the air conditioner by the door. There were rusted iron bars on the windows of the lower floor. 'Don't worry,' Deyon said, observing his expression. 'It's all good.' He keyed the lock. 'The old man will be watching one of his television shows about this time though, so be warned.'

The yellow door with the lion's head knocker opened onto the main living space, a raised kitchen and dining area visible in the background. An old black recliner with a protective plastic covering against the bare brick faced an open and blazing fireplace, above which was hoisted a flat tube widescreen television. The Pastor sat with his feet on the table in front of him observing the screen. He was balding but with significant tufts of grey hair either side of the scalp and impressive grey sideburns. Upon his substantial paunch rested a cup and saucer. On the table was a teapot and another white cup on a saucer with a spoon.

'Father,' Deyon said. 'This is the man.'

'The man has come,' the Pastor declaimed, distract-edly. He did not take his eyes from the screen for a second. 'Be seated, visitor.'

Cowan glanced anxiously at Deyon, who directed him to a three-piece sofa. He sat. Deyon poured cocoa into the cup. 'Your room is the second one on the right up the stairs,' he whispered. 'It's a mattress on the floor but you'll live. The bathroom is at the end of the hall.' He raised his voice. 'Mr Cowan can use your toiletries, father?'

'He may.' The Pastor said this in an offhand way, still fixated on his television show. It was a Sherlock Holmes mystery.

Cowan decided firing another perturbed look Deyon's way might be useful.

'It's all good,' Deyon hissed at him. 'I told you. I'm off now.'

'You are?' said Cowan, feeling panicked. 'You're going? You sure?'

'I met someone at the party. He works for Patton Boggs LLP. Say no more.' The Pastor shifted in his sofa, bothered by their low whispering. 'You'll be fine. Just sit with him a while, then go to bed. Wait till this show is over, though.' Five minutes after Deyon's hasty departure, there was a commercial break and the Pastor muted the television.

'Here's a question for you,' he said, now gazing deeply into the fireplace with the same intensity he had the screen moments before.

'Yes?'

'Where all these white people coming from? Tell me that?'

'I don't know,' Cowan said. 'I'm a stranger here myself.' The Pastor nodded, comprehendingly. 'Do not neglect to show hospitality to strangers, for thereby some have entertained angels unawares.'

'I'm no angel, sir.'

'And how would you know that?'

Cowan was contemplating a suitable reply when the Pastor raised his hand. The program had resumed. Nothing more passed between them until the next break in the action and the consequent muting. This was to be the rhythm of their conversation then.

'There are mysteries,' the Pastor declared, rather cryptically. Cowan inclined towards him, interested in listening now. 'And the white boy with the big chin solves them. He's very good. You like detectives?'

'I've kind of gone off them.'

'My son tells me you lost someone close to you.'

Cowan was surprised by this news. 'Yes, a child.'

'It is difficult.' The Pastor looked into the fire. 'I too lost a child. Deyontais is the third. My second was the prodigal. I lost him to himself, then the streets, then the drugs.'

Cowan actually heard himself say, 'I'm sorry for your loss.'

'It's beginning,' said the Pastor, cranking the volume up again.

Cowan wanted to hear a lot more about grief and recovery, a religious perspective on coping with overwhelming despair. He had to wait another fifteen minutes. The villain onscreen had been obvious to him from the outset.

'I remember him still as a child,' the Pastor said, resuming. 'The things he did, the things he said. I have memories of him. You don't lose the memories.'

'No.'

'What memories have you of your child? Which day do you remember most?'

'Many.'

'But there was one day you remember best. There is always one. Speak of it. No, wait.' He raised the remote again, clicked. 'Tell me later.'

The damn show was thankfully over at last, the crime solved, the hidden mystery explained, the wrongdoer exposed and punished. Credits rolled. If only life was like that.

'Didn't see that coming,' said the Pastor, shaking his head bemusedly at Cowan. 'Who would have known it to be her? She seemed such an innocent.'

The light from the fireplace flickered up the walls, the coals a fading orange.

'There was this one day,' Cowan began. 'I used to take her to fly her kite when she was a wee girl. She had a kite made of plastic and metal. It had a hawk emblazoned on the plastic so the further it stretched away in the sky, the more it looked like a bird, a raptor set to swoop. I remember that kite. That day we climbed the hill behind our house and I attached three reels of twine end to end and set it out in the sky till it was almost invisible, a distant dot, and she felt no tug on the line. It took her hours to rewind the coil. She didn't mind though. She loved it. She was always a bit of a tomboy, now I think of it.'

'The girl loved spending that special time alone with her

father,' the Pastor murmured and Cowan at once felt a pang deep in his chest.

'She asked me if the kite was so high a plane might catch the twine and pull her into the sky behind it. It scared her, but she felt it would be wonderful too, to be pulled up and trail behind a plane forever. I told her the kite wasn't that high. Planes were a lot higher. I said maybe a tiny plane could snag it. But it would take a big jet to pull her into the sky. She was very disappointed. See, she'd set her heart on flying. I told her what she needed to be careful of was the power lines. If the twine touched the cable she'd be electrocuted. There'd be a big flash and just a patch of black grass where she was standing. 'You wouldn't like that,' I told her. 'Would you?' She thought about it. 'No.' 'And your daddy wouldn't like it neither,' I said to her. 'What on earth would I do with myself then? What would I do if my wee lassie went away?''

The Pastor folded his hands upon his stomach. Cowan wasn't convinced he was even listening. He'd been yapping away more than any time since he'd been in DC. He'd been raving like a lunatic at the old man. Logorrhoea it was called, no? Verbal diarrhoea, that was it. You couldn't blame the old man if he'd just nodded off with boredom.

'She said she didn't know. That I remember. Her saying to me she didn't know.'

'I saw a little boy flying his kite in a park, high, out of sight in the sky.' Cowan was startled by the Pastor's voice. 'I said, 'Son, are you flying your kite?' 'Yes Sir!' he said.

'I don't see a kite,' I told him. 'Are you sure it's up there?' You know what he said?'

Cowan shook his head.

"Pastor Ferguson,' the boy said, 'I know that kite is up there because every now and then I feel it pulling on the string."

Cowan laughed. 'No offence, sir, but I think you made that story up.'

The Pastor turned his venerable head to look at Cowan directly for the first time, evaluating. 'It is possible. May I share some scripture with you?'

'Scripture is not my thing.'

'I would like to. It would do me good, if not you.'

'Well, I never say no to a bedtime story, sir.'

'You read bedtime stories to your child?'

'I did.'

The Pastor reached over to a side table and lifted from it a heavy bible. 'Tonight we're reading from Second Kings, King James Version.'

'Only version worth a damn.'

The Pastor opened the book. 'The text is:

And it came to pass, as they still went on, and talked, that, behold, there appeared a chariot of fire, and horses of fire, and parted them both asunder; and Elijah went up by a whirlwind into heaven. And Elisha saw it, and he cried, My father, my father, the chariot of Israel, and the horse-men thereof. And he saw him no more: and he took hold of his own clothes, and rent them in two pieces.'

The Pastor laid the book upon his chest, content with the
sentiment.

'Aye,' said Cowan. 'Chariots of Fire. I think I saw the
movie.'

'So, what has happened here in the Book? Elijah,
the prophet, has died. God, as a descending fire, consumes
him as he leaves this life. He is sucked into the whirlwind.
And Elisha is left behind. Three times Elisha says to Elijah
in scripture, I will not leave you, but Elisha cannot control
when Elijah leaves him. And so the chariot of fire has taken
Elijah from him, and Elisha is left alone. He listens to the
empty sound of the wind. Elisha is sad. Elisha is grieving.
And grieving is hard. He tears his coat in two.'

'I know that feeling,' Cowan said. 'Your son's been
telling me since forever to tear my own coat here in two. It's
a donkey jacket is how come it looks like this.'

'It is very ugly.'

'I suppose it is.'

'Monstrously so.' The Pastor looked sympathetically
upon him. 'But the lesson of Scripture here is that there is no
death. For what is death?'

'Excuse me?'

'Death is the process in which we are born to eternal life.
As in birth we move from one place, the womb, to a new
place, this world, so in dying we also move from this world
to another. The Lord calls this place Paradise, and there is
nothing in Paradise we should fear. But for those left behind,
death is hard. Our life is torn in two, as Elisha's coat was torn,

and it will not be mended. This is grief, the blackness of grief. For Elisha there is a great emptiness within. You know this emptiness, do you not? You feel it.'

'Yes,' Cowan said, very quietly.

'This is the grief. But grief is a mosaic, with pieces unique to each person. You've seen mosaics? In a mosaic, many pieces together form a pattern, and it can be a work of art. Think of how you feel when you see the light through a stained-glass window. How the mystery heals!' The Pastor held out his cup to Cowan. 'If I threw this cup in the fireplace it would shatter. It would be destroyed forever. You agree?'

'Yes.'

'No.' The Pastor shook his head, disappointed in Cowan's answer. 'An artist could gather up all the fragments and bring them together into a new mosaic.'

'I know you're working an analogy here, but I just don't get it.'

'Grief is like this. Something in our life shattered, and we are left with pieces. A daughter dies, say. We want our life to be normal again, but it never will be. Our task now is to partner with God, our heavenly artist. He alone can gather together the pieces of your grief and form them into a mosaic.' The Pastor patted his fat fingers on the Bible. 'Think on it again. Elisha picks up the coat. This is all he has left. The God of Elijah is now his. He rends that garment but he will wear it the rest of his days. And so it is with us. In whatever loss we have, there is a precious thing left to us. Our task is to pick it up, cherish it, and make it a part of our life. We partner with God, the heavenly artist, who makes our new mosaic out of the broken pieces of our life.'

Cowan could find nothing sensible to say to any of this.

'If things in your life are torn, if the cup is shattered, take inspiration from Elisha. So, you are grieving. Do as he did. Pick up what is precious from your past and begin to use it in a new way. Partner with a God who loves you. Make your mosaic with him.'

The firelight flickered, dying embers red-glowing. 'That was a scorcher of a sermon,' Cowan observed. 'Does it usually work? How many times have you delivered that beauty?'

'Many times. It's a standby.' The Pastor looked at Cowan through hooded eyes. 'It usually takes root in time though.'

'It won't with me.'

'At least you should thank God for what you have left.'

'What do I have left?' asked Cowan, his words tinged with bitterness.

'God.' The Pastor with some difficulty sat up straight. His belly splayed before him. He put the cup gently in the saucer and regarded Cowan with deep seriousness.

The old man's mad, Cowan thought. Mad as James Hampton fiddling with his sweetie-wrapper silver-foil Throne. There was a surplus of madness in this world.

'He is the Bread of Life; He satisfies your hunger. He is the Captain of our Salvation; He defeats every enemy. He is the Saviour of Men; He forgives the guilty.'

'I'm not ready for that.' Cowan was laughing nervously now.

'Wait, and in time He grants peace to your troubled soul. Wait, and in time He gives joy to your broken heart. Wait, and in time He cleans you up and makes you new.'

'You make him sound like an interstellar Stanley Steamer man.'

'Do you intend to reprove my words,' said the Pastor, smiling at Cowan now, 'when the words of one in despair belong to the wind?'

Cowan recalled that singular verse. 'That's from the Book of Job, right?'

The Pastor was positively delighted at Cowan's passing the theological test. 'You should go to bed now. You look very tired. There is hope for you yet.'

Cowan began ascending the staircase to the second floor. 'There's towels in the bathroom cupboard,' the Pastor called up after him. 'The hot water comes out the cold tap, which is not good.'

'I keep expecting something to come to me,' Cowan said to him, stopping halfway up and looking down into the murk below. 'To change me.'

The Pastor's voice rose up at him from out of the darkness. 'Spirit is invisible, like the wind. You cannot see it move or work. You see it act on things – as when it passes through a tree. You cannot see the wind, but how the leaves do sway! So it is with Spirit. The Spirit moves us, and we act. A work gets done, a work of kindness. What we see is not the Spirit itself.' The Pastor yawned and replaced the Bible on the side table. He clicked the TV back on. 'Mind that tap, child, or you'll get a scalding.'

★ ★ ★

It was 2am when Deyon called and woke him, sounding scared out of his wits. The body of a woman had been found floating in the Potomac earlier that day. It was all over Twitter. Her throat was cut from ear to ear. Cowan's heart sank like a heavy stone to the bottom of a great dead sea. His first thought was that Mary Barnham was not so protected after all. His next, and the one that settled like an ice floe in his soul, was that Kris had never responded to his earlier message.

11   TUESDAY (MORNING)

Cowan was sleepless till daybreak, feeling utterly distraught. Then, at last, a black dream took him. He was walking with Kris along an endless shoreline towards an ebony totem buried in sand. Warm shallow water swept shells on the shore. They walked and walked but never could seem to reach the totem. They seemed fated to walk forever. Deyon shook him into this world again at noon. Cowan recalled at once that Kris was dead. First it had been Catriona, and now it was Kris. He began to weep. For what else was there for him to do?

'Are you OK?' Deyon was ashen-faced, never having seen Cowan this vulnerable. His tears were embarrassing them both. 'It's the Barnham girl, isn't it? They got her. What are you going to do now? The police are going to be looking for you.'

'I'm heading over to Alexandria.' Cowan had a swipe at his wet cheeks with the back of his arm like a cat. 'I want a long blether with my pal the Senator.'

'Look, the police will just lock you up, that's your best option now. That's what you told me in the car the other day, remember? These other people will kill you dead.'

'They can try.'

'Won't they be expecting you to come after them?'

'I expect they might. They know I'm stupid that way, a real loose cannon, right?'

'But you're going anyway?'

Cowan shrugged. 'What can I tell you? I'm a fucking idiot walking into the lion's den. The writing's on the wall and the pipes are calling and all that, Danny boy.'

'Anything I can do?'

'Get us some coffee and a pile of Kleenex? I think I have allergies.'

'Besides that?'

'You've done enough, son. You're well out of this.' Cowan felt the need to change the tenor of the conversation before he wept again. 'How'd it go last night?'

'Spectacular.' Deyon smiled at him. 'Want all the juicy details?'

'I think I'll skip them for now. It's been a hell of a long day already.' Cowan wasn't telling Deyon anything about Kris. It was too much to share. He didn't need to hear any of that. 'Say, would your father happen to have a good razor?'

'Why? You going to slit your throat with it? We just wallpapered that bathroom.'

'And could you maybe rustle me up a small piece of plywood about so long and some masking tape and a screwdriver?'

'For what?'

'I'm thinking about building myself a kite, to pass the time.'

'Are you serious?'

'No, I'm not fucking serious. But could you get that stuff for me anyway?'

★ ★ ★

Foggy Bottom. Cowan was staring again at the platform where she stood that last night she existed. As long as he stared, that world remained in motion and as long as the world remained in motion, she existed.

Last week, he'd seen this place for the first time. It had not changed in the interim: a scatter of early afternoon commuters and map-gazing tourists, a long row of blinking yellow lights, and a chiming *Step back, doors closing*. Before today, he'd been a traveller here too, a wanderer in a search of God only knew what; an explanation of the way things were; a deeper comprehension of the death of another; a making of order out of chaos. He'd believed that nothing but the key was wanting. *Nil nisi lavis deest*. Another fragment dredged from an O Grade Latin class he failed. Memories of dead languages. *Step back, doors closing*. Memories of dead men.

If Cowan had taken that step back, the doors might have slid closed forever. Finding nothing of consequence, he would be a happier man, or a healthier one. But he'd done the opposite and taken three deliberate steps forward and let the doors cascade open. He'd lifted the keystone to find no hidden plate of gold underneath, and that the death he wished to explain so ardently was his own. The abyss was his open and gaping grave and the quicklime was at hand. He tried to imagine another version of himself, walking along a sun-drenched beach hand-in-hand with a red-haired girl whose eyes were like doves, besides springs of water, bathed in milk. She was dead now, too. He'd have been as well killing her himself. And Cowan had killed her in a way, he supposed. The more he imagined the soft sand warm beneath his feet, the more his imagined self became the real one, making this self sitting in darkness not real at all. He couldn't go to the police. He'd left a trail of bodies in his wake, like the ghost of manifest destiny. He was a man out of options. What was there left for him to do? To walk towards those who wished him dead. To make a sacrifice of himself. But he didn't want to die yet. He wasn't ready for that, not by a long chalk. Fuck that for a plan. He was no lamb to this slaughter.

The train plunged into the lacquer-black darkness and took him with it.

It was turning chilly and the late afternoon was sky blue. A sky so clear and true you could have put your fist through it. An ascending plane cut a diagonal swathe across the blue. He wouldn't have minded being up there, gazing down on our small insect life, an observer, oblivious to harm. It was 2.30pm. On the other side of the turnstiles at King Street, slouched a young man. His hair was cut in a fade and topped with a purple do-rag knotted in front, his wide-legged Rocawears bunched on a pair of reverse-laced red K-Swiss. He had the look, right down to the old RG3 sweatshirt over a snow-white tee, but was trying way too hard not to look at the arrivals. A blue knapsack nestled between his feet. It was the knapsack that was off. Cowan didn't care to find out what was inside it. He looped back past the escalator and took the rear exit. He crossed by the Amtrak depot and began the climb up Shooter's Hill to the Washington Masonic Memorial. Crossing Callahan, he looked back to catch a glimpse of a blue bag slung over a shoulder, a phone clamped to an ear.

The Memorial had been fashioned after the Lighthouse of Alexandria, although no Egyptian architect would have concocted nine floors of Doric, Ionic and Corinthian into a stone tiered cake monstrosity like this. Your Egyptian might have stuck the step pyramid on top and approved the double keystone light fixture that capped it. The information board was a dark and solemn blue. Open daily. No dogs allowed. No filming. Proper attire required. Cowan was well screwed. That fucking donkey jacket would be the death of him. On top of the board was a golden crest, sun at the top, moon at the bottom, columns at upper left and right surmounted with globes, sheaves of wheat, working tools and pomegranates. In the center was a G surrounded by a square and a compass and the year 1910. In bright crimson were three stars and two horizontal stripes: *In Memoriam Perpetuam.*

Cowan kept on up the hill, being asked to make choices now, picking the curving cement path on the left, the sinister he believed it was called, scaling another granite step tier, and then another. Up and up. Ascending. The grass embankment framing the steps was stippled brown; the landscaping minimal, sparse bushes ranged symmetrically. There was no cover, nowhere to hide, a blank and deserted place. One tier from the top was an enclosed glass case containing a reproduction of Brady's 1864 panoramic view of Alexandria.

The city of Robert E. Lee was grey and smoky, a military tent village erected at the west end where the train station now stood, a long row of arches, like some rich man's croquet lawn. Cowan read about the Ellsworth Avengers, glancing at the city of today and back at the sepia daguerreotype, his hands clutched on a rusted red railing. He wondered at the differences, locating landmarks then and today, and contemplated the vagaries of time, the hidden meanings of architecture. Directly in front of him, sloping downhill, was yet another representation of the main emblem: a stone G enclosed within the square and compass. To his right, casually leaning, was the young man he'd seen at the Metro station. The kid had followed him all the way up here. It wasn't for his autograph.

'Aight,' the young man said, tapping a finger on his do-rag. A blue-black tat of a spiderweb looked like a bruise on the side of his neck.

The pair stood in silence looking off at a distant horizon, low brown rooftops, a distant snaking blue, a far away Ferris wheel, unturning. A flag flapped on a flagpole causing it to creak. Cowan noticed the butt of a pistol protruding from the waistband of the boy's boxers. He was supposed to. He could feel his heart beat in his chest, erratic.

'What do you suppose the big G stands for?' he asked, huskiness seeped into his voice.

'Huh?' The kid stared at him like his question was mined.

'That big G on the stone there?'

'George.'

'You think so?'

'Uh-huh. George Washington, man, founding father, freed the slaves and shit.'

'You don't think it stands for God?'

The young man considered this suggestion. 'Nah.'

'Seriously? How about Geometry then?'

'Don't give a shit, cuz. Whatev.'

'You should give a shit,' Cowan said, angrily. 'There's a hell of a big difference between God and George. See, God doesn't have a name, that's what the theologians say. But if he did, I don't think it'd be George. Who could take a God called George seriously? 'Come out the burning bush, George, you're scaring the weans! George! Enough with the plague of frogs!' George doesn't have the right ring to it. Doesn't that bother you?'

The boy gave him the heavy-lidded look he probably reserved for homeless DC crazies. 'I ain't got to bother about nothin' but be black and die, slim.'

'What do you think God's name would be, then? If he had a name?'

'God.'

'Besides that.'

'Fuck is with you man?'

'Seriously. I'm just curious. If God had a name what'd it be? For you?'

'Somethin' like...' The young man pondered his knuckles, machinery grinding. 'Fuck, I know.'

'Come on, son. You're not even trying.'

There was an unnerving silence that lasted about seven years. 'Somethin' like Mabone maybe,' the young man spat at him, finally.

'What?'

'Mahabone. Yeah, there it is. I made it up. Got some serious ji voodoo vibe to it. See, I was God I'd want a serious motherfuckin' name, scare the shit out folks got me bent.' The speaker tilted his chin at the declining sun, contented. 'Mahabone, hell. I'm liking that. They all be shittin' their pants old Mahabone come round.'

'You got a name?'

'You hear me ask yours?' The kid held Cowan's gaze for 30 long seconds. Finally, 'Yeah, I got a name.'

'That's good,' Cowan told him, nodding with approval. 'I think having a name is useful. That's how come my cat is called Susan.'

The kid crouched and unzipped the blue knapsack at his feet. Cowan watched carefully, expecting a semi-automatic or worse. Instead, he extracted a two-thirds full 40-ounce bottle of Country Club. The cap was unscrewed. Amber fluid sloshed side to side.

'I see you brought your own urine sample.'

'You ever shut the fuck up, man? I'm here appreciatin' nature and shit.'

Saying this, the kid took a deep swig of the malt liquor and wiped his mouth on his sleeve. He had to hold the bottle with both hands to tip it, like he was playing a brass instrument. He took another slug, gulping it down.

'Did you know that real beer is made from barley?' Cowan asked. 'That rot gut you're drinking is likely derived from corn.'

The kid screwed the cap and adjusted the bottle on the stone parapet in front of them. He had a scratch at the hair under the front knot. 'Do I look like I give a fuck?'

'Right enough, that there is the only Country Club you'll ever see the inside of.' Cowan gestured at the Memorial behind them. 'Ever gone inside that?'

'I ain't ever been in that joint.' The young man rocked his head from shoulder to shoulder, grimacing slightly. 'Fuck is these creepy pillars and shit?'

A well-dressed couple in prosperous middle age climbed the steps near where the men stood. The younger man observed their approach, his eyes flitting from side to side, evaluating terrain and trajectories. The couple passed, deep in conversation, climbing the final tier to the entrance, where they paused in an attitude of worship. The man pointed out something of interest. A photo was taken. He had a selfie stick. Unbelievable! People who used selfie sticks needed to take a long hard look at themselves.

'I do dig them boxers,' Cowan announced, with surreal enthusiasm. 'Very pretty. Colourful, you know. I knew a girl had panties the exact same shade of blue, red and white. I think her name was Wonder Woman. Wait, maybe I'm thinking of my granny instead?' Cowan smirked. 'Would that be the new concealed carry underwear I've read about?

I'm just curious. What do you plan to do with the gun? Shoot your balls off?'

The young man tilted his chin at him. 'Kill your ass. Do the world a favour.'

'You're the fifth or sixth person who's said that to me recently.' Cowan extended his arms as though to embrace the landscape. 'You wouldn't do it here, with all these sight-seers seeing sights? Look, here comes Tiger Woods this time.' A tall man came down the steps backwards, stopping occasionally to snap a photograph on his phone.

He wore a green jacket.

'Tourists don't give no shit, neither. You know how they do. They from Minnesota and such.' The young man waxed philosophical. 'See no evil, know what I'm sayin'?'

'You all getting acquainted?' The photographer joined them. He wore a pair of too-large Locs sunglasses, a Redskins snapback high on his brow. 'What's good, cuz?' was his greeting to the other man. He offered his fist for a pound and the two performed an elaborate ritual handshake, thumb and fingers a blur.

'Man, I'mma keep it a hunnit, don't like this shit. Naw. Way in the open, know what I'm sayin'? Like we doin' business at the Kennedy Centre. Should be in the cut for a deal like this.'

'What you got there?' said the newcomer, gesturing at the bottle and shaking his head. 'You can't be doing that here. What the matter with you, Jalil? Get a grip.'

Jalil sighed. 'Listen to this motherfucker talk for five and you be drinkin' too.'

It was only when Prince Hall lifted off the frames that Cowan recognized him. 'Well, well. Who are you when you're at home? The gangsta twin brother of the slick arsehole works for Haley boy? Or is this your alter ego? Royalty, eh?'

Hall achieved a smile. 'I guess you could say that.' He walked around Cowan and finger-walked his jacket pockets, hunkering to track with his palms the inside seam of his jeans, his socks. He removed the wallet. 'I appreciate you hooking up with us today.'

'I didn't think we were that intimate yet.' Cowan was rolling his hips seductively. 'If you're feeling frisky, shouldn't you ask me out for a drink first?'

Hall finished up his search and palmed his chest pocket for a cigarette. 'Smoke?'

'Looking after my health.' Cowan grinned at him. 'Figuring to live a long time.'

Hall laughed, tossing the wallet to Jalil who immediately began rifling it.

'Next you'll be asking me if I want a blindfold.'

Hall lit up with the flick of a Bic and inhaled deeply. 'I'm not with you.'

'Before the execution. It's traditional. Like the last cigarette and the last supper? By the way, before you ask, it's steak and chips, and a pokey-hat for dessert.'

Hall blew out a streamer of smoke. 'That's a morbid thought.'

'I'm a morbid person,' Cowan said. 'I'm from Scotland.'

'So I've heard. I've heard a whole lot about you this week. Too much.'

'I do believe you're what is known in the trade as a trigger-puller, Prince. See, I've been doing my research on the mercenary profession.'

'You do what you have to do.'

'How many people you killed in your line of murder? I mean, work.'

'I'm going to finish this jack,' Hall announced, ignoring Cowan's remark. 'Then we're all going to take a stroll back around there and admire the fine architecture.'

'I'm not going anywhere with you,' Cowan told him, reasonably. 'Sorry. I like it here. I can appreciate the nature and shit, that right?'

Jalil sniffed derisively. 'I think we got a crazy. Talkin' to me about the name of God and some shit.' He'd finished with the wallet, finding nothing of interest, stuffing two twenty dollar bills in his pocket. 'We 'bout done here?'

'This fine specimen of humanity says the G in the block there is for George,' Cowan said. 'I say God. This is an interpretive disagreement. Want to be the casting vote, Prince?' Cowan blinked rapidly a few times at him, like eyelash semaphore. 'Prince! What a silly name. For a human being I mean. Unless you're Prince William or Prince Louie Louie of Lichtenstein or such. Good name for a gelding though.'

'Giblum.'

'You making that up?'

'Nope.' Hall examined the tip of his cigarette like it was a Rorschach, flicked dead ash. 'It means stone squarer.'

'I'm beyond surprised.'

'You get a free education when you serve. That's the point of signing the papers. You be all that you can be, no one tell you that? Haven't you seen the ads?'

'No, I mean I'm surprised you're a smoker.'

Hall took another long drag and squinted at Cowan through the wraith of smoke. 'It's my only vice, Detective Inspector. Obama was a smoker. It makes me feel less bad. In fact, it makes me feel Presidential some weekends.' Hall was looking in Cowan's eyes, almost regretfully. 'You'd have been better to never come here.'

'That's what practically everyone tells me. You know, you're the third person that has pointed a gun at me in three days. Everything in threes, like a fairy tale. The first man is in hospital and the second man is dead. Just saying. No pressure.'

The tourists came back down the steps and the men either side of Cowan exchanged a glance. Hall made a delicate gesture with his hands, an oblique sign.

Cowan turned to examine the sprawl of city below them. 'You get a good view from up here. Over there on Duke Street is where you took a potshot at me that day.'

Hall offered the tiniest smirk. 'I gave you a wave though. I like to be sociable.'

'I appreciated that. You were letting me know it wasn't personal.'

'Nothing is personal.' Hall looked more serious now. 'I just can't believe I missed, is all. I'm usually deadeye.'

'Where was it you served again? Afghanistan? Iraq?'

Hall shook his head sadly at Cowan. 'You don't want to know where I've been or the kind of things I done, trust me.'

'Actually, I kind of do want to know. It's interesting to me. You leave the service and end up doing this for a living? Or is it a dying? How's that work? Angie's list?'

'Imagine you spend the best years of your life riding high-speed boats and jumping out airplanes.' Hall sighed. 'What do you do after? Sell insurance?'

'I wouldn't buy life insurance from you. I'll tell you that for nothing.'

Hall laughed. 'I've been getting shot at my whole life, man.'

'Aye, see for me it's a recent annoying phenomenon.'

'What I've discovered is that the things I know how to do really well – urban warfare, sniping, close-quarter combat – are all worthless in the civilian world.'

'Unless you're a second-hand car salesman.'

'You can make more money in a month doing contracting work than you can in a year in the service.' Hall shrugged. 'So, it has its compensations.'

'The adrenaline rush must be addictive too, I bet.'

'Perhaps.'

'And I'm sure the chicks dig it.'

'If you say so.'

'The ones you don't kill, I mean. Painful business though.'

'Pain? Pain is just weakness leaving the body. Don't you know that by now?'

'Prince,' Cowan said, thoughtfully. 'It really is some kind of name. Say, you weren't named after the midget in the purple suit? The one sang 'Darling Nikki'?'

Hall ran his tongue across his teeth and narrowed his eyes slightly. 'Great song that,' was all he said.

The couple was still stopped on the lower level by the emblem. Hall tapped two fingers against the steel railing. The sun hung lower in the sky, an invitation to night.

'What about my little girl, then?' Cowan asked, his voice become a hoarse whistle. 'I'm assuming it wasn't personal with her, either?'

Hall glanced up at the flapping flag, his expression now troubled. 'No plan survives first contact with the enemy,' he muttered.

'Aye, but in this case, the enemy was a twenty-year-old girl and the wrong girl at that. You may as well fill us in on the details. I'm not getting out of this alive, am I? Haley's not coming to make a public apology, is he? He sent along his errand boy.'

Hall cleared his throat and spat over the parapet and didn't say anything.

'You owe me that much. You can tell me how you did for Kris, too.'

Prince looked at him and shrugged. 'I don't know anyone of that name,' he said.

At last, the tourists turned away from the emblem, satiated with masonry, and moved back along the right path. In two more minutes, they'd be out of sight.

'I'm not coming with you,' Cowan said, quietly. 'You'll have to do for me here, like this. I guess it'll be another mugging gone wrong, eh? What's one more?'

Hall's face was contorting. 'It was a mistake was all. I regret it. But your daughter was not a complete innocent in all of this. A file had been shared with her, too.'

'A file containing the draft manuscript of Mary Barnham's famous book?'

Hall nodded. 'Very good work. We got the wrong woman, yes. And it's because I chose the wrong vessel for the task, yes. My bad.'

'Carlton? Sounds like that boy was seriously limited in the skill department. See, I don't think I'd ever be employing any of my old pals from the council scheme on a hit. That's just a recipe for disaster. I'd have to pay them in Buckfast wine to start with.'

'It's the trouble with non-professionals. Keeping a clear head in a crisis.' Hall winced, remembering back. 'Carlton panicked when she went after him. She sprung at him, you see. Tried to wrestle the gun away from him. Nearly did. Everything got completely out of hand. Turned into a real shitshow.'

'That was my wee girl for you, Prince, reckless and wonderful. Not going down without a fight. I suppose the headshot must have been you then? Being professional?'

'Made a mess and been tidying it up ever since. These things happen.'

'These things happen?' Cowan cackled mirthlessly. 'In your world murder and mayhem just happen? Are you going to start making the big speech about how you need to crack some eggs to make an omelette next? Sorry, I'm the hardboiled type myself.'

Hall flinched slightly. 'It's a hard world. You know that. You're police.'

Cowan tried to access fury and found he couldn't. This was a good thing. He would never get out of this angry. He needed to be composed, think carefully and act quickly. For now, jabbering like an idiot would do. 'You don't work for Haley, right?'

Hall stared at him, his mouth like a slot.

'No. Haley is small potatoes, right? You're out on assignment. You're one of Gil Martin's boys. He signs the checks. Ever meet the man in person? Does he give orders directly? I suppose Mary must have contacted Haley with questions about what she had on Tubalcain and his own connections with them, which was a lot, or enough to get the Undistinguished Gentleman creeping up to her apartment on Fairfax in the small hours for a wee chat. Mary must have had some right awkward questions for him. Maybe she insinuated something about a video that didn't get hot-washed? Am I getting warm?'

'Where you're going,' said Hall, smiling, 'will be plenty warm enough for you.'

'Haley would have the wind up bigtime after that meeting. Gets on the blower to his financial paymasters at Tubalcain in a right old panic. Pissing his pants. This business about them knocking off all and sundry whenever they feel the urge gets out there, his Presidential aspirations are up in smoke. Was the meeting in his office that day a follow-up for you Tubalcain wankers to figure out how much she knew? Or was it to make her an offer she couldn't refuse? Which was refused. Did she tell you to go fuck yourselves?'

'You talk too much.'

'Everyone and their dog says that. Especially the dog.' Cowan spat a gob on the grass. 'Woof, woof.'

Hall took a long drag on his cigarette and wafted smoke in the air. 'The thing is, no one talks too much when the flies are walking across their eyeballs.'

'Must be hard for you, Prince. I do feel bad. You being so super professional and all, and you have to work with amateurs like Lil' Wayne here.' Cowan nodded at Jalil who had been struggling to follow the conversation for a while now. 'Boys from the old neighbourhood? Black men disposable as diapers. And Martin's got them slaving on his Wringhim plantation now. What's that make you, Prince? What's the expression?'

Hall ashed his cigarette on the railing and a slow rain of orange flecks descended. 'You have to use what's at hand when you're building,' he said, turning a complete 360, seeing no one for miles. 'Different tools for different purposes.' He flicked his butt on the grass, reached into his jacket pocket, made more significant eye contact with Jalil.

They couldn't shoot him there. They must have something else in mind. Something quieter. 'What about this tool here?' Cowan asked, edging his feet closer to Jalil as he spoke. 'When this is done, you going to do for him like how you took care of Carlton? Planning to dump this one's body face-down in the Anacostia River afterwards too?'

'What the fuck this crazy rambling 'bout?' Jalil asked.

'Forget to tell you about that, did he?' Cowan tut-tut-ted his tongue on the roof of his mouth. 'You didn't let Jalil know how royalty cleans up after itself? That's the last royalty call you get, son. That's what they call a sin of omission where I'm from, Prince.'

'I hate to be rude, but you're starting to bore me.' Hall nodded at Jalil, who didn't move.

His mouth clicked open and shut. 'What you got to do with Carlton?'

Cowan toe-shuffled closer, within arm's length of the bottle now. He could have used a decent slug of it. But that wasn't what he had in mind.

'You need to kill here, cuz,' Hall said, looking uneasy now. 'This one just trying to psych the situation.'

'I was askin' is all. I been thinkin' bout how that shit went down my own self.'

'We talk about this later, aight?'

'Hold up, but way Carlton was buggin'…'

Jalil didn't complete his thought because Cowan had

scooped up the malt liquor bottle with both hands and brought it down hard upon his purple do-rag. There was a dull hollow glassy thud and the cap popped. Blood and liquor sprayed on the stonework, a newer blend. Jalil staggered sideways like a stunned cow and Cowan hit him again, smacking him on the cheekbone with the big bottle so hard it shattered. Cheap-ass wine came in a cheap-ass glass. He was left holding the wide jagged neck. He regarded it seriously. Jalil's knees buckled, and his eyes rolled back like a man far gone in drink. which in a matter of speaking he was, being now well splattered in it. He toppled onto the grass embankment, where he thrashed for a moment, his legs kicking as though pedaling an invisible bicycle, displacing a wave of dirt. When he fell, the gun spun between the railings and onto the emblem, clattering across the gray stone.

Cowan was still trying to gauge where it went when Hall's body flew into his, a linebacker's hit, a full tilt concussive blow. The momentum of the collision sent both men across the railing and off the parapet. Coupled as Siamese twins, they fell with a hollow thud onto the carved square below. It was a four-foot drop, nothing too spectacular, but they crashed down hard and awkwardly on the big stone G. Cowan's back spat rapid sparks of pain. Only a tsunami of adrenaline and terror got him upright.

Hall was hurt worse, his right shoulder dislocating when it struck the stone. His arm hung limp by his side where he sat and he had the demeanour of a man who'd failed to accomplish a basic task, now targeting fury like a laser at his own ineptitude. He eyed his enemy through a mist of hurt and rage. Cowan scrambled across the stone searching frantically for the missing gun. He couldn't see it anywhere. Hall was back on his feet now and with the subtlest flick of his wrist, like a conjuror's trick, a small ivory knife appeared between his fingers. Cowan backed up across the stone G as Hall advanced towards him, at every step dabbing the knife tentatively at his chest. Cowan felt the indentation of the stone letter beneath his feet. Hall was in his element and trained to kill in situations like this, hand to hand. But he was injured, already switching the blade to his left hand, eyes moist with the agony of the dislocation. His status evened things up. The third time he awkwardly thrust with his left hand, wincing as he did so, Cowan skewered him on the wrist with the broken bottleneck.

'I'm going to kill you,' Hall snarled, baring his teeth. He looked at the bottleneck embedded in his wrist, the blood spurting soft around it. He took a step forward, his face crumpled with pain. 'I'm going to kill your ass. Kill your ass,' he chanted. But the knife hung limp from his hand, an empty threat. How much purchase did he have on it?

They circled one another on the stone emblem in the attitude of dancers. Hall crouched on the compass, Cowan on the square. Only one dancer was able to lead here. Cowan half-expected to be numbed by panic, but his mind was clear as a summer burn on Skye. He could have taught a class in homicidal mindfulness. This close to death, he felt untroubled, philosophical even, about mortality. He discovered he very much wanted to live and found he was no longer afraid.

When Hall made another pathetic lunge at him, Cowan tugged on the elastic in his sleeve and the razorblade embedded in plywood snapped into his fingers. He jinked to one side and stroked the blade with a neat downward motion across Hall's exposed cheek. It was such a Glasgow move, no mean city of the slash. The blade slit Hall, temple to chin. His skin tore like paper. He gave a cry and fell to one knee. Cowan booted him hard in the jaw and, dropping over his prostrate figure, plunged the blade into his neck. Scrabbling, his hand located a jagged rock in the undergrowth. He picked it up. There was a thick wet smack on contact. He felt it sink into the face and something broke, a crack and splitting of little bones. He didn't think about anything except his need to sponge that softness with the stone. By the time he was done there was no face anymore to speak of.

Afterwards, he sat on the compass edge, catching his breath, still watching. He tried to locate something to feel. He thought it important to be feeling something. The spurting was making a red tributary across the indentation of the square and compass. The blood lodged in the stone channels like the flooding of a river valley. The handle protruded from Hall's neck and the plywood quivered each time a jet squirted under the blade. 'Nobody's killed me yet,' Cowan muttered. Hall's thigh was twitching still and there was a soft wet blubbering, but the dead look had come to him now.

After a while of searching, Cowan found the gun in a bush below the parapet.

Jalil was up in a seated position now, feeling at his face with his hands. One cheek was badly swollen and one eye closing fast. Cowan noticed that his left ear was bleeding too. He jammed the gun in it. 'I told you drinking was bad for you,' he said.

'What the fuck you do?' moaned Jalil, blood seeping between his fingers.

'You've heard the expression hitting the bottle? This time the bottle went and hit you. I think you might be concussed, although that'd be hard to tell with you, son. You're already about a seven on the Glasgow coma scale.' Cowan tracked the cut on the top of the kid's head with his palm. 'You're going to need a doctor.'

'I don't believe in them,' Jalil groaned. 'Fucks stick you with needles and shit.'

'You need stitches. It won't hurt.'

"It won't hurt' always does,' Jalil noted philosophically, looking despondent.

Cowan grabbed him under the armpits and hauled him to his feet. The thing that had been Hall was twitching on the stone still, but just the one foot now, some muscle memory that didn't know yet, nerves firing messages, blanks, undelivered, electricity shorting. The blood-squirt rhythmic wet pulse of us all. Cowan jammed the gun into Jalil's neck forcing him to look at the body spread on the emblem, each arm forming a 90-degree angle, like some final signal of distress. Jalil didn't say anything about it. 'Head hurts like a motherfucker,' he observed.

'That could be you,' Cowan informed him. 'Him lying there. Just saying.'

'Could be. But ain't.' Jalil shrugged. 'I didn't like him much, anyways. He had a bad attitude, know what I'm sayin'. Now he doesn't so much.'

The blood spilling thick and viscous upon the emblem made the stone slippery. Cowan had never considered the slipperiness of blood on stone.

'Where'd the motherfucker's face go?'

'Take off your jacket,' Cowan ordered.

'It's a classic RG3, man.'

'Give us the fucking jacket.'

Jalil took it off and handed it to him. Cowan removed his own jacket. He looked at it nostalgically. They'd been through a lot together. 'Here,' he said, tossing the donkey jacket at Jalil. 'Wipe that stone off with this.'

'You serious? The stone?'

'Do I look serious?'

'I dunno what you look like.'

Jalil commenced scrubbing the stone with the jacket. Just then, the declining sun freakishly seemed to dart its golden rays to the centre. Both men looked up, for a moment disturbed by the solar interruption. Then they got back to the bloody task at hand.

'Move the body off first, obviously,' Cowan said, getting frustrated. 'And be careful you don't go and slip and fall. That would be embarrassing.' He hauled on the other man's sweatshirt. 'It's important not to embarrass yourself.' Cowan flipped up the hood and sat hunched like a monk, keeping the gun leveled at Jalil till he was finished wiping the stone. The hoodie made him very self-conscious. His back hurt and his legs had decided to start shaking again. He wondered if he was going into shock. That was all he needed.

'Now what?'

'Now, how's about you drag that corpse under that there bush, see it? For now.'

'You goin' to shoot me or what?'

'Depends on you.'

Jalil shrugged, like he didn't care one way or another. He dragged the body under the bush and kicked it into concealment. He wiped his hands clean on the grass when he returned. He kept sticking a finger in his ear every few seconds.

'You know how to make this all go away?' Cowan asked.

'How you mean?'

'I mean can you make a call to the people you work for, the ones who set this up, and make it go away? Like it never happened. You connected? Or is that what Prince did before he abdicated? Do you have any other number?'

'Maybe.'

'Fucking do it then. Make a call. Then you can go get some stitches.'

'I think I got a number some place. You not goin' to shoot me?'

'Nah. I want to pretty bad, but I might need the bullets where I'm going.'

'The safety is still on.'

'Yeah, I figured.'

'Can't shoot nobody with the safety on. You retarded?'

'Don't use that word. You going to make that call or not?'

'What do I say?'

'Tell them you fucked up. Say Prince is dead. Tell them the man you planned to waste got away. He's a slippery bloody bastard. Literally. Say he ran off in the direction of the Metro. Tell them you need a body disposed of and a ride to the hospital. Got it?'

'That's it?'

'That it. No texting though. Call. I want to hear everything said out loud.'

Jalil's eyes never once left Cowan's face while he spoke on the phone. Finished, Cowan took the phone from him and threw it against the stone emblem.

'The fuck?'

'Doing you a favour, son. Don't you know that the mobile phone is destroying the art of conversation? I read it in *The Beano*.'

'That a new fucking iPhone!'

Cowan took off the safety and leveled the gun at Jalil's groin. 'Go take a walk over yonder and find my wallet for me.'

Jalil came back with it. 'You take really bad photos, man. They do the licence over you ask, you know? Don't nobody have to go through life looking that ugly-ass.'

'You can keep the 40 bucks and put it toward a new coat.' Cowan stuffed the wallet in his back pocket. 'Then you do me a big favour and get yourself a new line of work. You're not cut out for this. Be an exotic male dancer or a postman or something.'

'You not goin' to shoot me?'

'Don't tempt me. You keep bringing it up, I'm liable to.' Cowan lowered the gun and took off down the steps.

'You really goin' to the Metro?' Jalil called after him.

Cowan turned around and aimed the gun at him. 'It matter to you?'

'I ain't say shit. No matter, now.' Jalil's lip was in a full pout. 'You sure you need to keep that jacket?'

'Uh-huh.'

'Aight bet. Redskins blow this year. Smith couldn't score in a whorehouse.'

'That's what I hear.'

★ ★ ★

He walked quickly along King Street, glancing nervously at the traffic headed east. The street whirled like the blades of a fan. He went into a Mexican restaurant, suddenly famished. Maybe that's what killing someone did to you: gave you a real appetite. He asked to be seated at a window table, one overlooking the main drag.

4.15pm, night fast falling, headlights coming on.

He settled back in his chair, looked around at the massive rack of glasses by the bar, the giant longhorns above the kitchen, the array of weird masks in rows on the brick walls. Even that scary-ass Frida Kahlo in the painting looked seductive tonight. He was safe. The waitress who took his order was checking him out. She was a young, leggy, sloe-eyed blonde in too-tight jeans and a low-cut blouse. He didn't attract that kind of attention from this young a woman anymore. In his early thirties, a cloak of invisibility had descended on him in that regard. He wondered if he had the look of a stone-cold killer too: maybe the danger he was exuding tonight made him more attractive to the females of the species. Something evolutionary.

The waitress returned with his Pepsi, big-eyeing him all the way across the room. She was staring at him so blatantly that he felt obligated to stare back, blatantly. She was pretty. He began thinking about Kris and how much he wanted to be with her and for a second drifted off into another pleasanter space. Then he remembered she was dead. When the waitress brought his order, she'd also put on the tray a glass of water without ice and a big pile of napkins. She leaned her breasts across him and he deep-whiffed her perfume as she whispered in his ear. 'Sir, there's blood. It's on your face.' He looked at her. 'It's, like, all over your cheeks.'

He took a napkin from her and dipped it in the glass of water and began wiping the blood away. There was a lot of it, caked and crusted, and it wasn't even his. He depleted the pile of napkins quickly. 'I think I must have cut myself,' he mumbled at her. 'Shaving.'

The waitress leaned into him again, giving him a look

of concern tinctured, he now realised, with horror. 'There's blood on your hands too,' she said.

There was.

12   TUESDAY (NIGHT)

A night turned chill. A wet wind swirling west, up the streets from the river. A slick of ice etched silver arrows on the pavement and a bright moon hung above like a new-laid egg. Up the darkened street, came a woman walking a small dog on a long leash. She scooped something from the sidewalk into a Safeway bag. She wore enormous black earmuffs, her face the white icing between, and in passing, Cowan offered her the same look she'd given the dog shit. The wind slashed through the jacket and stuck to his bones. Across the grass, dark leaves poured, a boa of them blown to the base of the brick wall encircling the Wringhim House.

He kicked a foothold in a mortar and levered himself up. He swung his legs over, hung dangling like a puppet, and dropped thief-quiet on the bare lawn. Small trees by the colonnade were frosted with orange light and in the pale-blue windows the full moon was yellow as an ivory skull. Sky crepuscular, a dark blue water with the sheen of moonlight on it, like he'd dropped into the painting of an Edward Hopper dream. He moved along the shadows in a crouch, smooth metal of the gun, cold on his palm, expecting a siren blare with every step he took. There would be cameras, alarm systems, infrared lasers, spotlights, motion detectors, and sensors. There would be security guards set to unleash vicious Alsatians. There would be… nothing at all.

No alarm, no camera, no dog, no meaning. Just a sky like an empty sea, frothed by the blaze of a single white star.

Cowan saw a seated figure on the bench at the back and froze, horror-struck. Then he recalled Thomas Jefferson, who was harmless here. He remembered the motto: *Visita interiora terrae, rectifando invenies occultam lapidem*, whatever the fuck that meant. On he slunk like the burglar he was, closer to the back entrance of the house. He'd come to kill or, failing that, be killed. Since leaving the restaurant, the problem of the universe had been revolving in him, and the enemy he sought had now swollen in his imagination into the very image of the ungraspable phantom of life and the key to it all. But in a garden that seemed strangely familiar to him, that enemy seemed just a man not at home. Cowan had come too far in his quest to go back. He gave Jefferson an affectionate pat on his hard head and touched a finger to the cold glass. No alarm still. He was the only one alarmed tonight. He could lob a brick through this window and nothing would happen. As if what was to come under this blazing star was presumed in advance, predestined centuries before his coming here.

'Mr Cowan.'

From the black lawn came a voice, sounding out of the darkness, identifying him. His own name seemed strange then and fear came in rippling waves, crawling across his skin like many small black flies. He was inking into the night. The handle of the gun shone with the sweat of his palm. The voice came from within the folly. Cowan walked towards it, surrendered to some mechanical impulse, as a medium under a mesmerist's veil. The pale humped shape, like a heaped snow hill, sat stock-still and squat beneath the five pillars: a ghostly thing under a rusted dome, with white smoke spiraling. Cowan held the gun at arm's length. His hand shaking like it held an icicle. He watched the trembling of it. Was the gun causing his hand to shake, or his hand the gun? Cause and effect was all garbled now.

'Come, please.' A voice so oil-smooth and pleasant. 'I've been waiting for you all this time. I feared you'd lost your way.'

Cowan commanded his feet to move and approached the folly. The wind picked up, gusting leaves around the white figure sat amid the pillars on a white wicker chair, a pipe curled in a white fist. Clouds of smoke rose, as if from an old puffer on the Clyde. Gil Martin was very fat and wore a white bathrobe and tiny red slippers delicate as a little girl's ballet shoes. His feet must have been very cold in those cloven red pointes. An elderly man with such dainty feet should not be sitting out in this chill.

'The Great Architect of Wringhim, I take it?'

'Oh, I just laid the cornerstone.' The accompanying Gallic shrug gave Martin the appearance of having a white pyramidical hump and his shaven head glistened in the darkness like a white cue ball. 'You look,' he said to Cowan, 'like a man has been rode hard and put away wet.' Martin laughed, bending slightly, his fat flesh a sudden snow-slide, his bathrobe belt trailing like a white snake.

Music rippled out of the folly, a drip of exploratory piano keys, a prelude to a gorgeous nocturne. The music seemed to flow around Cowan's body and trail behind him like a wake, immersing him in softness. It was as if he could see the notes ascend, give them visible shape, blue bubbles floating delicately on a stave of darkness. 'I had new speakers installed,' Martin explained. 'I'm more of a classic blues man myself, Robert Johnson at the crossroads and so on.'

Cowan examined the broad, milky forehead. Criss-crossed by the shadows of the pillars, it seemed a complex hieroglyph of wrinkles. The gun wobbled in the jelly mold that was his right hand. He laced the fingers of his left hand around his wrist to steady it.

'But why the long face? As the jockey said to his horse.' Martin opened his mouth wide to laugh and so offered a glimpse of the bluish pearl-white of the inside of his jaw. 'Things aren't so bad. Even a spotted pig looks black at night.'

Cowan was making the discovery that he could not speak at all.

'Tonight, you have broken and entered. You have torn down laws you swore to uphold.' Martin had a white dimpled smile of fathomless contempt. 'If anyone has cause to be upset, it would be me. Am I not the injured party? Speak you.' Martin tapped out his pipe on the white-wicker and the ashes dispersed as a white cloud. He rested a red packet of tobacco on the arm of the chair and refilled the pipe, tightly packing the bowl. 'You have piled upon this unfortunate visage the sum of all the general rage and hatred felt by man, since Adam spent too long in the garden listening to his wife regarding his diet. And now you come skulking here and have nothing to say?' He lit his pipe and puffed experimentally, sending up signals of tiny clouds against the dark.

'I'm going to kill you,' Cowan announced, at last locating his voice. He tightened his finger around the trigger but could not bend it.

Martin was unconcerned. 'After all this, don't you know who I am?'

'You're nothing.'

The shadows beneath the old man's almost transparent white skin seemed to knit in the murk. 'It's possible,' he muttered, morosely.

The wind whistling through the pillars was tinged with odours of autumn decay.

'Before I blow your brains out, how's about you indulge me with the truth?'

'Truth!' Martin's laugh was in the music. 'Dabble your toe in it and it's nothing. Wade in further and you feel the undertow, a pull so slow you scarcely notice, till it's too late.' Martin shivered, perturbed at the drift of his thoughts. 'Then the whirling plunge down and down into darkness.' He hoisted his pipe to his mouth, red coals glowing. 'They do say it's a dreadful thing to fall from the Grace of God.'

'I didn't come to be lectured by some fat corporate fuck about the nature of evil.'

'You didn't?' Martin gave Cowan a quizzical look that

was difficult to achieve without eyebrows. He appeared to be completely hairless, like a baby. 'I am more than corporate, I'm a statesman.' He examined a pocket of green light on his lap, then resumed his dissertation: 'A statesman is a student of history who has learned that a human being is a complex creature, neither good nor bad, and the good can come out of the bad and the bad can, as well, come out of the good, and the devil take the hindmost.'

'Know what my definition of a statesman is?' Cowan evacuated a gob of spittle on a pillar. 'A dead politician. I think what the world needs is a lot more statesmen.'

The old man rocked back in his chair rearranging thick folds of creamy flesh beneath his robe. 'A wise man said that when buying and selling are controlled by legislation, the first things to be bought and sold are legislators.' Martin examined the curved stem of his pipe and, again, the rectangular light on his lap, a phone perhaps. 'Weren't your own legislators bought and sold by English gold, a parcel of rogues?'

'Now you're a student of Scottish history as well?'

'Haven't you noticed the ways that history envelops you here in this place? Isn't it just uncanny? At any rate, I cannot be bought and sold.' Martin sighed. 'If I have a weakness, it is pride.'

'You don't say.'

'Where was I? Oh yes. The events with which you have concerned yourself are part of a process. Process in itself is neither morally good nor bad. We may judge results but not process. At this time results are, sadly, uncertain. But faith is hope in things unseen. In any case, a morally bad agent may perform a deed that is good and a morally good agent, a deed that is bad. Do you see my point?'

'No.'

'My point is: what if a man has to sell his soul to get the power to do good?'

Cowan raised his foot onto the stone rim of the folly and slowly lowered the gun onto his knee. His arm bucked in a bluster, melded with the dripping music, a musical wind or windy music, he couldn't tell. The marble floor was checkered, black and white squares like a chessboard, but liquefied now, black white, white black, the distinction blurred in some geometrical miscegenation. The pillars, fused in five points at the dome's chapiters, wind buffeted now, seemed to be detaching and the ceiling, studded with a design of triple tau triangles, strained upward to the sky. Cowan wrestled his gun barrel till it was pointed directly at the old man's skull.

Martin sat up, causing his great belly to quiver and ripple like blancmange. He tucked it in some, looking amused. 'You cannot kill me. Too much guilt involved.'

Cowan hauled back on the trigger. The muzzle flashes came and went as yellow eyes, percussion crashing into the sky. He poured bullets into the dark. One of the casings got up inside his collar and he felt hot metal sliding down his back. His ears were blasted out and everything was muffled, a watery ringing. The soil was littered with brass.

'A brilliant fellow, Calvin,' Martin said, unscathed and

yawning. 'Believed in the potency of the imagination, said you could solve problems in your dreams. Calvin's first proof of the soul was that human beings want to know why the planets move.' He put down his pipe and uplifted his two plump little hands to the heavens as if he might reach into the depths of the Milky Way and pluck a soul like a white grape with those thick fingers. 'They need to know why that star is arranged just so.'

Cowan was staring at the stupid gun still. What the hell? He had fucked up righteously. 'What would you know about souls?' he bawled into the folly, frustrated beyond belief. 'You take a bubble bath in other people's pain.'

A gust whipped up his hands and the gun scudded off into the black of the sky.

'Calvin believed all experience is visionary and all of us equally competent perceivers of any vision. For Calvin everyone was a visionary! How visionary an idea!'

Cowan examined his empty hands. He could see the little blue veins pulse between the thin bones. No stigmata there. He felt like crying or praying.

Martin was upright, balanced on the balls of his feet, so that the movement of his rising seemed a thing imperfectly perceived, an error of vision on the observer's part. The wind billowed the sperm-white robe around him and he resembled a great white mad monk. Cowan had to force his hands down by his side, leaning at a 45-degree angle now. The wind ripped at his clothes like a boy-band groupie. 'I suppose I'm dreaming, is all?'

A shiny bald mass of bone-white skull nodded agreeably.

'You want to tell me that I dreamed my daughter dead too? I can accept that.'

'No. She is dead and the dead do not return, as a rule.' Martin coughed. 'With notable exceptions. Those who made her so will soon all be dead also. Symmetries.'

'You'll find others like them.'

'No doubt.'

The hooded phantom was fading, a still voice from the centre of a whirlwind.

'And you get to swim away scot free?'

'No doubt.'

'I can't accept that.' Cowan's throat rasped hoarse. 'I doubt. I doubt. I doubt.'

The vision in the night enveloped in blowing white fabric, sheathed, hooded as a Klansman, like the wreckage of sails on a stricken ship. When Cowan stepped inside the folly to see, the night started to melt around him and the stone-work dripped oil black.

Cowan tried to force his eyes open. He really could have used a couple of matchsticks for propping his eyelids, like a cartoon cat. The headlights of the car were blinding white.

He closed his eyes again. His breathing was shallow in his lungs and he felt very hot.

He had no idea what the hell had happened. 'Everything alright now?' the woman asked, bending over him.

Cowan tried to get up and toppled backwards against

something firm and hard. His clothes felt damp, from sweat or who knew what. Jalil's jacket was tied around his waist like an apron. One of his pants legs was rolled up. 'I don't know,' he said to her.

His world reassembled brick by brick, giving him location first. He had his back to the long cold boundary wall of the Wringhim house, right outside the front gate. The woman now inquiring after his health was the Senator's wife, Yumi Ishiku.

'I must have had a wee turn,' Cowan said to her. 'A turn for the worse, that is.'

'You were passed out, I think,' she said, her hand on his arm. 'Lightheaded?'

Cowan brushed a caking of soil from his jeans, embarrassed. 'I'm...'

'Yes,' she interrupted. 'I know who you are. We met. My husband also told me about you. When I saw you laying here I thought you were a homeless person.'

'I get that a lot.'

'But then I recognised you. How did you get this close to my house without alerting security? You look awful. Do you think you can try to stand up now?'

'Yes, I think I'm about ready for something like that.' She helped Cowan to his feet. He went lurching on the pavement like a newborn giraffe on ice. He put the jacket on properly and pulled down his pants leg. He felt a little less ridiculous. Not much though.

'You should come in,' she said, with an expression of

vague concern. 'Till you're yourself again. Then we'll get you a cab, perhaps.'

Ishiku disarmed the security system by punching a four-digit code in a box on the wall. The gate whined open. She pulled her Mercedes sedan into the driveway and parked in front of the garage. Cowan tottered along behind her car. Two young men in dark suits, wearing coiled earpieces, scooted out of the shadows to intercept him. 'It's OK,' she called out of her window to them. 'He's visiting with me.'

'All right ma'am.' One of the men opened her door, bowing slightly as she exited, and then took her place in the driver's seat.

Cowan followed Ishiku along the colonnade. She wore sneakers and moved soundlessly on the gravel. The lawn was lit by little searchlights, illuminating the blue shoulder bag she carried. It had the logo of Jahbulon Yoga. Somewhere a dog snuffled and snarled. From beyond the border of the garden, further in the night, came a whiff of entrails of greenness and a rising scent like mildew, a soft rotten dampening. Ishiku unlocked the door with a click of her keychain and then disarmed a second security system. In the kitchen, she pointed to the high stool by an oaken table. Cowan sat on it and propped himself against the table's edge. His skull felt balloon-like. Ishiku poured a tumbler of water and scooped ice from the icebox and brought it to him. He gulped it down greedily, like a man just stumbled out of desert sands.

Leaving the kitchen for a moment, Ishiku returned

minus sweatshirt and bag and poured a tumbler for herself. The tap from which she filled her glass had a white filter. Cowan could observe her more closely now. She intrigued him. She was small and delicate, black hair feathered into bangs, eyes the same coffee-brown as the marbles he'd played with as a child.

'Feeling better?'

'I've had kind of a wild night to tell you the truth.'

'You look like it. What was it you came to see my husband about this evening?'

'My daughter.' Cowan streaked the condensation on the tumbler with his finger. 'I don't know if he talks to you about that.'

'We share everything.'

'Everything?'

'Yes.'

'You really are the quintessential Washington power couple, then.'

She smiled pleasantly at him, brushing a jet-black strand behind her ear, tucking it in. 'I heard it was a terrible accident. I feel so bad for you. The poor girl.'

She sat on the stool opposite him and conducted a thorough examination of her fingernails, green tipped and sharp. Her teeth were very small and impossibly even. She had an abstracted air, like her mind was elsewhere. She was younger than her husband, late-thirties, Cowan estimated. 'It wasn't altogether an accident,' he said to her.

She didn't acknowledge hearing him. 'I had the most

awful news tonight myself,' she said, meditatively, finger-nails still spread before her. 'A little while ago, I found out that someone very close to me has died also.'

'I beg your pardon?' Cowan assumed he was mishearing her now.

She was apologetic. 'I only learned an hour ago. I got a call. I think I'm still in shock. When I saw you in the driveway, I was confused. I wasn't sure you were real.'

Cowan wasn't always sure what reality was either. The two of them had that in common. He had to concentrate to stop his mouth dropping open like a basset hound's.

'He was in Louisville,' she explained, with a long sigh. 'This friend of mine. It was a massive myocardial infarction, so they tell me. One minute he was talking and then he just collapsed and couldn't be revived. He died on his way to the hospital.'

Cowan didn't know what to say. He tried, 'I'm so sorry.'

She took a sip of water. He watched the muscles move in her throat as she swallowed. 'To be honest, my friend did not look after himself. His diet was awful. Good eating habits are very important.' She pinioned the tumbler between her fingers. On the third finger of her left hand, she wore a pale green ring, an emerald he supposed, larger than was usual. 'But it's still a dreadful shock. Is it bad I can't feel anything yet?'

'The grief comes later,' he said. 'There's a delay. Then it hits like a steam train.'

'I have to fly down first thing in the morning to Kentucky.' She smiled uneasily. 'It's all so stupid and surreal. I'm still processing.'

'Yes,' Cowan said. 'It's a process.'

'I got the call at yoga and came home in a fog, to find you lying like a dead man by my gate. It's so strange to talk to you. Another?' She refilled his glass, this time no ice. She laid the tumbler before him. 'I'm sorry, I keep nothing stronger in the house.'

'That's fine,' he said. 'I'm loud enough without.'

'Mr Cowan… May I call you Charles?' He nodded, impressed at the fact she remembered. 'Were you named after the Bonnie Prince?'

'Could have been. I just hope it wasn't Charles Atlas.'

'Who was he?'

'A man who used to get sand kicked in his face.'

'How unfortunate for him.'

They sat in silence, an electric clock chirping like a cricket on the wall.

'Ishiku? That would be a Japanese name?'

She nodded. 'My parents came to this country many years ago.'

'It's a nation of immigrants this, right enough.'

'But I was born here.' She was adamant on this point. 'I was born a citizen.'

He wondered if her blasé reaction to death was cultural. That's probably how they could do what they did in Manchuria that time. The thought was racist. He had to work on that. He really did. A blue radiator ticked and hissed in the corner of the kitchen. She looked at him, soft brown eyes opaque, scrutinising and yet betraying no particular interest. As if it had occurred to her that before her now sat a curious specimen, something she might consider pinning on the corkboard of her insect collection.

'With my husband…' she began, hesitated, and resumed. 'In speaking on behalf of my husband, I am in a position where I can make certain… promises.'

'I'm afraid you've lost me, Mrs Factor. Promises?'

'Your face is very bruised,' she said, looking concerned. 'Do you know that?'

'Aye. I fell on a rock.'

'You fell on a rock. Goodness. Do you fall down a lot?'

'Apparently.' Cowan shrugged. 'Recently, at any rate.'

Ishiku eased her hand across the table and her fingers touched his sleeve. He wondered what she made of his jacket. It was a bit young for him. So was she. She spoke so quietly he could barely hear her. 'If Haley were here, he would want this to be over.'

Cowan looked at where her hand touched him. 'What 'this' would that be?'

'I have no wish to play games,' she said, sighing and withdrawing her hand. 'I am quite tired tonight.'

'Who's playing games here? You're the one talking like a crossword puzzle.'

Ishiku took a lung-deep breath and exhaled. It was probably a technique she'd learned in yoga. 'To my mind,' she said, tapping the tabletop three times for emphasis, 'these recent deaths have squared the circle.'

'Am I still dreaming?' Cowan asked her. 'Am I outside lying in your driveway?'

'No,' she said. 'You are here in my kitchen, Mr Cowan. You are not dreaming anymore.' She stood up and pushed the button on the intercom on the wall then sat down again. Her long nails tapped a percussive rhythm on the tumbler. 'Pym will be here in a few minutes.'

'What did you mean exactly?' Cowan asked. 'By promises?'

'I'd like for you to have no other...' She searched for the word. 'Problems.'

'Problems? You're all about the promises and the problems, aren't you?'

'Also.' It seemed to be taking her forever to open and close her eyes now. 'I'll see to it that steps are taken to ensure you and others are protected from further harm.'

The conversation was making him feel lightheaded again. How many levels were there to his dreams? Was his unconscious a parking garage? Was all he saw or seemed to see just a dream within a dream, like the wee drunk man said? 'Steps? What?'

'This is what I will do for you.' She put her hand again upon his sleeve. His arm felt warm where she touched it. He tried to think, but couldn't. These days Cowan always felt like a man who'd come to the coconut shy only to be handed an algebra test. 'I don't know what's keeping him,' she said, looking towards the door and shaking her head.

'Excuse me, what you're telling me here, is that no one else will die? And that you're in a position to make such promises on behalf of your murdering spouse?'

She pressed the tumbler against her mouth. She didn't drink from it, just let her lips bulge red against the glass. Her green ring blurred vermillion through the liquid in the fluorescence of the lighting. 'I made no promise about dying,' she said. 'I said nothing untoward would happen to you or anyone you know. On this you have my word.'

'Nothing untoward? I forgot you were a lawyer, lady. You've got a way with words. Or you get away with them. Tell me, what exactly is your word worth anyway?'

'A great deal.' She wrinkled her nose. 'De Gaulle said that since a politician never believes what he says, he is always surprised to be taken at his word.'

'Is this Asterix De Gaulle you're referring to?'

'But,' she added, ignoring him. 'I am not a politician yet.'

'Yet?'

'When my husband eventually retires from public service, as he someday surely will, I will naturally have to run for his seat.'

'Naturally.'

'The spouse always has some advantage in those circumstances. Elections are important. I'm sure you realise that.'

'There's nothing like an election day, especially for the elect. And you will win, of course, being the wife, having your husband's political machine behind you.'

'And I will win.' This Ishiku uttered dreamily, looking up at the ceiling.

'Aye, and that'll be another gala day for Haley's friends at Tubalcain.' The radiator burbled on as her eyes fixed him in place. It began whistling, a continuous shrill tone high and keening, like a thin jet of steam bleeding through a valve. 'You'll be in a position to do something then, though,' Cowan said, scanning her features, eager for confirmation. 'When you're a Senator. You can do something about them.'

'How so?' She seemed to be wryly amused at the intensity of his intonation.

'Wringhim. Tubalcain. Your husband lives in that corporation's back pocket. But do you have any conception of what that lot are up to? What they will ask of you?'

She said nothing, letting the water in her glass slosh back and forth.

'You ever meet the legendary Gil Martin?'

'No.' She covered her mouth demurely with her hand. 'I'm sorry. I'm not laughing at you. It's just... well, I'll let you in on one of the greatest secrets of all.'

Cowan waited, having no idea what she was about to reveal to him.

'There is no Gil Martin,' she giggled. 'He's a figure created by the company. He's just a convenient myth. You see they did a bit of dynamic modelling, consumer studies. Their business model depends upon guarantees of privacy and security but above all else, given what they do, with the military and the CIA and so on, absolute secrecy. That they are able to conceal and mislead so much about their own origins and founder is…'

'Evidence of their efficiency and dependability.'

'Exactly.'

'So the biggest secret is, there is no secret. There is no man behind the curtain.'

'No man. You might think of it as an issue of corporate personhood. In Citizens United versus FEC a very important principle was reaffirmed, Mr Cowan: that corporations are people. Tubalcain also affirms that principle in its own unique way.'

'It's a unique enterprise for sure, I'll give you that. Most people in my experience don't go scooting all around the globe knocking off anybody or anything that bothers them. That's unique. So, what you're telling me is that Gil is just a figure to divert us from all the horrific things they do, like the wee doggie nodding on a serial killer's dashboard.'

Ishiku shrugged slightly. Her eyes now seemed hard and bright without any depth to them. In her face, there was no trace of affect at all.

'You know a lot more about the Tubalcain business model than I expected.' Gazing into those cold eyes of hers, Cowan suddenly felt his stomach flip like a pancake on the griddle. 'That isn't just because your husband talked about them though, is it?'

'No. I'm on the Board of Directors.' She smiled, exposing a row of even white teeth, and it was only then that he realised that this little woman, seemingly fragile as a paper crane, scared him senseless. 'We are currently engaged in shifting resources away from security contracting, due to the extensive risks in that sector. I'm sure you can imagine. We're currently effecting a merger with other corporate security operations.'

'And this is how you can go making promises to me? And how you make my problems go away? There is no man behind the curtain right enough. It's a woman.'

'I will need to resign all of my directorships before I run for election, of course.' She presented him with a lofty empty smile. 'But that will be some years from now, obviously, when my husband is no longer capable of doing so himself.'

Cowan's mouth was parched and he suddenly felt very afraid. 'So there's a deal on the table for me, right now? What did you mean earlier when you said you would protect those close to me? Everyone really close to me is dead already.'

'Exactly what I said: nothing less, nothing more.' Ishiku smiled, turning to greet her entering bodyguard. Pym wore a grey suit, immaculately cut. At once, he commenced eye-fucking Cowan the exact same way Hall had a few days before. There was something in reincarnation, after all. Pythagoras had it right. That girl knew all the angles.

'Ready, ma'am?'

'You can bring her in now.'

Pym exited the room immediately at her command.

'I could go to the police,' Cowan said. 'Fill them in on everything I know.'

'To tell them what? No one will believe you. You poor man, you know nothing.'

'I could still make life pretty damn inconvenient for you.'

'Please.' Ishiku's look froze the blood solid in his veins. How could Cowan have ever known in a thousand years that the ultimate horror would be a pair of soft brown eyes? Flannelfeet was a rank amateur in this company. In the depth of these eyes he found some ultimate emotional vacuum, the bland banality of ledgers of profit and loss. The place where law and politics and business met was deep and dark and dull and looked like an old cemetery. It looked like Yumi Ishiku's eyes.

'At the Masonic memorial in Alexandria tonight there was an incident…'

'No. You are confused. Nothing at all happened. It is as it ever was.'

'When I was in Manassas yesterday…'

'There is nothing but dead fields of corn and spilled wine.' Ishiku stared off as if seeing the cornfields of which she spoke. 'You are tired and sick. Perhaps you've begun drinking again, Mr Cowan. Remember, you told me you fall down a great deal?'

When Pym returned, he brought Kris with him. He pushed her into the kitchen ahead of him. She stumbled a little, looking gawky and beautiful and terrified. Cowan was at once overcome with a great and unreasonable happiness, like one born again. Kris was dishevelled and bleary-eyed and obviously very frightened. He understood that.

She looked at him pleadingly. He'd got her into this. He was a prize idiot. She was wearing a t-shirt and sweatpants. It wasn't her look at all.

'I thought you were dead,' he blurted at her. 'I thought these bastards killed you. I wasn't coping very well with that thought at all, actually.'

'I'm alright,' Kris said, looking towards Ishiku. 'I'm just tired and scared. These people kept me here all last night. I don't know what it is they want with me.'

'You are a house guest,' Ishiku said, coldly. 'No harm has come to you here.'

'Did you buy the new outfit online?' Cowan asked Kris, taking her in his arms and dragging her close to him, needing once more to inhale all of her. 'Because, seriously, I think you might be due a major refund.'

Kris laughed nervously. 'Your new friends here kicked my door down and dragged me out of bed in the middle of the night.'

'Aye, they're like the Gestapo that way. I at least hope they let you bring your teddy bear hot water bottle with you? I know you can't survive without that.'

Kris buried her head in his shoulder. She was shaking. Cowan stroked her hair, murmured in her ear that everything was OK now. He didn't believe it for a second.

'The two of you have an intimacy,' Ishiku said, regarding them with disdain. 'I approve of intimacy. It does not, in every circumstance, connote weakness.'

'Well, as long we have your approval, Yumi, we're all

set.' Cowan took Kris by the hand. 'I guess we can bugger off home now in time for the *Late Show*?'

'I know all about the intimacy you share,' Ishiku continued, bleak and unsmiling. 'Because a film was made, of necessity. For your own protection even. The two of you together in a hotel room on Capitol Hill, I believe. In the small hours of the morning.'

Kris put her hand over her mouth.

'Well, I hope you enjoyed our performance,' Cowan said. 'If I'd known there was an audience we'd have done requests, like Congress of the Cow. Did you pick up some pointers? I'm sure there's some stuff on tape Haley could try in the bedroom? Could you leak it to the media now, so I can get famous and have my own television programme?'

'Chic,' said Kris, very quietly. 'I think you need to be quiet and listen.'

Ishiku looked at Kris and smiled. 'My dear, you are quite lovely, and quite smart. You work for St Clair and Abif, I hear?'

'I'm missing work today,' Kris said, shaking like a leaf. 'They'll be wondering where I am.'

'Oh,' Ishiku waved her fingers dismissively. 'They know where you are. We do rather a lot of business with them, you know. I'll take care of everything. Who knows, there might even be a promotion for you soon.' She turned back to Cowan. 'You should spend more time with this woman. She might civilise you.'

'Thing is, I'm not civilised at all. I came here to kill your husband, but now I've altogether changed my mind. It was a sad error of judgment. I want to kill you instead.'

'Yes.' Ishiku was bored with the conversation now, glancing towards Pym. 'This is why this affair must end here. All this talk of killing! Take this young lady out to the car, please, make her comfortable. Mr Cowan will be joining you all directly.'

Kris was looking right at him as she was escorted out. Her eyes begged him to play along, to do what he was told. As if doing the sensible thing was even a remote possibility for him. As if Cowan were ever capable of playing along with anything.

So, he was alone with her in the kitchen again. This time he would have to act. He needed to do the business very quickly. This house was crawling with armed men. He could never hope to make it out of here alive after, but still. How many deaths was this woman already complicit in? If he broke his tumbler against the table edge, it would only take a few seconds to stick the jagged edge into her carotid artery and hold it there. There might be a kitchen knife in one of those drawers too, so he could maybe just slit her throat, the same way her goons had done for Mary Barnham he supposed, or he could just throttle her with his bare hands, which would be for the best, for then at least no one would hear. Muffled into oblivion, there would be no more distracting screams coming out of this one. Cowan knew he was capable of it now, which made him infinitely sad. Then out of nowhere he had a vivid recollection of seeing the young Graham girl laid out on the cold slab all those years ago. He saw her red hair and bruised pale skin.

Ishiku reached for her neck, as though she'd read his mind. 'Please remember to give my regards to Mr Bannon if you see him,' she said. 'He's been very helpful to us in the past in so many ways. We do have a special relationship with you British.'

'He's a willing worker that Bannon.' Cowan frowned. 'The man's got all the attributes, except that nature played a cruel joke and made him a fucking moron.'

'He goes to the same yoga studio I do. On a different night.'

Pym came back into the kitchen. 'Finished, ma'am?'

'Did you happen to come across a gun outside on your travels?' Cowan asked. He pointed both forefingers at Ishiku, like a double-drawn gunslinger. 'No. There is no gun. I'm delusional. I forgot. I've been practically in an alcoholic coma all this time.'

Ishiku smiled icily and held out her hand to him. He was either supposed to shake it or kiss her ring, like you might the Pope's. He could see now that the stone was not an emerald. It wasn't a stone either. It was a green dragonfly, with folded wings.

'An heirloom?'

'Isn't it beautiful?' Ishiku splayed her fingers at him, admiring the gem. 'Beautiful things are my weakness.'

'Mine too.' He was thinking of Kris when he said that, of how much he needed to be with her now and so very far away from here. 'You should wear it when you run for higher office. It might bring you luck.'

Ishiku's smile was cold as a wasteland of Antarctic snow. 'I don't need luck, Mr Cowan. Don't you know that it is now and in this world we must live?'

Pym gripped his arm. Cowan still wasn't sure he'd make it back to the hotel alive. Which river would his body be destined for? 'Will I meet you again?' he asked her.

'The wind is picking up tonight,' she said, listening to the jangling chimes. The eyes of Yumi Ishiku were still two deep pools. Death lived in them.

'I think you might have got something big and nasty living in your folly out there, Mrs Factor,' Cowan said, mock-cheerily. 'You might want to call in pest control.'

'Goodnight, Mr Cowan,' she said, knifing her eyes into his. 'You are the only pest. Please go before I change my mind. I hope, for your sake, we never meet again.'

The armed men who drove them back into DC did not let him accompany Kris into her house; he was permitted to kiss her goodbye. Cowan assumed that it was only he who was to be disposed of then. The deal had been no more deaths but his, quid pro quo. He should really have been reading the small print. Then, much to his incredulity, the killers dropped him off at the front entrance of the Hyatt. Pym even wished him a good night. It was bucketing down again. The rain fell in black sheets and pooled in the awning.

'All alone tonight, sir?' asked the doorman, ushering him under an umbrella.

'Aye.'

'Oh, that's too bad.'

Cowan's key would not open the door of his hotel room. He had to go to the front desk. He scanned the lobby as he crossed it, nervous as a Christian Scientist with a severed artery. The clerk reminded him that he had agreed to switch rooms at the end of his stay. Finding the room still occupied, his luggage had been packed up and removed to a room on the fourth floor. Street view. Was the gentleman just getting back from somewhere? There had been concerns and inquiries.

'Is that standard practice?' Cowan asked her. 'To move a guest's stuff like that?'

She told him no. Usually the hotel would store the bags in checked luggage. In this case, however, the police had come and packed up his things. Telling him this, she smiled with bland inattention. It was all nothing to do with her. She just worked there. She gave him his new room number and the magnetic strip key.

He found his bag unpacked by the bed, underwear and socks arranged neatly in rows in the drawers. Shirts hung on hangers. It wasn't at all normal. There was a new toothbrush in clean cellophane on the sink and a note from McDonald on the pillow beside the mint. Cowan sucked on the mint as he dialed the number. 'Am I wanted for murder?' he asked as soon as the Commander picked up. 'I am curious, and yellow.'

'You're a hard man to find, Cowan.'

'Well, a hard man is good to find. Wasn't it Mae West said that?'

'I'll meet you in the lobby in twenty minutes.'

'I'm tired as a cactus,' Cowan informed him. 'I've been chased all over creation by the forces of evil for days. It's no fucking fun.'

McDonald had already hung up.

Forty minutes later, he strolled across the lobby bearing a rictus grin towards where McDonald stood waiting, tapping his foot impatiently and presenting a face like fizz. Cowan was just being fashionably late. He pointed to the carpet design under his feet. 'What does that pattern look like to you?'

McDonald examined the coloured loops. 'One of those things kids play with gets all twisted up. Whaddyacallums. You can walk them down a flight of stairs?'

'Aye, that's it exactly. It's a fucked-up slinky.'

'Right. One of those things.'

'That's why I can deal with you, Mac. You're a man after my own heart.'

'Just be thankful I'm not a man after your own ass. I could well be.'

They sat on a sofa close to the bar, but not so near as to be a problem. The waiter hustled over and they both enthusiastically ordered cokes, disappointing him. 'He's thinking about his tip,' Cowan said. 'Poor sod.'

'I come bearing good news, Cowan. You're not wanted for murder today.'

'But I was? I suppose the bad news is I'm wanted for crimes against humanity?'

'If you were a suspect, you'd have been in cuffs the minute you set foot in here. I had men watching out for you by the concierge desk. For 48 hours, you were being sought as someone who could help us with our inquiries.'

'And we all know what that means... And now?'

'Who knows? This investigation has been taken out of my hands.'

'By who?'

'This is a curious business you've got yourself mixed up in.' McDonald regarded him, narrowly. 'We were looking for a woman who was reported missing two days ago. Yet another one of those white GW girls, would you believe?'

'Seems to be a pattern.'

'It is that. This was your daughter's former roommate, would you believe?'

'Oh, I believe it. Don't tell me, she was the one whose body was in the river? Poor wee timorous bestie.'

'Before we dragged her out, there were a few items recovered from the desktop of her computer that were... well, I guess, a little delicate is the word I'd use.'

'That's three words. And this delicacy would be related to her employment situation?' Cowan rubbed his eyes, feeling beyond exhausted. 'Erin was the one I had you arrange my appointment with. I guess you remembered that, Sherlock?'

'Which is the main reason you were in such deep shit, my foolish Caledonian friend. Turns out she worked an exclusive clientele and kept extensive records of her appointments and business dealings, which is most unusual for someone in that line of work. That's what the agency was for. Discretion is the soul of valour in that profession.'

'It's like being in MI6 in that regard.'

'We located an online appointment book, a diary, and other compromising materials. A few local celebrities seem to have enjoyed her attentions.'

'Including politicians, I assume? I hear the little Catholic schoolgirl thing is very appealing, well to Catholics mainly. Not the priests, for obvious reasons. Wrong gender. Speaks to adolescent arrested development fetishism and all that. Like tennis.'

'So it seems.'

'Permit me to blow your investigative mind for a minute,' Cowan announced, winking at McDonald. 'This is going to be real good. Your expression I mean.'

'Well, there's a first time for everything.' McDonald sniffed. 'I'm waiting with bated breath, Cowan. Blow away.'

'You have found evidence that Congressman Griffith of Louisiana was one of that dearly departed Erin's very best customers.'

McDonald shifted uneasily. 'You do seem a step ahead. How is that?'

'It's called detective work. I'm going to offer online seminars, if you're interested after this. I'll give you a special discount. So is Griffith a suspect in her murder?'

'He has an alibi, like you. I'm telling you, Cowan, you

should thank God for surveillance cameras. We have you driving around Virginia highways and byways at a very good time for you. You've been on camera more than Ariana Grande Latte recently.'

'But what you found on Erin's computer is not good news for Griffith, regardless? Not if his name gets mentioned in relation to this young dead lady.'

'I wouldn't imagine it would enhance his election prospects in Louisiana any.'

'Why?' Cowan laughed. 'Because she wasn't immediate family?'

'I think Mr Griffith might be in similar difficulty if he had been caught getting a blow job from a horse.'

'From everything I've heard, I think that's a serious exaggeration, Mac. I do believe the Congressman would be the one performing equine fellatio in that scenario.'

McDonald bolted his coke in one sustained gulp. 'Give you gas knocking it back like that,' Cowan observed, looking offended. 'So what's bothering you, Mac? You got a face on you like a jellyfish in a string bag.'

'You bother me, Cowan. You're always bothering me. See, I can't forget you ranting on about your daughter's computer. How those tamperers were sophisticated.'

'You think someone got to Erin's computer? That Griffith is being set up?'

'Doesn't matter what I think.' McDonald shook his head. 'I'm not on the case. Feds are involved. I'm told there are national security implications to this shit.'

'No offence, but you sound as paranoid as I used to be, Mac.'

'I'm suspicious. Ever since you set foot in my office, I've been suspicious. Which is why I'm here now. You're about to tell me everything you found out.'

'I am? Unofficially?'

'If that's how you want it.'

'That my girl was murdered and that the man you said did it was the man that did it. I was wrong. I stand corrected. Carlton was guilty as not charged. I also have it on good authority that the second man involved in her murder has since then shuffled off this mortal coil also. I don't care to go into the details. It would not reflect well on me.'

'That sounded like a confession.'

'I plead the fifth. Also the sixth and the seventh, if they help.'

'That it?'

'Well, there's one more thing. It's kind of a side issue, but there's this giant corporation that has its tentacles in huge sections of the government and military and is corrosively corrupt and will kill anyone who tries to get in its way. It's the same evil corporation that probably recently arranged to get you taken off this case. I'd also have to say, this crew is extremely efficient at cleaning up after their inefficiencies.'

McDonald stared at him. 'I don't know if you're being serious.'

'Actually, for the first time since we met, I think, I might be.'

'I don't know what to say to any of that.'

'How's about wow. That's what I say to myself when I think about it. Wow.'

'You've said a lot of weird shit to me, Cowan, but this is right up there.'

'Tell me about it. You know, I was just this minute watching CNN breaking news upstairs in my room. Did you hear? How Haley Factor collapsed and died at a fundraiser in Louisville? That's why I was late getting down here. I was watching the coverage. Massive heart attack, natural causes, his diet was appalling. Happened an hour ago. TV was there. I saw the timestamp on the snuff film. Viewer discretion was advised.'

'Death happens.'

'What if I told you that I heard two hours ago about his dying like that?'

'You mean an hour before it happened?'

'Yes.'

'I'd say you were confused and messing up a timeline.'

'Uh-huh. Or?'

McDonald descended deeper into the sofa cushion. The Commander looked immensely tired and defeated. 'What you going to do about all you been digging up here?'

'Things are a bit complicated, honestly. If you fancy a wee flutter though, I'd put a few dollars on Haley's widow for the Senate seat and, if the odds are right, on her being very competitive in the next Presidential cycle too. After all, Bill Griffith has his issues with the call girl thing, even if it's a big hoax set-up. Then again, it's not like anyone would believe me about any of this. I'd sound like a regular nutcase.'

'You usually do. Thing is, I've started to think I might believe you.'

'Which would make you a nutcase, too. So, leave well enough alone. I'm serious. I like you, Mac, sort of. I think you're kind of a good man.'

'Thank you, Cowan.' McDonald seemed simultaneously surprised and perturbed at the assertion. 'I think you might be getting there yourself.'

'Tell me, you hear anything about an unfortunate death at the Vienna Metro?'

'Yes, a suicide. Man jumped on the tracks. He was all kinds of messed up. The toxicology was wild. Meth, opioids, valium, the complete pharmacy, out of his head.'

'And no video, right?'

McDonald stared at him, slowly comprehending.

'The camera was broke again, eh? I thought so. Talk about coincidence and damn bad luck. One more thing…'

'Oh yes, you haven't managed your inappropriate racist remark of the day yet.'

Cowan took a deep swig of Coke and leaned close enough to press the envelope firmly into McDonald's hand. He whispered, 'If anything happens to me, or to either of the two people whose names are on the front on that, in the next two years, no matter how much a death seems beyond suspicion, you open this. Otherwise, I'm asking you not to.'

McDonald was whispering too now. 'You think we're being recorded now?'

'Give it the works, an autopsy, the lot. Do that for me? Can I have your word?'

McDonald stared at him a long time.

'I trust you,' Cowan hissed between his teeth. 'I don't know who else I can.'

McDonald nodded, agreeing. The men shook hands, perfecting the performance. 'A sincere sensation it has been indeed,' McDonald said, normal volume resumed. 'Come visit us again, if you must.'

'Oh, I'll be back. Like The Terminator, right?'

'You do about the same amount of damage.'

'There's someone in this town I do want to see again. It's not you, though.'

'A woman is it?' McDonald let his eyes drift to the pocket where he had secreted the envelope with the names on it. 'What's her name?'

'I'm not telling you. I don't want you hitting on her when I'm in Scotland. I can just see you moving in on her like a creeping glacier.' Cowan shook his head adamantly. 'I have also been informed that once a woman goes black, she never goes back.'

'That's just because of our witty banter.'

'Well, that's always been my assumption,' Cowan said, grinning wildly at him. 'You'll make a decent policeman yet, Big Mac.'

13 THURSDAY

'You actually believed you met the man in charge?'

'Well, sort of. It's hard to explain. I wasn't altogether *compos mentis*.'

'How did the meeting go?'

'It went.' Cowan coughed nervously, recalling the strange events of two days before. 'Like I said, it's difficult to describe. He reminded me of someone else.'

They were walking near the place on Fairfax where they first met. That had only been a few days before but seemed a lifetime now. Kris had been babysitting Emma. Now she was babysitting him. As day dimmed, the two of them strolled towards the west bank of the river. Tourists sat on the benches outside the Torpedo Factory arguing about where to go to dinner. 'You know what I was doing earlier today?' Kris asked.

'No.'

'I was thinking.'

'Did I not tell you about that already? No good can ever come of thinking.'

Her laughter was deep and soft and satisfying, a good sound to hear. 'I was just wondering a thing.'

'Such as?'

'Whether you'd like me as much if I was different? If I had a blonde pageboy, or little stumpy legs like an alligator?'

She was biting her lip. She looked terribly good when she

was biting her lip, he thought. It wasn't every woman could bite her lip like that. With her, he believed more than anything in touch. The memory of the way her hair fell at night upon her bare shoulder left him weak as water. That's what he believed in now: her and the touching of her. It was all he believed in. Cowan harkened to the wallop of his heart. Kris was to him a seraphic unreality. He was love-daft is all it was. He snatched her hand up in his. 'What's down that way?' he asked, pointing along Strand Street.

'Just the Potomac, Waterfront Park.'

'Want to go sit there and look at the water? I like looking at water.'

'It's a bit scummy,' she said but pressed his hand in response anyway, acquiescing. Her fingers were cool to the touch.

There was a light on the other shore clarifying into a green dot.

'Is that Maryland over there?'

'It could be.'

They sat, legs dangling off a boardwalk. Wavelets lapped weeds. A fishing lure, discarded, bobbed on the night-tide. Who would fish in this at all? He felt discomfited, but pleasantly so, running his finger along her neck just to feel her shiver. The light turned slowly gold and the air tasted sweetly of the rightness of things. He heard his own breathing, quick nervous inhalations. Kris sighed. She turned to look at him, her eyes wide, and he bent over to at least graze her lips. Hers were eyes that deep-pooled, dark in the moonlight under a sky gone slick with stars, all too perfect.

'I'm still scared,' she said, her hand clawing at his arm, breaking the perfection.

'I know it.' Cowan went searching in his mind for words of reassurance, could find nothing adequate. 'But I think we'll be left alone now.'

'Those people frighten me. That woman! The way she looked at you. You're done with her now? Tell me you're done with all of this.'

'I'm done.' Cowan decided to change the subject. 'Who cuts your hair?'

'I go to a place called Bang. It's down on U Street, near Navy Yard.'

'It'd be a better name for a brothel than a hairdresser.'

'The girl who cuts my hair has so many tattoos. I worry about her.'

'You worry about everyone. You can't save the world.'

'There's only one person could ever do that.' Kris laughed when she saw his expression. 'Who cuts your hair?'

'Nobody. It leaves me too weak. It's a whole big Samson situation.'

'Yes. We can't have you pulling any more temples down.'

Cowan looked down at his feet. 'Not yet, anyway.' They didn't speak for a while. They just sat on a little wharf, content to be this close. Boats bobbed. A crisscross of jet contrails faded in the gloaming. Arriving planes now became distant lights, like foundered stars. All the lights in the world were coming out tonight. Cowan started up humming Delilah.

'Do you ever think about how there are more stars in the universe than there are grains of sand on every beach, in every desert, here on earth?'

'I can believe it,' Cowan said. 'But I prefer not to think about it.'

'I think all the stars in the universe are locked inside one grain of sand,' Kris said. 'And that that grain of sand is on a beach somewhere, and God walks down this beach early every morning, after breakfast, and leaves these deep footprints in the wet sand.'

Cowan looked at her, concerned. 'What's God wearing?' he asked, finally.

'Blue bathing suit,' Kris said, right away. 'And carrying a big picnic basket all bulgy with fluffy white towels.'

'Aye,' Cowan said. 'That's exactly how I see God too.' His phone beeped in his pocket. He looked at the number and stood up at once. 'I just need to take this,' he told Kris. 'It's business. I'm just going to walk over there a bit.'

'Is it bad?' she asked.

'No,' he said. 'I don't think so. It's just private stuff.' Cowan walked along Royal past the ticky-tacky little gift shops there. Wee teddy bears dressed in tartan trousers and tam o'shanters were arranged in a window display. 'Mr Gorham. How are you? Riotously amused as ever?'

'You can have three minutes only.' Gorham was staying true to his anti-social personality. 'No more than that.'

Cowan waited, listening to an elaborate sequence of clicks. She wasn't in the same place Gorham was, then. She was being patched through from somewhere far away.

'Hi,' she said, at last. 'I guess you know who this is, Mr Cowan?'

'I guess I can guess,' Cowan said. Her voice was different from what he expected, throatier somehow, distant, sadder. 'How are you doing, Miss Barnham?'

'Well, my living situation is difficult, temporarily, for a year or so maybe. But I'm well. I'm alive.' There was a long pause. 'I loved her very much, Mr Cowan.'

'Aye, I'm sure you did. That makes the two of us.' The next minute was silence.

'I... I still feel responsible. I mean, I was responsible. It was my fault. I am so very sorry. I... I have to live with that. I live with it every day. Every... day. I just wanted... I just needed to tell you how very, very sorry I am. The words are insufficient, I know. I don't know what else to say. There are no words for this. There are no words for what you must feel.'

'At least you're not sending thoughts and prayers.' Cowan sighed, searching for the words to comfort her. Maybe there was a language somewhere. Maybe we just never looked hard enough. 'It wasn't your fault. You weren't to know. You can't live a life with that guilt. No one can live a life with that guilt. My daughter would want me to forgive you. I know that. But I also don't think there's anything to forgive you for.'

'I wish it were that easy for me.' Cowan could hear her sobbing softly now.

'It is too that easy. You pick up the pieces and start over. You build something new. It's what the dead would want of us. It's what they'd expect of us.' Cowan could hear her soft snuffling softly so many miles away. 'How's your book coming along?'

'My book?' Mary sounded surprised. 'Oh, it's not being written. It never will be.' Her breathing sounded laboured now. 'That's the price I have to pay, Mr Cowan.'

'Don't worry about it. You did what you had to do. There's more than one way to skin a cat. And I'm from Glasgow, so I would know. We don't have cats anymore there.'

'I don't understand.'

'I'm not finished with those Tubalcain people, Mary. I'll write the next chapter of your book for you. It might take me a while, but I'm shooting for a bestseller.'

'Please be careful.' Cowan heard the distant intervention of another voice on the line, muffled but commanding. 'I have to go now. I'm sorry. I'm sorry. I keep saying I'm sorry. The words won't work right. Maybe someday it might be possible for us to meet?'

'I would like that, Mary.'

'Maybe. We could talk about Catri…' The line went dead.

Kris was still sitting on the dock where he'd left her. 'Everything OK?' was her greeting. 'You look pale as stone.'

'Everything is fine. I always look this pale. I'm from Scotland, remember, a place where the sun is mere rumour and speculation.'

'It's Thanksgiving,' she announced, as if he wasn't well aware of it.

'We don't have Thanksgiving in Scotland. It's like the sun in that regard.'

'Maybe you should have it now. You've got things to give thanks for.'

'Right.' He touched her cheek gently with a finger. 'I think that's true.'

She pushed his hand away. 'You do know you're a big closet romantic?'

'Ach, it's that awful Scots sentimentality.' Cowan didn't feel too good about that. 'Scratch the surface and it's there, like an open sore. It's a national failing.'

'I've never been to Scotland. What's it like, for real?'

Cowan shrugged despondently. 'It has potential, but it's not that real.' He tossed a little pebble in the water. Three skips and the ripples converged. 'Like this place here.'

Night descended, shadows merging into the dark of a murder of crows. The black water washed against the wharf and pooled debris. The green light in the distance was clearer now, a pinpoint. That little stick pile stranded there. Would it be flotsam or jetsam?

'I'd like you to come see me, soon. Could you manage that?' Kris was looking at him earnestly. 'I mean, I need you to. I need you to come back over here and see me.'

'I know it.'

'I'm sorry I made that sound so desperate.' Kris looked flushed and glorious. 'I just need to make this thing mean something now. Us. You understand? If I don't…'

'I know. Hush. I need to make it mean something too.' Cowan could hear his voice break, spiraling up an octave. 'I'll be back in no time. You can always come over there and see me too, you know. Like right away, even. Get rid of some of that grotesque salary of yours. I can take you around all the best tourist haunts too, which are all the places we massacred the English or got ourselves massacred by them.'

On the far shore that little green light still shone. Cowan remembered a little green dragonfly on a ring finger. He wondered at the ways his inner world flowed out into the landscape. He trembled a little knowing in his heart that he wasn't done with the cold eyes of Yumi Ishiku. He'd meant what he said to Mary. There was another chapter to be written in this story. What was a promise though? What did it entail? What was the apogee of all this hurting?

'I'm getting a promotion this month, would you believe,' Kris said. 'Just came out of the blue. But I don't know how to feel about it.'

'Give thanks, I suppose.'

'It's not a coincidence, is it?'

'No, nothing is a coincidence. Deyon texted me this morning to say he got some tuition refund cheque in the mail yesterday from the university. He didn't know what to make of it. He wasn't due any money back from them. I wouldn't be giving that kid any more discretionary spending. He'll only go buying more yellow trousers.'

'But it means he's safe? It means they're not going to hurt him.'

'I believe so. I told him he'd best take the money and not run.'

'You cold?' she asked.

'No.'

'You were shivering. You must be cold.'

'No, I'm just frightened of all the things I don't understand.'

'Let's walk back,' Kris said, looking worried. 'Let's go to bed.'

But they didn't move. They just sat there in the dark. Kris put her arm around his shoulder and pulled him close. Her kiss had a disturbing tenderness. Sinking into the warmth of those lips, Cowan felt all was well in this world. It wasn't a good world, no, but you made of it what you could. You made it a new one. You built it of more solid stone or at least tried to cobble a throne together from the detritus of the everyday. It was his daughter who'd brought him here, to this place. His only child, a lovely girl he named for the heroine in a long-forgotten book, a girl who loved daisy chains and laughs and skyscraping kites. He had loved her so. Had she brought him home at last, too? To this place that was not his home? Time would tell. He looked up into the all-encompassing darkness. The stars still sent dead light to this diseased spinning bulb. But it was in this world and no

other we must live. Kris took his hand in hers and squeezed
it tight.

Fear not.